GW00602693

A SMALL KEY
TO A BIG LIFE

Martin Gillard

Pen Press Publishers Ltd

Copyright © Martin Gillard 2008

All rights reserved

No part of this publication may be reproduced,
stored in a retrieval system, or transmitted
in any form or by any means, without
the prior permission in writing of the publisher,
nor be otherwise circulated in any form of binding or cover
other than that in which it is published and without a similar
condition including this condition being imposed on the
subsequent purchaser.

First published in Great Britain by
Pen Press Publishers Ltd
25 Eastern PLace
Brighton
BN2 1GJ

ISBN 978-1-906206-48-2

Printed and bound in the UK

A catalogue record of this book is available from
the British Library

Cover design John Gillard

Who looks outside, dreams; who looks inside, awakes.

Carl Gustav Jung

For my father.

A SMALL KEY
TO A BIG LIFE

Chapter 1

Bill Knight hated his life.

It was Friday night. The start of the weekend. He did not know how long he had been sitting there, but everyone else had gone home hours ago. Bill could not muster the enthusiasm to get up from behind his desk. His head felt so heavy that he just allowed it to hang forward like a dead weight. The photo of him and Angie happened to be in his eye line and he sat staring at it.

If Angie had just an inkling of how desperate he felt. And of how painful it was now to remember the extravagant plans he had as a young man. How stupid he must have been then. Stupid and naïve. He thought he would travel. He thought he would explore the world, go everywhere and experience so much. He would feel at ease anywhere in any company. What an idiot!

He would have an eye for a chance and use his wits to make a lot of money. Not for him a dead-end job working for someone else. Oh no! It was a big world out there and Bill Knight would live a big life.

The last thing he ever wanted was to be like his father. Wilf Knight had lived a small life. Apart from his three years in the army and his two trips to London to visit his brother, Les, he had spent his entire life in Bramport. Bill often wondered how his father had done it, working for the same ironmongers in Chapel Street for 43 years and always short of money. Now he felt just like a carbon copy.

Waves of rain had started beating against the metal-framed windows of Bill's office making him feel even more cut off from the world outside. And Bill's gaze had gone beyond the photo on the corner of his desk and was now settled in the far right-hand corner of the room. The corner where you could raise the carpet to reveal a small metal door. The corner where the money was.

His mother had always fussed about money. Every few weeks whenever the family finances hit a crisis point she would announce one of her 'purges', usually on a Friday night after opening Wilf's wages. Peg Knight would sit at the kitchen table and summon her two children to stand facing her, whilst she made it clear what a terrible effect their extravagance was having on the family.

"I've told you before. Your father's the only one bringing money into this house and we can't go on like it. You kids think you can have everything you want, but I'm telling you, you can't!"

And she would look back and forth from Bill to his younger sister Liz, as if she expected a response, but there was never a chance that either of them was going to utter a word to her in this mood.

"I'm telling you both now. There's going to be a purge with you two. Don't you ask for biscuits or Corona or the fancy tinned rubbish you both seem to like so much. You'll learn to do without for a change. There isn't the money coming in and that's that."

Peg Knight spoke as if people were disagreeing with her, but no one dared, not even Wilf.

Bill never understood how his liking for a glass of lemonade and a biscuit could cause such hardship to the whole family, but the need for purges always made him feel guilty and irresponsible, which was probably the main point of them. His mother would be very strict and determined about her economies for a week or two. The Corona man would bypass them on his Friday round, there would be no visits to the corner shop and the only vegetable on offer would be kale from the back garden. But after two or three weeks everything would gradually return to normal, until Peg's next reminder that you could not always have what you want in this life. It was only Wilf who noticed that a harder edge was developing in his wife's voice as the years went by, but he said nothing.

Bill's parents had a long marriage but he never regarded them as being particularly happy. They never seemed to have fun together. They were settled rather than happy. Bill often wondered how his dad must have felt when Peg started one of her purges, with the implicit reminder that he only earned enough at Holland's Ironmongers to provide his family with the mere basics of life. But Wilf never argued with Peg in those days, or she with him. They both had their roles clearly mapped out and they stayed within them. He went out to work and brought home the money, and she ran the house and looked after the kids and the family budget. That was the way things were, and that was that.

Looking back now Bill realised that the ambitions his parents should have had in their own lives were instead placed onto their children. Wilf and Peg seemed to ask for so little for themselves and yet had such expectations of him and to a lesser extent his sister Liz. Bill had never seen his parents as pleased as the day he came home from primary school and told them he had passed the 11+ to get into Bramport Grammar. Wilf passed the news to anyone who would listen, and everyone agreed that Bill was a bright boy, who could do whatever he put his mind to. Wilf regarded entrance to the grammar school as the passport to success.

"Get yourself your qualifications, Son. That's the key. With qualifications you can get yourself a position in a bank or an office. You must have qualifications in this life. I wish I'd had half the chances you youngsters have today."

Wilf Knight had a point. At an age when he should have been training for a profession, or studying at college, he was parachuted into Holland as a soldier in the 2nd Battalion of the Parachute Regiment, sent to capture the Rhine Bridge at Arnhem. He was repatriated by the Red Cross in January 1945 from a German hospital in Wiesbaden. After spending a further year in hospital in Bristol after repatriation, Wilf returned to Bramport. He had lost his left hand, the lower part of his left leg and all ambition to do anything more than live a peaceful life.

Before leaving Bramport to join the Paras Wilf had got engaged to Peggy Thornton and three months after he returned they were married in St Paul's Church. Alfred Holland, who had lost two sons in the war, offered Wilf a job in his ironmongers shop and promised him that he could have the job for life. And Wilf had taken him at his word.

Peg had been 17 when Wilf left Bramport in 1943. She had waited so long for him to return that by the time he did come back she had turned him into an ideal. She saw him in every film she watched at the Regent Cinema. He was Ronald Coleman one week, Robert Young or Clark Gable the next. Wilf was the handsome hero returning from foreign fields who would bring love and glamour into her life. But the reality was somewhat different, as it was bound to be. Wilf Knight was as strong and steady in mind as ever when he came home, but he was no longer a young man full of optimism. He had lost the exuberance of youth and instead craved only security and peace with the girl he loved in the town he knew. His injuries had left him with a pronounced limp, and he had the manner and gait of an old man, although when he came back to Bramport in 1946 Wilf Knight was barely 22 years old.

Whatever reservations Peggy Thornton may have had about marrying the fiancé who had become a stranger to her, she kept to herself. She gave up her job in Cromford's Tearooms and gave herself over full-time to looking after Wilf and having a family. It took her four years to fall pregnant, and there were times during those years when she wondered if the trauma of Wilf's injuries might have affected his ability to father children. Those had been her darkest years. The thought of spending her life with Wilf without children had kept her awake at night staring panic-stricken into the darkness. When young William finally arrived in the spring of 1951 it seemed that a new age had dawned for her and Wilf, and all the things they had once expected for themselves they now expected for and from their new son.

Bill grew up knowing very little of his parents' wartime experiences and nothing at all about his father's heroism. Wilf refused to talk about what had happened to him in Holland. His stock answer to an inquisitive child or a thoughtless adult was always the same.

"Lost the bloody things in a game of cards. Lost an arm and a leg. End of story."

Bill never heard his parents speak a word about their lives before he was born. So he grew up knowing only a disabled father who worked steadily at providing for his family, but who did not join in with his games very much, and a mother who worked dutifully for her husband and her children in the home. He was sure his parents loved him, but what he felt most, especially from his father, was a smothering concern about the direction his life should take.

His sister Liz was two years younger than Bill and she seemed to escape this burden of expectation from over-anxious parents. The irony was that Liz Knight relaxed over her studies and blossomed with the gentle encouragement of her parents, whilst Bill became stifled by their constant anxiety about his performance and progress. And because he felt that nothing he did came from himself, study became a chore and school, home and life in Bramport became a prison. Before long Wilf and Peg compounded their mistake by making one child the yardstick for the other. Bill never forgot the countless rows he had with his father.

"I don't know what's the matter with you, Bill, I honestly don't. When I look at your sister and see how she just gets on with her studies. She doesn't make all this fuss about it all. We've all got to work, you know, Son."

"That's not fair, Dad. I don't mind hard work. Look at me on Saturdays at the shop with you. I work harder than anyone."

"I don't want you working in a bloody shop. I do enough of that for the bloody lot of us. You've got to get a proper job, a career. Something with qualifications. For God's sake, boy, wise up, will you? You've got all the opportunities going. You can enter a profession or go to university. Whatever you want. I don't want you working in a shop like me."

"I don't either, Dad. I'm just saying I'm not afraid of hard work, that's all. I don't mind what I do as long as I can see something of the world. I want to travel and explore things."

"Explore things! What sort of bloody plan is that? I'm here to tell you, my son, I've seen the world out there and it's not what you think. I'm telling you, Bill, forget all that for now and concentrate on your studies. Get yourself qualifications and you'll have the choice of any position you want. Enter a profession and you're secure for life."

Thoughts and feelings were never explored too deeply in the Knight family for fear of what might be revealed, so father and son had little chance of understanding one another. To Wilf the idea of a position rather than a job was the difference between a life of status, respect and security, and a life of humility and making do.

To Bill both options represented drudgery. He went to sixth form to keep his parents happy, but from the first day he could not wait to leave. He wanted to learn about the world by seeing and doing, not by studying. Bill threw himself into sport and captained the school rugby team at fly-half while he was still in the lower sixth. He was fearless when it came to physical challenges, just like his father. At the age of 17 he was playing for Bramport first team, and Wilf Knight could always be seen at home games cheering his son on from the touchline, regardless of the weather. And often as not Liz Knight was there too, offering support to her father as well as her brother.

Bill was pleased he was able to do something so well that it made his father proud of him, and it made up for some of the guilt he felt knowing that he could not share his father's plans for his future.

By the time he started the upper sixth in September 1968 Bill's restlessness had become unbearable and he had already made up his mind what he had to do. He was determined to leave Bramport as soon as he finished his A levels. As much as he loved Wilf and Peg, he knew that he had to get away from the provincial life he shared with them. As soon as he finished college he would move to London to look for work. He would take on anything he could find, and when he had saved £100 he would start to live the life he really wanted for himself. He would travel the world.

Chapter 2

Even with his plan in place the hours sitting in college, and the extra hours sitting in front of books in his bedroom did not get any easier for Bill. The only good thing about the sixth form as far as he was concerned was meeting Angie Malpas. When Angie arrived after Christmas of the second year, Bill at last found an outlet for some of the feelings he kept so suppressed. Bill always maintained that he fell in love with her the first time they met at Mark Stone's party on New Year's Eve, 1968. But it was not just the physical attraction that mattered so much to Bill. Angie seemed like a kindred spirit. Her father was a pilot instructor in the RAF at Chivenham and she had been to many of the places in the world, which held such a fascination for Bill. He would talk to Angie for hours about her life in Germany, Cyprus, Singapore and Australia, and he would tell her about his own plans to travel, and about the opportunities that were waiting for those people who had the nerve to seize them.

Angie loved Bill too. She loved his strength and his courage and his unwavering feelings for her. She loved his family with its strong roots in Bramport. Whereas Bill felt smothered in the Knight house Angie felt cosseted and secure there. She had moved around enough in her short life, often being uprooted again just as she had settled into a new school and made new friends. And wherever they went, the arguments between her parents continued. She lost count of the number of times she lay in her bed in a house she hardly knew, listening to her mother downstairs crying and shouting.

"I'm not staying here so that you can screw your latest tart whenever you feel like it. You either get a new posting and get off this base, or I'm leaving!"

"For God's sake, Vera, keep your voice down, will you, or you'll wake up the girl."

But the girl was awake, and with each new move to a new place came the same argument. And with each argument came the same terror of not knowing if one or both parents would be gone in the morning.

So Angie saw the intrusive relationships in the Knight family and read them as closeness, and the claustrophobic routine that made Bill feel trapped made Angie feel safe.

Wilf and Peg had very mixed feelings about their only son's new girlfriend. Angie was so warm and affectionate to them, and to Liz, that they found it impossible not to grow fond of her, and it was plain for all to see that Angie was devoted to Bill. On the other hand Bill spent even less time with his books now that Angie was in his life, and this led to even more tension between father and son.

"But you'll have plenty of time for girls when you're qualified, Bill. You've got to get your priorities right now."

"Angie is my priority, Dad. I love her and I want to spend my time with *her*, not with Thomas bloody Aquinas."

"Don't you take that tone with me, William."

"I'm sorry, Dad, but you're just not listening to me. You go on about being qualified. Qualified for what? Spending my whole life in Bramport like you and Mum? Do you know the only thing I want to qualify for? To be a man with some get up and go, and the guts to do the things I dream of doing."

The words hurt Wilf but he did not show it.

"But what *are* your dreams, Son?" he said.

Bill was surprised by his father's sudden wish to know what he really felt and thought. But his answer came quickly.

"I want to be free, Dad. Free to be me. There's so much life out there and I want to grab it. Sometimes I feel desperate, Dad. I get so impatient waiting to do things and see places. That's why Angie's so important to me. I've never felt like this. It's all new. I get really excited about everything with her. You must understand,

Dad. I can't say no to those feelings and yes to things that drive me mad with frustration."

Wilf said nothing. He usually felt exasperated with his boy, but instead he felt only a need to protect him from the realities of the world he was so anxious to take on.

"Don't be in too much of a hurry, Son. There's plenty of time for everything."

Wilf knew that the love his son felt for this girl meant more than anything he could say to him. Wilf bowed his head and placed his good hand on Bill's arm.

"I just want the best for you, Son."

"I'm not afraid of life, Dad. I just want to get as much of it as I can. There's this huge world out there and I want to see all of it." And as he spoke Bill drew a large circle with his outstretched arms.

"There are so many chances out there, Dad, and I want to take as many as I can. I just can't stay in a backwater like Bramport. I want to get out of here and live a bigger life."

Bill eased himself out of his chair at Horseman's Heating. His whole body ached and he stood up slowly and coaxed each muscle and tendon back into use. It was getting dark outside and he went to the window to close the hanging blinds. The yellow neon lights had just gone on in the streets of the Lighthouse Industrial Estate and Bill looked out at the rain, which was still being driven in from the sea.

"A big life," he muttered to himself. "What a bloody big life this has turned out to be."

He sat down again at his desk and switched on the Anglepoise lamp. Twenty-one years he had been coming in and sitting at this desk. And it was 30 years now, almost to the day, since he had started work at Horseman's. He should get a medal for 30 years. Not that he took any pride in it. Thirty years in the same damned job was an admission of complete failure as far as he was concerned. And he still struggled to understand how he had allowed it to happen.

Getting Angie pregnant in the summer he left college had not helped, that was for sure.

Angie and Bill knew they were taking risks, but Bramport was a small town, where everyone knew everyone else's business, and in 1969 it was not the easiest place in the world to get contraception. Angie knew immediately that she would keep the baby and that Bill would stand by her. His mother was morally outraged by the news of Angie's pregnancy, of course, and she made it clear that she found Bill and Angie's behaviour 'disgusting'. Wilf did not seem at all surprised that something had intervened in his son's life to turn his youthful dreams to nought, just as his own dreams had been shattered by a German grenade. Bill never forgot the advice his father gave him at that time.

"It took a bloody war to ruin my plans, Son, but you've managed to bugger up your life all on your own. Still, you've made your bed, William, and now you must face up to your responsibilities like a man.

"And always remember, Son, the best thing any man can do for his children is to love their mother."

But Bill had not needed that advice then. He loved Angie so much that getting married and having a child seemed like an adventure in itself. Everything was so new and full of promise, and Bill saw no reason why he and Angie and the baby could not explore the wide world together. Being with them would make every new experience even better. He felt like a man of the world, empowered by his new situation. He and Angie were married in Bramport Registry Office on September 16th, 1969. There were a few friends, a spattering of relatives hiding varying degrees of disapproval, and Bill's closest friend, Stoner, was his best man.

The happy couple were oblivious to any negativity around them. Bill even felt sorry for his mates, Harry Woodford and Stoner, who were going off to university and art college. He knew they had always envied him for having Angie, who was by common consent the best looking girl in the whole sixth form. As far as Bill was concerned, Harry and Stoner were choosing to remain school kids, prolonging their childhood and coming home in the 'school' holidays to live with their mums and dads.

"Life's precious, Stoner. Yours'll be over before you have any excitement. Get out there into the real world and live a little. You've got to grab it now."

"I am living, Bill. I'm getting away from the oldies. That's the main thing."

"Three years in Bristol in a grotty bed-sit surviving on a pittance. I tell you, Stoner, you want to forget the theory and start getting in some practice."

"You've got it all wrong, Bill, my old mate. I'll be free to please myself at last and…."

"Yeah, and do what all your teachers tell you to do. I thought you and me hated all that. It's time to grow up, Stoner, and stop being a kid."

So Stoner and Harry went to study, whilst Bill chose an adult life with a pregnant wife, no job and the spare room at Angie's mum's house. Her father, Flight Lieutenant Alan Malpas, was now at home so infrequently that Angie always referred to their new home as 'Mum's House'. That Christmas Angie's father finally left his family and moved in with a girl not much older than his own daughter and Bill was promoted to the 'man of the house'.

As a wedding present Grandad Thornton gave the newly-weds £200 and the use of his Vauxhall Viva so they could have a honeymoon. Unlike Angie, Bill had never been abroad and he saw this trip as the start of the big adventure he was sure his life would be. Two days after their wedding Bill and Angie set off to drive to Greece. Angie was nine weeks pregnant. They had a two-man ridge tent and each other. Most of their family at home in Bramport thoroughly disapproved of what they were doing, but Bill and Angie did not care. To both of them it felt like rebellion and it felt good, especially with the comfort and security of having one another.

For Bill, being abroad for the first time in his life was everything he imagined it would be. He experienced more in those four weeks than he had in his whole lifetime. The drive across France to Switzerland. The Alps. Snowball fights in September. The Italian Lakes. Florence and Venice, where they sang for their supper in St Mark's Square and were nearly arrested. Bill felt so far away from everything that had formed his life up to that point. Then came the long drive through Yugoslavia, when Angie felt homesick for the first time. In Greece they drove right down to the south of the Peloponnese, where they snorkelled in the clear, warm water during the day, and made love on the beach at night. The experiences were so intense for Bill that he thought they would stay with him forever. And they had.

They both agreed that they had to get back for the sake of the baby Angie was carrying, and also to earn some money. They also agreed that there was no reason why all three of them could not continue their adventure the following year and go even further afield. So Bill looked for a job in Bramport that paid the best money, and ten days after returning from their trip he started delivering coal for Arthur Horseman for £28 a week, plus what he could fiddle by giving low weights at the posher houses.

Bill was not keen on working for Benny Horseman's father. All through school Benny had seemed to enjoy making enemies more than making friends. He was a big lad and he liked throwing his weight around. Even though he was spoiled with money by his father, Benny enjoyed extorting as much as he could from the younger children. One day he tried it on Liz Knight and Bill gave him a bloody nose for his trouble. Neither Bill nor Benny ever forgot it. Benny grew up to be lazy and charmless, and there was no one who seemed to like him. But the fact remained that his family had supplied every grate in Bramport with coal and coke for years, and his father was a relatively wealthy man. Although Arthur was usually as tight with his money as a man could be, he continued to spoil Benny with material things, whilst ignoring his son's increasing brashness and arrogance.

Bill meanwhile worked six days a week, sometimes ten or twelve hours a day and he earned steady money. He and Angie soon managed to get a rented flat on the Northcote Estate and a six-year-old Mini to run around in. Angie complained of feeling unwell when she got back from Greece and spent most of her days over the next six months at her mum's. Sometimes Bill would get impatient when he got home from work to find Angie was not there, but his main wish was for Angie to be happy and for the baby to be healthy. Bill got his wish. Michael was born on 24th

April, 1970 and was promptly known as Mickey. Bill was overwhelmed with love for his son and he had never seen Angie happier. Two days after Mickey was born Bill celebrated his 19th birthday. His life was full. This would do for now.

Chapter 3

It became clear to Bill very soon after Mickey was born that his little family would not be going on any adventures that summer. For a start both he and Angie were exhausted most of the time. For three whole months Mickey woke them up every night and Bill had to be at Horseman's yard at six o'clock every morning to load his lorry and start his rounds. All the other coalies would finish by midday and be off home, but Bill would finish his round by ten o'clock and then start another. The other men thought he was mad, but they had a grudging respect for this well-spoken young lad who worked so hard for his new family. Bill's motives were not quite so selfless. He was trying to put all the money from his second round on one side, so that he and Angie and Mickey could set off on another trip together, but somehow most of the extra was being spent on things 'Mickey just can't do without'.

Angie spent most of her days at her mum's house with Mickey. Sometimes she would meet Bill on his second round, if he was delivering in Bramport, and the three of them would have lunch together. They looked a strange sight, this little family, sitting on a grass verge at the side of the road on the Allenby Estate, or by the river in Bright Park. There was Angie in a summer dress with her black hair and pale skin nursing Mickey, and Bill with his face and arms blackened with coal dust sitting on the leather hood and back cover, which he wore to protect himself from the sharp edges of coal which stuck out through the heavy sacks he delivered all day.

They were good times. Bill adored his wife and child and he saw endless possibilities for their future. Secretly (because he never broached the subject) he could not understand why Angie did not

14

leave Mickey with her mum for a few hours a week, whilst she got a part-time job. They could do with the extra money if they were going to fulfil their dream of going travelling again. As it was they were saving next to nothing, and whenever Bill talked of going to America or Australia for a holiday, or even to find work there, Angie would make no attempt to encourage the idea or even add thoughts of her own.

Bill came to suspect that Angie was more interested in putting down stronger roots in Bramport than freeing themselves to explore together, and he was right. Angie had been moved around enough in her life, and having watched her parents' unhappy marriage she had learned to mistake an absence of change with stability and security. Slowly Bill's need to expand his world by travel and to grow through new experiences was overshadowed by Angie's need to have a home of her own, preferably near a good school for Mickey. But Bill loved Angie and his son, and he knew that Angie loved him. They were young, and if he gave her what she wanted now, there was still plenty of time in their lives to explore the world together, and for him one day to set up his own business maybe, as long as his eye for an opportunity and his spirit of adventure stayed with him.

Bill brought his fist down on his desk and cursed himself for having been so young and stupid and idealistic. Of course he had not explored the bloody world! Unless you could call camping in Cornwall and the odd week in Spain exploration.

Bill picked up the photo in the pewter frame from his desk. It was his favourite. Just the two of them on their silver wedding at the top of the Empire State Building. The wind was blowing in their faces and they were both laughing. It had been one of the happiest times of Bill's life. He had been amazed to find himself in places that for years he had only seen in film and books. They had to cut the trip short after five days because Angie had one of her panic attacks, and she had to get home. But Angie and Bill both agreed they should go back one day, and for weeks afterwards Bill told stories about the trip to anyone who would listen.

Walking around New York he experienced the same excitement he had felt during the adventure to Greece with Angie 25 years before. But ultimately their time in New York only served to show him even more clearly all the things he had missed out on in his life. Trips away with Angie had become increasingly difficult over the years. Whenever she spent more than a few days away from Bramport and her mother, Angie became nervous and anxious. The tablets the doctor prescribed helped a bit, but any attempt by Bill to rationalise the situation with her made matters much worse. The more rational he tried to be the more agitated Angie became, until finally she would have a really severe attack of 'nerves' which might go on for days.

Bill put the photo face down on his desk, folded his arms tightly against his chest and sat back in his chair. Each step he and Angie had taken in their lives had seemed so logical at the time, but every step had taken Bill further away from the dreams he had as a young man. It had seemed foolish to spend money on rent, so they bought a house on the Allenby Estate, heavily mortgaged of course, but convenient for young Mickey to start at the local school on his fifth birthday. By that time Angie was pregnant again and in May 1975 their second son, David, was born. Bill was delighted with his new son and for now little Davey more than compensated for the mind-numbing boredom he felt every day earning the money to keep his growing family housed, clothed and fed.

Then in 1978 Arthur Horseman died and the ownership of Horseman's Coal and Coke Merchants passed to his indolent son, Benny. By now Horseman's had fewer lorries on the road but they were still employing 12 full-time drivers. Benny must have been clever enough to realise that he had neither the character nor the intelligence to run the family business, because at this point he made one of the rare good decisions of his life.

"I'm ready to offer you the chance of a lifetime, Billy boy. How would you like to be the manager of Horseman's Coal?"

Bill asked for one week to consider.

Angie could not see there was anything to consider. She assumed that Bill would be thrilled to be manager of Horseman's by the age of 27. As soon as Bill told her of Benny's offer she went straight

16

round to her mum's with the news and then went out to buy new shoes for the boys.

Bill's feelings were not so straightforward. He would certainly be pleased to get off the lorries and away from the filthy coal and the filthy weather. He was pleased with the thought of the extra money too, and he knew how happy that would make Angie. Somehow though he realised that this step up was another step away from what he really wanted to do with his life. And Bill had another misgiving. He also realised that he could do a lot of good for Horseman's, and he was reluctant to be instrumental in making money for Benny.

For some time Bill had had the seed of an idea in his mind. It was clear to him, as it had been to old Arthur Horseman, that the days of coal and coke delivery were numbered. Lots of good customers were turning to electric storage heaters and oil-fired central heating. With the ever-increasing cost of oil, and with natural gas coming from the North Sea, many people were now installing gas heating in their homes. All the new houses in Westgate already had it. The problem for people in Bramport was that they had to go to Medford, 40 miles away, if they wanted new systems supplied and installed. There was no one in Bramport filling this gap in the market. Bill had plenty of the right entrepreneurial spirit and he was determined that he would be the one to fill the gap and make the money.

Bill spent the next few days putting his plan together and working out the start-up costs. He reckoned he would need £5,000 for premises, material, advertising and three months' wages for an experienced fitter. This should be enough to survive until he could create sufficient cash flow. When the bank only offered him a £2,000 overdraft and no one else would look at him, Bill knew that he would have to find the money himself. That night he put his plans to Angie, and they had one of their rare rows.

"Don't you see, Angie? It's the chance I've been waiting for. I can work for myself at last and make some real money. Think of all the things we could do if we had money. And we could make a fortune out of this."

"But we could lose a fortune too, Bill. It's taken us over three years to get this house just as we want it. And now you want to get rid of it and lose all the money we've got tied up in it."

"Who says we'll lose anything? I *know* I can make it work, Angie. It's what I've always wanted, a chance to go my own way. Trust me, Angie. I'll get you a house in Westgate when this takes off…"

"*If* it takes off, Bill, and it's a big if."

"For God's sake, Angie, you could have a bit of faith in me. I haven't let you down yet, have I? Are we just going to settle for this for the rest of our lives? Don't you want more than this for us? The same routine week after week. What about all the plans we had?"

Bill tried again and again to explain the details of his scheme to Angie, but he could find no way around the part which involved selling their home to raise money for the venture. Bill's efforts to reassure her were as doomed as her father's had been, whenever he had tried to convince her that uprooting her once again was the best thing for everyone and should not make her too unhappy.

"I'm telling you, Bill, I'll not let the boys go back into a rented flat. You must be mad to risk all this. And what about Mickey's school? He's so settled there."

It was unfair of Angie to bring the boys into it, but she knew that using them to play on Bill's sense of responsibility to his sons was her best chance of getting him to back down. She sensed his vulnerability and kept going.

"If it was just you and me, Bill, I'd do it like a shot, but we can't disrupt Mickey's schooling and take him away from all his friends. And Davey's just a toddler. He needs to be settled too at his age. Like it or not, darling, we've got to put their needs first. They're doing so well at the moment."

Bill knew the argument was lost.

"Please take the manager's job, Bill. Please don't risk spoiling everything for us all."

In later years Angie's words often came back to haunt Bill, and so did his own weak response.

"Well, if I don't do it, someone else will," he said. "It's such a great idea I've got here. I know somebody's going to make a bloody fortune out of it."

Bill's prophecy proved correct, but not for him. He became manager of Horseman's and made Benny Horseman into a millionaire.

Bill held on to his idea for as long as he could, but as the demand for coal diminished quarter by quarter it became clear that lorries would have to be sold and men laid off. These were Bill's friends and he could not sit back and watch the firm that employed them slowly go under. So Bill put his scheme to Benny, who was only too happy to take a risk as long as someone else was doing the work and the worrying. Gradually coal lorries were replaced with vans for the plumbers who installed the systems that Horseman's supplied. Some men were retrained and others were redeployed in the warehouse. Not one person lost their job. Within six years Horseman's was the largest central heating firm in the county. Over the next 25 years Bill Knight led the expansion into double-glazing, damp-proofing and insulation and Horseman's was taking work off the Medford firms. Benny Horseman, who had never done a proper day's work in his life, was a multi-millionaire and lived like one, whilst Bill Knight lived in a comfortable semi with neo-Georgian windows on the new estate on the edge of town.

So Bill Knight sat head-bowed in his office on a Friday night at the end of another week at Horseman's Heating and Supplies. He was 48 years old and he hated his life.

If only he could express his anger, but it was all inside him sitting somewhere in the pit of his stomach, where it turned into anxiety and a restlessness that he feared could drive him mad. How could Angie be so content with everything? She had her weekly routine worked out and appeared happy enough with it. She did the housework most mornings and went down to the Co-op at Crossways. And she would look in on her mother every day to have lunch with her. She did not seem to notice how much she got on his nerves nowadays. If only she could feel some of the frustration that he felt, maybe then they could still break away and do something together. He laughed dismissively at the thought.

For some time he had known that if he was to do anything it would have to be on his own.

The boys did not need him any more. Dave had a good job at Horseman's and Mick had set up on his own as an electrician and was making good money. His wife, Cheryl, ran her own private nursery and was doing so well that they had been able to afford a detached house in Westgate. According to Angie it was only right that children should overtake their parents in this way.

Dave was a joker. Everybody liked him, especially the women, which is probably why year after year he was the top salesman at Horseman's.

"You lot in your comfortable little offices would be out of work without Dave the Dealer," he would say.

Bill joined in the banter and he was proud of his son, but Dave's words rankled with him. He wondered where any of them would be if he had not turned up day after day for the past God-knows-how-many years and made Horseman's what it was.

But nothing and no one made Bill feel worse about his life than Benny Horseman. He swanned around Bramport like the lord of the manor, which strictly speaking was what he was. Ever since he bought Aldrington Hall and the title that went with it. The Bramport Chamber of Commerce had even held a gala dinner to celebrate Benny's 20 years 'at the helm of Bramport's largest and most successful business'. Then they had made the uncouth fool Bramport Businessman of the Year 1998.

Benny had come over to Bill and Angie as they sat at their table and put an arm around Angie's shoulder. Bill noticed the Rolex Oyster on his wrist. Benny was drunk.

"Angie darlin', you tell Billy boy here to stick with me. Horseman's is going places."

"Yeah, down the bloody drain if you were in charge of it." But Bill only thought the words. He could not say them, because he knew that Benny was stupid enough to sack him for something like that. And where would that leave everyone who relied on him?

Chapter 4

"Bastard," said Bill, as he snapped out of his daydream. He looked up at the clock over the door of his office. Ten to seven. Bill felt exhausted but he still could not be bothered getting up and going home. He pulled a lever on the right-hand side of his chair and leaned back. That was much better.

If only he had a fraction of the money that Benny had, he could do so much. He did not need to own a house or a car or all the things that Angie valued so much. He would love to do what Harry and Stoner had done when they left university in '71. Pack a rucksack and go around the world, taking as long as he wanted to. Experience something new and unexpected every day. Everything the exact opposite of his life now.

He imagined himself walking along a waterfront somewhere in the Far East. The sun was shining and he was unshaven and going nowhere in particular. He sat down at a table outside a bar and started chatting to the people around him. They were as relaxed as he was, and everyone was swapping stories of their most recent adventures. He was what he wanted to be, a world traveller at ease anywhere in any company. As Bill returned slowly to the present he realised he had a big smile on his face. Then a thought entered his head that would not go away.

Why not live out this dream now?

And the more Bill tried to dismiss the thought, the more strongly it returned until it took root and would not budge.

"I'm going to do it," he said out loud. "I'm going to bloody well do it."

And Bill realised very clearly, very positively, very soberly, that instead of wondering and wishing and waiting any more, he was going to do exactly what Harry and Stoner had done. He was going to pack a rucksack and explore the world. "My God," he said, "I really am going to do it." And Bill jumped up from his chair and started to pace from one side of the room to the other as the excitement took hold of him. And he knew that this time he was not daydreaming, and that for once in his life he was not going to allow practicalities to drag him back. He knew he was going to follow his decision through. He knew that he had to follow it through.

Bill kept pacing from one side of his office to the other as he dealt with the implications of his decision. He knew that he still had to consider Angie. He would not allow her to dissuade him this time, but he had to make some provision for her. The days when he had hoped she might share in his dreams were long past. His thoughts followed in quick succession. The greatest problem to overcome was money, not so much the cost of his own plans but the money Angie would need to maintain her life at home in Bramport while he was away. Bill reckoned that he needed very little for himself. The whole point was to face the unknown and the unexpected and survive on his wits. He needed a one-way ticket to Mumbai or Sydney or wherever, and then he could make up the rest. But Angie would find it impossible to survive on the few thousand they had in savings without his money from Horseman's.

Bill sat down at his desk and picked up the pen in front of him. He had to fight to remain calm. He leaned forward with the pen poised over a blank sheet of paper and attempted to solve this problem in the same practical way he had solved so many others during his years at Horseman's. He wrote down the words 'sell house'. But he knew right away that Angie would never allow him to do it, and that he could not allow himself to be so selfish. Bill drew a heavy line through the words and wrote 're-mortgage' underneath. But they had already re-mortgaged for the conservatory and the room in the roof. If he funded his trip by raising even more money on the house he would have to work into old age to pay it back. Another heavy line.

Then Bill wrote 'Benny'. Perhaps Benny would lend him some

money to fund his plans and hold his job open for a year, like a sabbatical. After all, Bill had done enough for Horseman's over the years. As quickly as Bill had that thought, he threw his pen on to the desk and laughed scornfully as he realised that such an imaginative, generous gesture was hardly part of Benny Horseman's makeup. "Damn, damn, damn," he muttered to himself as he tried to reconcile the absolute certainty that he had to go through with his plans with the growing awareness of the problems he faced.

Why did everything always have to come down to money?

Bill stayed at his desk and swivelled in his chair as he allowed ideas to run freely through his head. Most were dismissed in an instant, some with a wince as he realised how outrageous they were, but one idea would not go away, even though it was the most outrageous idea of all. It too involved Benny Horseman.

Benny had come into the office that afternoon at about four o'clock. There was nothing unusual about that. He often popped in on a Friday if he was in Bramport. He seemed to think that his 20 minute visits were vital to the successful running of the business. In fact all he did was offend the women in the office with his clumsy, crude remarks and disrupt Bill as he checked the week's invoices.

"Hello, girls. Come on, form a queue. Benny's here with his one-eyed trouser snake."

Only Cindy laughed, but she had only been at Horseman's for one week and had not yet learned that it was best not to encourage Benny in any way. He homed in on her.

"And there's the girl to charm it out of its basket and make it perform."

Benny put his hands behind his head and thrust his groin in Cindy's direction. Benny had little concept of preserving dignity, his own or anyone else's. Cindy's face reddened and she suddenly found some urgent paperwork on her desk that demanded her full attention. Benny lost interest, turned, and opened the door of Bill Knight's office.

"Hello, Billy boy, how have we done this week then?"

"It's been a very good week, Benny. One of the best."

Every time Bill spoke to Benny he had to make an effort to hide his loathing for him, and over the years he had found the best way was to be as formal and businesslike as possible.

"We signed the Meads contract with Swallow on Wednesday for 75 units."

"Yeah, yeah, whatever, Billy boy," was the best Benny could offer.

Bill knew that Benny did not want any details of the week's work, even if Bill had just signed the best deal ever for Horseman's. The contract with Swallow Homes to supply and fit all the plumbing, insulation, and state-of-the-art solar panels for the new development of 75 executive homes in Medford would make Benny another small fortune. But Benny was not interested in details. It was only the bottom line that interested Benny, and he paid the best accountant firm in Medford to make sure that every penny that passed through Horseman's was accounted for.

"I want to put some readies in the safe, Billy," he announced.

Benny often kept a few thousand pounds in the office safe for his personal use, but today there was much more than usual.

"Me and the missus are off to Florida next week and I'm going to need some readies."

And with that Benny went to the corner of the room furthest from the door. He lifted the edge of the carpet to reveal a heavy, hinged opening about a foot square set into the concrete floor. Benny entered a combination which only he, Bill Knight, and his accountant Harry Woodford knew, and opened the door to the office safe. He reached inside his coat pocket and took out the money. He held up 20 wads of £1,000 each and counted them out one by one before placing them into the hole in the ground. He had a smirk on his face as if he was teasing Bill by drawing the process out.

"Sleep tight, you little beauties," he said. Then he turned to Bill as he went to the open door of the office. "I'll pick them up around ten on Monday, Billy boy. Have a good one."

"Okay, Benny, I've still got a few things to finish off here. I'll see you on Monday."

Bill watched Benny as he walked from his office. Benny's huge frame seemed to intimidate everyone as he walked past them. He paused to whisper something in Cindy Turner's ear on his way out and then Bill heard his booming laughter coming from the stairs. Bill felt no new distaste for Benny's latest lapse of decency, just the same loathing as always.

It had been well over two hours since the last person had left Horseman's and wished Bill goodnight. For the last 20 minutes his eyes had become fixed once more on the carpet in the far corner of his office. The phone rang. It was Angie.

"Is that you, Bill? What are you doing? I've been really worried about you. Do you know what time it is?"

Bill looked at his watch. Twenty-five past seven.

"Sorry, love, I've been having a terrible time sorting out these invoices," he lied. Bill wished he could be more honest with Angie, but he had always had a problem telling her things he knew she would not want to hear.

"Look, Bill, Mum's been taken poorly and I'm going over to see her. She's in a bit of a state so I've promised I'll stay over 'til the morning. You'll be alright, won't you? There's food in the fridge."

Bill was hardly listening as Angie went over the rest of the domestic arrangements. Throughout the conversation he could think of little but the £20,000 beneath his office floor. When he put the phone down he got up, went over to the safe and opened it. He stared at the money for a long time. Twenty packs of used £20 notes. Each pack with a band of white paper on it. On each band was printed '£1,000'. Bill took the money out and laid it on the carpet. He had no moral objections to taking every penny of it. He reckoned that he had made three or four hundred times that for Benny Horseman over the years. If anyone was owed that money it was Bill Knight, and it was just enough to keep Angie going for a year while he was away.

However hard he tried to rationalise it, Bill knew he could not simply steal the money. He could stage a break-in, but what if he was found out? He might be prepared to take the risk for himself, but he could not bring the consequences of such an action down on Angie's head too. And what would the boys think of him? But Bill also knew that he had to do something. He had passed a point of no return. His life had to change somehow or the crushing frustration of it all would destroy him. Recently he had even started to wish illness on himself so that he could at least have an excuse for leaving Horseman's and escaping the trap that his life had become. Even Angie would have to accept change then.

Bill realised how grotesque his situation had become if he was allowing himself such thoughts. Nothing he did now could be as absurd as wishing, almost on a daily basis, for some sort of illness to force a change in the direction of his life.

He came to a decision. He would not steal the money, but he would take it and make it work for him. It was time for once in his life to take a chance, and with any luck he would have Benny's money back in the safe before he even realised it was gone. Bill took £1,000, divided it into £200 lots and placed the folded notes into his right trouser pocket. He put another £9,000 in £1,000 bundles inside his jacket pockets. From his desk he took a money belt, which was used for trips to the bank, and he put the remaining £10,000 in the belt under his shirt. Bill closed the safe and put back the carpet. He then went through the ritual of securing Horseman's Heating for the night, as he had done thousands of times before, and went out into the wet October night. Bill got into his car and set off towards the International Casino in Medford, on a journey that would change his life.

Chapter 5

As he drove the 40 miles to Medford Bill struggled to hold on to the emotions that had brought him this far. He needed the anger and excitement to spur him on, but he also had to be calm to have a chance of winning. Slowly he began to rationalise his actions so that he could still carry through the night's plans.

He had not yet stolen the money, because all £20,000 was still safe in his pockets and the money belt. As long as he only gambled what he could afford to pay back he was only borrowing it. He would go as high as £5,000, and then he would get up and leave, no matter what. Losing £5,000 would not be a disaster, but there was always a chance he could win enough money to make a real difference to his life. He owed it to himself to take that chance for once and to try to change things for himself. By the time Bill arrived at the International he had no nerves and no more doubts.

He would start by only betting £200 at a time and he took some comfort in persuading himself that this was a sensible, cautious approach. Bill had been to the casino before with Angie. Their old friend, Harry Woodford, and his wife, Alison, lived in Medford and the four of them had gone out for dinner one night and then on to the International. Bill had been fascinated just watching people as they played. Some tried to act nonchalantly whether they won or lost, as if it was a matter of indifference to them either way. Perhaps it was to some people. Others were more prepared to show their disappointment or their joy as the wheel played with them. Strangely the people playing for the least money were usually the most demonstrative. Those playing for hundreds or even thousands appeared the most nonchalant. Perhaps it depended on what was at stake.

That night with Angie they had placed their bets together. Angie was adamant they would gamble only £50 with 50p chips. Bill had wanted to pepper the table with chips, but Angie more cautiously placed the minimum two chips at a time on the even bets, black or red, odd or even. Whilst Bill lost quickly, Angie painstakingly built up a pile of chips and then insisted on changing them for cash, ignoring Bill's pleas to let him have one more go with her winnings.

Tonight Bill would follow the Angie method. He would lay sensible bets with a reasonable chance of winning, but he would play for much higher stakes. Bill resisted the temptation to go to the bar and instead made straight for the table with the highest limit. There was a £100 limit on a single number at 35-1, and a limit of £2500 on the even bets. Although the casino was already quite busy, Bill found the perfect seat halfway down the table. He waited for the croupier to pay out after the last spin and then placed £200 in £20 notes on the green baize.

"Twenty-five pound chips, please," he said. He was nervous but determined. All his thinking and agonising had been done.

"Changing £200 for eight £25 pieces," confirmed the croupier. The pit boss glanced over the young man's shoulder and nodded his approval at the accuracy of the transaction.

Bill looked at the last number. Twenty-three red. He placed all his chips on black. The croupier took the small white ball between thumb and forefinger, spun the wheel in one direction and rolled the ball in the other. There was a flurry of activity as hands appeared all over the table placing chips according to whatever infallible system their owners had worked out. As the wheel slowed, the ball lost its centrifugal force and started bouncing from one number to another.

"No more bets now, please," ordered the young man.

Finally the ball bounced into a number and this time did not bounce out again.

"Two black," he announced. And then next to Bill's eight chips he placed eight more.

Bill decided to let the bet ride. The wheel was spun again. The ball bounced and settled again in one number.

"Twenty black."

This time 16 chips were placed next to the winning pile. Bill tried hard to suppress a smile. A good start, but nowhere near enough. Thirty-two chips. Eight hundred pounds. He wondered if he should leave so much on one bet, but there was no more time to think as the croupier spun the wheel again. Bill watched the ball as it bounced indecisively from one number to the next. He looked at the eight hundred pounds worth of chips that he still had on black. At the last moment he decided to hedge his bet and he moved half the chips to the even square.

"Twenty-nine black," announced the croupier, and he swept up the losing chips and paid out for the third time in a row on black. Bill cursed the over-caution that had caused his loss of nerve. He could have £1600 now instead of only eight. He left the winning chips on black and reached into his right-hand trouser pocket. He unfolded all the notes and put £800 on the table. The croupier counted it out.

"Eight hundred pounds. Thirty-two pieces at £25."

Bill decided he had to play longer odds, but nothing too reckless. He had to stay calm and focussed. He decided on a 2-1 gamble, that the winning number would be between 13 and 24. He placed 32 chips on the middle third, stared at the table and listened as the ball started to bounce. A voice in his head repeated the mantra, "Black, middle third, black, middle third…." At last the croupier spoke.

"Three red."

Bill let out an audible sigh and kept his hands clasped on his lap, still staring down at the table. It was time for a cool nerve. He must not panic. Stay calm. One more good win and he could have it all back. Bill reached inside his jacket pocket, took out £1,000, and broke one of the basic rules of gambling. He started to chase his losses. As he placed a £1,000 bet on red, nothing seemed real any more. It certainly did not feel like £1,000 piled in front of him, as the croupier announced the winning number, cupped his hands around the chips and toppled the pile into a hole in the table in front of him.

Two thousand pounds down, but he had come here for higher stakes than that. There was plenty of time to recoup. One thousand pounds on a 2-1 bet and with any luck he would have it all back in one go. There was no luck. Three thousand pounds down. Bill went back to safer even bets and doubled the stakes. Two thousand on black. In the distance Bill heard the croupier call out some number or other and with it the word 'red'. Five thousand pounds down.

Although he was surrounded by people, there was no one for Bill to talk to as his plans unravelled. Everyone was too busy in their own private world of winning and losing. Anyway, it was not a disaster yet, but he had to get at least some back. He could not leave with a £5,000 loss.

Bill had reached the stage where the only way lay forward. Another £1,000 disappeared on black. Everything was happening so quickly, and yet with each loss the chance to win on the next spin of the wheel could not come fast enough. After each spin the croupier cupped his hands around Bill's chips and drew them back across the baize towards him, where they clattered down the hole into the inner workings of the table. Bill reached inside his jacket pocket and took out his last £1,000 bundle. He felt that he had to prolong his chances of winning by making smaller bets at longer odds. He started placing £100 bets on single numbers at 35-1. The odds stacked against him were just too great. In the end he felt a numbness beyond panic. His neck and back were so stiff that he could hardly stand. He stumbled to his feet and searched for the washroom.

He found a cubicle, locked the door behind him and slumped down on the seat with his head in his hands.

"You bloody idiot, what the hell have you done?" he repeated to himself, and suddenly the anger, frustration and sense of grievance, which had brought him to this point, seemed to have lost their validity. As he thought of himself in his office that afternoon all he could see was a weak, selfish man full of self-pity, who was too stupid to appreciate what he had. Bill tried hard to regain his composure, think clearly and work out his options. But try as he might he could not keep down the rising sense of panic centred in his stomach. Bill put his head in his hands and rocked slowly back and forth. He had wanted change in his life and he certainly had that now. The consequences of his actions came to him quickly, and his fears came to him in their familiar order of priority.

'Angie will be frantic when she finds out.'

'What will Dad say?'

'What will the boys think of me?'

Then he thought of the pleasure Benny would derive from his downfall. Good old Bill Knight, everybody's mate. Mr Honest, Mr Clean, Mr Reliable caught with his hand in the till. It would confirm Benny's view that in the end everyone was like him, motivated by greed and self-interest. Benny would do nothing to prevent Bill's humiliation. The Horsemans had not been generous employers and Bill had not earned a lot of money during a lifetime of hard work, but he had earned the respect of everyone who had dealings with him, and he knew that Benny would get great pleasure in taking that away. Benny would make the sacking as public as possible and then call in the police.

Bill's panic reached another level at this thought. He stood up and leaned forward with both forearms against the cubicle door. Bill closed his eyes and breathed deeply as he tried to gain control of his mind and body. It was not the thought of Benny or the police or even prison that panicked him, but the thought of how Angie would cope with the changes this would bring about. He could not imagine what would become of her without his money coming in and without him being there for her. Bill imagined Angie in a flat somewhere in Bramport with her husband in prison, and he thought that he could work 100 years at Horseman's and put up with any frustration just to have his life back again. Strange that he could put up with anything for himself, but it was the thought of hurting Angie that finally caused his emotions to run over.

Bill heard someone come into the washroom and open the cubicle next to him. He fought for composure and took a tissue from his pocket. As he did so four black chips fell to the floor. He picked up the three at his feet and looked around for the fourth. It had rolled behind the toilet and was underneath the waste pipe in some filthy liquid. Bill crouched down and leaned forward over the bowl. He had to turn his head and almost rest his right cheek on the toilet seat, so that he could feel blindly with his fingers for the last £25 chip. He felt with his fingertips in the foul-smelling filth and finally managed to pinch the chip between his middle and index finger. Bill raised himself from the floor, opened the cubicle door and washed his hands and the chips in the sink, taking care not to glimpse himself in the mirror. Then he opened the door into the casino and went out to face the consequences of what he had done.

Bill was surprised to see that everything remained just the same on the gambling floor. The rhythm at the tables had not stopped for a minute. As Bill passed the scene of his earlier madness he paused to watch the croupier sweep up another mountain of chips. He put his hand on his stomach to check that the money belt was still there, as if somehow there was a chance the remaining 10,000 might escape on to the table.

"No chance," Bill muttered to himself, and he even managed to smile at the thought that he would allow such a thing to happen.

Bill approached the table, pressing the money belt harder against his stomach with his left hand, whilst rolling the four black chips around in his right. He reasoned that he might as well get rid of these last remnants of a ruinous night and then leave. Bill sat down and looked around the table. He decided to perform these last rites quickly and chose a number to suit his mood. He reached across the table and put his last £100 on zero at 35-1. Before the ball stopped bouncing, searching for a number, Bill stood up, resigned to the inevitable disappointment. The ball bounced for the last time and Bill slumped back in disbelief.

"Zero," announced the croupier without emotion.

Bill calculated quickly. One hundred pounds at 35-1. Three thousand five hundred pounds. The croupier paid out the lowest odds first, leaving those with the highest odds until last. Eventually the croupier guided 35 pieces of bright green plastic across the table towards Bill. Each piece was the size of a credit card and worth £100. By the time Bill had a chance to work out how this might change anything for him the wheel was spinning again.

"No more bets now, ladies and gentlemen, please."

It was too late to bet, but Bill was glad of that, until he heard the croupier announce once more, "Zero".

Bill banged the edge of the table at not being more alert to what was going on. The elderly gentleman to Bill's right noticed his reaction and leaned towards him.

"You're alright there, old chap," he said, "you're in again."

Bill was puzzled. "What do you mean? I didn't bet on that one."

"Yes you did. You didn't take off your original chips. You've still got £100 on it."

Bill looked over to see the jenny perched on top of his four chips, proclaiming his win. Then 35 more pieces of green plastic were pushed in his direction. Another £3500.

"You're doing well," ventured the gentleman to his right.

"Not really," said Bill. "I've been having a terrible night."

Bill smiled to himself at the thought of just how terrible it had been.

"Sorry to hear that." The elderly gentleman nodded in the direction of the young croupier. "They'll be changing him soon," he confided. "He's getting into too much of a rhythm. He's rolling the jack and the wheel with the same movement and pressure every time. The jack keeps coming back to the same place. That's the fourth time in a row we've had zero or the neighbours."

With this he pushed a card in front of Bill with a picture of the roulette wheel on it. "Leave your chips on zero, old chap, and bet on the two numbers either side of it on the wheel." He whispered the advice in Bill's ear as if the system he had discovered could get him into trouble. Then the elderly gentleman placed five chips on the table with the request, "Zero and the neighbours".

"Zero and the neighbours by £125," confirmed the croupier.

As the wheel spun and the jack began to bounce, Bill hurriedly followed his mentor's lead and placed five pieces of green plastic on the table.

"Zero and the neighbours," he heard himself say.

"Zero and the neighbours by £500," came the confirmation.

Bill had little time to enjoy his change of fortune. His newfound equilibrium was rocked again as he heard how much he had just gambled. He resolved that this would definitely be the last spin of the wheel for him, and then he would leave with at least £6500 intact. As the jack slowed and bounced he looked down to see which numbers lay either side of the zero. Twenty-six and 3 on one side, 32 and 15 on the other. Bill just wanted the ball to settle down in one number so that he could get out. This was madness. He was mad. All he wanted to do was escape.

"Fifteen black."

"There you are, old chap. Told you. They'll be changing him soon."

The elderly gentleman spoke as if he disapproved of the young croupier who was bringing him such good fortune.

Bill's reaction to his new good luck would also have confused anyone who bothered to look at him. As another £3500 were pushed towards him, he wiped a thumb against one eye and a forefinger against the other as he tried to keep his emotions in check. There were no celebrations. He was exhausted. He looked down at the plastic in front of him and almost laboriously made five equal piles of 20 pieces. Each pile contained £2,000. Ten thousand pounds in total. He had been to the brink but now he had his life back. He could return the money to the safe first thing on Monday morning. Benny would never know it had gone. Angie would never know how close he had come to ruining their lives. No police. No disgrace. No sacking. Thank God. With utter relief Bill pushed back his chair and started to raise his aching frame. Then he felt strong hands on his shoulders pushing him back down in his place.

"Aye, aye, Billy boy, fancy seeing you here then?"

"My God. Benny. What are you doing here?"

"Don't sound too pleased to see me, will you?" Benny replied sarcastically.

Bill struggled to find the control that he usually exerted when dealing with Benny, but for once his usual feeling of superiority eluded him.

"Sorry, Benny," he mumbled.

"I never knew you came to the International, you sly dog," continued Benny. As Bill got up to face him, Benny spotted the chips on the table where Bill had been sitting.

"Bloody hell, Billy boy, looks like you've been having a bit of luck."

Bill was still so shocked that he was barely coherent.

"I was just going, Benny. Can't believe my luck tonight. I was just on my way out. I just fancied a night out."

"Don't often see you without Angie, Bill. Got someone in tow, have you? Anyway, how much are you up?"

"Ten thousand, I think. Incredible, isn't it? Total luck. I was just on my way out."

"Not so fast, Billy boy. This is Jasmine, by the way."

Benny stood aside to reveal an attractive young woman Bill had never seen before.

"Jaz, this is Bill Knight. He works for me."

Bill stepped forward to shake Jasmine's hand and as he did so Benny side-stepped him and sat himself down on Bill's chair at the table, knocking into the elderly gentleman who promptly got up and left. Benny turned around to Bill and Jasmine.

"We've been at the crap table and our luck's been crap an' all, hasn't it, Jaz?"

"Yes, terrible," said Jasmine. She took Bill's arm and whispered in his ear. "He's lost over £3,000."

"I tell you what, Billy boy, I fancy playing some more, but I'm potless. I'll borrow your ten here and pay you back on Monday out of what's in the safe."

Before Bill could think of a reasonable objection Benny was placing £100 bets wildly around the table.

"Benny, I really need that money," Bill implored him. He sounded like the type of whimpering schoolboy that a younger Benny had loved to bully.

"Bloody hell, Billy. You know I'm good for it. Tell you what. I'll give you 11 thou' out of the safe on Monday. That way you're up a grand. Can't be fairer than that, can I?"

Benny turned back to the table. "What a prat," he muttered at the thought of Bill Knight's fussing. He turned back and dismissed Bill and Jasmine as if they were two impatient children waiting for their father to come out the pub.

"Go and enjoy yourselves. Get a drink at the bar or something. Put it on my tab. I'll be along in a minute."

Jasmine took Bill by the arm and led him to the bar area where she ordered two large cognacs. Jasmine tried to make polite conversation, but Bill could not concentrate on anything she was saying. He was too busy trying to work out what he would do if Benny lost all the money. Bill reasoned that he could still salvage the situation. He would return £9,000 to the safe first thing on Monday morning, and when Benny came in to the office he would tell him that he had already paid himself back. That way Benny would only expect to see £9,000 in the safe anyway. Everything would be alright. Bill heaved a sigh of relief at the thought. Jasmine mistook the sigh for boredom.

"I'm very sorry if I'm not interesting enough for you, Mr Knight. I'm never surprised when Benny totally ignores me, but you struck me as more of a gentleman."

"I'm terribly sorry, Jasmine. I didn't mean to be so rude."

Bill looked at Jasmine properly for the first time. She was probably no more than 23 years old. Her eyes were green. Her hair was the colour of gold and fell in loose curls onto her shoulders. She was wearing a simple red dress and red lipstick to match, and she was beautiful. She looked straight into Bill's eyes as he spoke.

"It's just that Benny turning up and taking over like that has thrown me a bit. To be honest I'm a bit worried about the money. I wonder if we should go and see how he's getting on."

Jasmine took Bill's arm with both hands and pulled him towards her.

"Don't do that. Please keep me company. Besides, Benny hates people watching him play, especially when he's on a losing streak."

"Do you think he's going to lose then?" Bill did not intend to sound quite so anxious. "I'll be in a right mess without that money."

"Don't worry, Bill. Benny said he'll pay you back and he will. It's not because he's particularly honest, you understand. More the fact that he won't want to lose face with you."

Bill recognised the accuracy of Jasmine's description of Benny and he relaxed again.

"You're an astute girl, Jasmine. I just can't understand why you're…"

"Shit and bollocks. The bloody wheel's rigged."

Benny was back from the tables.

"Ten grand straight down the pan. The damn numbers are all over the bloody place. I'm telling you. That bloody wheel's rigged."

It was the best Benny could offer to explain his poor performance at the tables.

"I wish I could have some of your bloody luck, Bill Knight. You know, Jaz, this fellow's a real dark horse. I've known him since we were 11 years old, and I never thought he was a gambling man. Now I owe the lucky bastard ten grand."

"Wasn't it 11,000, Benny?" said Jasmine.

"Bloody hell, you stupid tart, you just cost me another 1,000 quid."

Bill wondered if everything Benny Horseman did and everything he said were actually designed to stoke up anger and frustration in him. It took all his resolve to stay calm and not throw himself across the table and throttle the meddling, ignorant fool. But Bill had a lifetime's practice in hiding his true thoughts and feelings and his reply was as measured as always.

"I suppose I'm not really a gambler, Benny. Angie and I have been here before with Harry and Alison Woodford, but Angie's staying with her mum tonight and I fancied a night out on my own."

Benny was not listening. He turned to Jasmine. "Well, come on, sweetheart, let's leave this lucky man and see if we can still make this a night to remember." Benny went to put his hand up Jasmine's skirt and winked at Bill. Jasmine pushed Benny's hand away and slapped his arm.

"Come on, Jaz," said Benny, as he pulled her from her seat, "you're going to make me a lucky man tonight. See you Monday at ten, Billy boy."

"It was very nice to meet you, Bill," Jasmine said, and she reached out her hand to him. Bill stood up and took her hand in both of his.

"And you, Jasmine. Please take care of yourself."

Bill did not have to wait until Monday morning before he heard from Benny again.

Chapter 6

Bill did not go home after he left the casino. He had driven five miles out of Medford when he was overcome with exhaustion from the stress and strain that he had been feeling for weeks, and he could drive no further. He stopped at the Travelodge on the Medford bypass and booked in for the night.

The sound of someone shouting in the corridor outside his room the next morning woke Bill from a long, deep sleep. He looked at his watch. It was 9.31am. As he lay there it took him a minute to put in some order the events that had led to him waking up in this strange room. His heart rate soared as he thought of the money and Benny and the casino, but then slowly he was able to reassure himself that everything had worked out okay. He sat up in bed and went through what he had to do next.

"I go to the office and…No, phone Angie first. Tell her I'm alright. Then go to the office. Put £9,000 back from the money in the belt."

Bill quickly felt under the pillow next to him to check that the belt was safe, and he sighed with relief at finding all £10,000 intact inside.

"Thank God for that. Then on Monday morning Benny comes in at ten, and I tell him that I've already taken the £11,000 he owes me from the safe."

Bill lay there for a few more moments checking whether there was anything he had not considered.

"No, I think that's everything," he said in a calm, almost cocky voice. He felt exhilarated now by the risk he had taken and by the way he had got himself out of a huge mess. He jumped out of bed and caught sight of himself in the mirror. He turned to face himself.

"And you're £1,000 up on the night, you stupid, lucky, stupid bastard."

Bill was ready now to get home to Bramport and put everything back in place. But first he had to phone Angie and let her know he was alright. He had no intention of ever breathing a word to her about the real events of the past 12 hours.

Bill searched in his jacket for his mobile phone. The display showed nine missed calls. Bill had managed to sleep through all of them. He searched through the options to display the numbers of the people who had been trying to reach him, and his stomach churned over. All the calls were made between 8.12am and 9.28am. There were four from Angie's mum's house, three from his own house and two from Benny's mobile.

"What the hell…?"

Bill tried to piece together what might be happening in Bramport in his absence, if Angie and Benny were so anxious to contact him. He pressed 'return call' to his own home. After half a ring Angie answered.

"Hello? Angie?"

"Bill, is that you? Where are you? I've been worried sick…It's Bill," she said to someone else in the room with her.

"Angie, what's going on there? Benny's been trying to phone me."

"I'll tell you in a minute. Where are you?"

"I'm in a hotel just outside Medford. I was too tired to drive home last night."

"What are you doing in Medford? Who are you with?"

"I'm not *with* anyone, Angie, for Christ's sake. Why should I be *with* someone? Please tell me why Benny's trying to contact me."

"There's been a robbery at Horseman's. Benny discovered it this morning. Someone's got into your office and taken £20,000 from the safe."

Angie reported the theft of £20,000 in such a deadpan voice that it seemed to be a minor matter to her, compared with the news of Bill's presence in a hotel room in Medford.

"Why are you in Medford?"

"Forget that, Angie. Listen to me. Tell Benny to wait for me to get back to Bramport and not to call the police yet."

"The police are here now, Bill. Bob Fulton's in charge. He wants to talk to you."

Inspector Fulton was an old school friend.

"No, Angie, no. I don't want to talk to him now. Tell him I'll be there in about an hour. I don't want to talk any more now, love. I'll see you soon."

"Bill, you're worrying me. What's going on?"

"No more now, Angie. I'll be home in an hour."

Bill switched off his phone and slumped down on the bed. Sweat poured off him.

As Bill drove back to Bramport it took a great effort of will for him to focus his thoughts. There was so much he did not understand. Why had Benny gone to the office so early on a Saturday morning? When Benny found the money wasn't in the safe, why didn't he contact Bill to find out if he knew anything about it? Then Bill remembered that Benny had made two calls to his mobile, but he had been sleeping so soundly that he had not heard it ring. If only he could have talked to Benny then he might have been able to stop him involving the police. Perhaps it still wasn't too late to sort it all out with Benny and convince the police it was all a misunderstanding. He had to try.

Bill pulled in at the next lay-by and turned on his phone. He found Benny's missed calls and pressed the recall button.

"Billy boy, where have you been? Everyone's trying to track you down."

Bill found it strange that Benny sounded almost playful, and not like a man who had just been robbed of £20,000. He decided against confessing anything to Benny right away.

"Tell me exactly what happened this morning, Benny. I thought you'd still be in Medford with Jasmine."

"Bloody hell, Billy, I can't talk about that now, you prat."

It was obvious that Benny's wife, Sandra, was in earshot.

"Just tell me what you were doing in my office this morning, will you?"

"I don't have to explain myself to you, Bill Knight. I own the bloody firm, remember?"

Bill realised how stupid it would be to antagonise Benny in any way. At this moment Benny was the only person who could save his skin.

"Sorry, Benny. Angie's given me the bare outlines. I'm just uptight that's all. Please tell me what's happened."

"Some bastard's robbed me of 20,000 bloody quid. That's what's happened!"

Benny was not playful any more.

"The funny thing is there's no sign of a break-in, and the safe must have been opened by bloody Raffles. Or someone with the combination."

Benny left the suggestion hanging in the air and Bill felt he had to fill the silence.

"So that's you, me or Harry Woodford?"

"That's what I've told Bob Fulton. He's already asked the Medford police to have a word with Harry. They should be with him now. But I've told them Harry's my accountant and he's not going to rob me. I've said the same about you, Billy. I've told them everyone knows Bill Knight's as honest as the day is long."

There was sarcasm in his voice. Bill knew that Benny was playing with him and enjoying every minute, and he knew that he was in the worst position possible. At Benny Horseman's mercy.

"Look, Benny, I think I can throw some light on all of this. Can I come over and see you now at your place? I'll be about 45 minutes."

"I think you better had, Billy boy. I'll look forward to it."

Bill phoned Angie to tell her he would be delayed. Her mother answered.

"Angie's in a bit of a state with her nerves, Bill. I've told her to lie down. Inspector Fulton's still here."

"Tell them both I'll be a couple of hours, will you, Vera. I've been delayed."

Bill did not wait for an answer. He hung up and switched off his phone. He needed time to think.

Aldrington Hall lay six miles outside Bramport on the Medford road, so it took Bill only 30 minutes to reach it. It was a magnificent Georgian country house, built in 1761 for Thomas Aldrington, a gentleman farmer, corn merchant and ship owner, and the first in a line of local magistrates and sheriffs of the county. Now the Hall and the 30 acres of parkland surrounding it belonged to Benny Horseman, who had grown rich as the non-working proprietor of Horseman Heating and Supplies. Bill Knight tried never to visit the Hall. The sight of the grandeur his hard work had provided for Benny was too much for him to stomach.

Bill parked next to Benny's S-Class Mercedes and Sandra's Porsche Carrera. He climbed the wide steps, which led to a large porch supported by two Doric columns. He pressed the white porcelain button set in a large circle of moulded antique brass. Coming from the entrance hall he heard the electric chimes of *Greensleeves*, and then Sandra's voice.

"I'm going, Benny."

Bill felt sick to his stomach as the large door swung open. In the next 30 minutes he had somehow to put things right with Benny, or his life would fall apart.

"Hello, Bill," Sandra said. "Thanks for coming over. Isn't this an awful business? Benny's expecting you. He's in his study. He's in a very strange mood."

It was obvious that Benny had shared none of his suspicions with his wife.

Bill followed Sandra across the large entrance hall. Sandra knocked on the door of Benny's study and showed Bill in. She announced Bill in the same way she used to announce visitors when she was a secretary at Horseman's. Being Benny's wife did not appear to have raised her status very much.

"Bill Knight to see you, Benny."

"Yeah, alright. Now leave us alone and no interruptions. Understood?"

"Yes, Benny." Sandra closed the study door as quietly as she could.

Benny was sitting at his desk in a large leather chair, which just accommodated his bulky frame. Behind him was a floor-to-ceiling window overlooking the parkland. He did not get up when Bill walked in, but gestured to him to sit down on a straight-back chair in front of the desk. Bill immediately felt twice as uncomfortable as before, like a nervous interviewee. If that was Benny's game, then Bill had to acknowledge that he was playing it very well.

"Well, Billy boy, this is a right mess and no mistake. You said on the phone you could shed some light on it."

"Look, Benny, I don't want to play games. I…."

"Play games. Who's playing fucking games. Some low-life shit has stolen my fucking money! That's no game to me, pal!"

Benny's vehemence shocked Bill.

"I've done something really stupid, Benny. I think I must have had a mental breakdown or something."

Bill knew he sounded pathetic, but he knew he was at Benny's mercy and that Benny wanted to see him grovel.

"*I* took the money from the safe, Benny, and I went to the International with it. I was only borrowing it, Benny. I intended to have it back in the safe before anyone missed it. You said you didn't need it until Monday. I'm really sorry, Benny. It's totally out of character. I'm so embarrassed about it. Tell me what you want me to do to put it right and I'll do it."

Bill was talking too fast and saying too much. At last he stopped and waited for Benny's reaction. Benny leaned back in his chair.

"That's it, is it? I put you in a position of trust and you steal my money? You say you're sorry and we forget about it? You're a bit embarrassed so we'll just pretend it never happened? You must take me for a right fucking prat."

"Please, Benny, I've got £10,000 right here now." Bill took off the money belt and placed it on the desk. "The other £10,000 is what you saw me with the other night. The ten you lost."

"Oh, it's my fucking fault now, is it? I stole it now, did I?"

"No, Benny. Wait. Let me think. I didn't mean it like that. I know. You've got £10,000 on the desk. The other £10,000 is what you gambled with. I'll tell you what I'll do." He leaned forward and held out his hands. "I'll pay you back the other £10,000 over the next 12 months. With interest. That way I pay for your losses at the tables last night and you're well up on the deal."

Benny fixed his eyes on Bill and smiled. He leaned forward too and glared at him. His voice was cold and full of hate.

"You wanker, Knight. You steal my money and then you come grovelling here and expect me to just forget it. How are you going to pay me back anything when you haven't got a fucking job and you're in fucking prison?"

Bill fought for composure. He must ignore the provocation, stay calm, and try another tack.

"I've worked for you and your father for over 30 years, Benny, and you must know I've been responsible more than anyone for the success of that business. I know I've done something really stupid here and I'm asking you for some understanding and some help. Please, Benny, let's settle this between ourselves and leave the police out of it. It's in your interests to keep me in the firm making you money."

"You don't get it, Billy boy, do you? You're not the boss. I am. You chose to work for Horseman's and we've paid you for it. All you are to me is an employee caught with his greedy, mucky, little hand in the till. Now you can fuck off and stew in your own shit."

Bill knew everything was lost. It was pointless to try to rationalise with Benny Horseman. He stood up and looked down at him.

"You're an ungrateful bastard, aren't you, Benny? You've got all of this because of my ideas and other people's hard work, and you're so thick you don't even realise it. God knows why you hate me so much, Benny, but I get some comfort out of knowing you're condemned to live your whole life being just as stupid as you are now."

Benny rose up from his chair and leaned over his desk, his face red with rage.

"That's why I hate you, you little prick. Because you think you're so fucking clever and so fucking perfect. You think you know everything. Everybody likes you and thinks you're so bloody marvellous. But you're a wanker. You make me fucking sick!"

Benny was shouting so loud that it brought Sandra to the door. She knocked repeatedly but stayed outside.

"Benny, are you alright in there?"

"It's alright, Sandra. Benny's just a bit upset, that's all. I'm leaving now," Bill called to her. Then he turned to Benny, who had sat back down in his chair and was trying to catch his breath.

"You're wrong about me, Benny. I don't think I'm clever at all, and I sure as hell know I'm not perfect. You can't damage me more than I've already damaged myself. But I'm sorry we couldn't work this out. I don't know who's going to pay the bigger price, you or me."

When he arrived home Bill was relieved to find that Bob Fulton had given up waiting for him and had gone back to the station. Angie was lying on the sofa in the lounge and her mother, Vera, was sitting with her holding her hand. Angie looked scared to death. Bill could stand up to any number of bullies like Benny Horseman, but he had no defence against the guilt he felt at seeing how he had hurt Angie.

"I'll make us all a cup of tea," said Vera and she went out into the kitchen.

Bill was grateful that Vera did not interfere between him and Angie. He went straight over to Angie and took her mother's place on the sofa.

"Oh Bill. I've been worried to death. What's going on? Whatever it is, please tell me everything's going to be alright."

"Everything's going to be alright, darling," he lied. "Just let me explain everything gradually, will you?"

The phone rang in the hall. Vera came out of the kitchen to answer it.

"Hello, Mick. Yes, your dad's back now, love. I don't know, love, he's just this minute walked in. He hasn't said anything about it yet. Hold on, love, I'll ask him. Bill, do you want to talk to Mickey?"

"Tell him I'll phone him back later, Vera, will you? Tell him not to worry. But I can't talk at the moment."

He turned back to Angie. He could see that she was terrified at what he might be about to tell her and decided that the kindest thing to do was to be completely honest from the start. He stood

46

up and started to pace, as he usually did when he was nervous or excited.

"Angie, I'm really sorry, darling, but I've done something unbelievably stupid."

"Oh, God, Bill, no," she whimpered and drew her knees up to her chest to protect herself.

"I had a bit of a brainstorm last night and took some money belonging to Benny. I only meant to borrow it, but Benny found out and now he's accusing me of stealing it."

"I don't understand. Why do you need to borrow money from Benny?"

"You'll just think I'm stupid if I tell you."

"It's another woman, isn't it? I know it is. Just get it over with and tell me straight out." She put a clenched fist to her mouth and Bill saw fear in her eyes.

"Angie, it's not another woman. For God's sake. I'm not your bloody father." Bill remembered Vera was in the other room and lowered his voice.

"For the umpteenth time, Angie, there is no other woman. There never has been. That is *not* the problem. I took the money because…God, I feel stupid…because I wanted to have time off from Horseman's to travel and see a bit of the world."

"Oh, my God, not that again, Bill. You mean all this is about you wanting to go on holiday."

"That's the trouble, Angie, you never hear what you don't want to hear, do you? You know I'm not talking about a holiday, but you refuse to accept what I'm saying. You know how much I hated my job. Horseman's was killing me. I had to do something."

"What do you mean, Horseman's *was* killing you?"

"Benny's sacked me."

"But he can't sack you. Not after all you've done for him. You've got to talk to him …explain…apologise."

"I've been up to the Hall. I've just come from there. There's no reasoning with him. He's bloody furious about it. I always knew we weren't exactly friends but I had no idea he hated me so much."

"Hate you? Why should he hate you? He'd have nothing without you."

"I can tell you, it's not the way he sees it. There's absolutely no way back with him. Not that I want one."

"Bill, what's got into you?" Angie sat upright on the sofa. "You've got to find a way back. How are we going to live otherwise?"

"I don't know, Angie. I'm trying to get my head round it all. Right now we've got to stay calm and..."

"I can't stay calm until you tell me what this is all about. All I know is you were in Medford last night...God knows why...the police were here this morning looking for you...and now you tell me you've lost your job. What are you trying to do to me? You're driving me mad! What the hell's going on?"

"You must stay calm Angie, or we'll never get anywhere." He knelt down and took her hand. "I'll tell you everything, but we must stay calm. Okay?" Angie nodded and Bill stood back up.

"I was in my office last night after everyone left and I was just feeling desperate. I was so frustrated about everything. Horseman's, Bramport, the job."

Angie sighed. How many times had she heard this before?

"But not you and the boys. You know that," Bill added quickly, mistaking the signs. "Benny had been in earlier, showing off with all his money and he wound me up so much. He put all this money in the safe. Twenty thousand pounds just so he and Sandra can go to Florida. Think what you and I could do with that money. I thought, 'I can change my life with that money. I can take time off, travel a bit, relax, save myself from having a bloody heart attack or something.' So I took it."

"What a stupid thing..."

"No, Angie. Please let me finish. So I took it. I reckoned I had a right to take it. But I wasn't stealing it. I don't know if anyone will ever believe me, but I was not stealing it. I was always going to put it back. I'm *not* a thief."

"What were...?"

"Please, Angie, let me just tell you. I took it to the casino in Medford. I thought I'd try and win a few thousand, so that I could have a bit of a break from everything. I don't think you realise how desperate I've been feeling over the past few months. I know you've had your mum's illness and everything, but things have just built up with me to such a point I…"

"I'm sorry, Bill, but what you're saying just sounds pathetic." Angie stood up and went to the sideboard. She snatched a tissue from the box and sat down again on the sofa.

"So I take it you didn't win then?" she said.

"Oh, it's like that, is it, Angie? You've suddenly heard enough, have you? Well, believe it or not, I did win. But guess what? Who should suddenly arrive to turn everything to shit again, but good old Benny Horseman? I was just leaving to put the money back, when he turns up and borrows £10,000 and loses the bloody lot. Can you believe it? Benny bloody Horseman. I'm in the shit again because of Benny bloody Horseman."

Bill started pacing faster.

"It still would have been alright because I only had to put £9,000 back in the safe this morning, and I had that. But what happens? Benny bloody Horseman goes into the office this morning at the crack of dawn, for the first time in his whole bloody life, thinks he's been robbed and calls the bloody police. Now they're going to arrest me."

Bill stopped pacing and slumped in an armchair.

"My God, Bill, I feel as if I don't know you at all. I do believe you've wrecked our lives. You've lost your job. We'll lose the house. You'll be in court. It'll be in the papers. The whole of Bramport will know. It's an absolute nightmare. I don't think I can stand it. I think I'm going to go mad."

Angie stood up and rushed into the kitchen. She slammed the door so hard Bill was sure she must have cracked the glass, but he did not bother looking up to check. Then he heard the sound of Angie sobbing and the sound of her mother fighting to give her reassurance. Bill knew that Vera would do a better job than he ever could. He got up, took his car keys and left.

Chapter 7

As Bill drove to the police station in Bramport to see Bob Fulton he wondered how many of the familiar faces he recognised knew about the 'robbery' at Horseman's. News travelled fast in Bramport. Everyone he knew seemed to be acting normally towards him. Some smiled, others nodded and a few waved as they saw him. Everyone seemed to have time for Bill Knight, but right now he would give anything for the anonymity of a big city. Soon the whole of Bramport would know what he had done, especially if Benny had anything to do with it. Bill could not decide if it made matters better or worse that nobody would be able to believe he was capable of such a thing. Then he realised that he had to speak to the boys and his parents before the news spread. When Bill reached the station he stayed in the car and called Mickey.

"Hello, Mick, it's Dad. Sorry I couldn't speak earlier."

"Hi, Dad. What the hell's going on today? Why do the police want to see you?"

"What have you heard, Son?"

"It doesn't matter what I've heard. It's what you tell me that matters."

Bill told the truth as clearly as he could see it, as if he was still teaching his son the difference between right and wrong.

"I took some money from the safe in my office, Mickey. I shouldn't have taken it, because it wasn't mine to take. I persuaded myself that I was only borrowing it, because I knew I would pay it back somehow. But it was stupid and now I have to account for myself. But I'm not a thief, Mickey."

"You don't have to tell me that, Dad. You're the most honest person I know. You don't have to say any more."

His son's absolute faith in him broke straight through Bill's emotional defences. He had to clench his teeth hard to stop himself from breaking down. Even so his eyes filled with tears.

"Thanks, Son. I've got to go now."

"Can I do anything to help you, Dad?"

"Yes. Don't worry about me. Just look after yourself and Cheryl. Mum's with Nan. Perhaps you could call her for me, could you, Son? Tell her I'm with Bob Fulton. She'll know who that is. And tell her I'm fine."

"Okay, Dad, will do. Take care. Bye."

The tears rolled down Bill's face and he shouted at himself to snap out of it.

"Stop feeling sorry for yourself, you bastard. Don't you start that!"

He shook his head from side to side in an attempt to regain his composure. He dialled the personal mobile of his younger son, Dave, but there was no reply and the answering service clicked in. Bill listened to his son's outgoing message.

"You've reached the voicemail service of Dave Knight. If you are female and not a close relative, leave your number and I guarantee I'll call you back. If you are male and I owe you money, I guarantee I won't, but leave a message anyway."

"Hello, Dave, you silly bugger. Your old man's got himself in a bit of a mess but nothing I can't sort out. I can't say much about it at the moment. Don't worry about me. Speak to Mickey if you want to know more. Bye."

Bill was surprised to find that he was smiling as he ended the call. His voice had been lighter and more relaxed and now his mood was lighter too. Dave had that effect on people. He was one of the few people in Bill's life who was guaranteed not to judge him. Dave seemed able to accept anything and move on. Bill envied him for that.

Bill's final call was to his mum and dad. As soon as his mother answered the phone Bill decided to say nothing about the trouble he was in. She immediately started to complain about Wilf, and it was obvious they knew nothing about the events of the past 18 hours.

"Your father's not here. A waste of space he is. Never around when he's needed."

Bill felt sorry for his father. He had aged terribly since he retired and his disability seemed more pronounced than ever. Wilf had withdrawn into himself over the years and Peg moaned continually about the time he spent out in his garden shed. Wilf's shed had become a bit of a family joke, as he kept it permanently locked and would allow no one else inside. It was obvious to everyone except Peg that his shed was the only place where he could find some peace.

"You really ought to make an effort to get over this weekend, William. You know how much it means to your father."

"I'll try, Mum, but I'd better not promise anything at the moment. But I will get over as soon as I can though."

"Oh, well, if you're too busy, I suppose that'll just have to do us. Your father will just have to learn."

There was no pleasing Peg, and Bill had stopped trying long ago, but the bitterness that had slowly grown inside her made it hard on those who still loved her. Especially Wilf.

Bill ended the call and sat for several moments studying the blue and white sign in front of him. 'Bramport Constabulary'. God knows what either of his parents would have to say if they knew of the events that were unfolding in their son's life now.

Bill entered the police station at 12.30. He gave his name at the desk and asked to see Inspector Bob Fulton. Bill had known Bob Fulton since they'd played rugby together at Bramport Grammar. Later they'd played together for Bramport Chiefs and were quite good friends at one stage. Bill gave up his rugby soon after Mickey was born, but Bob went on to play representative games for the county. He was 6ft 8 in his stockinged feet and when he came out to meet Bill Knight he was an imposing figure. He held out his hand and greeted Bill with genuine warmth.

"Hello, Bill, it's so good to see you. It must be 20 years."

"And the rest, Bob."

They both laughed and continued chatting as Bill was shown down a long corridor to a door marked 'Interview Room'. There was one table with two chairs on either side. Fixed to the wall was a tape recording machine, and in the far corner stood a water dispenser. The only window was covered by a venetian blind, which was half closed.

"Thanks for coming in, Bill. Take a seat. This is my colleague, Detective Sergeant Tony Parker."

Sergeant Parker was in his early thirties. He nodded at Bill from across the table. He made no gesture to shake Bill's hand or any attempt to exchange pleasantries. Instead he turned and occupied himself with the tape machine. Bill sensed the change in mood and suddenly felt very nervous. When Bob Fulton spoke again his voice was still relaxed but less friendly.

"We need to talk to you about the disappearance of £20,000 from the premises of Horseman's Heating in Argyle Street, which was reported to us this morning at 8.06. The money was taken from a safe, which we understand is situated in your office. We obviously need to know if you can shed any light on this matter. I do have to say to you at this point that you are not being accused of anything and you are not under arrest, but I have to caution you that at a later date it may harm your defence if you do not mention when questioned something which you later rely on in court. Anything you do say may be given in evidence. This interview is being taped and you are entitled to have a legal representative present with you before you say anything to us."

"Do you think I should have a legal representative present?" Bill asked.

"That depends entirely on you and on what you are going to say to us. As I have explained to you, you are not being accused of anything. We merely want to find out if you can help us in this matter."

"Can I ask you a question?"

"Yes, certainly."

"Who reported the theft?"

"The theft was reported by Benjamin Horseman, who I believe is known to you."

"Yes, of course, he's my boss," said Bill. "What time did you say he reported it?"

Sergeant Parker examined a single sheet of paper in front of him.

"The theft was reported to this station at 8.06 this morning."

Bill considered this information for a moment. He had intended to tell Bob Fulton everything just as it had happened. To him it was only right that he should face the consequences of what he had done. But now he changed his mind.

"I do want to speak to a solicitor but I also want to say one thing before I do. It was me who took the money from the safe, so you can stop questioning Harry Woodford in Medford about it. That's just ridiculous."

"I thought it was ridiculous when your name was mentioned, Bill," said Bob Fulton. "For God's sake, man, don't say any more before you see a solicitor. You can wait in here."

The only solicitor Bill knew was Tom Wiltshire whose firm, Wiltshire, Stanford and Cross, dealt with all of Horseman's legal work. It took Bob Fulton an hour to track him down and get him on the phone to Bill.

"Hello, Bill. Tom Wiltshire here. Bob Fulton's told me about your little problem. Look, Bill, you have to understand that it's very likely that Benny Horseman will be contacting me on this matter and strictly speaking he is my client, even though I deal mostly with your office at Horseman's. Frankly, Bill, I'm no great loss to you on this one. Most of my work is contracts and employment law and such. I've been in touch with Robinson and Reed in Church Street. They've got a young lady there who's very good on the criminal stuff. Her name is Natalie Barry. She should be with you in about an hour."

Natalie Barry arrived at two o'clock and was shown into the interview room. Bill stood up as she entered. He was surprised how young she looked. Although Ms Barry could not have been any more than 30 years old, she immediately took control of the situation.

"Mr Knight, my name is Natalie Barry. Call me Natalie, and I'll call you…?"

"Bill."

"We might as well be on familiar terms, Bill, because we are going to have no secrets from one another. I want you to tell me everything that's happened. Don't leave anything out and don't try to distort the facts. I'm not here to judge you. I'm on your side and I'm here to help."

Bill liked Natalie Barry. He told her everything from the moment Benny entered his office the previous afternoon, right up to the present moment with the two of them facing one another across the table at Bramport Police Station. When she finished she stopped making notes and looked directly at him as she spoke.

"There are four elements to theft, Bill. One, you must appropriate some property. You appropriated £20,000. Two, the property must belong to someone else. In this case Mr Horseman. Three, the appropriation must be dishonest. In other words, you had no valid reason to take it.

"Those three do not make you guilty of theft on their own, according to the 1968 Theft Act, but number four might. Number four says you must intend to deprive the original possessor, Mr Horseman, permanently of his money. That is the key point here, Bill. Did you intend to keep his money indefinitely?"

"No, Natalie, I didn't."

"You say you did not, and in your favour is the fact that you have already been to Mr Horseman and returned £10,000, and offered to repay the rest to him. An offer he refused. Also in your favour is the fact that you had the other £10,000 at the casino ready to repay him, but Mr Horseman appropriated that from you and subsequently lost it at the table."

She paused and tapped her pen lightly on the table as if distracted for a moment, and then continued.

"I must say I find that episode most bizarre, but we'll come back to that later. You also say that there is a witness to these events at the casino. Someone you only know as Jasmine, who was a companion of Mr Horseman's. It's going to be important to contact this Jasmine, so that she can verify that you had all of Mr Horseman's money intact at that time."

"I'm sorry, Natalie, I don't know how to contact her. I'd never met her before."

"We'll worry about that later. On the negative side is whether we can prove that you always intended to repay the money. It will be crucial to show that you were only borrowing the money and that you always intended to return it."

"I did intend to return it."

"If you had lost the whole £20,000, could you have returned it on Monday morning?" Natalie asked him.

"No, not that quickly, it might have taken a few weeks to raise the money."

"That is our biggest problem, you see. Most people accused of theft would say they will return the money once they're caught, if that means they can escape punishment. In law we have to show that you *always* intended to return it. The prosecution will argue that the probable consequences of gambling the money on roulette would be that you would be unable to return the money. That makes it theft."

"So it's all about my state of mind on Friday when I took it, and how good I thought I was at roulette. God, what an absolute fool I must seem to you."

"That's not important right now, Bill, but your state of mind on Friday evening is."

"My state of mind on Friday? Oh, I don't know. I was stressed and frustrated, I suppose. I was angry with Benny, angry with myself, desperate to do something to change my life. God, it sounds so juvenile. I was excited, determined, confused. Take your pick, Natalie. But there is one thing I know to be true. I was not running away. I was going to face the consequences of what I was doing, and I was going to pay back any money that I lost. I just wanted a chance to win and to change things for myself. If only Benny hadn't butted in, everything would've been okay."

"I must say I find Mr Horseman's role in all this very puzzling."

"So do I, Natalie. Why the hell was he in my office at eight o'clock this morning?"

"I'm sure the police have asked him that. They'll have his statement by now. We can surmise that he was worried about his money. Perhaps when he saw you at the casino with so much money he put two and two together."

"So when he found it was missing, why didn't he contact me first to give me a chance to explain? Why go straight to the police?"

"Perhaps he did try to contact you."

"No, Natalie, that's what surprised me when Bob Fulton told me Benny reported the theft at 8.06 this morning. Benny tried to get through to me twice on my mobile this morning. I got two missed calls from him. One at 9.24 and another at 9.28. And I bet that was after he'd made his statement to the police."

Bill was too agitated to stay in his chair. He started to pace up and down.

"Hold on, Bill. Sit down and stay calm. I can't stand overreaction. It is possible that Mr Horseman tried to contact you at home. Do you have an answer machine?"

"Yes."

"Have you checked it?"

"No, not this morning. But my wife, Angie, will be there."

"I'll go outside to phone your wife. You try to relax, and remember that none of this makes Mr Horseman guilty of anything."

"No, but it would show he was pretty keen not to let me put things right with him first. He was pretty keen to involve the police so I couldn't show I intended to pay the money back."

When Natalie left the room Bill found it impossible to relax. He could not escape the feeling that somehow he had played right into Benny's hands, and it made him as mad as hell. After a few minutes Natalie returned. Her calm professionalism reminded him how he normally acted in a crisis and he realised how far he had fallen.

"I've spoken to your wife."

"How is she?"

"She seems quite upset, and it took her a moment to understand exactly who I was, but she was able to clear this up for us. Your wife tried to contact you at your home this morning from her mother's house at about eight o'clock. When there was no reply at your home, and no reply on your mobile, she went round to your house at about 8.45. She confirms that there were no messages from Mr Horseman on your answer machine. Mr Horseman phoned your house at about 9.20. He told your wife about the 'theft', as he saw it, but was unable to tell her where you were."

"So after the casino he suspected me of taking his money. He goes to the office really early to make sure I don't get a chance to put it back. He phones the police right away and says there's been a robbery, knowing all the time that I had his money. And he doesn't phone me until later so that I'll have no chance to put it right. What a complete bastard!"

"Bill, I've told you before, do not overreact. Inspector Fulton will want a statement from you soon. You are going to need to keep your wits about you and keep emotions out of this."

"I'm sorry, Natalie. All I want to do is tell the truth. I know the truth about what I did and what I intended, and I just want to be honest about it. If I'm going to retain any self-respect I have to tell the truth."

"As your legal representative I would advise no less, Bill. But I find the truth can be very elusive. There's the truth as you see it, and then there's the truth as someone else, like Mr Horseman, sees it. Truth is not an absolute. It changes according to one's perspective and according to the limits of our knowledge. Our job is to persuade others to see the same truth that you see now. Later on even your own perspective may change, and you may see all of this quite differently."

At 3.30pm Natalie Barry informed Inspector Fulton that her client was ready to make a statement. This time there were four of them around the table and Bob Fulton was more formal than ever with Ms Barry there.

"Mr Knight, I must advise you that you are still under caution and that this interview is being tape recorded. Could you please tell us in your own time what you know about the disappearance of £20,000 in cash from the safe in your office at Horseman's Heating and Supplies, between approximately 4.30pm yesterday the 22nd of October 1999 and 8am this morning?"

Bill went over the same events once again, determined to tell the truth and leave nothing out, but it soon became clear that Bob Fulton was not going to give him an easy ride.

"You say you only intended to gamble £5,000 of Mr Horseman's money, because you knew if you lost it you could pay that amount straight back. Why then did you take all £20,000 with you?"

"I suppose I wanted the possibility of playing with more if I needed to."

"So had you lost all 20,000, how were you going to pay it back?" Natalie interrupted.

"Let's not talk hypothetically, Inspector."

"I'm trying to establish your client's intentions when he took the money, Ms Barry. Mr Knight, how did you intend to pay back the £10,000 that you admit you lost?"

"I would have taken out a loan or something. I wasn't going to run away. I was always going to pay back whatever I lost. I know I can't prove that, but I know that's the truth. But surely you know I've paid back all the money to Mr Horseman, if you've already spoken to him this morning. I gave him £10,000 this morning at his home. I gave it to him in a money belt. And he borrowed the other £10,000 from me at the casino last night. So it's all been paid back anyway."

"Ah, well that's where we have a problem you see, Mr Knight, because Mr Horseman has made no mention of you returning any of his money to him at any time. Can you prove that you've returned any of his money? Do you have any witnesses?"

Bill looked at Natalie and she saw the fear on his face. She remained calm as she spoke.

"You will of course put these discrepancies to Mr Horseman, won't you, Inspector, and remind Mr Horseman of the penalties of making false statements on this matter?"

"We will certainly be speaking to Mr Horseman again following our interview with your client, Ms Barry."

"But wait a moment," said Bill, "there *was* a witness at the casino. Benny was with a young woman called Jasmine. She saw Benny take the £10,000 and lose it."

Then Bill paused and spoke quietly, almost to himself.

"Actually she didn't see him lose it. Neither did I. But she did see that I had the money and that Benny took it off me at the table."

"You mean you gave it to him?" asked Inspector Fulton.

Bill continued to talk as if he was trying to work something out as he spoke.

"No, it was lying on the table in chips. Benny just sat down at my chair and took over from me."

"And this Jasmine can confirm this, can she?"

"Yes, she can."

"Can you give us her full name?"

"No, I'd never met her before, but Mr Horseman could."

"No, Mr Horseman has told us that he *was* at the casino with this young lady, but according to him he had met her only 30 minutes beforehand for the first time in a bar."

"No, he's lying. They definitely knew one another. It was obvious."

Bill was getting too excited. Natalie grasped his arm firmly.

"Of course, Inspector, you will be able to examine CCTV footage from the casino to try to support my client's account of these events," she said. "And, of course, this young lady must have signed the visitors' book before she was allowed in."

"Thankyou, Ms Barry, we will follow up all these points, as you say. However, there are a few other details I'd like you to clarify for us, Mr Knight. If you had all £20,000 of Mr Horseman's money on you when you met him at the casino, why didn't you return it to him there and then?"

"Because I wanted to put it back without him realising it had gone. I just wanted everything back to normal. I guess I wanted to keep my job and not let anyone know what a fool I'd been. Which is a bit ironic now, I s'pose."

"So why didn't you go straight back to Bramport and put the money back that night?"

"Because I was exhausted. I thought I could do it in the morning. Benny never ever goes into the office that early, and definitely not on a Saturday."

"How could you be so sure?"

"Because he doesn't give a damn about the business as long as he gets good profits from it. Because he's a lazy so-and-so, who…"

Bill felt Natalie grasp his arm again and shake it. He knew she was angry with him.

"I'm sorry, Natalie, but I have been absolutely stitched up here."

"I hope that's not an accusation against us, Mr Knight," Inspector Fulton protested.

"No, I'm sorry. I didn't mean you. I meant Benny Horseman has stitched me up."

"Mr Horseman has committed no crime, Mr Knight. You on the other hand admit to taking £20,000, which you knew belonged to Mr Horseman. You took this money to a casino to gamble on roulette, but insist that you intended to pay it back, although it's clear that you had no immediate means of doing so. You failed to return to your home after taking the money, and only returned when you knew the police wished to interview you. It's not looking too good, is it?"

Bill shook his head.

"My client needs a break now, Inspector."

"Right, interview suspended at 15.56pm."

Bill and Natalie were left alone in the interview room drinking tea from polystyrene cups. Natalie sat calmly at the table whilst Bill walked from one side of the room to another.

"I see what you mean about truth now, Natalie," he said. "There's more than one version, isn't there?"

"I'm afraid so, Bill."

"I didn't do very well, did I?"

"It certainly would have been preferable if you had not got so agitated. But if it's any consolation, I believe what you're saying. I'm afraid to say, though, that I think they will charge you. On the evidence I think they have no choice. But we'll insist that they question Mr Horseman again and see if he acknowledges this time that you have paid him back all the money you took from the safe. If he lies, he's a fool. If we can prove he's lying, it could do your case a lot of good. We really need to find this Jasmine character. Leave it to me. That's what I'm paid for."

"We need to discuss your fees, don't we?"

"Not yet. We'll see what happens here first. Then we'll look at all our options. Your main job right now is to stay calm and hold on to what you know is the truth."

At 5 o'clock Natalie handed Inspector Fulton Bill's written statement. Since his account had not changed since the interview, Natalie was informed that there would be no further questioning that afternoon. Twenty minutes later they were summoned to the charge room where Bill was formally charged with theft. Everyone stood as the charge sheet was read out. Bill was informed that he would be released on police bail to appear at the magistrates' court on Friday, 5th November to answer the charges. No one joked about the date. Bill was reminded that if he failed to appear, a warrant would be issued for his arrest, and that he was to have no contact in the interim with Benjamin Arthur Horseman, who would be appearing as a prosecution witness.

When he found himself in the car park 15 minutes later with a copy of the charge sheet in his hand, Bill was in a daze, and he thanked God that Natalie Barry was there with him. Her tone was as calm and measured as always as they walked to her car.

"It's not very pleasant all that, but we'll deal with it all step by step. We'll enter a plea of not guilty on the fifth and probably elect for a jury trial at the Crown Court. That will give us six months to find witnesses at the casino to corroborate your story. By the way I meant to ask, did anyone witness you returning the money belt to Mr Horseman this morning?"

"It's hard to think, Natalie. I'm still in a state of shock."

"Look, Bill, I know it's difficult right now, but this is no more or no less than it is. You acted foolishly under severe stress, and have already put right your uncharacteristic mistake by repaying all the money you are accused of stealing."

Natalie was already rehearsing his defence and he could have kissed her for making him sound so innocent. It made him think more clearly.

"No, Natalie, the only other person at the Hall this morning was Benny's wife, Sandra, but she didn't see me return the money."

"Never mind. Can she at least testify that you visited her husband this morning?"

"Yes, she showed me in."

"That's good. It's then up to us to persuade the jury of the positive intention of your visit. Of course it is possible that Mr Horseman will change his story upon further police questioning, and admit that you've already repaid the money."

"Would they drop the charges then?"

"Possibly. Under those circumstances the CPS might consider that you've only been guilty of a mere breach of trust with no criminal intent and decide not to proceed. Or they may consider you stole the money and only returned it because you were discovered. On the other hand, if Mr Horseman sticks to his story that you stole his money and he hasn't seen it since, they will almost certainly go ahead. But one never know with the CPS. They are, shall we say, unpredictable. But don't worry. There's a lot we can work on."

They had reached Natalie Barry's car.

"Natalie, I can't tell you enough how grateful I am. You must think I'm a complete idiot."

"Stop worrying about what I think of you, Bill. It's not my job to judge you. I don't even have to like you in order to defend you well. You don't have to please me about anything, as long as you're telling the truth."

"I'm sorry, Natalie. I understand all that."

Natalie took a step towards him and placed her hand on his forearm.

"Look, Bill. I'm your lawyer not your doctor, but from what I've learned of you already it's pretty obvious you've acted somewhat out of character here. You're obviously a man under considerable stress. I think you need to look clearly at what's going on in your life to make you do something like this. Is there a friend you could talk to, or your wife perhaps?"

Bill sighed but said nothing.

"Will you be alright to drive home, Bill?"

"Yes, of course I will, Natalie. It's very good of you to concern yourself with me like this. It's very late. I've kept you long enough."

He stepped back and shook her hand.

"Thanks again."

"Okay. If you're alright, I'll be off then, Bill. I'll phone you in the next day or two to let you know of any developments with Mr Horseman, or with tracking down the mysterious Jasmine. Take care."

Bill waved as she left the car park. As he walked over to his own car he was surprised to feel tears running down his cheeks.

Chapter 8

When Bill got home he found the house in darkness. Angie had left a note in the kitchen telling him to call her at her mum's as soon as he got in. Bill could not face talking to anyone right away, least of all Angie.

How was he going to tell any of his family that he had been charged with theft? That he had disgraced them and was not the person they thought he was? Angie could not rely on him; the boys could not admire him; his parents and his sister could not be proud of him. They thought he was strong and honest and dependable, but they were wrong. He was a fool and a thief.

As he stood in the kitchen with his head resting on his arms on the worktop, he could not decide whether the tears he was shedding were for the people he loved, or for himself. At the thought that he might be crying for himself, Bill stood up and made the tears stop. He did not deserve them. He strode into the lounge and threw his jacket onto a chair. He had to make himself strong again and see this situation through. He decided to call Angie and to be as upbeat as possible.

"Hello, Angie, I've just got back, love. How are you and your mum?"

"Bill, we've been worried sick. What happened at the police station?"

"Oh, they haven't made up their minds yet. I'm sure they all think I've been a complete bloody idiot, which is true, of course. But the lawyer was very good, excellent in fact."

"What did she say about it? She phoned here, you know, about half past two."

"I know, love. She was very good. She told them I'd acted completely out of character and that I never had any intention of keeping the money. Benny's been lying about whether I returned the money to him, so if he keeps that up he could be in as much trouble as me."

"What do you mean?"

"He's making a false statement by denying I've given him the money back. He could be in a lot of trouble for that."

"So do you think he'd have to give you your job back then?"

"God, Angie, I'm not even thinking about that. That's the least of my worries."

"I'd have thought it was our main worry. How are we going…?"

"Please, Angie, I just can't talk about that now. The police still have some things to look into, so I can't tell you much more at the moment."

There was silence at the other end of the phone.

"I'm sure everything will work out okay, Angie. Don't worry, love. Leave it with me, will you? Are you coming back tonight?"

"I'm not sure, Bill. I can't pretend I'm not worried. And this has really taken a lot out of Mum. If you're telling me everything's going to be alright, I think I ought to stay with her."

"Okay, Angie."

"If I did come back tonight, you and I would only be going over it all again, wouldn't we? I've had enough for now."

"Yeah, me too, love. It's probably a good idea. Look after your mum and have a good night's rest. We'll sort it all out in the morning. Night, love. I love you, Angie."

"I love you too, Bill. See you tomorrow."

Bill was relieved that Angie was not coming back that night. He needed comfort and some reassurance, but knew that she could not provide it. Natalie was right. He needed to speak to someone, but it had to be someone who would not judge him and who would not increase his feelings of guilt. For now Bill could think of no one, and he searched for comfort and distraction instead in a bottle of Courvoisier and the football on the TV.

The next morning at ten o'clock Bill watched Angie park her Nissan Micra on the drive and walk towards the front door. She was still beautiful. Her hair was the same colour as when he'd first met her, and the little weight she had added over the years made her even more attractive to him, if anything. Whenever he saw her in unguarded moments, he always felt love for her and a need to protect her. Their life together ran very smoothly as long as the daily and weekly routines were not disrupted. They had learned over the years not to discuss anything in their lives too deeply, because that was when the gaps between them became too exposed. They talked instead about everyday things that carried no threat, but gradually the lack of real communication between them had become the greatest threat of all to their marriage. Bill knew today would be difficult, and he was not looking forward to it.

He opened the front door for Angie and kissed her on the cheek. He tried to sound as normal as possible.

"Alright, love? The kettle's boiled. Do you want a cup of tea?"

"Yes. Thanks. I'll be there in a minute."

Bill went into the kitchen and after a moment Angie followed him.

"So. I want you to tell me everything that happened yesterday," she said, "and Mum says you must try to explain to me why you did all this. I've had a tablet, so you can tell me everything."

Usually Bill hated Angie taking Valium, but they helped stop her panic attacks and in the present situation it was probably for the best. They stood in the kitchen as they talked.

"Okay, Angie. To be honest I didn't tell you the whole story last night because I wanted you to get a good night's sleep."

Angie put her tea down, closed her eyes and folded her arms.

"Go on. I knew there was more," she said.

"Well, they did charge me yesterday at the station. I have to appear at the magistrates' court in two weeks on the 5th November on a charge of theft."

"Okay, I'm going to stay calm. What happens then?"

"If Benny tells the truth that I've already paid him back the money, it might not even go to court. They may drop everything."

"And if he doesn't?"

"We have to prove he's lying. There was a girl with him at the casino who saw him take half the money back. Natalie Barry's trying to track her down. If she confirms that Benny's lying, I could be in the clear."

"And if she backs Benny up?"

"Then I don't know. We'd have to deal with that if and when it happens."

"Whatever happens though, your job's gone, has it?"

"I'm afraid so, but I can find something else. And we can survive for a few weeks on our savings."

"If you say so. There's lots I could say, but I'm just staying calm. So you don't think we'll lose the house or anything?"

"No, no way. I promise you, Angie, whatever I have to do, you won't lose this house."

"Okay. If you say so, I'll take your word for it. So now the big question. Why on earth have you done all this?"

Bill started to pace.

"If you can't stand still, let's go and talk in the front room."

"Do you mind if I have a brandy?" Bill asked. "I think it might settle me down a bit? Do you want one?"

"God, no. Not at ten o'clock in the morning. Not with these tablets."

"Sorry, I forgot."

Angie sat on the sofa. Bill poured a drink and walked to the window.

"I'm not sure I know myself why I did it, Angie. I'll try to explain, but if I am going to be honest with you and with myself, you mustn't get upset about what I say."

"I've had a tablet. I'll be alright. I want to know."

"The first thing is…I hate my job. I know that doesn't excuse what I've done, but I can't tell you how relieved I am not to have to go into that bloody office tomorrow."

Bill expected an objection but it did not come.

"I'm so fed up with the life I've been leading."

"Are you fed up with me?"

"No, Angie, I promise I'm not fed up with you. But I am fed

68

up…no, not fed up…disappointed with the way our lives, my life, has turned out."

"In what way?"

Bill could see Angie did not like what she was hearing, but at least she was remaining calm.

"There's no excitement, no adventure. Don't get me wrong, Angie, I love you, I really honestly do, but my God our lives are so deadly dull and boring. I can't stand the routine of bloody Horseman's for one more day, and I can't stand working for that bastard Benny."

"Well, you won't have to now, will you?"

Bill ignored the sarcasm.

"I think I can tell you why I did it, Angie," he said.

He paused and poured himself another drink.

"I took the damn money because I wanted to take a risk. I wanted to live on the edge. I wanted something to change. I wanted to do something adventurous."

"Are you mad?" said Angie. "Do you call this an adventure? Losing your job, being arrested, appearing in court. How's that being adventurous?"

"It's not what I would've chosen, but at least I've put a stop to what I hated most. There's been no outlet in our lives, Angie. We never go anywhere much…"

He paused and spoke more softly.

"…because of your attacks and everything. I still think of our trip to Greece in Grandad's old Vauxhall. I thought my whole life was going to be like that, but it turned out that was the bloody high point."

"Oh, for God's sake grow up, Bill. You're not some kid on an adventure holiday who gets upset when he has to come home."

"You can make me sound as stupid as you like, and I know I must sound stupid to you, but I also know that what I'm saying is true for me. I want my life to amount to more than it has."

"Shall I tell you how I see my life, Bill?"

"Yes, Angie, I really want to know."

"I see my life as a wonderful adventure. I see having two strong, healthy boys as a wonderful adventure. Having you and having them has been all the adventure I've ever needed. We have everything. We have our family. We're all healthy. We've got this lovely house. No money worries. You had a steady job. Think of all the people who would love to have a secure job like yours. But it's not good enough for you, is it? It's all a mill-stone round your neck."

Angie stood up and walked towards the kitchen.

"I think you're bloody spoilt and selfish," she said, as she passed him, "and I don't appreciate you blaming me for everything."

Bill said nothing, but went to the table and poured himself another drink. Any validity he had tried to give to his actions had disappeared with Angie's words. He expected to hear sobbing coming from the kitchen but there was none. He pushed the door open gently.

"I'm not upset, Bill, if that's what you think. I'm just bloody angry. You seem to blame your terrible life on me."

"I'm not saying my whole life's been terrible, Angie. I agree with everything you've just said. Of course I'm grateful for what I've got. You and the boys are everything to me. I don't take it all for granted."

"I think you do."

"I don't. I can only tell you how I feel. I'm not saying I'm right to feel it. I feel as guilty as hell about being like this. But you have your problems with your panic attacks, and I don't tell you that you're wrong to have them."

"You don't make me feel very good about it, considering that's what makes it impossible for me to go very far. You're saying that's what's stopped you from travelling and having your so-called adventures all this time."

"Well, it's not helped, but I don't blame you for it."

"Don't you?"

Bill said nothing.

"You're not going to answer that one, are you?" she said. "I knew this boiled down to you being fed up with me. I knew that's where it was all leading. If you were happy here with me, you wouldn't need anything else."

"I am happy with you, Angie. I do love you. All that I've been saying doesn't go against that."

"I'm not staying here watching you getting drunk and waiting for you to drop more bombshells. I'm going back to Mum's for a few hours."

"That's right, run to your bloody mother every time we need to have an adult conversation. Don't stay and resolve anything."

"How can I have an adult conversation with you? You're turning into a spoilt kid right before my eyes. And remember that 'my bloody mother', as you so nicely refer to her, has a weak heart that could kill her at any minute, and all of this is not helping her one little bit."

"I know, I know, I know. I'm sorry. Must you go?"

Angie collected her coat and car keys and stood with the front door open.

"Yes, I must. And by the way, I don't know whether this will mean anything to you, since you have such a long list of your own priorities, but our son Michael called yesterday while you were at the police station. Cheryl's pregnant. We're going to have our first grandchild. I don't know if that counts as any sort of an adventure for you."

Angie closed the front door and walked to her car. When Bill called after her she ignored him and drove off. Bill went straight inside to the phone and called Mick and Cheryl. Mick answered.

"It's fantastic, isn't it, Dad? We haven't been saying anything to anyone, but actually we've been trying for this for over six months. We were getting so desperate we were both going to have tests if Cheryl wasn't expecting by Christmas. It's been awful for her surrounded by other people's babies all day at the nursery, and worrying whether she could ever have any of her own. Still, everything's fantastic now. They reckon the birth will be around the 20th June. How do you and Mum feel about being grandparents then? And Dave will be an uncle! It's incredible, isn't it?"

Bill had not heard his son so excited since he was a small boy. His heart overflowed for him.

"Mick, I can't tell you how happy I am for you. It's the best news I've ever had, except for you and Dave, of course. I'm so proud of you and Cheryl, and I know Mum is too."

"Yeah, can I speak to Mum? She was talking yesterday about going to Mothercare and I wanted to tell her a few things."

"She's just popped out to see Nan. I'll tell her to call you later."

Mick picked up on his father's change of tone.

"Are you alright, Dad? I forgot to ask you about yesterday."

"Don't you even think about all that, Mickey. That is so unimportant next to what you've just told me. You leave all that to me. I'll sort it all out. I don't even want to talk about it."

"Okay, but remember I'm always here for you, Dad."

"You're a wonderful boy, Mickey, and I love you so much..." Bill's voice started to crack.

"Are you sure you're alright?"

"Yes, of course I am. I'm just so pleased with your news, and I'm a bit tired, I guess. Give my love to Cheryl and tell her 'well done'. And all my love to you both."

As soon as he put the phone down the damn burst. Before this weekend he had not cried for 25 years but now tears seemed to be ready to break through at any moment without warning. He tried to make himself stop, because he still was not sure who or what he was crying for. Were they tears of joy for his son and his baby? Tears of regret for not appreciating how much of real value he had around him all this time? Tears of guilt for taking everything so much for granted? Or were they simply tears of self-pity for the mess he had got himself into? He did not know, but no matter how strong and determined he tried to make himself, he could not make them go away.

Angie came back in the late afternoon and found Bill fast asleep on the sofa. She made some dinner and woke Bill up when it was ready. She noticed the redness and puffiness around his eyes, but said nothing. They ate in total silence. At nine o'clock Angie announced that she was going to bed. Bill was relieved to be left alone without the excruciating silence between them. He felt desperate for things between him and Angie to be back to normal, but there was one thing he knew he did not want to change. He knew that he could not have done another day at Horseman's and was relieved every time he remembered that he did not have to go back there in the morning.

Over the next two days the same pattern continued. All conversation was kept on a practical, non-threatening level, but both of them knew that sooner or later the deeper issues between them would have to be raised again. For now though the matter was shelved, because they both needed to regain some emotional equilibrium, and because they both feared where further arguments could lead them.

Chapter 9

On Thursday morning Natalie Barry phoned.

"Sorry I haven't been in touch earlier, Bill, but we've been working hard on the CCTV footage at the casino and tracking down Mr Horseman's friend, Jasmine. But first of all, Mr Horseman. He's been interviewed again by Inspector Fulton and his story stays the same, I'm afraid. He insists that he only gambled with his own money at the casino and that he didn't see you with any money there."

"He's lying."

"Hold on. It gets worse, I'm afraid. Mr Horseman confirms that you visited him on Saturday morning at his home, but only to confess to the theft, to apologise and to throw yourself on his mercy. According to him you admitted that you'd gambled away all his money on Friday evening, but offered to work to pay it back. He informed you that the police were already involved and reminded you that it had always been company policy to come down hard on any theft of company property by employees. He said that you had been forced to implement that policy on some occasions yourself."

"And what about the bad news?"

"I'm pleased you've managed to retain a sense of humour, Bill. I have copies of the CCTV tapes here. Perhaps you'd like to pop in to my office and go over them with me later today."

"Two o'clock okay with you?"

"I'll see you then."

Natalie Barry's office at Robinson and Reed was on the top floor and at least twice the size of Bill's old office at Horseman's. It was also much plusher. Her firm obviously thought a lot of her to look after her so well. Natalie poured Bill a coffee from the percolator on the sideboard and placed a video into a machine built into her desk. A black and white picture appeared on the television mounted on the wall by the window. Natalie closed the vertical blinds.

"This is Mr Horseman arriving in the reception area with a young lady who I presume is Jasmine."

Natalie froze the picture.

"Yes, that's her," Bill confirmed.

"Very attractive, isn't she?"

"Yes she was, and far too young for Benny."

"Ah, well, the reception staff assumed she was Mr Horseman's daughter. She signed in as Jenny Horseman and gave the same address as Mr Horseman."

"She's definitely not his daughter, Natalie. Benny hasn't got any children."

"No, quite. They obviously want to hide her identity, but there's nothing too sinister in that. Most people having an affair want to keep it secret. But the girl on the reception that night knew Mr Horseman, but had never seen this Jenny-Jasmine character with him before."

"It's a strange thing, you know, Natalie. I thought at the time she was much too refined for Benny. Frankly, she gave the impression that she knew him, but couldn't stand him near her. Mind you, most people who know Benny can't stand him near them."

"So that leaves us to surmise that their relationship may be of a different nature."

"What do you mean?"

"Goodness, Bill. You strike me as a man of the world. Can't you guess?"

"What, you mean he'd hired her. Like a prostitute or something?"

"You're shocked, aren't you? It does you credit, Bill."

"I know you're making fun of me, Natalie, but honestly she didn't seem like that at all. Not that I know…"

"Well, maybe she's a high-class escort. That's the conclusion I came to already, and we've checked all the known agencies in Medford, but she's not known anywhere. Our enquiries, as they say, have drawn a blank. We've printed some copies of this freeze frame and we'll show it to some contacts we have in Medford."

"My God, you have been busy."

"Well, we were hoping to blow a hole in Mr Horseman's statement before the hearing on the fifth, but it looks now as if we will have to go to the Crown Court."

"Unless I plead guilty to stealing the money and take what's coming to me."

"I wouldn't advise that at all. You couldn't then refute Mr Horseman's version of events."

"What would I get if I did plead guilty?"

"A person in a position of great trust, who steals a considerable amount of money from his long-term employer to gamble away at roulette, is not going to get away lightly. We could claim you acted under stress, of course. When did you last see your doctor?"

"Not in the last ten years."

"That makes you lucky with your health, but unlucky in court. But you have lived an exemplary life. I think you'd get between six months and three years."

"Three years! Oh my God."

"The maximum for theft is seven years. That's why you're not going to plead guilty. But don't panic. I'm here to stop you going anywhere near prison. But we do need to find a way of proving that you returned the money and that Mr Horseman is lying. Let's look at the footage at the tables."

"Just before we do, Natalie. I assume the time on that freeze frame is the time Benny arrived."

"Yes, he confirms that."

"It's nothing really, but it's just a few minutes after I went in. I know because I turned off my mobile when I went in and it was exactly 8.35."

"And Mr Horseman signed in at 8.37pm. Is it possible he saw you enter the casino?"

"I don't know, but when he approached me at the tables just after nine he certainly was acting as if he'd just spotted me."

"Unfortunately, the CCTV of the tables doesn't show the faces of the players, only their hands. The camera gives a bird's-eye view of the table to see if there are any irregularities in the play or the payouts. The camera is actually there to monitor the dealer more than anyone."

Natalie went over to her desk and inserted a different tape.

"Now, this is the tape of the only table which allows £100 chips. The one where you say you were playing. And here we are at 9.08."

"That's me!" Bill said. "I've just piled up my winnings into five equal piles, see. Typical of me that. Benny comes up now, so I stand up. See, my hands have gone from the table. In a minute Benny sits down. There you are. Now those are Benny's hands, not mine. Damn! If it was in colour and not black and white you could tell it was someone different, but it just looks the same here."

"I'm afraid it is rather inconclusive. You both have a gold band wedding ring and you are both wearing a dark jacket with white shirt cuffs. It doesn't help us very much."

"Is there no footage of the casino in a wider view, so we can see it's Benny?"

"Not now. That footage is on a 24 hour loop, so it was recorded over on Saturday night. They only keep the table footage for 72 hours, so we were lucky to get this."

"It's no good to us, is it? If we can't prove who's playing here, it's useless to us."

"I'm afraid so. I still think our biggest hope of refuting Mr Horseman's statement is by finding Jasmine. We'll keep going on that tack. We've also asked the casino management if any of their employees can help us, but they made it clear that no one there will get involved in a matter like this."

"That doesn't surprise me," said Bill, as he studied the television screen.

"Natalie, is this tape still on?"

"Yes, it is. Why?"

"Benny's not playing."

"What do you mean?"

"When he first sits down he puts on a few chips, but after that he's not playing. In fact, if you look now he's taking the chips away from the table a few at a time."

They both watched as every 20 or 30 seconds Benny picked up more chips and took them away from the table.

"You're right, Bill. He's definitely not laying any bets. But how does this help us?"

"It doesn't help us at all, I'm afraid, Natalie. It just shows that I'm a bigger bloody idiot than ever."

Bill got up and started to pace up and down.

"He didn't lose the money at all, you see. He put it in his pockets and then came over to me and Jasmine and pretended he'd lost it. He just wanted to make sure I didn't get it back. The tight-fisted swine. He's got the whole 20,000 nicely tucked away, and there was I on Saturday morning pleading with him to let me pay him another £10,000. God, what a fool I am. He must be loving all this."

"Why is he doing this to you?"

"I don't know, but I'm going to find out."

"Bill, don't you go anywhere near Mr Horseman. Do you understand? If you do, I shall refuse to represent you any further."

Bill was shocked by the severity of Natalie's tone.

"Of course, Natalie. You've been marvellous to me. I'm completely in your hands. I'm sorry if I get carried away. Sometimes the pressure just gets to me. The worst thing is knowing I've brought all this on myself. I have no one else to blame. I just feel that if Benny had one ounce of decency he could stop all this."

"I must say he does seem to have gone out of his way to make it as difficult for you as possible. But he has made one big mistake, and that is making a false statement to the police. That's what we're going to work on. Your first priority is to stay as unstressed as possible. Did you take my advice and talk all this through with someone?"

"No, not yet. It's strange when you get down to it, how few

people you have in your life for things like that. There's an old school friend, but I think I'm just too embarrassed by it all."

"Take my advice, Bill, phone him. What's his name?"

"Mark, but everyone calls him Stoner."

"You phone your friend Stoner and tell him you need to speak to him. We all need a safety valve, Bill, and you have a long time before all this is resolved. The legal process refuses to be rushed, I'm afraid. And see your doctor and explain how stressed you are. It's the truth and it will help your case.

"I'll be in touch if there are any more developments, otherwise I'll see you on the fifth. All you need to do in court is confirm your name and address and I'll do the rest. Nothing to worry about."

"Oh, I'll be an old hand by then, Natalie. I've got to answer a summons for speeding on the third. I was caught by a damn speed camera on my way to the casino. And it's my first ever driving offence. It must've been a mobile unit or something because I didn't even know I'd been flashed."

"You're not having much luck, are you, Bill? Plead guilty by letter is my advice. We don't want the magistrates getting too used to seeing you."

Chapter 10

Once Natalie confirmed that Bill would have to appear in the magistrates' court on the fifth, he knew he had to tell his parents about the whole affair, before they heard about it from someone else. Bill arranged to call around to see them on Friday morning before they went out to the weekly market in Bramport.

Peg and Wilf still lived in the same house that Bill and Liz grew up in. The newlyweds had bought it in 1946 when Wilf came out of the army. As Bill pulled up the short drive he passed the nameplate, 'Shangri-La', that had been there as long as he could remember. As a young girl in the late thirties, Peg had seen the film *Lost Horizon* at the Regal, and she always remembered the name of the idyllic valley in Tibet where everyone was gentle to one another and everyone lived to an advanced age. She had always promised herself that any home she shared with Wilf would have that name, and she'd had the plaque made up while Wilf was still away fighting. For Peg it had been an act of faith, but even before they moved into the house she had begun to regret the name she had chosen.

Wilf often told his children that their mother was a 'saint' and he would not hear a word said against her. And it was true that Peg worked hard for her family. They ate wholesome food, their clothes were always darned and washed, and the house was always clean and tidy. The garden that Peg tended was a never-ending source of fruit and vegetables, and Bill could even remember her on occasions being up a ladder doing repairs on the house. What he could not remember was ever feeling much warmth from his mother, or a sense of fun.

The only time Bill remembered his parents really laughing together was when he was about seven years old. Liz must have been about five, and all of them were together in the back garden. It was a hot day, so it must have been summer. It was unusual because his father was playing football with him and Liz, whilst his mother worked in the garden. Wilf did not usually join in any strenuous sports because of his disabilities. But on this occasion he seemed to be really enjoying himself, which made the whole thing so much more fun for Bill and Liz.

Wilf must have been getting carried away because he decided to kick the ball with his left leg, which was artificial from below the knee. And he kicked the ball with such force that it sailed into the air over the neighbour's fence and into the garden two doors down. They all looked up and tracked the ball as it flew through the air and were amazed to see Wilf's leg following the ball in the same arc. The ball landed safely in the garden whilst Wilf's leg became lodged in the branches of a sycamore tree. The force of the kick, combined with the sudden release of his leg, had meanwhile given Wilf considerable backward momentum and he had fallen into a privet hedge, where he remained looking stunned.

Bill remembered waiting to see the reaction of his parents before he could be sure whether he had just witnessed a tragedy or something as hilarious as it immediately appeared to him. Suddenly Peg dropped her hoe and started to laugh. At this Wilf also started to laugh and, after a quick check with one another, so did Bill and Liz. Peg was laughing so much that she had to sit down in the soil where she had been working. Wilf was on his back in the hedge with one and a half legs in the air, holding his stomach and laughing as much as Peg.

After a while he said to Bill, "Better go and ask Mrs White if you can have your ball back, Son."

"Yeah, and while you're over there," added Peg, "ask her if your father can have his leg back, please."

And with that their laughter started all over again. Bill remembered how he and Liz kept looking at one another not quite sure what to make of it all.

The fact that his mother was capable of such fun made it even sadder that Bill never saw her like that again. She seemed to regard life as a job that had to be done, and she was forever steeling herself to get through it. As a child Bill received mostly instructions and judgements from his mother, and not half enough love and encouragement. When he told his parents about the trouble he was in with Benny Horseman, Peg's reaction was predictable.

"I'm sorry, William, but I've got to say I'm dreadfully disappointed in you. Frankly, I'm quite ashamed of you."

"Please, Mum, try to be a little more understanding. I've tried to explain the pressure I've been under at work. It's been going on for some time now. People do silly things when they're under stress."

"But that doesn't give you the right to steal, William! Do you think your father and I don't know what stress and pressure are? I can tell you a few things about all that, you know. But neither of us ever stole anything that wasn't ours."

"I know, Mum. You can't make me feel any more foolish than I do already. I know I've let everyone down, and I'm really sorry."

"I don't know," she said, as she brushed imaginary crumbs from the dining table where she sat across from Bill, "when I think of all the sacrifices we've made so that you and Elizabeth could get on and do well. First her divorce, and now this with you. I don't know what it's all been for. Everyone lets you down in the end. No one sticks to anything any more."

"Now come on, Peg, don't upset yourself," said Wilf from his armchair by the fire. "They're not children any more."

As soon as Wilf spoke Peg turned on him.

"Don't upset yourself, he says." Peg got up and stood over Wilf in his armchair, waving a finger only 6 inches from his face.

"You sit in that chair all day doing nothing, or you're in your blasted shed doing I don't know what. Our two make a complete mess of their lives and bring all this on us and you do nothing. You're more useless than the lot of them."

"Please, Mum, don't take it out on Dad for what I've done. It's not his fault. It's nobody's fault but mine. And surely it's not Liz's fault if her husband runs off with another woman."

"Oh, no. Nothing's anybody's fault any more. No one takes

any responsibility nowadays. You can all sort it out for yourselves," she said, and she turned and headed for the kitchen clutching the bottom of her apron like a handkerchief. "I'm just fed up with the lot of you."

Bill sat at the dining table feeling 12 years old. After a few minutes the two men heard Peg's footsteps on the stairs and Wilf sighed deeply. He knew she would stay in the bedroom for most of the day, but he was happy to forego his lunch for a few hours' peace.

"Come out into the garden with me, Bill," he said eventually.

Wilf had walked with a stick for years, and as they went down the two steps at the back door he linked Bill's arm. Bill remembered how as a boy he had been repelled by his dad's artificial hand. It had been made of wood and was a mass of hinges, and Bill could not stand to touch it. Liz used to be happy to clean it for her father, but Bill had never been good at dealing with illness and injuries. Now his father seemed frail and dependent and Bill was happy to link arms with him and hold his flesh-coloured prosthesis as if it were a normal hand. The two men walked slowly down the garden path.

"I'm worried about you, Bill. This isn't like you at all, you know. I've never known you do a dishonest thing in your life, even when you were little. And you always seemed to be doing so well at Horseman's."

"I'm sorry to worry you, Dad, but I'll sort all this out. I did enjoy it at work in the early years, when it was a challenge to build it all up, but if I'm honest, I've hated going in there for a long time now."

"But that doesn't explain what you've done, Bill. Lots of people hate their jobs but they don't steal from their employer. I just don't understand."

"I know how stupid I've been, Dad, and if I could turn the clock back I would. What I have to do now is try to explain it to myself."

"And can you, Son?"

"I don't know. I think there were two things that were getting to me. First off, I couldn't stand working for that Benny."

"They've always been tight-fisted, the Horseman's. They reckon that's why Arthur's wife left him with the boy. Because he was so mean with his money."

"No, it's more than Benny being a bad payer, Dad. You must know there'd be no Horseman's at all without me."

"Everyone knows that, Bill."

"That business should've been mine, Dad. I had all the ideas. I've done all the hard graft. It should be me in Aldrington Hall with all the fancy cars and fancy lifestyle. Can you imagine what it's like seeing Benny Horseman with everything that I've worked for? And he treats everyone with contempt, and he treats me like a hired hand. He's been a right bastard to me."

"Calm down, Son. It's not like you to get so worked up."

"I know, Dad. This is the stress I've been talking about."

"But lots of managers work hard to make money for their employers, Son. That's what they're paid for."

"I've done more than that, Dad. I've built the business up from next to nothing. I don't know whether you remember all those years ago when I was offered the job as manager. I wanted to start my own firm doing what Horseman's are doing now, but Angie talked me out of it. The whole business should've been mine. We could've made a fortune."

"So a lot of this is about wasted opportunity, is it? And the feeling you're owed more than you've got?"

"Yes, I suppose it is up to a point."

"And you blame Angie as well for a lot of it, do you?"

"No, I don't blame Angie. We were both very young. I shouldn't really have listened to her, I suppose. I should've been more insistent. Should've stood up for myself more."

The two men had reached the end of the garden and were standing by the wall under the trellis. Wilf let go of his son's arm and they both sat down on the garden bench.

"Do you know, Dad, if I'm really honest with myself I think I do blame Angie to a certain extent. I feel she's held me back over the years, but I feel so bad saying it. She's been such a good wife, and a wonderful mother to the boys."

"That's the main thing, Bill. Everyone has regrets in their life, God knows. But the main thing is to hold the family together. You've had a good life with your Angie and you've got two smashing kids. You've got to deal with this mess like the man you are, start earning again and pick up the pieces. Your first priority must be Angie and the boys. In the end it's only the family that matters."

"Is that how you managed to stick out 43 years at Holland's?"

"I was pleased to have the work, Son. I've seen a lot of men out of work over the years, but I brought money into this house every week of my life. I know it wasn't much but it got us through."

"Didn't you find it too much sometimes?"

"Of course I did! There were times when I hated the slog of it. That's why I wanted things to be different for you."

"Well, I did 30 years at Horseman's, but it seems like nothing next to the 43 you did. I don't know how you put up with so much, I really don't."

"I couldn't see I had a choice, Bill. I was lucky to find any job when I came out of the army. It's just the way things are, and you just have to get on with it. Anyway, I don't want to talk about all that. Two reasons, you said. Two reasons why you did what you did. What was the other one then?"

"Oh, I'm not sure I can tell you now, Dad. I feel stupid saying it at the best of times, but now it just seems pathetic."

"Go on, nothing can shock me any more."

"Do you know, Dad, I remember standing in this garden saying this to you over 35 years ago.

"The fact is I've always wanted to travel. I don't mean go on a holiday. I mean take off and explore the world for a year or two, or more. Follow your nose and pit your wits against what the world has to offer. Do you remember me saying that to you?"

"I can't say I do really, Son."

Bill put his hands to his face and rubbed his fingertips hard against his forehead.

"Oh God, that's really ironic," he said. "I listened so much to your advice then and you can't even remember what you said."

"I expect I told you to wait until you'd established yourself, did I?"

"Yes, you did. But that's the point, isn't it? Once you establish yourself with a job and a family, life has you chained up and you can't break free. If you do break free you create one awful damn mess all around you and feel as guilty as hell. That's why I needed to borrow that money. I needed to make just enough to keep Angie's life intact whilst I broke free a bit. But look at the damn mess I've made now."

"Dear God, Bill, you're just like your mother."

"What? I'm nothing like my mother," Bill protested.

"Oh, yes you are. Why do you think she's so bitter and frustrated nowadays? She didn't used to be like that, you know. When I first met her she was so much fun and always laughing. She had what you'd call a zest for life. She sounded just like you're sounding now with all your talk of travel and breaking free."

"I don't remember her like that."

"No, it all changed when I came back from the army. She's been like a bird in a cage really, a bit like you and your chains, I suppose. It didn't really strike me how much she'd changed until you and Liz left home. We were always too busy to think about things much. And it's not been easy since I gave up work."

Wilf leant forward resting both hands on the top of his stick, and staring into the distance.

"I think your mum's found it very difficult with me over the years," he said, "because there was so much I couldn't do that she wanted to do. She's always been marvellous about it, but I think it's all starting to come out more now. It's no one's fault really."

"I don't think you can blame yourself, Dad. I love Mum, but I've got to say I don't think she's very nice to you sometimes. I think you ought to stand up for yourself a bit more."

"It's not a question of blame or standing up for yourself, Bill. It's just that everyone's made different and we have to make allowances, that's all. Peg's made allowances for me over the years, and now I'm making allowances for her."

"So what do you think I should do now then, Dad?"

"It's funny, isn't it, Son? Years ago you didn't want my advice but I gave it anyway, and now you ask me for advice and I'm

86

struggling to find the right things to tell you. All I can say is that you should do what's right, and only you can decide what that is. But don't be angry with everyone, Bill. And don't live a life of bitterness and regrets, Son. They'll just eat away at you."

"Regrets are all I seem to have at the moment. Do you ever regret spending all your life in Bramport, Dad? Let's face it, it's a bit of a one-horse town, isn't it?"

"No, it's my home. I've been lucky, I suppose, because I found out at a very early stage of my life that everyone and everything I need is right here."

Wilf shivered. "Come on," he said, "it's getting cold. Let's get back in and see how your mother is. Help me up, Son."

As they set off back to the house Bill could feel his father trembling.

"I've really enjoyed our little talk, Dad."

"Me too, Son. I wish now we'd talked a bit more over the years. You've always been a good boy."

"You know, Dad, there's something I've been meaning to ask you for ages."

"Go on then."

"What have you got in that bloody shed?"

Wilf laughed.

"Memories, Son, memories."

Chapter 11

When Bill got home at Friday lunchtime there was a message on the answer machine from Natalie Barry asking him to call her. He dialled her number right away.

"Hello, Bill, thanks for calling back. I've just found out something which might interest you."

"That sounds intriguing."

"Yes, it is. You remember you told me yesterday about a speeding ticket you picked up last Friday night on your way to Medford. Well, for no particular reason I checked the Magistrates Court list for next Thursday, 4th November, when your speeding summons comes up. Guess who else is on that list?"

"I don't know. Go on."

"Mr Benjamin Horseman."

"Oh well, I'm glad he's having some bad luck too."

"No, that's not the point. This morning I asked the police for copies of the photos taken by the speed camera on the pretext that you and Mr Horseman were my clients and that we might be contesting the evidence."

"Yes, I'm listening."

"Well, you were clocked at 7.56pm and 51 seconds going at 38 miles per hour through Westacott Village, which is a 30 zone."

"That's right."

"Mr Horseman was clocked at 7.56pm and 57 seconds doing the same speed by the same camera. He was right behind you, Bill!"

"You mean…"

"He was following you on your way to Medford."

"What?"

"We have to find out what his motives are for doing all this. Have you any idea why he wants to see you in all this trouble?"

"I know he doesn't like me, but I'm more use to him in my job than in a prison cell. It just doesn't make sense."

"Well, he can't be made responsible for you taking the money, but he's really gone out of his way to make it difficult for you since. We'll certainly question him about it in court."

"I'd like to have a quiet word with him about it now."

"Bill, I cannot emphasis enough to you how important it is for you to stay away from Mr Horseman. A conviction for attempting to pervert the course of justice carries a maximum sentence of life imprisonment. Do you understand me?"

"I won't go anywhere near him. I promise you, Natalie."

"I should think not. You do not need any further complications right now."

"I understand."

"There's one more thing about this speeding photo. Mr Horseman is not alone in the car. There's a woman with him, and I think it's the same woman who's on the casino CCTV."

"Jasmine?"

"I'm pretty sure of it."

"Jasmine was in the car with Benny?"

"We might have a job proving it in court, but I'm sure it's her."

"So Jasmine comes from Bramport?"

"Not necessarily, but it means that she was in Bramport on that Friday."

"This is becoming very weird, Natalie. I just can't get my head round it at the moment."

"The important thing is to find her. We need her if we're going to challenge Mr Horseman's version of events."

"Is there anything I can do, Natalie?"

"No, definitely not. You leave it all to me. I'll see if we can find any trace of her here in Bramport. As soon as we have any news, I'll let you know."

Bill was relieved when the weekend arrived. His presence in the house on a Saturday and Sunday was at least normal. During the week every minute he spent there was a constant reminder to him and Angie that their lives were being turned upside down. Nonetheless Bill made every effort over the weekend to stay out of Angie's way as much as possible. Saturday became a good time to renew the felt on the garage roof, and on Sunday both cars needed a thorough clean. By Sunday lunchtime the weekend seemed so normal that Bill ventured to discuss his plans for the coming week, prior to his appearance in court on the Friday.

"I'm going to start looking for a new job this week, Angie. I promise you I'll be bringing money into the house again soon."

"Whatever you say, Bill, but I'm not in the mood to talk about any of this at the moment."

"I just want to reassure you, love. That I'll make everything alright. That's all."

Angie's knife and fork clattered against her plate as she brought her hands down hard onto the table.

"I mean it. Not another word!" she said.

Her voice was so full of anger and tension that Bill became more and more concerned for her as the silence grew deeper. In the past he had always been there to sooth Angie's tensions, but for the first time in their lives he was now the main cause of them, and neither of them knew how to deal with this new situation. Both were relieved when the meal was over and Angie left to take her mum over to Mickey and Cheryl's. Normally Bill would have gone with them, but it was understood without a word being spoken that his presence was not required. Bill sat on his own at the table for a long time after Angie left. His role within his family was changing, and he found it hard to bear.

Over the next few days Bill stayed away from the house and away from Bramport as much as possible. He did not want to see anyone he knew. Every morning he drove the five miles down to Sinton Bay and walked along the beach, which stretched for three miles out to Rook Point. On Wednesday morning it was unseasonably warm as he began his walk.

That morning he had received a letter from Tom Wiltshire, the solicitor for Horseman's, which contained his P45. They regretted the present situation and thanked Bill for his contribution to the firm over the years. Since he had admitted to Mr Horseman a serious breach of trust they had no alternative etc etc. A decision about Bill's pension rights would not be made until the 'resolution of ongoing legal proceedings'. Bill was forbidden to enter the premises of Horseman Heating and Supplies, but if he would inform Wiltshire, Stanford and Cross of any personal belongings that he wished returned from the firm, they would be happy to organise it.

Tom Wiltshire was a decent sort and Bill had dealt with him a lot over the years. He knew Tom would get no pleasure out of writing that letter, but he could not help feeling another stab of embarrassment at the thought of how ridiculous he must appear to all the people he had previously dealt with on equal terms. In his personal and his professional life he felt his status being stripped from him at an alarming rate. And he was struggling to cope.

The rift with Angie was the hardest to bear. He could understand her anger and frustration with him, but he had always thought that the two of them could tackle any problem as long as they stuck together. Perhaps it was too early to expect such understanding from her, but he knew that he could put up with all the rest if he had Angie on his side.

 The situation with people like Tom Wiltshire and Bob Fulton made him feel foolish and embarrassed. With Benny he felt anger and resentment. With Mickey and Dave and Wilf and Peg he just felt sorry. But the situation with Angie made him feel a little of all of these, plus deep, deep sadness. He stopped on the sands and wiped his eyes. When he looked back he saw the hotel on the headland from where he'd started his walk. He had worked as a porter in the hotel during his first summer in the sixth form and he smiled at the memory. The hotel was a long way off now. He had not realised how far he had come. His inclination was to keep going, but people might worry about him and he had to go back.

As he turned he clenched his fists and called out. "I can't do this on my own," he said. "I can't do it on my own."

As he retraced his steps along the beach he made up his mind to follow Natalie's advice. He would phone his old friend Stoner as soon as he got back.

Bill picked up Mark Stone from his flat in Bramport at seven o'clock on Thursday evening. Bill wanted to get out of Bramport so they drove out to the Three Tuns in Hadworthy, a village a few miles to the north.

Bill and Stoner had known one another since they arrived at Bramport Grammar from different primary schools in 1962. On arrival at their new school the boys were separated from the girls, and then separated again from anyone who came from the same primary school, the idea being that they would then have to forge new friendships. When Bill looked around from his allocated desk he saw Mark Stone to his left and Harry Woodford to his right. The boys could not have been more different, but something happened in Bill's first hour at his new school that made him like Harry and Stoner right away. They became friends on that first day and had remained friends ever since.

The day started with a uniform check in the form room. First year boys had to wear short grey flannel trousers, long grey socks and black shoes with laces, along with the school's bottle-green jacket, green and yellow-striped tie and a cap, which was divided into segments of the same green and yellow. Peg had taken a photo of Bill in his uniform in the back garden the day before he started, and it still stood on the sideboard at Shangri-La. Peg had instructed him to smile and relax, but the boy in the picture was doing neither. He stared straight at the camera looking serious and ready for anything.

The uniform check was carried out by their form teacher, 'Dai' Thomas, a geography teacher and rugby fanatic. Dai had a large Mercator map on the wall at the front of his classroom, and a big red arrow pinpointed the exact centre of the map. Dai assured the class that he had measured the dimensions of the map exactly to find the precise centre of the world.

"And I have to inform all you unfortunate Englishmen that the official centre of the world is Wales. And to be even more precise…"

Dai went over to the map and, peering over the top of his horn-rimmed spectacles, he pointed to the tip of the arrow. His voice rose to a crescendo.

"...to be even more precise the exact official centre of the world is Llanelli, the home of the greatest rugby team in the world."

He remained at the map, his outstretched hand still pointing at Llanelli, as if giving his young pupils time to absorb the enormity of the truth he had just revealed to them. Then he turned suddenly and strode to the front of the class.

"Right, uniform check! Class, stand! Good God, you look like a load of wine bottles."

He surveyed the class and pointed to Mark Stone.

"You boy, come 'ere!"

The rest of the class were just relieved that they had not been chosen, but Stoner went to the front as if he did not have a care in the world. His blond hair hung over his ears in a pudding-basin cut, the knot of his tie had disappeared into his shirt collar and one part of his shirt hung over the front of his trousers, which were not the regulation grey. Dai put his hands on Stoner's shoulders and turned him around to face the class. Stoner appeared totally unfazed by this uncalled-for attention and smiled at his new classmates. Then Dai surveyed the boys again and Bill felt sure he was about to be chosen, as Dai's gaze lingered on him. Then suddenly the teacher raised his arm and pointed straight at Harry Woodford.

"Come here, young man, if you please. The rest of you, sit!"

The remaining 20 boys sat down, all counting themselves very lucky, whilst Harry made his way to the front of the class. He was placed next to Stoner. The contrast could not have been greater. His hair was neatly cut and his parting was held in place by a helping of Brylcreem. His tie was secured by a tight knot and all his clothes appeared to have been ironed. Even his short trousers had smart creases in them. With his black-framed glasses he looked every inch the perfect swot. Dai put his hand on Stoner's shoulders and demanded, "Name, boy!"

" Er...Mark Stone...er, sir."

"S-t-o-w-n-e-r, is it?"

"And you, boy?"

"Harry Woodford, sir."

"Harry. Now there's a nice name for a proper English gentleman."

Then Dai began to highlight the obvious differences between the two boys' sartorial presentation.

"You see before you the elegance of a gentleman from good old Harry on my left 'ere, and the shambles that is Stoner on my right."

And every time he mentioned Stoner's shortcomings he would tap him on the back of his head. As Dai continued to compare the merits of the two boys at very great length, it would have been expected that both Harry and Stoner would have shrunk with embarrassment, and in Stoner's case, cowered with fear. But the opposite was the case. In spite of Dai's booming voice and the frequent taps he was receiving, Stoner retained a quizzical smile on his face throughout, and at times seemed to be nodding in agreement with what Dai was saying.

Meanwhile Harry Woodford lowered his chin and gazed over his spectacles at the class, mouthing a speech in perfect imitation of the Welshman. Dai seemed so caught up in his own verbosity that he had not realised that his two young stooges were completely stealing his show. By the time the boys were sent back to their seats, the rest of the class were trying as hard as they could to stifle their laughter.

Thinking the mirth was for his own performance Dai smiled at the class and announced that he was going to the office to collect the register. In later years the boys realised that Dai's frequent departures halfway through the lesson to collect something that he had 'forgotten' were only excuses to have a quick Park Drive, to which he was addicted. Once he left the room the boys let out a collective sigh of relief and spontaneously applauded Harry and Stoner. They both rose from their seats, stretched across Bill to shake hands and bowed to the class. The two boys most likely to become victims in school became instant stars, and Stoner was stuck with his nickname forever.

Years later, when Bill was playing rugby for Bramport Chiefs and Dai Thomas was one of his greatest supporters, he stood in the bar with his old teacher and told him the story of Harry and Mark in that first registration.

"I always did that with the new boys on the first day, Bill. It helped to break the ice, see. Settled their nerves a bit."

Dai proved to be a marvellous geography teacher and Bill remembered him with great fondness. He had just the right mix of humour and firmness, combined with an eccentricity that kept his pupils constantly on their toes. He had a great passion for his subject and he inspired Bill with his love of other countries and other cultures. It did not surprise Bill one bit to discover that Dai had manipulated the situation on that first day just for Harry and Stoner's benefit.

As a result of it Harry and Stoner became great friends, and since Bill sat between them he soon became included in their conversations, and eventually in their friendship. The three boys were very different, but they all had the same sense of mischief and fun. The interests they did not have in common they learnt over the years to share, so things that could have separated them brought them closer together. Because Bill excelled at sport, whenever there were teams to form for lunchtime football or cricket he was always one of the captains who took turns to choose a player. Normally Harry and Stoner would have been left on the side, but not when Bill was around. They always got into his team, and no one objected. Harry loved study and helped both his friends through some of the toughest work. He also had a sharp sense of humour and was a natural mimic.

Stoner was a law unto himself. Nothing seemed to disturb his equanimity. To those who did not know him well he seemed disorganised and disinterested, but that was not true of him. Stoner was passionate about art and music and the right to be how you wanted to be, and not as others wanted you. He was always in trouble for minor infractions of the uniform code at Bramport Grammar, and for making next to no effort in the lessons that did not interest him. If he had not made such a major contribution to music in the school and to the set designs for all the school productions from the third year on, he probably would not have lasted at the Grammar. If it had not been for Stoner, Bill and Harry would never have appeared in *A Midsummer Night's Dream* as Puck and one of the lesser fairy elves, but all three of them were prepared to do things together which they would never have done on their own.

Stoner, much more than his two friends, was a free spirit. He never settled down after leaving art college. Whilst Harry joined an accountancy firm in Medford, and Bill took over the running of Horseman's, Stoner set off to see the world and did not stop for 25 years. He busked all over Europe; he chartered boats in the Caribbean, and worked on sheep farms in Australia. But in between his travels he always returned to Bramport to see his family and his old friends. Whenever Bill met Stoner during those years he was always surprised that his friend had no stories to tell. He could never understand why Stoner had no tales of adventure, when he had been so far and seen so much. He would talk instead of a piece of music he had heard, or a meal he had shared with someone. That was Stoner, a law unto himself. Eventually he went to Tibet before the Chinese took over, and spent months at a time with monks in retreat. He would return to Bramport for a few weeks every summer to work at Horseman's to earn enough money to return to the monks in Tibet, and later Northern India. Bill and Angie had often let him stay with them during these times.

In 1996 Stoner returned to Horseman's to work temporarily again, but this time he had not left. Instead he rented a flat in Bramport and when Bill asked him about his plans Stoner said that he felt it was time to stay in one place. So now he worked for Benny as a factotum, doing all the jobs that Benny could not be bothered with. Stoner was one of the few people who could get on with Benny, because he was so laid-back and self-contained that Benny's ways did not affect him. Bill knew that Stoner would always take anything he told him in his stride and not judge him.

On the way to the Three Tuns Bill asked his friend what was being said at Horseman's.

"Not a lot really, Bill. People just tend to get on with their lives, I guess."

"Well, it's nice to know I'm missed."

"They've put Hugh Turner in charge," said Stoner.

"Hugh Turner! He can't tell a toilet from a tap!"

"Yeah, he's a nice bloke, old Hugh, but he's not the sharpest knife in the drawer, it's true. Perhaps they like the fact that he'll never be able to remember the combination to the safe."

"Ooh, that one hurt, Stoner."

"Well, you've got to laugh about it, haven't you, Bill?"

"I'm not sure I can see the funny side of any of it yet."

"Oh, you will, my old mate, you will."

Bill parked outside the pub and Stoner slapped him on the back as he followed him through the small front door of the Three Tuns. Bill got two pints of Thoday's at the bar and they found a table in the corner.

"So, Bill, tell me truthfully, where have you hidden the money?"

Bill tried to smile.

"I know you're only joking, Stoner, but seriously I've already given it back to Benny, every last penny of it. What's he said to you about it all?"

"Benny? He hasn't said a word to me. He knows he can't involve me in any of this. He knows you and I are mates."

"I don't know how you can work for that bastard, Stoner."

"That's rich coming from a man who worked for him for 30 years."

"No, I mean I don't know how you can spend so much time in his company."

"I take as I find, Bill. Benny's always treated me alright. I feel quite sorry for him really."

"Sorry for him! Why the hell would anyone feel sorry for Benny Horseman?"

"Because he's angry about everyone and everything, and basically he's a very bitter and sad man."

"God, Stoner, you'd see something good in Jack the Ripper, you would."

"No, I don't mean I can't see how twisted and devious Benny is," said Stoner. "I know how he uses people…It's just that it's a matter of what you choose to make important in your life. I know what Benny can be like but I don't allow him to be important to me."

"Well, I don't either," Bill protested.

"Yes, you do. Your problem is you've made him too important to you and now you're getting as angry as he is. People like Benny draw you into their web, if you let them. I just don't let him affect me."

"Maybe you're right," Bill said. "I've sure as hell got tangled up in his bloody web now. I've been an absolute bloody fool, haven't I, Stoner? I don't know what you make of it all."

"Well, you know I don't wish you any pain or hardship, my old mate, but frankly I think it's bloody hilarious."

"You what?"

"What you've done, it's bloody hilarious. There you are sitting in your office, and you think to yourself, 'What shall I do next? I know, I'll nick 20,000 quid from the safe. I'm sure nobody will mind too much'."

Bill started to laugh.

"Then what do you do with it? You take it to the casino, gamble it on bloody roulette and lose the lot. It's bloody magnificent. Even I would never have thought of that. I take my hat off to you, mate."

Bill ignored the errors of detail and laughed even more.

"Then you come home and announce, cool as a cucumber, 'I'm terribly sorry but I seem to have mislaid your money. Terribly inconvenient, I know. Hope none of you mind too much'."

Both of them were now laughing so much that other people in the pub were looking over and smiling at them.

Bill tried to catch his breath to speak.

"And do you know why I did it?" he said.

"No, I don't. You must tell me."

"I wanted to go on holiday."

And they both dissolved into laughter so much that Bill had to stand up and bend over double to contain it. After a minute the spasms subsided and he gestured to the man behind the bar.

"Sorry, landlord. I had to get that out of my system. God, Stoner, I needed that."

"I should say you did, my old mate. You're strung out like a piano wire. I'll get another pint."

Bill watched his friend make his way to the bar. Trust Stoner to see everything from a different angle. For the first time in weeks Bill was starting to relax. Stoner came back with the drinks.

"That's what Angie thought when I tried to explain all this to her, you know," Bill said.

"What did she think?" asked Stoner.

"She thought I'd taken 20,000 quid so I could have a nice holiday. Can you believe it?"

"You couldn't get her to understand then?"

"You're joking! No, not at all. I feel terrible towards her. But how can I explain any of it to her when I can't even explain it to myself."

"I'll try to explain it to you, if you like," Stoner offered.

"Yes, please!"

"You took that money because you're a dreamer."

"How the hell do you work that out?"

"You're an idealist, Bill, a romantic. You always have been."

"I can't see that, Stoner. No one's had their feet planted more firmly on the ground than I have over the years."

"Yes, and I bet that's what you see as your biggest problem too. I know how practical and organised you are, Bill, and I know there's no one who can graft like you, but you were never as one-dimensional as that."

"Aren't I?"

"No. You were always an idealist. You've always wanted to create a perfect world around you. I'm not criticising you, I think in many ways it's admirable, but it makes life bloody difficult for you."

"I'm not sure I get what you mean, Stoner."

"Well, look at you at school. You always wanted to make everything safe and secure for everyone in our little circle of friends. You wanted to protect all of us from the bullies, didn't you? From the Benny's of this world. It was admirable, and I for one was bloody grateful, but it didn't make your life easy, did it? Then there's your sport. You weren't just *in* the team. You were the team. You took responsibility for every game. And it's been the same at

Horseman's. You wanted to make it as right as possible for everyone who worked there."

"You make me sound like a right pain in the arse," Bill said.

"Not at all. It means that you're a reliable friend and a hard working boss and a lot else besides. Everyone's always been able to depend on Bill Knight and that's great for them. The only person you're a pain in the arse to is yourself. Everyone else is saying, 'Thanks very much, Bill'."

"How does that make me an idealist?"

"Because you think it's possible for you to create this ideal world around you and you can't. And the more you try and the harder it is, the more frustrated and angry you become. And the more resentment you feel towards the ungrateful people who prevent your perfect world from existing."

"The only person I resent is Benny Horseman, for what he's doing to me now."

"Maybe, but I imagine it goes a bit deeper than that."

Stoner leant forward and took a long drink.

"Anyway what do I know? I should be charging you 100 quid an hour for all this crap. Let's change the subject."

"Yes, I'm sorry, Stoner. But I really appreciate you talking it over with me."

"That's alright, mate."

"But there was just one more thing you said. You said I was a romantic. What the hell do you mean by that?"

Stoner put his pint back on the table.

"Well, if you must. You're a romantic, Bill my old mate, because you believe there's a perfect existence somewhere. Having failed to create it here, you think it exists elsewhere, and that if you travel long enough and far enough you'll find it."

"So I should learn to appreciate what I've got already?"

"You should learn to know what you want and recognise it when you have it."

"A lot of what I want is here with Angie and the boys, but it's not enough."

"Then you've got some changes to make or some compromises to reach. Anyway, another pint?"

"No, it's my round," said Bill, "I'll get them."

Bill stood at the bar waiting for the drinks. It was true. He did have a picture of himself leading a different life. He had had it on that Friday night in his office. A picture of him relaxed and at ease with himself, but at the same time excited by all the possibilities that life offered. The picture always used to have Angie in it, but not any more. Not for a long time, if he was honest. Bill went back to Stoner with the drinks.

"So what were you looking for on all your travels, Stoner?"

"Simple, Bill, nothing. I found lots of things, but I was never looking for anything in particular. I don't have your romantic notions, you see, so I never went searching for adventures. I never liked living my life with great emotional highs and lows."

"So you just take everything as it comes along."

"And if possible accept it. I've never wanted the sort of drama you've got in your life right now."

"Neither have I! I'm not recommending police interviews and court appearances as a recipe for a happy life, Stoner.

"But the strange thing is though; I have got very mixed feelings about all that's going on at the moment."

"How come?"

"Well, most of the time I'm really bloody terrified about all that's happening, and all that could happen in the future because of what I've done. I've never felt so insecure and vulnerable in my life. But do you know what, Stoner? I wouldn't go back. I feel that lots of things are going to have to change now and I'm just trying to prepare myself for it."

"It could just be the three pints talking."

"No, really. I haven't admitted this to anyone else, maybe not even to myself 'til now. On the night I went to Medford I stayed in a hotel, and in the morning I woke up and realised what I had done, and at that point I thought I'd got away with it. I'd taken the money, gambled with it, and made £1,000 profit. And do you know what? I was really fired up by it all. It felt really good to have taken such a risk for once. Of course, I then found Benny had gone to the police, so the feeling didn't last long."

"Just as well, I reckon."

"God, Stoner. You do say the weirdest things sometimes. How the hell do you work that out?"

"Well, let's say you had got away with it. You covered everything up and made a £1,000 on your little adventure. Where would you be now?"

"Well, I wouldn't be in court tomorrow on a charge of theft for a start."

"No, I'll tell you where you'd be. You'd still be at Horseman's getting more and more peed off, and in a few days or weeks it would all have come to a head again. At least now you're on your way to working things through. You obviously needed to have a good look at your life, which is probably why you did it in the first place."

Bill looked at his friend in disbelief.

"What? Are you now trying to tell me that I did all this on purpose just to turn my life upside down?"

Stoner smiled back at him.

"For such a clever fellow, Bill, you can be a bit slow sometimes," he said. "Of course that's why you did it. Isn't it obvious?"

Stoner stood up and put on his coat, whilst Bill sat shaking his head like a confused child trying to work out what Stoner had just revealed to him.

"Come on, my old mate. Let's get something to eat. Give me your keys. I'll drive. You've got enough problems."

Chapter 12

The next morning Bill met Natalie Barry at her office at 11 o'clock and they walked together to the Magistrates' Court in Sudeley Square next to the town hall. Bill's committal hearing was at 11.30. Outside on the main steps there were small groups of people drawing on cigarettes and looking nervous. Bill followed Natalie through the revolving doors. The courthouse was a Victorian building and the entrance hall and all the corridors had marble floors and were lined with dark oak panelling, giving a clear impression that serious business was conducted there.

There was no place here for Stoner's humour and understanding.

Natalie sat Bill down on one of the benches that lined the walls and told him to wait whilst she saw to some formalities. Within a few minutes she was back and he stood up as she approached.

"Sit down, Bill. We're up next. In Court 2. I'm going in now to prepare a few things. You stay here. Listen for your name to be called and make yourself known to the usher over there. He'll show you in to the dock. And under no circumstances sit down until the magistrate tells you, even if everyone else does. Alright?"

"I think so."

"Don't worry, Bill. You'll see me in there. I'll be sitting in front of you. You just leave everything to me. Alright?"

She smiled and touched his hand and then she was gone. About ten minutes later his name was called and the usher showed him in. They recognised one another but neither acknowledged it.

From the dock Bill kept his eyes on Natalie who was sitting at a table in the well of the court below him to his right. Raised up in front of him were three lay magistrates on the bench. Bill was relieved when he recognised none of them. The clerk of the court announced the case and Bill was asked to confirm his name and address. He was not told to sit.

The CPS prosecutor referred the magistrates to the papers relating to the case and Bill was asked to plead. Natalie answered that her client pleaded not guilty and wished to opt for trial by jury at the Crown Court, and to be granted a continuance of bail. There followed some discussion between the magistrates and the clerk of the court and the case was referred to the Crown Court in Medford and the defendant was released on bail.

The whole process had taken less than 15 minutes and before he knew it Bill was walking back briskly with Natalie to her office at Robinson and Reed in Church Street. He was relieved to be released for now from a world where he felt he had absolutely no control over events.

"I've got to say I didn't enjoy that one little bit, Natalie. I never realised before what was meant by 'the full weight of the law', but I do now."

"The law is blind and all-powerful, Bill. It's not there to respect your feelings. But all that was just a formality really. As I told you, they have to let you go to Crown Court if you opt for it."

"What's next then, Natalie?" he asked, as he fought to keep half a step behind her.

"They will inform me of a date for Crown Court for about six months hence. It's always a long wait but at least it gives us plenty of time to prepare. You must let me know whether you want me to instruct a barrister on your behalf."

"Can't you represent me?"

"Well, I do have my certificate of advocacy for the Crown Court, so I can if you wish."

"Yes, I'd really appreciate that, Natalie. And I really appreciate all you did today."

They stopped outside her office.

"You're very welcome, Bill. I must say goodbye here. I have a very busy day ahead of me. I'll be in touch when I get the court date and I'll send you some information on applying for legal aid."

"I've got a feeling I'm going to need that."

"If you're unemployed and you have less than £3,000 in the bank you'll qualify for it automatically."

"Oh, I definitely qualify alright."

"Chin up, Bill. I'll keep you up to date on any new developments, and remember you can contact me at any time."

"Thanks, Natalie."

They shook hands and Natalie disappeared into her offices. Bill waited for a moment before he crossed the road and went into the Black Lion for a large whisky. The first mouthful made him shiver and then feel a lot better. He pulled up a bar stool, took out his mobile and switched it on in case Angie had been trying to contact him. There were no messages on his voicemail. Bill finished his drink and walked back to his car. As he got to the NCP car park his mobile rang. It was not Angie.

"Hello, Bill. It's Harry Woodford."

"Hello, Harry, this is a nice surprise. How are you?"

"I'm fine, Bill. More important, how are things with you?"

"How long have you got, Harry?"

"That bad, eh? Listen, Bill, I got a call from Stoner this morning and he said he saw you last night. I already knew about what had been going on with you. I'm sorry I haven't been in touch earlier."

"That's alright, Harry. I know how things are."

"The thing is, Bill, I need to talk to you, but not on the phone."

"We could meet in a pub somewhere."

"No, it has to be somewhere private. There are things I feel you have a right to know. Can you come to my house, Bill?"

"Come to Medford, you mean?"

"Yes, is that possible?"

"I can come tonight, if you like."

"Yes, tonight's fine. About seven?"

"Seven's good, Harry. I'll see you then."

Bill left Bramport just before six to give himself plenty of time to get to Harry's by seven. He did not want to be late for Harry. He could not believe that only two weeks had passed since he drove along the same road to the casino with £20,000 of Benny Horseman's money. He kept looking in the mirror and wondering how he had failed to notice Benny's silver Mercedes following him all that way that night. He slowed down to 40 miles an hour and counted out six seconds, the time between them registered by the mobile speed camera. He guessed that he travelled about 100 yards in six seconds. Benny must have stayed two or three car lengths back to conceal himself.

Bill remembered how exhilarated he had felt two weeks before at the risk he was taking. He had been so sure that no one would suspect he was capable of such a daring act, and that thought had given him added satisfaction. And all the time Benny had suspected him, and had been tracking him all the way. No doubt he had found it all so amusing and would probably have been bragging to Jasmine all the time about how clever he was.

"Bastard," Bill shouted, and he hit the steering wheel with the palm of his right hand. He had to calm down before he reached Harry's house. Bill was very apprehensive about seeing Harry Woodford. He did not want to face any more embarrassing or belittling situations today. Bill could not imagine talking to Harry about anything too personal in the same way he could with Stoner. He had remained good friends with Harry over the years, but when they met up it was always with their wives, and the talk was usually of families and holidays and business.

At one time Bill would probably have said that he had more in common with Harry than with Stoner. They were both well respected in the business community, and as the accountant for Horseman's for nearly a quarter of a century Harry had a lot of dealings with Bill on a professional level. But since Stoner had come back to settle in Bramport Bill found he had far more in common with him than with Harry. He liked the way that Stoner was not bound by what most people considered normal. He seemed to be able to take on any event or idea and give it thinking space. Bill wondered if that came from all the things Stoner had seen and experienced on his travels, but that could not be the only answer.

Harry had done very well since he left school. He had gone to Durham University to study mathematics and then taken his articles with a firm of accountants in Medford whilst he studied to become a chartered accountant. It was there that he met his wife, Alison, who qualified a year later than Harry. Then they had set up their own firm, Woodford and Woodford. They had struggled for a few years, and in the early days it seemed that they had made a mistake in setting up their own business rather than staying in secure, salaried jobs. Then in 1978 Horseman's in Bramport got a new general manager, and he made Woodford and Woodford the new accountants for the firm. As Horseman's diversified and expanded under the new manager, he gave more and more business to Woodford and Woodford and Harry and Alison's financial position improved. Their reputation spread and their business grew until they were the largest accountancy firm in Medford. By the early nineties they were the largest in the county and employed 26 staff. Harry remained forever grateful to his old friend, Bill Knight, for the help that saved them.

Bill pulled into Cathedral Close in Medford at 6.55 and parked outside the former bishop's residence. Harry and Alison bought the Tudor hall in 1997 at some astronomical price. They held a moving-in party on the night of the general election, and Harry joked that he had to "buy now, before New Labour takes it all off me". Bill was genuinely pleased with his friend's success. He felt none of the envy or bitterness that he felt towards Benny Horseman. Far from it. Harry was decent and fair and had worked hard for what he had. In Bill's eyes that gave him every right to have it and enjoy it.

When he looked at Harry Woodford and then thought of his own fortunes, Bill had only one misgiving. Two of Harry's children were already at university and the third was at private school and about to follow in their footsteps. Bill had few regrets about cutting his own education short, but he wondered if he had done the best for Mickey and Dave. They had had no trodden path to follow like Harry's children. Bill had felt under such pressure from his own parents when he was at school that he had been determined not to do the same to his own sons. Angie had insisted that as long as the boys were 'happy and healthy' nothing else mattered, and most of the time Bill agreed with her. But because there was no expectation that Mickey or Dave would go to university, there was never much chance that either of them would. Bill realised that he had repeated the mistake of his father in letting his own attitudes have too much effect on the progress of his children. And he realised this most of all whenever he met up with Harry.

Harry might be a little eccentric, but he was also an astute man who sometimes used his eccentricity to mask great intelligence and focus. Everything he did seemed to be measured and considered, and the future of his children had been determined by options and choices that were clearly explained to them. At school it had been Bill who seemed to have all the answers. He was sporty and strong and sociable, and Harry and Stoner would have liked to have been more like him. Now Bill felt that both his friends had grown up with more wisdom than him and that he had a lot to learn from them both.

When Bill got out of the car he could smell the smoke from the fireworks. As he pressed the central locking, someone called out to him.

"Hello, Bill, I'm over here."

Bill turned and saw Harry on the green in the middle of the Close, peering anxiously into the sky and shaking his fist at the fireworks as they exploded.

"Damn Guy Fawkes, causing all this trouble. It's the thatched roof, you see. Could go up if one lands on it."

Harry strode over to Bill and held out his hand.

"Good to see you, Bill. Thanks for coming all this way. I hate Bonfire Night."

"Hello, Harry. Nice to see you too."

They walked up the pathway to the front door.

"I never thought of the risk to the roof, Harry. It must be worrying for you."

"I've got two lads at the front and two at the back, keeping an eye out."

He turned back towards the green and shouted to two teenagers who were chatting away about 50 yards from the house.

"Hey, you two! You're meant to be looking up! If you see

anything at all, you come and get me. Understood?"

The two boys waved in recognition of their instructions and peered into the sky.

"Bonfire Night costs me £100 for firewatchers. It's like the Blitz. Incendiaries everywhere. The Close survived the Baedeker Raids in 1942, but every November it gets worse. Crazy. Crazy. Come in, Bill."

They took off their coats in the hallway.

"Alison's gone with Melissa to a bonfire party, so we won't be disturbed. Come into the drawing room. Can I get you something?"

"A whisky would be nice, Harry, to keep out the cold."

The two men sat in armchairs by the fire and sipped their whisky.

"Cheers, Bill. So, how are you coping with all this fuss?"

"I don't know how much you know, Harry."

"Assume I know everything. Tell me how *you* are."

"I'm okay, Harry. I was in court today."

"Oh yes, how did it go?"

"It was just a formality. To tell you the truth, Harry, I feel extremely embarrassed talking about all this. To be honest, I feel very foolish in front of you right now."

"There's no need for that, Bill. We're old friends."

"I know we are, but I doubt whether you can understand how I got myself into this mess."

"Well, I rather assumed you'd had some sort of breakdown through stress or something. You wouldn't be the first."

"Yes, I have been under stress for a long time," said Bill, "but it's not overwork as such. Stoner tried to explain it to me last night. It's stress that I've put on myself because of the sort of person I am. It makes sense when he says it. You'd be better off talking to him."

"He wouldn't say anything to me, Bill. You know what he's like about confidences."

"Yes. He's a good man is Stoner."

"S-t-o-w-n-e-r!" said Harry in perfect imitation of Dai Thomas. The two friends laughed. Bill leaned forward and studied his whisky as he swirled it around in his glass.

"Stoner says that I try to control too much. He says that I have this idea I can make everything the way I want it, if I just try hard enough. When it doesn't work out, I get angry and frustrated and that's what drove me to act so stupidly. It seems a nice, neat explanation."

"Don't be too hard on yourself, Bill. We all make mistakes."

"Yes, but I've started to feel my whole life's been a mistake, Harry. Nothing's the way I wanted it to be."

"But you're a great success, Bill. You're so loved and admired."

"It's really good of you to say that, Harry, but I don't feel very deserving of love and admiration at the moment."

"But your family love you, and we all think the world of you. You need to think rationally about all this, Bill."

"I've tried to do that, Harry. Before I took the money I tried to give it a rational explanation, and I've tried to explain it rationally since, but I can't. It was an irrational act, plain and simple. I just have to accept that. Stoner has this weird idea that I had this secret desire to turn everything in my life upside down. He wouldn't say that if he could be in my shoes now."

"Perhaps when people are really unhappy they do find strange ways of showing it, Bill, almost like a cry for help. It depends how desperate they are. Maybe all this is your cry for help."

"Hold on, Harry, you're starting to sound just like Stoner. You'll be eating yak's porridge in Tibet if you're not careful."

"No, but seriously, Bill, if it's not a cry for help, why else would you have done it?"

"Well, I can tell you why I think I did it. I wanted to get away from Horseman's and get away on my own for a while. I just needed some money to make sure Angie was alright while I was gone. So I took a risk and it didn't work out."

"That's a bit ironic really, isn't it, when you think how many risks you've taken for Horseman's that have paid off so handsomely for them?"

"Yes, I do find it a bit hard to take."

Harry took Bill's glass and poured them both another drink.

"How is Angie, by the way?" he said.

"She's fine. We're just helping one another through it all."

"That's good. Please give her our love from Alison and me."

Bill could not possibly tell Harry that he had hardly seen Angie for days, and that when they were together they hardly spoke.

"So, Harry. What is it that you want to tell me?"

"Oh, this isn't going to be easy, Bill. But you've got to know."

Harry stood up and went over to the window, which looked out onto the green. He eventually turned and faced Bill.

"Have you ever heard of a company called SCP?"

"Yes, they're that big French firm, aren't they?"

"Yes, that's right. Their full name is Societe de Chauffage de Paulhan. They're in the same line as Horseman's, but on a much larger scale. They've expanded into several other countries in Europe over the last ten years, and now they're looking to come over here."

"Yes, I remember reading about it. They bought out that firm in the West Midlands recently, didn't they?"

"Yes, that's right, Bill. Well now they're buying Horseman's."

"They're what?"

"My firm and Tom Wiltshire have been in negotiations with SCP on Benny Horseman's behalf for about ten weeks."

"Why wasn't I told about it?"

"Benny didn't want it, and he's the sole proprietor of Horseman's remember. It's a privately owned business and legally he has no obligation to tell any of his employees about such plans at this stage. My firm is professionally obliged to follow his wishes. But if I'd known what you were going to do, Bill, I would have given you some indication. If only I could have known."

"Why, Harry? What difference would it have made?"

Harry went over to the sideboard and brought his whisky glass down heavily on the walnut surface. Bill had rarely seen him so agitated.

"SCP intends to keep Horseman's intact apart from the key managerial roles, which will be taken over by people from their West Midlands operation."

Harry turned round to Bill.

"They were going to make you redundant, Bill. Along with the finance manager and the works' manager, Phil Durrant and George Harper."

"Redundant? I don't believe it. That would've been the answer to my prayers. What sort of pay-off would I have got?"

"Your statutory entitlement wasn't much, Bill. Only about £6,500."

Bill leapt from his chair.

"Six and a half thousand pounds for 30 bloody years! What's the big deal about that, Harry, for crying out loud?"

"People in your position don't settle for the statutory minimum, Bill. Benny would've had to have made you a substantial ex-gratia payment to ward off any potential tribunal claim."

Bill felt weak at the knees and sat down again.

"What's the bottom line, Harry?" he said.

"Well, it's quite customary for senior managers to receive one month's gross salary for each year of employment. I know that your salary at Horseman's was disgracefully low. I pointed this out to Benny on many occasions."

Bill stared straight ahead and gripped the arms of his chair. "What's the bottom line, Harry?" he repeated in a monotone.

"I explained to Benny that a specialist employment law solicitor would be able to negotiate a substantial severance package, given your position and length of…"

"Harry! For God's sake. What's the bottom line?"

"I'm so sorry, Bill. They were going to offer you £150,000 as a lump sum, and a fully enhanced pension payable after three months' notice."

Chapter 13

By the time Bill got back to Bramport it was past midnight and Angie was already in bed. Bill knew that he had no chance of sleeping for hours. Harry had been reluctant to let Bill drive home in the agitated state he was in, but Bill was insistent. He was angry with everyone, especially himself. If only he had waited another week, he would have had everything delivered to him on a plate. Everything he could possibly have hoped for. It was too much to bear.

In his own mind he turned his anger on everyone else, even Harry. Why had Harry not confided in him earlier? Everything could have been so different then. Bill imagined Harry and Benny and Tom Wiltshire discussing his redundancy while he worked on in his office at Horseman's, oblivious to all their plans. How dare they sit there trying to work out what he was worth? All three of them with their expensive houses and their fat incomes and their self-importance, discussing Bill and his pathetic salary. Forty-five thousand pounds a year for the general manager of a company that was being sold for £12 million.

Bill paced from one side of the living room to the other, not knowing how he was going to live with what he had learnt tonight. One more week and he would have had £150,000, an income for life, and none of this stress and anger and hopelessness. He sat down on the sofa. His teeth were clenched as hard as his fists, and he stared out blankly not able to deal with any more thoughts. When he woke up three hours later his fists were still clenched and every muscle in his body ached.

Bill looked at his watch. Ten past five. It was Saturday. Angie would be up at about eight and would be taking her mother shopping in Waitrose later. God knows how he was going to tell Angie about all this. Bill shuffled into the kitchen like an old man and put the kettle on to make a cup of tea. Behind him he heard the door open. It was Angie.

"I'll have one of those, if you're making one," she said. Her voice was flat. Bill tried to sound more upbeat.

"Sorry if I woke you, love. I was trying to be as quiet as I could."

Angie sat down at the kitchen table and pulled her dressing gown over her bare legs.

"I was awake anyway. I couldn't sleep," she said.

After a few seconds, which seemed much longer, she broke the silence.

"So what was this vital information Harry had that was so important then?"

Bill let out a long sigh. He was not ready for this yet.

"Do you mind if we leave it 'til a bit later, love? I'm absolutely done in. I'd like to…"

"Please yourself," Angie said, and she got up, slammed the door and went back upstairs.

Bill felt his stress level rise again. He was on the verge of running after her, and shouting and screaming and releasing all his frustration, but he was too frightened to allow it. For the first time in his life he was not sure if he could control his anger once he released it. His heart was pounding and he breathed as deeply and deliberately as he could. When he was sure his anger was safely contained within him, he went to the foot of the stairs and called out to Angie. A smothering numbness made his voice sound calm and normal.

"I'm sorry, love. Your tea's here, if you want to come and talk about it all."

After a few minutes Angie reappeared. She took Bill's calmness for granted and was huffy.

"I only wanted to know what's going on. It's not too much to ask, is it?"

"No, I want to bring you up to date with everything, love. I was going to have a shower, that's all. To wake myself up."

"Do you want to tell me now, or not?"

"Yes, of course I do. It was really interesting actually. Harry was telling me how he's had to argue with Benny for years to pay me anything like a decent salary. Apparently Harry always thought I should be on a profit-sharing scheme, but Benny would never hear of it."

"You're always going on about Benny and how tight he's been towards you. What is it between you two? You're fixated with him."

"You don't understand, love."

"Yes, I do. We've done alright out of Benny. We've got this lovely home. The mortgage is nearly finished. The boys always had what they needed. We've always been happy here. What more could we ask for?"

"What more could we ask for?" Bill repeated, as if in a daze.

Angie snapped at him. "Don't start that again. I don't want to hear about how unhappy and unfulfilled you've always been. How do you think that makes me feel?"

"It's not about you. Angie. It's about me. About how I feel about myself. About my life. What I've achieved and done in my life. I love you. I've always loved you, but this is about me!"

"Then why do I feel you're blaming me all the time?"

"I don't know why you always feel like that. That's your problem."

"Thank you very much, Bill."

Angie got up to leave the room.

"No, Angie. We've got to deal with this."

Bill grabbed her arm. It was the first time he had ever touched her with any aggression. His voice was raised.

"Don't walk away every time you don't want an adult conversation."

"Let me go!"

"You stupid bloody fool! Do you want to know what Harry really wanted to tell me last night? They're selling Horseman's. Benny's going to make £12 million. Twelve million bloody pounds! Do you understand that?"

Angie wrenched her arm loose. She shouted back at him.

"I don't care what Benny Horseman makes. He can make £12 *billion* for all I care. All I care about is keeping my home!"

"Keeping *your* home. It's *your* home now, is it? Alright, you'll love this bit then. I was going to be made redundant. They were going to give me £150,000 and a half salary pension for the rest of my life."

The colour drained from Angie's face and she cupped her hands over her nose and mouth. She sat down slowly on a kitchen chair.

"Oh my God, Bill. What have you done? What have you done?"

"What have *I* done? What have *I* done? Oh, I see. It's alright if I take the blame now, is it?"

"What have you done?" she repeated. Angie sounded scared, but Bill could not protect either of them from this.

"I'll tell you what I've done. I've stood up for myself. That's what I've done. I've fought back. I've said, 'I'm not doing this any more.' I'll tell you now, I'm not going to be a sad old man like my father."

"We could have paid off the mortgage, bought all the things we've been putting off," Angie said to herself, still in a state of shock.

"You're not listening to me, you stupid fool. You never really listen to a word I say to you."

Angie snapped back to the present.

"You idiot, Bill! You idiot! If you hadn't taken that money everything would've been okay."

"Well, I didn't know, did I? Because nobody thought of telling me."

Bill took a step towards Angie. There was a gentler tone in his voice but he sounded desperate.

"I can't stand the frustration of this, Angie. I can't take all the blame on my own. It's too much."

"Well I didn't steal Benny's money, did I? You're the only one to blame for that."

Bill stepped back as if someone had punched him hard.

"What are you trying to do to me, Angie, drive me crazy? Benny's money? You think that was Benny's money? That was my money!

116

I've had all the ideas at that place. I've done all the work. It would've all been mine if you'd gone along with me in the first place."

"What do you mean by that?"

"When I was offered the manager's job right at the beginning. I wanted to raise money on our first house to start my own business, but you wouldn't have it."

"That was years ago. That doesn't mean anything now."

"It may not mean anything to you, Angie, but if you'd spent 30 years seeing all the money you make go to a cretin like Benny Horseman, you might have a different angle on it."

"So if it wasn't for me, you think it would be you getting the £12 million now and not Benny, do you?"

"Well, I would, wouldn't I?"

Bill looked over at Angie. A taboo had been broken and he was nervous, but he was also relieved that at last he had managed to speak the truth.

"We ought to be more honest with one another, Angie, and say what we really think. It would help us to deal with our frustrations together. We've got to start saying how we really feel, and really listen to one another."

"You must hate me," Angie said.

Bill saw that she was trembling. Her skin looked clammy and there were beads of sweat on her forehead.

"I don't hate you. I love you, but I hated the life I was leading. I hated it, but you would never listen to me."

"I knew this would all be my fault. I knew it was because you were fed up with me."

"Don't do this Angie. It's not about that. Please let's trust one another. We must be able to be honest with one another."

Angie stood up. She was taking short, shallow breaths and she held her right hand to her chest.

"I knew you blamed me. I've got to go. Let me go."

"Please calm down, Angie, and stay and talk. Let's sort things out together."

Angie started to climb the stairs.

"I'm going to Mum's for a while."

Bill stood at the foot of the stairs and shouted after her.

"No, Angie, you mustn't run away all the time."

"I've got to go."

Bill sensed the anger and frustration he was going to feel if she left him alone now with nothing resolved.

"That's right, run away as always. No wonder I got so pissed off with everything. I'm married to a bloody child. Every time you don't like something you run to Mummy."

He knew he was being cruel, but he needed to provoke a response. When there was none it made him worse. He shouted once more up the empty stairs.

"Your so-called panic attacks are just an excuse to never do anything. If you don't want a conversation you just have an attack. If you don't want to go somewhere you have an attack. Do you hear me? They're just a pathetic excuse."

He waited for a response but there was none. Barriers were being broken down which had stood for 30 years and some part of him was scared. But he could not stop.

"No wonder I'm so damned fed up. We can't ever do anything or go anywhere, or 'Angie might have one of her attacks'. It's just bloody childish. This is childish now. Can you hear me?"

More silence.

"I remember when being together used to drive us forward. Now it just holds us back. Think of all the things we could've done, if you'd behaved more like an adult. You've done nothing for years except hold me back. Angie? Are you listening to me? Angie?"

She still refused to speak.

"Damn you then!"

Bill waited at the foot of the stairs. And waited. How could she just stay up there and ignore him? He knew the things he was saying would be cutting deep into her and he could not understand why she did not cry out. Surely nothing would stop her, if... Then a terrifying thought entered his head and he bounded up the stairs two steps at a time. Now he was screaming her name, "Angie! Angie!" He burst into the bedroom and saw her lying on the bed. Her eyes were red with tears and she was curled up like a child with a handkerchief pressed against her face.

"Angie, I thought…Oh God, I thought you…"

He went over to her and took her in his arms. All his anger and frustration turned to deep, heavy sobs.

"I'm so sorry, darling. I thought something had happened to you. Thank God you're alright. I'm so sorry for everything I've done. I didn't mean what I said. I love you so much. I'm so sorry. Forgive me, Angie."

Angie did not speak and she did not move. He held her and brushed her hair lightly back from her forehead and kissed her face. He could feel her breath on him but she said nothing and he feared that he had lost her forever. Then she put her arm around his neck and stroked the back of his head. "Thankyou, Angie. Thankyou, darling," he sobbed. He brought his legs up onto the bed and lay down next to her. They were both crying now and the tears running down their faces washed together. For a long time they just held on to one another and cried until they both fell asleep.

It was the sound of the phone ringing in the living room that woke them. They both lay there waiting for the answer machine to click in, before either of them decided whether to take the call. At the sound of Dave's voice Angie leapt out of bed and hurried downstairs. Bill turned and looked at his watch. It was 10.30. He could hear the muffled sound of Angie talking to their younger son.

Angie was a wonderful mother. She always saw the best in her sons. She had always had so much patience with Mickey and Dave. She would spend hours helping them with their homework, or preparing things they needed for school or clubs or for simply playing with their friends. Why had he not had that sort of patience with them? Why did he use to come home from work and find their questions and demands so annoying, whilst Angie managed to find such pleasure in it all? It was difficult for Bill to admit to himself that at times his own children had felt like a burden to him. Such feelings seemed like a sacrilege, and he was surprised that he was now owning up to them. But in his present mood it was just one more thing for him to feel guilty about, and he tried unsuccessfully to put it out of his mind.

He thought of his own mum and dad. He had not expected his father to share everything with him. He could not remember Wilf spending a lot of 'quality time' with him, and he did not feel he was neglected by his father. Quite the opposite. He wished the silly old fool had not meddled so much in his life, trying to push him in this direction or that. If only he had been left to find his own way more. Then he thought of Peg. If Angie was the greatest supporter of her children, then Peg was the greatest critic of hers. Nothing he or Liz ever did was right or good enough for her. Liz lived in Medford now and would have little to do with her mother. If only he…

"Bill, Dave wants to talk to you," Angie shouted up to him.

Bill put on his dressing gown. He touched Angie's arm as they passed on the stairs.

"I'll be back down in a minute," she responded.

Bill picked up the phone.

"Hello, Dave, how are you, Son?"

"I'm alright, Dad. Where have you been? I thought you'd fallen off the planet."

"Yes, I'm sorry I haven't been in touch. There's been a lot going on lately."

"No need to be sorry. I thought I'd pop over and see you later. Will you be in about two?"

"Yes, I'll be here. We'll catch up on all our news then. See you, Son."

Bill was making tea when Angie came into the kitchen.

"Dave's coming over later."

"Yes, I know, he told me he wants to see you."

"What about, do you know?"

"About what happened yesterday, I expect."

"At the Magistrates Court?"

"No, at Horseman's, between him and Benny."

"What happened between him and Benny? What are you talking about? Tell me quickly."

Angie sat down with her tea.

"This is why I find all this so worrying and upsetting. I don't know where it's all going to end," she said.

"What happened, Angie? Tell me."

"Dave resigned his job yesterday."

"No! He mustn't do that. He was doing so well. He was earning more than me. I don't understand."

"I know," said Angie, "I'm really worried about him. But at least he's just got himself to think about. I just pray Mickey doesn't do anything stupid. Not with the baby coming. He's always got a lot of work from Horseman's."

She rubbed her hand against her forehead as if she could wipe the worry away.

"Why would either of them do anything like that?"

Angie snapped at him.

"For God's sake, Bill. I was determined to stay calm this morning, but you do drive me bloody mad recently. Why the devil do you think your sons would do it? Because they think the world of you, that's why. They worship you. Are you too wrapped up in yourself to see that? Dave's trying to stand up for you."

Bill wiped his eyes and said softly, "The dear boy. The dear boy."

Angie looked at him and took a gentler tone.

"I'm not sure I can take much more of this, Bill. I don't know where we all are with you any more."

Bill stood with his arms wrapped around his chest, staring ahead of him.

"Look at you now," Angie said, "I've never seen you like this before. I haven't seen you cry in over 30 years. And look how angry you're getting. You really frightened me last night."

"I know. I'm sorry, love."

"We used to be so settled. I always knew I could rely on you. I don't understand what's happened."

"I know, Angie. I don't either."

"If you were ill, or you had an accident or something, we'd tackle it together. But you seem to be blaming me and I can't take that."

"I'm not blaming you."

"Yes, you are. You said some terrible things to me yesterday, but I don't want to go over it any more. This is going to make me really ill, if I'm not careful. I think we both need some peace and quiet, and time to think. I'm going to move in with Mum for a while."

Bill was not surprised.

"For how long?" he said.

"I don't know. For as long as we both need."

"No, Angie. That's not fair on you. You stay here. I know you love it here. Get your mum to move in with you for a while, if you like. I can stay at Stoner's. He said I could when I saw him on Thursday. Maybe he saw this coming before we did. He seems to have a sixth sense, does Stoner."

"That was nice of him to offer. Are you sure you'd be alright there?"

"Yes, darling, I'll be alright. Come here."

Angie went over to him and they held on to one another for a long time.

"I love you, Angie," Bill said between his tears. "I'll try to put all this right. I want you to be able to depend on me again. I never wanted to let you down."

Angie pushed her head into his chest.

"I feel so insecure, Bill. I'm just so frightened. Please try and make things the way they were. We were alright before all this, weren't we?"

"I'll try as hard as I can, Angie. You know I've always loved you, and I promise I always will."

They agreed not to make too much of Bill leaving, so Angie went over to her mother's and left Bill to phone Stoner and pack a bag. He said he would be gone by the time she got back. Bill put the bag out of sight under the stairs and waited for Dave to arrive at two o'clock. When he walked in they embraced, as they always did when they had not seen one another for a week or two. Over a beer Bill brought his son up to date with everything that had happened over the past few days. Dave was as chirpy as ever and it helped Bill to be with someone who saw the funny side of most things, and the positive side of everything. The only thing he kept from his son for now was the decision he and Angie had made that morning.

"So what's this Mum's been telling me about you giving up your job, Son? What made you do that?"

"Oh, that. It was a bit of a laugh really. Benny was in the office yesterday for his usual Friday inspection visit. He was as cocky as hell, making the big announcement about this takeover business. He was shooting his mouth off about how he'd managed to safeguard everybody's job through his... what did he say? ...'tough negotiation and personal intervention'. That's a joke. We all know he couldn't give a damn if we all got the push from this French firm. Anyway, he hadn't noticed that I'd come into the office. He was saying that the guy who replaced you...."

"Hugh Turner."

"That's the cookie, Huge Turnover. He was saying that Huge Turnover would be redeployed and only two people would be made redundant. 'This was most regrettable,' blah, blah, blah, 'but he, Benny Horseman, had insisted that they get the most generous severance package, blah, blah'."

"The bloody liar! I know for a fact that he was trying to get away with the statutory minimum."

"Well, anyway, he then started to have a dig at you."

Bill felt his stomach churn.

"What was he saying?"

"Do you want the lot?"

"Yes, I want to know."

"He was saying that the proud story of Horseman's had nearly been ruined right at the end by someone they all thought they could trust being found to be a thief, or something like that."

"The bastard!"

"Steady on, Dad. No one liked it, I can tell you. There was definite unrest amongst the ranks. Then he started talking about money going missing in the past, and how there were more revelations to come."

"I've never taken anything before. I've told the God's honest truth about all this. He's the one that's been lying about it all."

"Calm down, Father, or I shan't tell you the good bit."

"There's a good bit?"

"Yes, of course there is. I wouldn't be setting the scene for you otherwise, but you keep interrupting. Let me tell my story."

"Sorry, Son."

"Benny hadn't noticed, see, that I'd come into the office and was standing right behind him, just as he was telling everyone how marvellous he was and how you'd let the firm down, blah, blah. I let him rabbit on for a while. He was the only one in the room who hadn't seen me. Everyone else knew I was bound to do something. So then I grabbed hold of the collar of his jacket from behind and pulled it over his shoulders and halfway down his back, so his arms were pinned to his side. Then I put a wicker wastepaper basket over his head so he could just see out and see everyone laughing."

"You idiot! What happened then?"

"Then I kicked him up the arse."

"Davey, you're a madman."

"Listen who's talking. Honestly, Dad, you would've loved it. Benny was trying to shake this basket off his head, and he was trying to kick out at me at the same time. He was knocking things over like a drunken elephant. Eventually someone took pity on him and helped him out of it. He was cursing and swearing at me. 'You effing Knights. I got your effing father and I'll effing well get you.' I said, 'Benny, you're as much use as a one-armed juggler with an itchy arse. Your sole purpose in life seems to be to serve as a warning to others.' He seemed to take that as my resignation speech."

Bill laughed but with little enthusiasm.

"You shouldn't have thrown your job away over me, Davey."

"You don't really think I was going to stand there and let him say those things about you, do you? Would you let him talk about me or Mickey like that?"

"No, I wouldn't."

"Well, there you are then. I was ready for a change anyway. One door closes, another opens. That's what I say. You do *not* have to worry about me."

"You're a wonderful boy, Dave. I'm grateful for you standing up for me like that."

"I don't care what you've done, Dad, because I know deep down you're a decent bloke, and I won't have a lowlife like Horseman bad-mouthing you."

"Thanks for saying that, Son. It means a lot to me."

"The truth is, Dad, I think I may have contributed to your problems a bit."

"Of course you haven't."

"No, listen. I haven't always got on so badly with Benny Horseman, and I've chatted things over with him in the past from time to time. Just casual conversations now and again, you know. But I'm afraid I may have said something to him recently that he's latched on to."

"What sort of thing?"

"Well, you were saying in the summer about how you'd had enough of your job, and how you only needed 20 or 30 grand to change your life. How you were desperate to see the world before old age kicked in. You remember?"

"At the barbecue at Mickey's place."

"Yeah, then and on a few hundred other occasions. When you've had a beer or two you never shut up about it. I just took it as the ramblings of a drunken old fool."

"So, what's the problem?"

"The problem is, I remember talking to Benny about how you were feeling. It was very casual. It wasn't even a serious conversation. You know I wouldn't break your confidence."

"I know that."

"Anyway, he asked me how much it would take to tempt you, and I said 'about £20,000'. It was just a joke. I remember him saying, 'I'd better watch my back then'."

"When did he say that?"

"The Friday before the Friday you... you know, before you took the money."

"This is just so weird, Dave. It's as if Benny's planned everything that's happened to me."

"Yeah, but he couldn't make you do what you did, could he?"

"No, but I think everything must've fallen just right for him somehow. He must be laughing his head off about me."

"Well, he sure as hell wasn't laughing yesterday when he was stumbling around with a waste-paper basket stuck on his head."

"No, I'd love to have seen that."

"Have you any idea why he's got such a grudge against you, Dad?"

"Not really. But he seems to be incredibly envious of me for some reason. That's a joke for a start."

"Why shouldn't he be envious of you? You've got me as a son, and old Mick, and a beautiful wife. And you're in pretty good shape yourself, for an old has-been. Benny's about as popular as a fart in a phone box."

"Oh, I know how lucky I am to have such a wonderful family, Dave. I'm sorry I'm such hard work at the moment. I know I'm not the best of company. In fact I've decided to give your Mum a bit of a rest from me for a while."

"How do you mean?"

"I'm going to move in with Stoner for a week or two to give Mum a break from all this."

"It's not permanent, is it? You're not getting divorced or anything?"

"Good God, no."

"Well I hope not. I know Mum can get a bit stressy, and you're obviously having one hell of a midlife crisis. But it's nothing the two of you can't work out, surely."

"No, we'll work it out."

"There's no way you're taking me to McDonald's and the zoo every other Saturday, I can tell you."

Bill laughed half-heartedly.

"No, Mum and I are still in all of this together. I told her I'd tell you what we're doing and she's seeing Mickey later. I promise it's just for a short while 'til I can sort all this out."

"And how do you intend to do that?"

"Well, I reckon I could sort it all out in ten minutes if I could get Benny down a quiet alley somewhere. I might just persuade him to tell the truth about me giving him his money back."

"Don't you dare do that, Dad. Do you hear me? You could be charged with all kinds of things if you tried something like that."

"Don't worry, Son, I'm only joking. I've already promised my lawyer I won't go anywhere near Mr Horseman. But I'd love to get back at him somehow."

"Well, why don't you play him at his own game and concentrate on his weaknesses?"

"Like what?"

"Everyone knows that Benny's as tight as a camel's arse in a sand storm. He likes to keep hold of his money even if he has to bend the rules. Why don't you ask your mate Stoner about the rents he collects for him? I've got a friend who knows some tenants of Benny's, and they get a choice when they pay their rent. It's either £500 a month cash, or £550 if it's a cheque. Now why do you think that is?"

"He keeps it off the books, you mean?"

"Well, it aint 'cos he hasn't got a bank account, that's for sure."

"But Benny hasn't got that many properties."

"Oh no? He's got a damn-sight more than you or the tax man know about. I bet it would be interesting to find out how much he's hiding every week. It makes you think, doesn't it?"

"It certainly does, Son. I'm seeing Stoner later. I'll ask him what he knows."

Chapter 14

As Bill made his way to Stoner's flat, the smoke from the previous day's fireworks and bonfires still hung in the air. The flat was on the top floor of a Victorian terrace in Castle Square in the centre of Bramport. It was the type of house that would once have been occupied by one family, probably with a housekeeper living in the basement. In the 80s it had been divided into four flats, which were all now regarded as spacious in their own right. Stoner rented the two-bedroomed flat on the second floor. Bill's bedroom was a room in the roof with two Velux windows.

He had only brought a small bag with him, with two spare shirts, socks and underpants and some toiletries. As he unpacked, the reality of leaving the home he shared with Angie hit him harder than he expected. There was no excitement in going to Stoner's, only apprehension. He fought to reassure himself that he was doing this to help Angie. "Make things the way they were," she had said to him before he left. But Bill knew that things could never go back to the way they were before he took the money.

When he went down to the kitchen Stoner was sitting at the table reading the paper.

"Got everything you want up there, Bill?" he said without looking up.

"Yes, fine. Thanks for letting me do this, Stoner. It shouldn't be for too long."

"It can be as long as you like, my old mate. Come and go as you please, like I do, and look after yourself, like I do. You can start by making me a cup of tea."

"I see, it's like that, is it? You want an unpaid domestic."

Bill looked in every cupboard for the tea, but eventually he had to give up. Stoner turned to him and spoke in mock exasperation.

"For God's sake, man, the tea's in the tea caddy. Two measures in the pot. Turn the kettle off as soon as it starts to rumble. Brew for three minutes. Make sure it's strained. No milk or sugar for me, or I'll evict you."

Bill looked at the black pellets in Stoner's tea caddy.

"Sorry, Stoner, I am quite domesticated really but I'm just not used to making tea from what looks like rat droppings. I think we'd better have separate catering arrangements."

"Suits me, my old mate."

"But I must give you something towards your rent, while I'm here."

"Could you stand to pay rent to Benny Horseman then, Bill?"

"You're joking! This is one of Benny's places? Yes, I suppose it would be, wouldn't it? With you working for him, I mean."

Bill placed a mug of green liquid in front of Stoner, who held it up and sniffed it as if it were fine wine. He put it down again without tasting it.

"I can't believe the irony of this, Stoner. My life comes crashing down because of my stupidity… and Benny's vindictiveness… and I end up giving money to the person who's screwing me out of every penny he can."

"I think it's rather magnificent, finding shelter under your enemy's roof. There's a beautiful balance and symmetry about it somehow."

"Well, we might have to agree to disagree there, Stoner."

Bill took a sip of his tea. It was bitter and smoky, and quite undrinkable.

"Stoner, I need to ask you another favour."

"No! You can't have Tetley tea bags."

"Seriously, I need your help with something."

Stoner looked up from his paper.

"Go on, Bill. I'm listening."

"If I can't prove that Benny's lying about me returning that money to him, I face going to prison. Angie will lose the house. It's a nightmare."

"How can I help you with that? Do you want me to talk to Benny?"

"Do you think it would do any good?"

"Well, I'm not his friend, but then Benny doesn't really go in for friends. But I don't threaten him in any way, and I might be able to appeal to his better nature."

"Does he have one?"

"He has humanity, and where there's humanity there's hope."

"I'm sorry, but I don't think I put much faith in Benny Horseman's humanity. I think there's more chance of persuading him if we grab him by the balls and squeeze."

"Well, I won't be doing that. That's for sure."

"I don't mean literally, Stoner."

"I won't be doing it literally or metaphorically."

"But I have to put some pressure on him, to make him tell the truth."

"What sort of pressure?"

"Well, there's a rumour that I've heard. Apparently Benny owns lots of property in Bramport and Medford that he lets out."

"That's no rumour. He's quite open about it."

"The rumour is that he's not open about all of them. I've heard there are several properties that he keeps from the Inland Revenue and avoids paying 40% tax on. I've heard that some tenants pay a reduced rent if they pay in cash, and it all goes straight into Benny's very large back pocket."

"And you've obviously heard that one of my jobs is to collect Benny's rents, so I must know all about it."

"Well, do you know about it?"

"I don't think that's the point, Bill. I think the point is that you want to involve me in your personal feud with Benny. He's been petty and vindictive to you, so you're going to be equally vindictive back. Where does it all end?"

"It ends with my life in ruins if I don't do something."

"Why are you always talking about your life being in ruins? According to you, your life was already in ruins before Benny did a thing to you. What ruins are we talking about this time?"

"This isn't a time to get smart over all this, Stoner. I need your help. I'm begging for your help."

"I'm your friend, Bill. I'll always try to help you, but I'm not sure that what you're asking me will help you at all. You don't want to get locked into a feud with Benny. Rise above it."

He put the paper down and turned to face Bill.

"You're always trying to control things and put them right. It's time to stop. Take this mess and make it into something good for you. Take time for yourself. Take this opportunity to find out what you want from your life. Don't get bogged down in trivial things."

"Stoner, going to prison is not trivial."

"Who says you're going to prison? Maybe you won't. Maybe you will and you'll learn something important from it."

"Bloody hell, Stoner, I'm in your home, accepting your hospitality, so I know I have no right to insult you, but you're talking bloody nonsense. How can anyone think that my going to prison might be good for me? All I'm asking for is a little information to help my case."

"No, you're not. You're asking me to encourage you to get deeper and deeper into this mess with Benny. You have a wonderful opportunity here to look closely at your life and decide what you want to make of it. Take the opportunity you've been given for the first time in your life to take stock. Spend time with Angie to find out what she wants. Maybe it would help her if she didn't need her house so much. You both seemed pretty happy to me when you had nothing but one another. Now you have one another and two wonderful children. How fantastic is that?"

"So you won't help me then."

"Bill, my old friend, I'm trying to help you. You just don't see it."

Nothing that Stoner said could make Bill see his situation differently, or lessen his anger towards Benny Horseman. Maybe if Stoner had shouldered the same responsibilities as Bill in his life, he might take a different view of the world. Maybe if he had worked a lifetime and then been cheated out of his lump sum and his pension just as he needed them most, he might not be so bloody saintly in his attitude to Benny Horseman. At eight o'clock Stoner went round to his local, but for once Bill did not want to go with him. Now even the company of his oldest and closest friend annoyed and frustrated him. By ten o'clock Bill could not sit alone with his thoughts a moment longer and he decided he must get some fresh air.

But strolling around the streets of Bramport proved to be no way to relax. At any moment he was likely to bump into someone he knew, and he became more tense and self-conscious as he turned every new corner. By the end of 20 minutes he was walking with his collar up and head down, quickening his pace to get back to the anonymity and seclusion of his attic room. But the walk had at least enabled him to make up his mind about two things. First of all he knew now that he had to get out of Bramport before the constrictions of the place drove him mad, and secondly, for the sake of Angie's welfare and his own sanity, he had to confront Benny before he left.

Chapter 15

Having a conversation with Benny was not going to be easy. The main problem would be finding a time and a place where there would be no witnesses. If there were witnesses Benny would go straight to the police and accuse Bill of intimidation, he had no doubt about that. He had to confront him where he could be sure there would be no one else around.

Aldrington Hall was isolated, and if he waited until Sandra went out he might find Benny at home on his own. But then he would have to get round the security cameras. Benny was very keen on security cameras and all the main rooms in the Hall had one. Bill was sure to be picked up on one of them and then Benny would have an even tighter grip on him. There was really only one place to confront Benny, and that was in the grounds of Aldrington Hall. He had to get to him somewhere far enough away from the house so that they would not be seen or heard.

The next day was a Sunday and Bill decided to drive out to Aldrington Hall to survey the ground. The main entrance to the Hall was on the road to Medford. The gates were electronically controlled from the house, and anyone wanting to gain access had to stop and press a security bell and show themselves on camera. Bill drove past the gates and carried on for another 200 yards along the high hedge, which screened views of the Hall from the road. The hedge looked thick and impenetrable, and anyway the road was far too busy for there to be a chance of getting in unseen.

After 200 yards Bill turned left off the main road and went down a quiet country lane. The lane ran away from the Hall, and the further he drove down it the more farmland there was separating the lane from the tall hedge, which skirted Benny's property. About 400 yards further on a narrow track ran between two fields. Bill stopped and peered down it. It turned to the right after about 100 yards and seemed to lead up a gentle slope to a small wood. Bill backed the car into the track and got out. If anyone needed access to the track he was blocking their way, but the lane was too narrow to leave the car anywhere else. With luck the farmer would not be out and about on a Sunday.

Bill started to walk up the track. If anyone challenged him he was simply out for a walk on a clear November morning, working up an appetite for Sunday lunch. It already felt better to be out of Bramport and at least he was now taking the initiative. Benny had been getting things his own way far too much recently, and the least Bill could do was let him know that he was not going to get away with his pack of lies unchallenged.

As the track turned to the right, Bill saw that it led to a gate where it entered the wood. On the gate was a notice, which read 'Private Property – Keep Out'. The hedge surrounding Aldrington Hall seemed to go behind the wood to his left. Bill looked around. There was no one in sight, just his car at the bottom of the slope. He climbed the gate and saw that a barbed wire fence ran from it around the wood. Once on the other side Bill recognised the same mixed feelings of excitement and uncertainty he used to get as a child whenever he did something he thought might be unwise.

"Why are forbidden places always so deathly quiet?" he wondered. He stopped and listened. There was not a sound. He walked on through the wood and felt increasingly uneasy.

"This is ridiculous," he said to himself in a whisper. He started to hum quietly to provide some noise and normality, but it did not help. He looked around again but there was neither the sight nor sound of a single living thing. He had come about 100 yards and the gate looked a long way back.

"For God's sake, Bill, behave yourself and do what you came here for," he said in a fuller voice, and he set off down the track trying hard to feign confidence.

When he had walked another 200 yards Bill thought he saw open ground beyond the trees. Realising he was reaching the edge of the wood and that he might be seen, he ran forward, bending as low as he could, and hid behind a tree. There below him, about 100 yards away, was Aldrington Hall. Parked in front of it were Benny's Mercedes and Sandra's Porsche. They were both at home. This would be a prime spot to watch their comings and goings. At last Bill felt that he was doing something to fight back. From here he could find out if Benny ever went walking in the grounds on his own, and then work out a way of intercepting him and confronting him.

His thoughts were interrupted when the front door of the Hall opened and Sandra came out and walked over to her car. Bill saw the amber lights on her Porsche flash as she released the central locking. She paused for a moment and looked up to the wood where Bill was hiding. He ducked behind the tree and then peered out slowly. Sandra was standing by her car waving at him. This was impossible. Surely she could not see him from down there. He ducked behind the tree again and heard the Porsche fire up. Then he heard the tyres on the gravel as Sandra drove away from the Hall. Bill took a longer look down towards the house. There was no movement. Then for the first time he noticed something red out of the corner of his eye, about 20 yards away to his left on the edge of the wood. It was a quad bike. It did not take long for him to work out the implications of all that he had just witnessed.

"Oh shit," he said out loud. Then as he turned to find out exactly who Sandra had been waving to, he found himself staring down the barrel of a 12-bore shotgun.

"You do turn up in the strangest of places, don't you, Billy boy?" Benny said. He pressed and prodded the barrel of the gun hard against Bill's chest as Bill sat back against the tree.

"You can't get anything right, can you, you loser? Why don't I just shoot you now and put you out of your misery?"

Benny had a big smile on his face and he looked triumphant. Bill struggled to regain some composure and stared back at him with contempt.

"Why don't you do just that, *Benny boy*?" he said. "I like the thought of you spending 15 years in prison. I'd die happy knowing you were going to pay that much."

"Who's going to put me in prison? You're on my land. It's obvious to anyone you're up to something. They're going to think you came here to attack me."

"Attack you? So where are your injuries, you thick bastard? And how did I manage to attack you sitting down next to a tree? Explain that away."

Benny's face hardened.

"You cocky sod, Knight. Maybe I should get the police out here then and say you came here to threaten me, to get me to change my statement. You should get at least a couple of extra years for that."

"Think it out, Benny. All I've got to do is say I came out here for a walk and some fresh air, and then you stuck your gun in my face. It'll be your word against mine." Bill started to get up. "If you were twice as smart, Horseman, you'd still be stupid."

"Sit down, Knight," Benny screamed.

"I'm not staying down for you or anyone else, Benny, so you'll just have to bloody well shoot me."

Benny stepped back and brought the gun up to his shoulder, as if taking aim. Bill ignored him, whilst he brushed the leaves and dirt from his clothes.

"Put the damn gun down, Benny, you haven't got the balls to shoot me and you know it." He looked around him. "Mind you, it looks as if you've shot everything else in here that can't fight back."

"Don't get too cocky with me, Knight. I still might shoot you, just for the hell of it."

Benny's tone was more menacing, and Bill decided not to push him too far for now. Besides, he needed Benny to give him some answers, and he knew he might not get them unless he conceded some ground first.

"The truth is, Benny, I've had enough of all this. I've decided to go away for a while before the trial comes up, and I had to get some answers before I left."

"Answers to what?"

"Well, I know now *why* you did it, but I still don't know *how* you did it?"

"And you think I'm going to tell you. Do you think I'm really that stupid? Open your coat and unbutton your shirt."

"What the hell for?"

"You're wired, aren't you, you little shit? You thought you could get me as easy as that?"

"No, I'm not, Benny," Bill protested, as he unbuttoned his shirt just as Benny had ordered. "Look, there's nothing there."

"Empty your pockets. Turn them inside out, so I can see them."

Bill put the contents of his pockets on the ground in front of him. Wallet, keys, tissues, chewing gum, and finally, a portable tape recorder.

"Throw that over here, you sneaky bastard, and sit down."

Bill threw the tape recorder over to Benny's feet, and Benny stamped it into the ground. Bill sat down again by the tree. It was time to be more submissive and to let Benny gloat.

"For God's sake put the gun down, Benny. I can't get to you from here anyway, and the bloody thing could go off by accident." Bill put his hands up in front of his face as if to protect himself.

"Oh, you can't keep up the hard man act any more then, Billy boy. Got you a little worried at last, have I?"

Benny lowered the gun, but kept his distance from where Bill was sitting. "You're not worth it, you snivelling little rat, thinking you could come creeping onto my land."

"Okay, Benny, let's save the insults. Are you going to tell me how you did it, or not?"

"What can't you work out for yourself then?"

"How you knew I was going to take the money that night."

Benny laughed. "Oh, you fell for that one a treat, didn't you, you twat? Jasmine and me couldn't believe our luck when you did that."

"I know you followed me to Medford, but how did you know I had the money with me?"

Benny was still laughing. "Because we saw you take it, you fucking idiot. There you were strolling up and down. I thought you were never going to take the bait, but then in you go, hook, line and sinker. It was beautiful to watch."

"I still don't understand how you could see what I was doing."

Then Bill paused, as Benny laughed, and he realised what Benny had done. "You had my office bugged, didn't you, you bastard?"

"And you say I'm thick. You took your time, didn't you, Billy boy? I had two pin-hole cameras in your office for a month trying to catch you at something. And before you say anything, it's perfectly legal if an employer suspects a worker of wrong-doing. I've had it checked. Anyway, they're not there now."

"But I've never put a foot wrong working for you. What the hell did you suspect me of?"

"Nothing. That's the beauty of it. You were always so squeaky clean. I couldn't see I had a chance of getting anything on you. Then that cheeky little brat of yours tells me I'm not tempting you with enough, and hey presto, Daddy's in the shit. I love it."

"So where were you watching me from then?"

"Jasmine and me were sitting in the Merc just around the corner, watching you on a split monitor wired up to a video. Clever, wouldn't you say, Billy boy?"

Benny laughed again and looked down at Bill waiting for a reaction, but Bill was determined to stay calm for now and tease out as much information as he could.

"So why did you need Jasmine there?" he said.

"She was Plan A. I didn't think in a month of Sundays you'd take the bait with the money, not Mr Honest and Superclean. That was a long shot. Jasmine was the main bait. She was going to go in and say she was looking for a friend or something. Then she was going to come on to you, get you down to some naughty stuff. I reckoned a video of that might not go down too well with Harry Woodford's fucking tribunal, or with your snotty wife, come to that."

"You are one despicable bastard, Benny, trying to involve a young girl like that, and my wife. I'm going to make sure you pay for all this."

"It doesn't look like it from where I'm standing, Billy boy. It looks to me like you're paying for everything." Benny started to laugh again. "I reckon I've saved at least half a million from your payout and pension, and I'll even get another 20 grand from the insurance when you're convicted. It's a fucking scream. And you

138

didn't even get a freebie from Jasmine. And she's a little cracker, I can tell you."

Benny was laughing so much now that it would have been a good time for Bill to have rushed him and taken the gun off him, but he decided against it. He needed to draw Benny out for as long as possible and learn as much as he could.

"Very good, Benny, very good. So you got lucky when I took the money. I suppose you got lucky when I went to the casino too."

"You're not kidding. I said to Jaz, 'Where is this daft fucker going with my money?' I thought you were going to London or Dover or something. I said to her, 'Mr Big, making a run for it with a measly 20,000 quid'. Then when you made for the casino it was like a fucking pantomime. I was standing ten feet behind you when you lost that ten grand. Then I followed you into the toilets and heard you blubbing like a fucking girl. When you came out again and started winning I had to think quick. So I told Jaz to get you away from the table while I stepped in and 'lost' the money. That was an inspired move, even if I do say so myself."

"So you didn't lose the money then?"

"No, you twat, just a couple of hundred when I knew you were watching me. Then I came over and made out I'd lost the lot. Pretty sweet, you must admit."

"Oh I do, Benny, I do."

"Then it was round the corner, grab a bottle of champagne and back to Jaz's place. I threw the ten grand on the bed and I was shagging her silly before you got back to your car. Sweet as a nut."

"And then you get round to my office the next morning to 'discover' the theft, before I can replace the money."

"And even better, you come round here a couple of hours later and give me back the other ten grand. And the joke is, you then go to the police and admit everything. You could've said we'd agreed to go to the casino together to gamble with the money. No one could prove any different. It would have been your word against mine. Your trouble is, Billy boy, you're too bloody honest."

"Yes, the irony of my situation hasn't escaped me, Benny. I am learning."

As he spoke Bill started to get up. He decided it was time for a change of tactic. Benny immediately raised the gun to his hip.

"Sit down! I didn't tell you you could move," he snapped.

"I don't give a damn what you tell me, Horseman, you bloody fool. I'm nearly frozen down there. I'm standing up whether you like it or not."

"Don't move from the tree then, or I swear I'll shoot you and say it was an accident and take my chances."

"My God, even with a gun you're scared of me, aren't you, Benny? You're still the bully you always were, and like all bullies you shit yourself when someone stands up to you. Well, don't worry. I have thought about beating the crap out of you over the last two weeks, but I'm not going to."

Bill took a step forward and Benny moved back.

"But I am going to get even with you."

"And how do you think you can do that?"

"By being a bit cleverer than I have been up 'til now. I think I might start by finding Jasmine and getting her to tell the truth. I expect she has the same loathing for you that everyone else has."

Benny smiled and looked relieved.

"Is that all you've got? I wish you luck there, Billy boy. I think I can safely say that Jasmine will never be seen again. Your chances of finding her are less than nothing."

"What the hell do you mean by that, Benny? Have you done something to that girl?"

"Mind your own fucking business, and if that's all you've got to threaten me with you'd better start greasing your arse ready for your prison time."

"Oh, I've got a few other ideas, Benny."

"Such as?"

"Such as where you get the cash from that you put in the safe on Fridays."

"Whose business is that anyway?"

"Well, it might be the Inland Revenue's business if you're trying to avoid paying tax on it."

"Who have you been talking to?" Benny barked at him.

"Never you mind, Benny boy. There are plenty of people out there who are ready to dish the dirt on you. I haven't even started digging yet."

"You're a cocky bastard, Knight, even when you know you're beaten. I fucking hate you."

"Yes, I think I do realise that now, Benny, but I still don't understand why. Look at everything you've got around you. You've got a perfect life here. You're about to pick up another 12 million quid. Why the hell go to all this trouble just to save paying me a few hundred thousand? Are you bloody sick, or something?"

Benny looked down at the ground and shook his head like an angry bull. Then he stared back at Bill with hatred in his eyes.

"Do you really think this is about money? Do you think I give a fuck about the money?" His voice rose as he spoke and with his right hand he pointed towards the Hall and then swept his arm violently behind him. "I don't give a shit about any of this."

"What the hell is it all about then?" Bill shouted at him.

"Respect, you bastard! It's about getting the respect I deserve."

"What the hell are you on about?"

"Fucking respect for me! That's *my* business you stole from, *my* firm, *mine*. It says Horseman above the gates, not fucking Knight."

"So?"

"So you've been sitting in my fucking chair all these years doing everything I wanted to do, and getting everything I should've got."

"But everything from Horseman's went to you, you bloody idiot. What the hell is wrong with you, Benny?"

Benny was red in the face and shouting with fury.

"I told you. I'm not talking about the fucking money! I'm talking about credit… recognition… respect. All that you've had that should've been mine. But nobody ever gave me a fucking chance, because they thought I was too *stupid*. But I'm not so stupid now, am I?"

Benny raised the gun towards Bill.

"And God help me, Knight, if you ever call me thick or stupid again, I'm going to blow your fucking head right off."

"Okay, Benny, okay," Bill replied in a voice as calm and reassuring as he could muster.

"Do you know what my bastard of a father said to me before he died?"

"No, Benny, I don't. Tell me."

Benny spoke in a high-pitched, mocking voice. "'Benny, I don't want you taking over the business. 'Cos you're not bright enough. Give the job to Bill Knight, Benny. He's smart. He's got all the ideas. He'll do much better at it than you ever could'. And do you know what that was to me?"

"No, Benny, I don't."

"A fucking life sentence. That's what it was. He could never take it back, so I'm stuck with it. And do you know what the old bastard did?"

"No," said Bill shaking his head.

"He made it a condition in his will…in his fucking will, mind…that the business had to be sold if you turned down the general manager's job. That's how much fucking faith the old sod had in me. But you knew that, didn't you, you bastard?"

"No. I didn't know any of this, Benny. How could I?"

"You fucking liar! I saw all the quiet chats you had with him. Turning him against me. I remember. Always the blue-eyed boy, weren't you, you little fucker? …He was always going on about how hard you worked. And what great ideas you had. 'Why can't you be more like Bill Knight, Benny?' The stupid old bastard. He was tight with his money alright. It drove my mother away. But fuck me, when it came to a kind word he was fucking super-tight. I'm telling you. I hate him even more than I fucking hate you. And I hate everything that you and that old bastard have ever given me."

"I'm sorry, Benny. What can I say? I didn't know any of this."

"Well, I don't fucking believe you. Anyway, none of it matters now. 'Cos I've got rid of you and I'm getting rid of Horseman's. Now the great Bill Knight can learn what it's like to eat a daily dose of shit. Life's not so good, is it, when I'm the clever one and you're the stupid bastard?"

"Look, Benny, this is crazy. You've got to believe me. I never suspected any of this. I never knew anything about you and your dad or any will. Okay, if I'm honest I have resented you over the years as much as you've obviously resented me. But can't we stop all this now? You can sell Horseman's, enjoy your life in peace, but tell Bob Fulton you got it wrong and let me have my peace too."

"Make everything right for you, you mean? Make myself out to be a liar and look like a fucking idiot again in front of everyone?"

"No, Benny. I mean, just call a truce."

"Play my usual role of Benny the thick, mean bastard, while you become Mr Knight, 'look-I-was-right-all-the-time'. You cheeky fucker. For once you're made to feel like the villain and you can't handle it. You fall apart after two weeks and come whining back to me."

"No, Benny, that's not why I'm here."

"Yes, you are. You're here to whinge and whine. Or maybe you came here to threaten me, eh?" He waved his gun towards Bill. "Now, fuck off, or I'm going to fucking kill you."

"What's the matter with you, Horseman? Can't you be reasonable just for once in your life?"

"Your time's running out, Knight." Benny raised the gun to his shoulder and took aim.

Bill bent down and started picking up his possessions from the ground in front of him.

"Okay, I'm going," he said. "I suppose I ought to leave before you get hurt. You'd look even more stupid with a shotgun sticking out of your arse."

As he looked up he saw Benny turn the gun around and grasp the barrel. As Bill started to get up Benny charged at him holding the gun above his head like a club.

"You cheeky fucker!" he screamed, as he bore down on Bill.

"No, Benny!" Bill shouted, and at the last moment he threw himself forward from his crouching position into Benny's shins. The impact tipped Benny up and he was pitched forward face first into the trunk of the tree which had been at Bill's back. At the last moment Benny turned his face away, which saved his nose from being smashed. Instead the side of his head took the impact.

When Bill looked around Benny was lying face down at the foot of the tree. He was groaning and blood was pouring from a gash above his right eyebrow. His cheekbone appeared to be broken and blood was coming from his mouth.

"Stay still, Benny," Bill said, as he moved him onto his side into the recovery position. He opened Benny's mouth and put two fingers inside to check that he had not swallowed his tongue, and that his airway was open. He cleaned Benny's mouth of blood, saliva and fragments of teeth and checked that he was breathing freely. Benny tried to move onto his back, but Bill stopped him.

"Stay on your side, Benny," he said as calmly as he could, "you're going to be alright. I'm going to get you help."

Bill searched in Benny's pockets for his mobile to call for an ambulance. If he dialled 999 and left the mobile on they could trace the call and find Benny later.

"No, they might not find you for hours," he muttered to himself.

Benny moaned louder and tried again to turn himself onto his back.

"No, Benny, you must stay on your side."

Bill put him once more into the recovery position and decided he would go into Aldrington village and call from a public phone. He would have to be quick.

"I'm sorry, Benny, I've got to leave you. You know what shit I'll be in if they find me here with you. But Benny, you must stay on your side or you could choke. Can you hear me?"

Benny groaned and Bill got up and looked down on him.

"You stupid bastard," he said.

Bill wiped his fingerprints from Benny's mobile and picked up the pieces of his tape recorder that Benny had smashed earlier. Then he searched the wood floor for anything else that could give away his presence there that morning. When he was satisfied that no one could prove he had been there, Bill started running to his car as fast as he could. The quicker he could get help to Benny the better. He had gone about 50 yards when he stopped.

"Shit, shit, shit," he cried. He took out his mobile, dialled 999, and went back to Benny to wait for the ambulance and the police.

It took 40 minutes for the police and the paramedics to arrive. They had to carry all their equipment up to the wood, because "some selfish idiot has blocked the path with his car". Benny had not regained consciousness during this time, and Bill had struggled continuously with Benny's 20-stone frame to prevent him turning onto his back. As soon as the paramedics arrived Benny appeared calmer. Their main concern seemed to be his neck, which soon had a large white collar around it.

"You've done a good job here, mate. It can be very nasty with a head injury. A lot of people fit and choke on their vomit, or swallow their tongue. You've probably saved your friend's life here."

Bill looked down at Benny lying on the stretcher with his head bandaged and his face covered in blood.

"He'll be alright, won't he?" he asked.

"He'll get a brain-scan, and we need to take care with his neck. I can't say more than that at the moment."

When the two policemen had finished helping the paramedics to lift Benny onto the stretcher, they turned their attention to Bill.

"So, sir, why did you want us here?"

"The guy lying down there is Benny Horseman."

"Yes, I recognise Mr Horseman, sir. And you are?"

"My name's Bill Knight. I used to work for Mr Horseman. There's some trouble between us at the moment, and I wanted the police here so I could explain what's happened. I don't want to be accused of doing this to him."

"Yes, I've heard about your 'trouble', Mr Knight. I thought I recognised you from the magistrates' court on Friday. You're out on bail for theft, aren't you? Theft from Mr Horseman, wasn't it?"

"Yes, it was."

"Someone in your position shouldn't be within a million miles of all this. You realise that, don't you, Mr Knight?"

"Yes, I do. I think I can explain."

The other policeman had picked up Benny's gun. He opened it and put the cartridges in his pocket. Then he smelled the barrel.

"Is this your gun, sir?"

"No, it's Mr Horseman's. I think he was hunting in the woods or something."

One of the paramedics interrupted them.

"We're ready with this guy now. We ought to get going as soon as possible. We'll need two of you to help. He weighs a ton."

Bill took one corner of the stretcher and the older of the two policemen walked behind them carrying the shotgun. They eventually manoeuvred Benny over the gate and walked back towards the spot where Bill had parked earlier. The ambulance and the police car were both blocking the lane with blue lights flashing. In the distance Bill saw a car reversing away from the obstruction, back to the main road. The sight of emergency vehicles and the flashing lights made Bill shake his head in disbelief. How much further could his life spiral out of control like this? Then he looked down at Benny and realised that he felt no loathing or contempt for him any more. He understood that all the trouble between them did not matter. All that mattered in the end was life itself. Bill looked up at the clear autumn sky and felt a huge sense of release, as he prayed silently for Benny Horseman to live.

Chapter 16

Bill stood with the two policemen watching the blue lights of the ambulance disappear as it rushed Benny Horseman to Bramport General Hospital. Bill's attempt to collect his thoughts was interrupted by the older police officer.

"I take it then that this is your vehicle blocking the path, Mr Knight? Not very considerate, was it?"

"Look, that hardly matters now, does it? I want to go to the hospital to make sure he's alright."

"I'm afraid you can't do that, sir. You said you wanted us here to explain the situation, and I think it's important that you give yourself the chance to do just that. Who's in charge of your theft case back at Bramport?"

"Bob Fulton. I mean, Inspector Fulton."

"Inspector Fulton's on duty later today, so you'll be able to speak to him."

"Oh, good. I suppose it's good. I don't know what to do."

"I'm not arresting you, Mr Knight, but I am advising you to come to the station with us. Will you do that, sir?"

"Yes, of course."

"Well, follow us then, sir. Are you alright to drive?"

"Yes, fine," Bill replied.

Twenty minutes later he found himself back in the same interview room in Bramport Police Station, trying desperately to get hold of Natalie Barry. The answer machine at Robinson and Reed gave him an out of hours contact number, but it was past three o'clock before he got through to anyone. The man on the other end took down some details and said that he would try to contact Natalie. By the time she eventually arrived at the police station, Bill had been there for nearly four hours. He felt a huge sense of relief when she walked through the door of the interview room.

"Natalie, I am so pleased to see you," he said, as he got up to greet her. She was dressed casually in jeans and a cashmere cardigan, but her manner was cold and businesslike. She ignored his outstretched hand.

"I can't say I'm pleased to see you, Mr Knight. If what I've been told is true, I am going to be extremely annoyed with you. Now sit down and tell me exactly what you have said so far to the police."

Bill felt as foolish as she intended he should, and he sat down as he was told. Natalie sat opposite him with a pen and notepad in front of her.

"I haven't said anything to them yet. Can you please tell me how Benny is? They won't tell me anything."

"Mr Horseman is undergoing tests to find out the full extent of his injuries. That's all I know. Now what have you said to the people here?"

"Nothing. I refused to be interviewed before you got here. Not after what happened last time. Bob Fulton's here apparently, so he knows all about this."

"I don't think he knows why you were found with the bloodied, unconscious body of the chief prosecution witness in your pending court case. I think we'd all like to know the answer to that question."

"I'm sorry, Natalie. I've let you down. I've learned a lot about Benny over the past week or so, and it's obvious he's been out to get me. I had to have it out with him."

"Stop there a moment, Mr Knight." Natalie Barry spoke slowly and without emotion and it added extra authority to her words.

"This is not a playground squabble that might end up with you or Mr Horseman with extra homework or an hour's detention. If the police can prove that you went onto Mr Horseman's property to threaten him or to do him harm, you will almost certainly go to prison. If they prove you caused his injuries you will serve at least three years, more likely five. If he dies, you will probably serve 20.

Now considering all this, how important do you think this need 'to have it out with him' really was?"

"You really are angry with me, aren't you?"

The tone of Natalie's voice did not change.

"You gave me your word that you would not go near Mr Horseman and I believed you. You have betrayed my trust. I simply expected better of you, that's all. I misjudged you."

"I'm very sorry, Natalie. I feel terrible towards you and towards Benny. I've never knowingly lied to you about any of this."

"Well, tell me what happened and be honest to me and to yourself. I'd like them to be one and the same thing for a change."

"So much has happened over the last two weeks. My wife and I have separated because of the strain of it all. Then there's the police interviews, and the court appearance on Friday. It's all been too much. I learned on Friday night that I was going to be made redundant from Horseman's. I was going to get a huge pay-off. I didn't need to take that money in the first place. Isn't that the biggest irony of all? I thought that was the reason Benny's been going out of his way to make things as bad as he can for me. I thought he just wanted to get out of paying me. I'm sorry, Natalie, but I had to let him know he wasn't going to get away with his lies. I just needed to tell him that I was going to fight back. I never intended to hurt him. I didn't hurt him, I swear."

"Slow down and focus on today. How did you meet Mr Horseman today?"

"I drove out to the Hall on the Medford road. I parked the car in a track by the side of the lane to Aldrington Village."

"Did you try to conceal the car?"

"No, it was in broad daylight. It was in people's way, if anything."

"Carry on."

"I wanted to get close to the Hall to see if I could work out a way of seeing Benny. But I didn't expect to see him today."

"So where did you go?"

"I walked up the track and came to a wood. I climbed the gate and walked to the other side of the wood. The wood was at the top of a small hill and you could look right down onto Aldrington

Hall. I thought I'd just stay there a while and see what Benny was doing. See if he went for walks or anything. See if I could get a chance to speak to him. Try to work out an end to this mess. I don't know. I don't know what the hell I was hoping to do."

"Was there any indication at any time that you were on Mr Horseman's property?"

"Yes. The gate to the wood had a private property notice on it."

"And you ignored it?"

"Yes."

Natalie leaned forward and placed her forearms on the table. Bill leaned away from her as she fixed her eyes on him.

"This is the second time in 16 days that you have undertaken something with a very high risk factor. Taking the money and going into that wood both involved you in something with no clear, safe outcome. Do you realise that?"

"Yes, I suppose I do. I just felt I had to do something."

"Look, Bill, you seem intent on changing things in your life, but what you're doing is causing seismic changes. It's clear that you're on a self-destructive path. Can't you see that?"

Bill hung his head.

"Taking risks like this involves the possibility of losing something you value. You've taken a risk with your job and your marriage and your liberty. You need to work out how much you value these things… I'm not sure you're even fully aware of the risks you're taking. You need to think very calmly about what you really want to change and start taking more gentle steps."

"A friend of mine gave me exactly the same advice recently."

"Well, he sounds like a good friend. Listen to him."

"I will, Natalie, I will. And thanks for dropping the 'Mr Knight' and calling me Bill again."

"I can't stay annoyed with you, Bill, because I honestly think you need help. You appear to me to be angry with two people. One is Mr Horseman, and the other is yourself. Mr Horseman is lying in hospital with serious injuries, and I dread to think what's going to happen to you if you go on like this."

"I'm not angry with Benny any more, Natalie. I saw his hatred for me today and I understood it. I don't think it's justified, but I think I understand how he feels. I also realise that he's condemned to a miserable life unless he gets rid of all his bitterness. When I saw him like that, I could see myself. It's ugly. I don't want to be like him. I actually feel sorry for Benny now. I just want him to be alright."

"I'm very relieved to hear you speak like that. But please don't underestimate the amount of trouble you could be in here. Tell me now how you met Mr Horseman and how his injuries occurred."

"I was looking down at the Hall and he came and stuck a shotgun in my face. I didn't even know he was there."

"And then?"

"We talked for about half an hour. He told me how he set me up after I took the money, by lying to the police about me giving it all back. He said he'd had my office under video surveillance for about a month. He was trying to set up a honey trap with this Jasmine girl. He'd been trying to get something on me for ages apparently. He just wanted to ruin my life. None of this is about me stealing from him. His anger towards me runs very, very deep, I can tell you."

"Did you get any proof of all that he's done?"

"Not a thing. It's still his word against mine."

"Did he threaten you with the gun?"

"All the time. He threatened to shoot me more than once. For a while I really thought he was going to do it. Eventually he got so mad that he did attack me. But he tried to hit me with the gun rather than shoot me with it, thank God. He charged at me, and I threw myself out of the way and he fell forward into the tree. I called the ambulance and police and looked after him until they arrived. I told one of the policemen about the history between Benny and me, and he advised me to come down here."

"I'm very pleased you called the police as well as the ambulance. That shows you didn't want to hide anything. I must ask you, why didn't you just leave Mr Horseman and get out of there?"

"He would've died, Natalie. He was in a terrible state. I just pray he's going to be alright. I didn't intend him any harm, but if I hadn't gone there, he wouldn't be in hospital now. I feel responsible for what happened to him."

"You have to be very careful when you say things like that. You may have a lot of moral responsibility for what happened today, but that's for you to think about and deal with later. Right now we have to consider how responsible you are in law."

"Thank you for helping me, Natalie."

"Based on what you just told me, there's going to be no evidence to suggest that you inflicted the injuries on Mr Horseman. The blood on your hands and clothes are consistent with the first aid you rendered him. There are no injuries to your hands, or marks on your shoes to suggest you have beaten or kicked him. I can take all this for granted, can't I? They will examine you, you know."

"Yes, Natalie, absolutely. I've been completely honest with you."

"Good. That leaves us with the more tricky business of explaining why you were there in the first place. There was no injunction against you, but it was pointed out to you that you should not seek to have contact with Mr Horseman. If you happened to meet in the street or in a shop by chance, no one could suggest any ulterior motive on your part. The fact that you were found on his property is your big problem. I think you have to choose between two scenarios. I want you to listen very carefully to what I am saying to you. Okay?"

"Yes, I'm listening."

"The first scenario is this. You have grown very angry with Mr Horseman, increasingly so over the past few days. The tension caused by this has even led to a separation from your wife. You feel that Mr Horseman has deprived you of a large sum of money that should be yours by right. Your feelings for him are nothing short of hatred. You decided today that you had to confront Mr Horseman over all the injustices you feel you have suffered at his hands. You therefore deliberately went on to his property this morning to challenge him, and to make him somehow change his statement to the police. When you saw him you argued with him, and you threatened him. You were looking for an argument and you got it. A fight ensued, as you expected it might, and in this fight

Mr Horseman was seriously injured. Is that the full truth? Yes or no?"

"Well, it's partly the…"

"Answer yes or no to this question, Bill. Is that the full truth?"

"No, it's not right."

"So, stop there and listen to my second scenario, will you?"

"Okay."

"You have been very stressed over recent months by your work. This led you to make a serious error of judgement two weeks ago, which led to your dismissal. This act was completely out of character and you immediately put your mistake right by making full restitution to your employer of any losses he may have incurred. Unfortunately your employer has lied about this restitution, and it has become clear that he has gone out of his way to make your unfortunate error of judgement appear far worse than it was. The stress of all this has led to a temporary, amicable separation from your wife.

"This morning you went for a walk near Aldrington Village to clear your thoughts. You had not walked there before and you were not quite sure where the walk would take you. You made no attempt to hide your presence there. You entered some woods marked 'private' out of curiosity and found yourself near Aldrington Hall. You did not know that this would be the outcome of entering the wood, and you certainly had no intention of visiting the Hall.

"You were about to return to your car, when you were accosted by Mr Horseman carrying a shotgun. Up to that point you had no idea that Mr Horseman was in the wood. Mr Horseman threatened you with the gun. You tried to persuade him to talk calmly and put the gun away, but he was too agitated. Mr Horseman attacked you using the gun as a club and he fell and sustained his injuries by hitting his head against a tree. You called the emergency services, including the police, and kept Mr Horseman alive until they arrived. Is that the full truth? Yes or no?"

Bill looked at Natalie and she held his gaze, showing no sign of emotion.

"Yes or no?" she repeated.

Bill understood. "Yes," he said, "that's the full truth."

"Good," Natalie replied, as she stood up and collected her notebook and pen, "then that's what we tell Inspector Fulton. I'll tell him we're ready to be interviewed."

Bill was examined by a police doctor who confirmed that he showed no signs of being in a struggle with Benny. One of the police constables who attended the scene confirmed that, according to the paramedics, Bill had probably saved Benny's life. Inspector Fulton sat back with his arms folded and stared at Bill whilst a police sergeant took the statement that Natalie had outlined. Within 50 minutes of Natalie Barry's arrival at the police station Bill was allowed to leave, with no new charges brought against him.

As Bill and Natalie went out into the car park it was already starting to get dark.

"You're a wonderful lawyer, Natalie. I don't know how you did that, but I'm very grateful."

"I've told you before, Bill. Truth is not an absolute. It's three dimensional and looks different according to where you're coming from. It's difficult to accept sometimes that any number of people can look at the same situation, view it honestly and still see it totally differently."

"Yes, I understand that more now," Bill said, and he thought of Benny in the wood.

"In law it all comes down to proof. Inspector Fulton knew that he had nothing to challenge our view of what happened today. Don't think for a minute that you would not still be in there if he had." She turned and pointed a finger at him. "Don't you dare take any more risks with the law, do you hear me? I've warned you once already."

Bill shook his head.

"I've got to go now, Bill. I'll stay in touch."

They shook hands and Natalie made her way to her car.

"Thanks again, Natalie. I'm very sorry to have ruined your Sunday."

Then he thought for a moment and shouted after her.

"Natalie, there must be something I can do to help my case that won't get me into trouble like this."

"There is," she shouted back. "Find Jasmine."

Chapter 17

Bill's decision to get away from Bramport for a while made more and more sense over the next few days. News of Benny's 'accident' appeared in the local press and rumours of Bill's involvement began to circulate. Angie took it as further proof that Bill was turning into someone she 'just couldn't recognise any more'. Mickey believed every word of his father's version of events, and made it clear that no one had better suggest anything different while he was around. Dave on the other hand did not believe a word of the official account of events, and remained convinced that his dad had finally given Benny 'the slap he deserved'. Having achieved some sort of hero status in the eyes of his younger son, Bill found he did not want it. Not for this.

Bill could hardly believe that the overwhelming feeling he now had towards Benny was guilt. But why not, he reasoned. He felt guilty towards everyone else in his life, so why not add Benny Horseman to the list? He had seen the bully in the woods, full of his usual bluff and bluster, but he had seen something else too. He had seen a man consumed with anger and frustration, because he had not lived the life he had always wanted. Someone who could not appreciate what he had, because he felt cheated out of something which by right he thought should be his. Stoner was right. Benny did have humanity, but it had been corrupted by bitterness, and it was his bitterness that had made him vindictive, petty and cruel.

There was no news from the hospital on Monday. Stoner phoned Sandra late in the afternoon but the results of the scans and tests were not yet ready. Bill hardly slept on Monday night. On Tuesday

Stoner went with Sandra to the hospital. As soon as Bill heard Stoner return, he was out of his chair.

"How is he, Stoner?"

"It's good news and bad. The good news is that Benny's not going to die, and he's regained consciousness."

"Thank God for that," Bill said as he flopped down into a chair.

"Who are you most relieved for, yourself or Benny?"

"That question's not worthy of you or me, Stoner."

"No, it's not, but then you haven't seen the state Benny's in."

"How bad is he?"

"Where shall I start? His right cheekbone and eye socket are smashed. He might lose the sight of that eye. His jaw has to be rewired, and he'll need a bloody good dentist. It's going to take weeks for him to fully recover."

Bill could not remember seeing Stoner as agitated as this.

"I know what a lousy human being Benny can be, Bill, but he didn't deserve this."

"I know, Stoner. I made a big mistake going anywhere near him. It was a stupid thing to do and I really regret it. I just thought I could sort things out with him."

"We went through all that! We talked about how you can't always make things the way you want them to be. You must've known you wouldn't be able to get through to Benny by meeting him like that."

"That's why I was asking you for some information. I wanted to have something to bargain with."

"And this is precisely why I wouldn't help you, Bill. Because I wanted to avoid something like this happening. It's not your damn job to bargain with Benny. You have lawyers and courts and judges for all that. You have to let this go, Bill, and let the law take its course. If Benny's been lying, the law will sort him out."

"You have that much faith in our legal system, do you, Stoner?"

"You have to. If everyone acted like you just have, we'd have anarchy."

"Well, I used to think the law was fair and objective, but recently I've seen how it can be shaped and manipulated in all sorts of ways. And God help you if you're the one on the wrong side of it."

"So you're not going to take my advice then, and use this time to work things out with Angie, and with yourself?"

"I'm too restless, Stoner. I can't settle to anything. I've got to get away from Bramport. I'm going to stay with my sister, Liz, in Medford for a few weeks. I've phoned her and Angie's okay about it. I was planning to go on Thursday."

"And what will you do in Medford?"

"I'll be anonymous, that's the main thing. I'm going to try to find some work as well. Angie's been really worried about our finances, so that should ease her concerns a bit."

He decided in the circumstances not to tell Stoner one of the main reasons he was going to Medford. To find the girl who had been with Benny on the night he took the money.

"I hope I haven't made you feel unwelcome here, Bill."

"Not a bit of it, Stoner. I know what a good friend you are to me. I'm sorry if you feel let down over all this."

"I don't do guilt trips on people, Bill. It's up to all of us to take responsibility for what we do. You decide how much responsibility you take for this and deal with it yourself. But you need to search your conscience for one thing."

"Go on. Tell me."

"Is there one small corner of you that feels even slightly better now because you no longer feel the only victim in all this? Does it feel better because you know that Benny's an even bigger victim than you? Maybe that's part of the reason your anger and frustration have eased a bit?"

"I'm not…"

"No, don't answer now. You don't even have to tell me. But you need to know the answer and you need to deal with what you find out about yourself."

"God, Stoner, I don't know where you get all this wisdom from. I will give it a lot of thought."

The two friends sat in silence together for several minutes. Eventually Bill spoke.

"Stoner, can I ask you to do one more thing for me while I'm in Medford?"

"As long as it doesn't involve you and Benny Horseman, or casinos, or shotguns, or God knows what else."

"No, I can safely promise you it doesn't. The thing is, will you look after Angie for me while I'm away? We've always been such good friends, the three of us, and I think it would help her a lot to be able to talk things over with you."

"Of course, Bill. I'll keep in touch with Angie."

"All this has really shaken her up, you know. She's always depended on me so much, and now she finds her rock has become like shifting sands."

"Do you want her to depend on you like that?" asked Stoner.

"I'd like her to be able to, but at the moment I just can't take the responsibility. I feel I've got enough problems just dealing with myself."

"Angie's an adult, Bill. You don't have to protect her from everything."

"I feel she needs me so much. The truth is, I've always loved Angie. I always will, but my love for her used to drive me on. Now I feel it's holding me back. You don't mind me talking like this, do you?"

"Do you have to ask?"

"No, I'm sorry, Stoner. I couldn't talk to anyone else about all this."

"You go to Medford, Bill, and try to get some peace. Don't worry about Angie. I'm sure she's a lot stronger than you give her credit for."

Bill moved out of Stoner's on Thursday morning. The last person he called before he left Bramport was Natalie Barry.

"I'm glad you told me of your plans, Bill, because the police have to be kept informed of any change of address."

Bill did not like to admit that he had already changed address once without letting anyone know.

"I was going to call you later anyway," Natalie continued. "Mr Horseman has managed to make a statement to the police about what happened on Sunday."

"What does he say?"

"Well, let's just say that his version of events varies in certain key details from your own."

"Such as?"

"According to Mr Horseman he was walking in the wood when you approached him from behind. You issued vague threats towards him before launching a vicious attack. Before he had a chance to defend himself you had thrown him forward into the tree. He had no further memory of events after that until he woke up in hospital on Monday morning."

"Do the police believe him?"

"I'm not sure, but it doesn't really matter. They can't prove or disprove either version of events, so there's complete stalemate. I take it you haven't heard from the police?"

"Not a thing."

"There you are then. If they could prove that you had attacked Mr Horseman in the manner he claims, you'd be in Medford Prison on remand by now."

Natalie's words made Bill shiver.

"I don't want you getting worked up about this again, Bill, and making any further attempts to contact Mr Horseman."

"Absolutely not, Natalie. I want nothing more to do with him. I've decided to let go of my hatred towards Benny. I just feel sorry for him that he's still wasting time being like that towards me."

"That's better, Bill. I can't tell you how pleased I am to hear you talking like that."

"I've been doing a lot of thinking since I saw you on Sunday, Natalie. I just want to clear up this business with the money and move on with my life. One of the reasons I'm going to Medford is to track down Jasmine. If I can find her I might at least get a fair hearing over the theft. Then I'm prepared to take whatever's coming to me."

"What makes you think you'll find her in Medford? We've already tried that."

"She must be there. It's something that Benny said in the wood. He was boasting about how he'd tricked me out of the £10,000 I had at the roulette table that night."

"What did he say?"

"He said that he pocketed the £10,000 and left me at the bar. But then he let slip that he went straight around to Jasmine's place."

"So her place must be in Medford?"

"Exactly."

"But Medford's a big town, Bill."

"Yes, but he said that he was back at Jasmine's place before I had time to get to my car. So it must be quite near the casino. He also said that on the way there he picked up a bottle of champagne round the corner, so there must be an off-licence or something between the casino and her place. It's a start anyway."

"Good for you. You're a right Sherlock Holmes, aren't you?"

"More Inspector Morse, I like to think."

"Have you got one of our photos of Jasmine to show people?"

"I've got the freeze frame of her as she enters the casino. It's not marvellous, but it'll have to do."

"Of course you do realise that finding her is only half the problem. We would then have to persuade her to testify that Mr Horseman is lying about you repaying the money."

"I know it's a long shot, Natalie, but at least I'll be doing something positive."

"Good. But remember, Bill, if you do find her you must check with me before you do or say anything which might be misconstrued."

"I will, Natalie. You can trust me on that."

"I hope so, Bill, I really do. Good luck, and keep in touch."

Chapter 18

Liz had asked Bill to arrive sometime between six and seven so that she would have time to get home from work and prepare the evening meal before he got there. Bill had not seen Liz or the children since February when they'd all met up at the Royal Oak Hotel in Westacott, midway between Bramport and Medford, to celebrate Wilf's 75th birthday. Bill and Liz kept in touch by phone every week or two, but a lot had happened in both their lives since they had last seen one another.

Liz lived about half a mile from Medford city centre in a redbrick Edwardian semi. She had bought the house with her husband Steve only two years previously. They were both teachers and had met at work and married after knowing one another for about six months. They were both in their early 30s then and saw no point in delaying any further.

Liz still taught French in the same school, Redland Mill Comprehensive in Medford, but Steve had moved on to be Head of Science at a sixth form college. It was there that he'd met a married English teacher called Charlotte, who was 20 years younger than him and had a degree from Oxford. They had moved in together over the summer and had left a trail of devastation in their wake.

Bill pulled up to Liz's house at about 6.45. When she opened the front door to him they embraced with genuine warmth, and she held on to him for much longer than usual. She ushered him in and called up the stairs.

"Suzanne, Jonathan. Uncle Bill's here."

"Coming," answered a girl's voice from somewhere on the first floor.

Bill left his suitcase in the hallway and followed Liz into the kitchen.

"Don't expect too much of a welcome, Bill. They're at that age."

Eventually Suzanne joined them in the kitchen. She was 15 years old, and dressed in blue jeans and a white school blouse.

"Hello, Susie. Don't you look great? You have grown up since I saw you last."

"I think we all have," Liz muttered to herself as she lifted a saucepan from the hob.

"Hi, Uncle Bill," Susie said as she gave Bill a peck on the cheek.

"When's dinner ready, Mum?"

"In about 20 minutes. Ask your Uncle Bill if he wants a drink."

"No, I'm fine, Liz, thanks."

"There's some red wine there if you'd like a glass, Bill. You can top me up too."

"Can I have a glass, Mum?"

"No you can't, miss. Go and call your brother."

"He'll be in his room on his computer," said Susie. "You won't get him down here, the miserable little squirt."

"Well, please try anyway."

"Can I do anything to help, Liz?" Bill ventured.

"No, he's been very difficult since his father left," replied Liz, misunderstanding the nature of his offer.

"Jonathan! You're wanted down here *now*!" Susie shouted from the bottom of the stairs.

"Don't disturb him, Liz. I'll take my case up and pop in on Jonathan on my way."

"That would be nice, Bill. You're in the spare room in the front, and Jon's room is right up the top. You're a brave man."

Susie had gone into the living room and Bill heard her flicking through the channels on the TV. When he reached the spare room he could see the effort his sister had made to make him welcome. The wardrobe and drawers had been emptied and fresh towels had been laid out on the bed. On the bedside table stood a bottle of whisky and a glass. Bill picked up the whisky and studied the label. Glenmorangie single malt. "Bless her," he said to himself.

Bill made his way up the stairs to the room in the loft extension and knocked on the door.

"Go away, I'm busy."

"Jon, it's Uncle Bill. Sorry to disturb you. Can I come in?"

"Yeah, if you want. It's open."

Bill opened the door and went in. His nephew did not look round to greet him, but kept tapping away on his computer. Jonathan was still dressed in his school uniform of grey trousers, white shirt, navy jumper and black trainers. His school tie had been discarded onto the bedroom floor. He looked younger than his 13 years.

"I've just come up to tell you your dinner's ready."

"I don't want any. What is it anyway?"

"I'm not sure, but it sure as hell smells good. Smells better than a fart in a phone box, as your cousin Davey would say."

Jonathan looked around and nearly smiled at him. "What did you say?"

"Your mum's cooking. It smells better than a fart in a phone box."

Jonathan got up and walked to the door. "I like that. I'm going to tell her what you said." And he bounded down the stairs.

Bill followed him in mock panic. "No, Jonathan, don't say that. You'll get me in all sorts of trouble."

Jonathan rushed into the kitchen.

"Mum, guess what Uncle Bill said? He said your cooking smells like a fart in a phone box."

"No, I didn't, Liz, honestly," and Bill reached out to give Jonathan a clip round the ear and deliberately missed.

"Have you got any more like that, Uncle Bill?"

"Help me lay the table and I'll give you more sayings from your Cousin Davey's black book."

"Mum, have I got to lay the table?"

"My God, Son, you're as much use as a one-armed acrobat with an itchy arse," Bill said. "Now let's go and get this table laid."

Jonathan laughed and Liz looked on in amazement. Susie came out to see what the strange noises were. Soon Bill was laying the table with the two children. He came back into the kitchen to get some plates and Liz turned and smiled at him.

"You're a miracle worker, Bill. I haven't heard Jon like that for weeks. Not since Steve left. I'm so pleased to have you here."

"It's good for me too, Liz. We'll have a good chat later and catch up on everything." And he put his arm around his sister and kissed her on her forehead.

The children went up to their rooms around ten o'clock. Bill and Liz stayed at the dining table and chatted over a second bottle of wine that Bill had brought with him. The mealtime had been enjoyable but hard work. Bill had to walk a tightrope to stop the tensions between Liz and Susie and Jonathan from boiling over. The squabbles between the two children were routine enough, but the really worrying part was the boy's attitude to his mother. His tone towards her bordered on contempt, and more than once Bill came close to stepping in and saying something about the boy's behaviour. At the end of the meal he still wondered whether he should have done.

"I bet you're finding Jonathan hard work at the moment, aren't you, Liz?" he said.

"Oh, he's terrible, but I can't bring myself to be too hard on him right now. I know he's only like it because he's missing his dad so much. He's so miserable and he doesn't know who to blame."

"So he takes it out on you?"

"Yes, and it's getting worse, if anything. It's the one thing I can't forgive Steve for, leaving his son at the age he is."

"What about Susie?"

"Oh, it's affected her badly too, but not half as much as Jonathan. She's got her friends and they talk things through between them, but Jonathan hasn't got anyone to talk to. He bottles it all up, whereas Susie and I have a good cry, or more often than not a good moan. She thinks her father's been a big shit, and I think she's told him as much."

"She takes after her mother then?"

"Yes, she doesn't take any prisoners. We all have to watch our step with Miss Suzanne."

Liz poured them both some more Cote du Rhone.

"Do you know, Bill, Steve moved out on the 25th July and ten days later Jon had his 13th birthday? What a way to celebrate becoming a teenager, eh? I don't wonder the poor love's becoming so difficult. I just don't know how best to deal with it."

Liz's voice trembled and for a moment it seemed that she would break down, but she recovered quickly and instead her tone became sharp and angry.

"Do you know, Bill, I see so much of this at school. If you have a good kid who suddenly starts to misbehave, or lose interest in their work, or just not give a damn any more, nine times out of ten it will be because of a parental break-up. The number of times I've called parents in because their son or daughter has suddenly started to act up, and I just wait for the mum to say, 'Of course, his dad and I are going through a separation at the moment'. Or a divorce or whatever. Sometimes I feel I can save them the trouble of saying it. I feel I can just say, 'So, Mrs So-and-so, your son has suddenly changed character. When exactly did you and your husband decide to split up?'"

"It's that bad, is it, Liz?"

"Yes, it is. And Steve's seen it as many times as I have, and still he's done it to his own children. I could throttle him for this. If he had to do it, why couldn't he wait until the children were older?"

"I don't know, Liz, it's difficult to write the rules for what we do in life. Look what I've done recently."

"That's not the same thing, Bill. You haven't deserted your family."

"Well, I'm not with them right now, am I?"

"But your boys are grown up. You would never have left them when they were kids. You know that as well as I do. It's all about integrity, and you've got it and people like Steve haven't. You're the same as Dad. That's why the two of you have always been my heroes." And she placed her hand on his forearm and squeezed.

"That's a very generous thing for you to say, Liz, but I don't know. I understand Dad being a hero, because of whatever he did in the war, but I don't see how I am."

"No, I don't see Dad as a hero for being a soldier. He's a hero for working for his family for over 40 years in that damned shop.

And so are you for sticking it out at Horseman's for 30 odd years."

"I don't know how you work that out, Liz. I look at my life and I look at Dad's life and I feel we've been more like cowards than heroes. We've just taken all the drudgery that life can pile onto us and haven't had the guts to say, 'That's enough. I'm not taking any more'. I feel Dad and I took the easy option more than anything. But I guess you've always been closer to Dad than I have."

"Girls always get more hugs and cuddles from their fathers than boys do, Bill. It doesn't mean that sons are loved any less."

"I know that, Liz, but if I'm honest, Dad's always got on my nerves. He still does really."

"Why do you say that?"

"Because he's always taken so much crap from everyone. He took all that crap at work for 40 years and then he came home and took a lot more from Mum. He takes even more from her now, and he never answers back. And he wasn't happy until he saw me in a job where I had to take my daily dose of crap, just like he did. He never encouraged me to do what I wanted to do with my life, you know, and I told him clearly enough."

"You can't still blame him for that."

"No, I don't. I blame myself good and proper. I should've had the courage to break the mould years ago."

"But that's what I'm saying, Bill. You didn't break anything because you put your family first, just like Dad did. And that's why you're a hero to me. Maybe Dad set you a great example and showed you something really precious."

"I'm sorry, Liz. I'd like to see it like that, but I can't."

Liz was quiet for a moment. She poured some more wine and then smiled as she recalled a distant memory. Eventually she spoke.

"Do you remember going to the Gaumont and the Regal when we were kids, Bill?"

"I certainly do. That's one of the few times when Mum got really excited, when she took us to the pictures."

"She used to let us have thrupence each for sweets and you nearly choked on a gobstopper. I remember Mum rushing out with you under her arm while you were choking to death."

"Yeah, and I swear she stopped at the exit to watch Alec

Guinness fall on the plunger and blow up the bridge over the River Kwai while I was fighting for breath."

"It wouldn't surprise me, the old bag," said Liz.

They both laughed at the thought of their mother's cold-hearted devotion to the cinema.

"Nothing came between Mum and her films," said Bill, "not even my imminent demise."

"That's one thing I've inherited from Mum. My love of films. And I hope it's the only thing. Do you know my favourite film of all time?"

"The Blackboard Jungle?"

"No, seriously, my favourite film of all time is *The Magnificent Seven*."

"1960, Yul Brynner. Daa da-da dum, daa-da-da-dum."

"That's right, and there's a scene in that film that I've watched a thousand times because I love it so much. It's got Charles Bronson in it. He's one of the seven protecting the village. I remember his character's called Bernardo O'Reilly, and he's talking to some small peasant boys who really admire the Seven because they fight against the baddies, while the villagers do nothing to protect themselves.

"One little boy says, 'We are ashamed to live here. Our fathers are cowards.' And then Charles Bronson slaps the little boy hard across the face. It's quite shocking to watch, even when you know it's coming. He's really angry with the little boy and I remember every word he says to him. He says, 'You think I'm brave because I carry a gun. Your fathers are much braver because they carry responsibility for you and your brothers, your sisters and mothers. And this responsibility is like a big rock that weighs a ton. It bends and it twists them until finally it buries them under the ground. And there's nobody says they have to do it. They do it because they love you, and because they want to. I have never had this kind of courage. Working every day with no guarantee anything will ever come of it. This is bravery.'"

Liz took Bill's hand in hers. "And that, Bill, is why you and Dad are my heroes, and why Jonathan's dad is such a shit."

The next morning Bill stayed out of the way whilst Liz and the children went through their morning routine. He heard raised voices and slamming doors. At eight o'clock he went downstairs and caught Liz just as she was about to leave.

"I was wondering, Liz, if you'd like me to do dinner for us all tonight?"

"That would be wonderful, Bill."

"What do people like? What's Jon's favourite?"

"KFC."

"I'm not sure I can get the recipe for that. Anything else?"

"Shepherd's pie. He loves shepherd's pie."

"Shepherd's pie it is then. I'll do all the shopping."

"That's great, Bill. I'm so glad you're here. I've got to rush. The kids are in the car. You've got your keys. Take it easy."

Liz gave him a kiss and shut the door, and the house was suddenly very quiet.

After breakfast Bill cleared up in the kitchen and phoned Angie. She was fine, she knew no further news of Benny, and she was in a hurry to get round to her mum's. Bill thought about phoning Stoner but decided against it. Just after ten he left the house to walk the half mile to Medford city centre. Although the sky was overcast, Bill's mood was lighter than it had been for weeks. The conversation with Liz had made him feel much better about himself, and it felt good to be in Medford where he was unlikely to meet anyone he knew.

When Bill was a boy, a trip to Medford had been a major event. He remembered going there on the train once with Liz and his parents. There had been long preparations and long lectures on what young children must do if they get lost in the 'big city'. Bill must have been very young, because the warnings scared him to death and he spent all day clinging on to his mother's hand, and she spent all day tutting and telling him not to be such a baby.

Medford was really only a city in the sense that it had its own cathedral and was an Episcopal see. Nowadays the bishop lived in a modern house next to the new cathedral shop and restaurant. The less practical bishop's residence dating from the 16th century was now occupied by Harry and Alison Woodford. Bill made a detour around Cathedral Close to avoid walking past their house, and he was soon in the area that had once been the medieval centre of the city.

Bill did not see much to admire. There had once been residential squares and narrow lanes full of shops here, but most of the historical centre had been destroyed by bombs in the spring of 1942. The cathedral, the close and the former bishop's residence had survived intact, but much of modern Medford owed its appearance to the architecture of the 50s and 60s. Some remedial work had been done in the past ten years to produce some mews housing and a pedestrian area in the centre, but shop facades with a mock-Tudor top half and a plate-glass bottom half had done little to restore the beautiful city that had existed before the war.

Bill made his way to the bottom of Gardner Street where the International Casino had stood since 1978. He passed the spot where he had parked his car exactly three weeks ago to the day. He was confronted by so many thoughts and emotions at returning to this spot that he decided not to dwell on any of them. The job in hand was to try to find Jasmine, and the first thing to do was to retrace her steps when she left the casino with Benny.

'Round the corner, grab a bottle of champagne, and then back to Jaz's place' were the words Benny had used to describe what they had done that night. Bill looked down the road. The end of the street was only 30 yards away. In the other direction Benny and Jasmine would have to have walked 100 yards before they got to the end. And half way up there was a road leading off to the right. Bill realised this was going to take longer than he thought.

He walked the 30 yards to the bottom of Gardner Street and looked left and right down Beechers Road. The road was lined with small shops with living accommodation above. Bill turned right and had only gone a few yards when he came to an off-licence. This fitted Benny's description perfectly. Bill could not believe his luck. Benny must have left the casino with Jasmine, walked down the road, round the corner and into this off-licence. Bill went in and chose a bottle of wine to have with dinner. As the young man got Bill's change, Bill took out the photo of Jasmine.

"You don't know this young lady by any chance, do you? I think she lives round here somewhere."

"What's she done?"

"She hasn't done anything wrong. She's a family friend, and we haven't heard from her for a while, and we're getting concerned about her."

"Let's have a closer look."

"She was seen coming in here three weeks ago today. She came out of the casino and bought a bottle of champagne here. She was with an older guy, late 40s. Big fella, barrel-chested."

"I don't remember her or him, and I work here every Friday," the young man said. He studied the photo more closely. "I think I'd remember a gorgeous girl like that buying champagne. What time did you say?"

"It was about half past nine."

"In the evening?"

"Yes."

"Oh, well it wasn't here then. We close at nine o'clock. It gets too iffy round here to stay open any later than that."

"Are you sure? Sorry, stupid question. Of course you're sure. Are there any more places round here where she could buy champagne at that time of night?"

"There's a pub, the Sentry Post, about 200 yards away if you turn left on your way out. All the offies round here are the same as us. They don't stay open after nine."

"Thanks for your help."

Over the next hour Bill walked half a mile up and down Beechers Road in both directions. No one in the Sentry Post recognised Jasmine from that night or any other night. He walked up Gardner Street, and down the small street off it to the right, which contained only lock-ups and small workshops. When he got to the top of Gardner Street Bill reached the road known locally as the Gables. Some of the shops and houses had escaped the destruction of the war and still had their original black timber, white render and small gable windows. The far side of the street curved back in a gentle arc and there was an area of green in front of it. There was a village atmosphere in the Gables and the number of estate agents and building societies lining the street pointed to the steep premium on property prices here. Bill was beginning to regret buying the bottle of wine one and a half hours earlier. He was tired of carrying it around. He went into a café and sat down at a round table in the window. The café was airy and modern. A young woman came over to take his order.

"A coffee and a cheese sandwich, please."

"Latte, cappuccino, espresso or filter, sir?"

"An ordinary coffee with milk, please."

"Would you like the baguette with camembert and rocket?"

"Yes, I suppose so."

"Would you like cranberry jelly with it, sir?"

Bill turned to face the waitress. She had a grin on her face.

"Are you trying to confuse me?" he asked, smiling at her.

"What would you really like?"

"Wholemeal bread, cheddar cheese and some onion."

"It's not on the menu but I'll see what I can do."

Minutes later she was back with exactly what Bill had ordered. He glimpsed the name badge on her tee-shirt.

"Thankyou, Hayley. It was nice of you to go to the extra trouble."

"You're very welcome, sir."

"Hayley, do you think you could help me with something else?"

"I'll try."

"Is there anywhere around here where I could buy a bottle of champagne?"

"Not here, I'm afraid. There's a Waitrose down past the roundabout."

"Is it far?"

"About 15 minutes if you're walking."

"Is there anywhere nearer than that?"

"I don't think so."

The waitress looked at the bottle of wine on the table.

"It looks like you're celebrating something."

"No, unfortunately it's not for a celebration. Not yet anyway. Thanks again."

Bill left the waitress a tip, which he considered generous given his circumstances, and walked towards Waitrose where he would buy the groceries for tonight's dinner. He had passed only three shops when he realised he had not shown anyone in the café the photo of Jasmine. He stopped and half-turned whilst trying to make up his mind whether to go back. In front of him he noticed a big sign painted on the front of a convenience store. 'Open non-stop 7-11'. He went in and approached the counter where alcohol and cigarettes were on sale.

"Do you have any champagne?" he asked.

The man behind the counter pointed to half a dozen bottles on the shelf behind him.

"I've got a couple cold ones in the cooler, if you want," he said.

"How late do you stay open?"

"You are joking, right? This is a 7-11. Now, can I get you anything?"

Bill decided against showing the photo or asking any more stupid questions. He went outside and looked around him. If this was where Benny and Jasmine came after the casino, 'her place' must be somewhere in the Gables. The area was full of commercial premises with living accommodation above and it was possible that she had a flat here somewhere. But Benny had been confident that Jasmine would never be found, so it seemed more than likely that she had already left Medford. Bill knew that his chances of finding her were slim, but he decided to have one more try on Monday morning when he could sit in the café and watch people as they left their homes for work. If Jasmine did appear with her long golden hair, she would at least be unmissable. He decided to get to the café before eight on Monday morning and try his luck.

Chapter 19

Jon and Susie came home from school at four o'clock. Bill was already in the kitchen preparing dinner. At home Angie did most of the cooking, but there had been occasions over the years when Angie had not felt up to it and Bill had tried his hand. He had surprised himself at how much he enjoyed it, and now he liked nothing better on a Sunday than shutting himself in the kitchen with a bottle of wine and some music and preparing a roast. His repertoire had broadened over the years and luckily it included shepherd's pie.

Susie popped her head around the kitchen door.

"Hi, Uncle Bill. Mum said to tell you she won't be home 'til about six. Reports to write or something. I'm going to get my homework done, alright? I want it out the way."

"Sensible girl."

Susie came into the kitchen and inspected the ingredients laid out on the worktop.

"This is seriously weird, seeing you cooking. Dad never cooked a thing."

"I just happen to enjoy it."

"What are you making?"

"Shepherd's pie and green beans."

"Jon'll be happy. It's his favourite. But he'll want baked beans."

"Well, he'll just have to like these for a change, won't he?" said Bill with a smile. "If you're going up to do your homework, could you ask Jon to come down and have a word with me, please, Susie?"

"I will do that thing. See you later."

It was several minutes before Bill heard Jon making his way very slowly down the stairs.

"Susie said you wanted to see me," the boy said with no enthusiasm.

"Thanks, Jon. I was hoping you could give me a hand here."

"I'm no good at cooking. I did it in Year 8. I hate it."

"Well, everyone tells me I'm doing your favourite."

"What?"

"Shepherd's pie."

"It's alright."

"Well, don't get too excited. The last time I did it was a disaster."

"Why? What happened?"

"No one seemed to like it, so I gave the leftovers to the dog. It must've been bad because I saw him licking his arse trying to get the taste out of his mouth."

Bill looked over his shoulder towards Jon, who had a very serious look on his face. Jon thought over what Bill had just said and started to smile. Bill smiled back and then they both started to laugh.

"Is that true?"

"Of course it is. Would I lie to you?"

Bill passed a bottle opener to Jon.

"Come on, matey, open that bottle of wine. You don't want to see a man die of thirst, do you?"

"I don't know how it works."

"I'll show you."

And Bill took off the foil from the top of the bottle and started to turn the corkscrew. He handed them both to Jon.

"Now you keep turning. Well done. Now push those two arms down and out pops the cork. Keep going. That's it. Good lad. Now pour a glass for your poor old Uncle Bill before I lose the will to live."

Bill glanced at Jon to see him holding the bottle with both hands, anxious not to spill a drop. Bill came over and took the glass and held it up to the light.

"Ah, the colour of priceless rubies, with excellent legs." He sniffed. "Ah, the aroma of strawberries and blackcurrants caressed by a light summer shower." Then he took a drink and swilled it around his mouth. "My God, it tastes like a wrestler's underpants!" And they both laughed again.

"No, Jon. I'm joking. It's really very nice. Now, can you provide the chef with some music? What have you got?"

"I'll bring down some CDs, shall I?"

Jon disappeared out of the kitchen and Bill heard him racing up the stairs.

He reappeared with an armful of CDs.

"I've got Oasis, Green Day, Red Hot Chilli Peppers. And before you say anything, that's a band not something for the pie."

Bill turned round and waved a spoon at him.

"Very good, Jon, very good. I think you're catching on. That's 1-0 to you."

When Liz came home at six o'clock she heard music coming from the kitchen. Bill was at the sink and Jon was mashing potatoes.

"Hi, Mum. It's nearly ready."

"Wow, I can't believe it. What a sight for sore eyes," she said.

"Jon, how about pouring your mum a glass of wine?"

Jon left what he was doing, carefully poured a glass for his mother and handed it to her.

"Here you are, Mum."

"Thank you, darling. What a lovely welcome home."

"Don't thank me too much. It tastes like a wrestler's underpants."

"Jonathan!" cried Bill in mock disapproval, and they both laughed. Liz looked pleased but confused.

"I'm taking my wine upstairs and leaving you two lunatics to it."

"We'll call you when it's ready," Bill shouted after her.

The dinner was a great success. Jonathan and Bill took equal credit for the cooking, although Jonathan was at great pains to point out with each mouthful exactly what his contribution had been. Everyone was in high spirits and the mood was completely different from the previous evening. Jonathan was animated and wanted to involve himself in the conversation. Each act of politeness and consideration was infectious and led to another, and another. By the end of the evening it was unthinkable that anyone would be unkind or unpleasant about anything.

Susie and her mum decided that they would go shopping together on Saturday, whilst Jon took little persuading from Bill to go to watch Medford United play at home in the third division against Doncaster Rovers. At the end of the evening Susie kissed her mother and Bill goodnight. Jon hugged his mum and gave Bill a high-five. When they had gone to their room Liz had a big smile on her face and tears in her eyes.

"That's the first time he's shown me any affection in months," she said. "I can't tell you how grateful I am to you, Bill."

"You don't need to be, Liz. It's just wonderful for me to feel I'm being of some use for a change. I've been getting so much wrong recently and letting so many people down. It should be me thanking all of you."

"Hardly."

"No really, Liz. You're giving me the chance to feel good about myself again, and I'm really grateful for that. They're good kids anyway. You take the credit for that, not me."

"Yes, they are good kids, aren't they? I think I've lost sight of that recently. I'm really looking forward to having a girls' day out with Susie tomorrow. She's hardly ever any trouble, you know, and I think I've neglected her a bit."

"She's a lovely girl. She's so confident and thoughtful. I thought girls of that age were meant to be moody and difficult."

"Oh, she has her moments, believe me."

"I know all about boys, you see, Liz, but I don't know much about bringing up girls."

"Boys are far more sensitive, Bill."

"Yes, I know that from my two. Mickey's always been sensitive. He's quite highly strung really. I suppose he gets that from Angie. Dave's more like me. He gets very restless, and he doesn't always think before he acts."

"They're lovely boys, your two."

"Yes, they are. I feel quite guilty towards them sometimes though. I feel I didn't spend enough time with them when they were younger. Angie always had so much patience with them, but I was always tired when I came back from work. I hate to admit it, but I just wanted them out of the way most of the time."

"Well, Angie wasn't out working all day, was she, like some of us have to? You came home from work tired out, I expect."

"That may be, but it doesn't make it right. When I think of all the time and priority I gave to my work over the years, it makes me quite angry. Why don't we see what's important until we're so much older? I suppose that's why I'm looking forward to my first grandchild so much. So that I can give them all the time they want from me. That's supposing I'm not locked up in Medford Prison next June when the baby's due."

"Don't think like that, Bill. I'm sure it won't come to that. And stop feeling guilty about everything. I keep telling you, you're a great father."

"Thanks, Liz, but I was thinking about what you said last night about the effect on Jonathan of Steve leaving. We fathers have so much power, don't we? And half the time we don't even realise it. Do you know Dave gave up his job last week, just to stand up for me? And last Sunday I met a man the same age as me who you'd think had everything he could wish for. Millions in the bank, a country mansion and the freedom to go wherever he wants…"

"Benny Horseman?"

"Yes, Benny Horseman. And do you know, I found out that in spite of all he has, Benny's lived his whole life in torment because of one thoughtless word and one callous act by his father. And he can't escape it. And he can never be happy until he comes to terms with it. I feel so sorry for him."

"You feel sorry for Benny Horseman? Now you have shocked me."

"I've been thinking about him a lot this week, and I've realised something else which must be difficult for him to bear. He's got no children of his own so that he can put it right. He doesn't have the chance to be a better dad than his own father was."

"You know, Bill, it strikes me you're always feeling bad about what you've done or haven't done, and you're always feeling guilty towards other people. It's really not necessary."

"I don't feel guilty towards everyone. I don't feel guilty towards you."

"I should hope not. But you say you feel guilty towards your boys, and you've always acted that way towards Angie."

"Well, I did make her pregnant when she was 17."

"There you go again, taking everything on to yourself. *You* made *her* pregnant. Don't you think she should take some responsibility for her own actions? Maybe she should feel guilty towards you. You were only a kid yourself."

"But I shouldn't have let it happen, Liz. She was so upset at the time and I couldn't help feeling responsible. I was worried she was going to do something to herself. I promised her then that I would make everything alright for her."

"And you have made everything alright. But how long does it all have to go on for? She's not a damn child. I know I'm probably overstepping the mark, Bill, but honestly, Angie can be a right pain in the arse."

"I know she can. And I won't pretend things have been easy between us recently, but I do love her."

"I know you do, but she doesn't half play on it at times."

"I've been a pain in the arse to her as well you know, Liz. It works both ways. She's had to put up with a lot from me."

"What, for example?"

"My restlessness. This dream I've always had of travelling, knowing she hates going anywhere. I've been unsettled for years."

"And why should you apologise for your dreams? Good God, Bill, you've worked all your life. Why shouldn't you be allowed your dreams? Stop blaming yourself for everything."

"I don't just blame myself. If I'm honest, I have started to blame Angie a bit recently. And I suppose I blame Dad a bit too."

"Why blame Dad for anything?"

"It's what I was saying earlier about the power fathers have over their sons. I think you should encourage your children and guide them gently, but if you see there's something they have their heart set on, you shouldn't stand in their way. Dad knew what my dreams were but he insisted I stayed on at school, and I hated it. So here I am 35 years later with the same dreams he should've allowed me to fulfil as a young man. The strange thing is, I was talking to him the other day and he couldn't remember even discussing it with me. But he was my father so whatever he said was bound to have a big influence on me. He should've realised that."

"You don't feel too bitter towards him, do you?"

"No, not bitter. Just a bit fed-up with him sometimes. I get a bit impatient with the old duffer. Probably because I'm afraid I'll end up like him."

"Don't talk about him like that, Bill. He's such a wonderful man. I hate the thought of you thinking badly of him."

"Sorry, Liz. I know you were always closer to him than I was. I don't mean to upset you."

"I've told you. Stop apologising for how you feel! I just think you should perhaps try to look at people in a different way. You've managed it with Benny Horseman and it might be a good idea to start looking at other people in your life differently. I think you could start by forgiving Dad for what you feel he's done."

"I don't need to forgive him."

"Yes you do. I think we all have to forgive our parents at some stage. It's only then we can really grow up and be free of our childhood. Forgiveness is liberating, Bill. It's the only thing that will help my Jonathan in the end."

"What do you mean by that exactly?"

"He needs to forgive his father for leaving him, before the anger and the pain he feels can go away. At the moment the poor boy's trapped by the anger he feels. And the worst thing is, I know that I hold the key to it all."

"How do you work that out, Liz?"

"Because Jonathan's got to see me forgive the rotten bastard first."

The next morning Liz phoned Steve to see if he wanted to go to the match with Jonathan and Bill. He had made no attempt to see Susie or Jonathan for nearly three weeks, and both children were getting more impatient and angry with him. This time he was sorry that he could not make it, but he and Charlotte had been invited to lunch with Charlotte's parents and they could not possibly change the arrangements. It was clear that for now the new woman in Steve's life was going to take precedence over everyone else, including his own children. Bill heard Liz making excuses to Jonathan on Steve's behalf, and he admired his sister for hiding her own anger in an attempt to protect her child's feelings as much as she could.

Bill admired his young nephew too. Jonathan was very quiet on the way to Medford United's home ground on the northern outskirts of the city, and Bill left him in peace to deal with his feelings in his own way. The phone call between his mum and dad had left Jonathan withdrawn and feeling insecure and isolated, but for once he fought against these feelings and reached out to his Uncle Bill. Bill sensed the boy struggling to surface through his anxiety and his heart went out to him. Slowly they built up a conversation about Medford's chances and the merits of each player in the match programme, and by the time they got to the ground Jon was quite animated again.

It was a close game with plenty of opportunity for shouting, barracking and generally letting off steam. All his life Bill had enjoyed the bonding that sport can bring, and it was good to feel that happening with his young nephew. Medford lost the match 3-2 and most Medford supporters were blaming Hopkins, their centre half, for scoring an own goal and conceding a penalty, all in the final 15 minutes. As they filed out into the darkness Bill and Jonathan passed their own judgements on him.

"Useless as a chocolate saucepan," suggested Bill.

"Useless as a concrete canoe," offered Jonathan.

And they both laughed in appreciation of their combined wit, as they made their way towards Pizza Express. Whilst they were waiting for their food Jonathan wanted to know if he could ask Bill a question.

"Anything you like, Jon."

"How long are you staying in Medford?"

"I don't know exactly. A few weeks, I expect. I've got some

business to see to here and I might even look for some work."

"Can I ask you another question?"

"I tell you what, Jon. You're allowed to ask me anything you like, and I promise to answer as truthfully as I can. How about that?"

"Okay. Are you and Auntie Angie getting divorced?"

It was not the question Bill had expected.

"No, we're not," he said. He tried to stay as matter of fact as he could. "We're having some time apart at the moment, but I'll be going home to Auntie Angie in a few weeks."

"Do you still love one another?"

"Yes, we do."

"I don't understand why grown-ups have to have time apart if they love one another."

"I think it's because people who live together have problems and they may start to argue, and it gets too much sometimes, and they decide to have a break from one another. But they still love one another, so when they feel better they can stop arguing and get back together again."

"Is that what'll happen with Mum and Dad?"

"I said I'd be honest with you, Jon, so I've got to say I'm not sure. It's a bit more complicated when you're married if one of you falls in love with someone else."

"Is that what's happened with Dad?"

"I expect so. I don't think he would ever leave you or Susie or your mum otherwise."

"But Mum says he still loves us, and I don't understand why he wants to leave us if he still loves us. He doesn't seem bothered about us at all any more."

"I can promise you one thing, Jon, because I know it's true. Your dad loves you and Susie as much as ever. That will never ever change. He'll always love you whatever happens."

"Then why did he leave us?"

The waiter brought their drinks and Bill waited until he had gone before he tried to answer the question.

"He didn't leave you or your sister, Jon. He left your mum. I know he wants to be with you, but he can't at the moment."

"Doesn't he love my mum any more then?"

"He may do. I don't know. None of this is easy. But the thing is, he thinks he loves Charlotte more than he loves your mum at the moment, so he chooses to be with her."

"That means he loves her more than he loves me or Susie then. I hate her."

"No, he doesn't love her more. I promise you. It's just a different kind of love which can be very powerful at first, and it makes people do daft things."

"You mean sex."

"Yes, that's part of it. When things settle down, your dad will be more available. You'll see a lot more of him."

"I might not want to, if he doesn't want to see me."

Jon slumped back in his chair and Bill leaned towards him.

"It's natural for you to be angry with him. Mums and dads aren't perfect, Jon. We make stupid mistakes like everyone else, and we might even hurt people we really love."

"Why can't someone talk to him then, and tell him not to be so stupid, and just make things the way they were? I hate the way things are now."

"I know you do, Jon. This is very difficult for you, and you're just going to have to be very brave about it and very patient with your dad."

There was a silence and Bill took a sip of his beer.

"Do you think Mum and Dad will get divorced?" Jon asked him. Bill hesitated.

"The honest answer is, I don't know. It's possible. It's also possible that he might realise he's done something really stupid and want to come back."

"Do you think Dad's stupid then?"

"I think not being with a wonderful boy like you, and a wonderful girl like Susie, and a wonderful woman like your mum is really stupid. But I also know that we mustn't be too hard on him, because we all know we can do stupid things sometimes."

"I wonder sometimes if one of us did something wrong. I wonder if Mum did something to make him leave and she won't tell us."

"No, Jon. Your mum hasn't done anything wrong. She's very hurt, you know, and she's being incredibly brave at the moment. You all are. You must be good to your mum and help her all you can."

"I know."

"Think how bad you feel about all this, Jon, and then remember that your mum is hurt just as badly."

"So you don't think it's anything we've done then?"

"No, I promise you this has nothing to do with anything you've done. You haven't caused this. You do know that, don't you?"

For the first time Jonathan's bottom lip started to tremble. Bill pulled his chair round to be closer to the boy.

"Don't ever think you're to blame for this, Jon."

"I… I'm…"

Jon struggled to talk as his whole face started to crumple into sobs. Suddenly he stood up and ran out of the restaurant. Bill hurried after him and saw him disappear into a side alley where he stood facing the wall wiping tears from his eyes, trying to control himself. Bill went to put his arm around him.

"Leave me alone! All of you just leave me alone!" Jon shouted and he shrugged his shoulder away from Bill's arm. Bill spoke softly to him.

"Jon, if there's something in particular that's really worrying you or upsetting you, you must tell someone. You'll feel so much better, I promise."

Slowly Bill placed his hand on Jon's shoulder. This time Jon let him keep it there.

"Let me help you, Son, if I can."

"It's just…" And Jon started to sob again. "It's just that I think Dad may have left because of me."

"No, Jon, I promise you that's just not true."

"But he did!"

"Why would you say such a thing?"

"Last summer I brought my report home… and it was terrible. All the grades were bad. And Dad said it was really embarrassing for him because he knew all the teachers…and he said I'd let him down."

"That's not so bad though, is it?"

"But then he said he was ashamed of me… and a few days later he left."

And with these words Jon's sobs started again and Bill knelt down and put his arms around him. Jonathan struggled to speak.

"I just wonder… if I'd got a good report… he might not have wanted to leave me," he said, and his whole body shook as his emotions at last flooded out. Bill stroked Jonathan's head and tried to comfort him, and the words of his own father came back to him from 30 years before. "Remember, Son," Wilf had said when Bill told him Angie was pregnant, "the best thing a man can do for his children is to love their mother."

They got home from the match at about eight o'clock. Bill had paid for the drinks at Pizza Express but they decided to go somewhere else to eat. They walked home from the centre of town and Jonathan was much calmer about everything. Bill asked Jonathan if he was allowed to tell Liz about their conversation earlier, and Jon agreed that he should. After Match of the Day Susie and Jon went to bed and Bill and Liz stayed up talking into the early hours. The next day Liz spent a long time on the phone with Steve, and on Sunday evening she spent an even longer time with Jonathan and Susie in their rooms. She came back downstairs looking emotionally drained.

"The poor little mites have been through hell," she said, as she fell back into an armchair, "and heaven knows how I'm going to teach a five-period day tomorrow."

"How have you left it?"

"There's not much more I can do for Susie or Jonathan at the moment. They both need to have a good talk with their father and tell him how they feel. I've told Steve that and he's coming over on Wednesday to cook them dinner and spend the evening with them. I thought maybe you and I could go to the pub or something."

"Sounds good to me."

"And if he cancels on them on Wednesday, I'll shoot the bugger."

"And I'll buy the bullets, Liz. But I'm sure he won't."

Liz smoothed the fabric on the arm of her chair, just as her mother did when she was considering something before she spoke.

"I have mixed feelings about them seeing Steve on Wednesday, you know, Bill," she said.

"In what way, Liz?"

"Well, on the one hand I want things to be resolved for the children so they know where they are. But on the other hand I feel that by coming to some sort of understanding with Steve, I'm giving the situation my approval. Do you know what I mean?"

"Yes, I understand that, Liz. But the most important thing is for children to have stability and routine, and to know where they are. You were the one telling me that."

"Yes, I know. I'm just not sure yet how I want things between me and Steve to work out. Whatever he agrees with the kids, I have to accept for their sake, but it may mean I'm accepting the split's permanent. I know how selfish that must sound."

"As long as Susie and Jonathan get a feeling of safety and security, I wouldn't worry too much about anything else at the moment, Liz. Let's face it, we adults know the real truth."

"And what's that?"

"That nothing ever stays the same."

"He might want to come back next week, you mean."

"I mean, who the hell knows where we're all heading."

Chapter 20

On Monday morning Bill was at the café in the Gables by eight o'clock. He sat at the same table by the window and the same waitress came up to serve him.

"Good morning, Hayley," he said.

"Good morning, sir. It's nice to see you again. Did you get your champagne?"

"Yes, I did, thanks. In a manner of speaking."

"And what would you like this morning?"

"Breakfast, please."

"Freshly squeezed OJ, croissant or muffin, with filter coffee is £3.85."

"OJ?"

Hayley bent down to whisper in his ear. "Orange juice, sir," she said.

"How about bacon and egg?"

"The nearest we have to that is a BLT baguette."

"Hell's bells, this is like being in a different country rather than dear old Medford! Please translate for me."

"A sandwich with French bread filled with bacon, lettuce and tomato, sir"

"I'll have that. With OJ and a CWM."

"A CWM, sir?"

"Coffee with milk."

"Thankyou, sir," Hayley said, and as she walked away she looked back over her shoulder and smiled at him.

A few minutes later she returned with his order.

"Thanks, Hayley. Do you have a moment or two you could spare me?"

"Certainly. It's not too busy yet. I can give you a minute."

"I just wondered if you've ever seen this girl around here." He passed Hayley the photograph of Jasmine.

"What a stunning girl. Do you know, I think I have seen her, but not for about four weeks."

"Really? That's marvellous. Was it around here you saw her?"

"Yes, definitely in the Gables, but not recently."

"And do you know anything about her?"

"For example?"

"Where she lived or worked?"

"No, sorry. But I'm certain it was her I saw." She leaned in to him and whispered, "What's the big mystery?"

"The mystery is where she came from and where she disappeared to."

"Are you a policeman?"

"No, the exact opposite. This girl could keep me out of prison."

"Goodness. How exciting! What have you done?"

"It's a long story."

"I'd love to hear it," she said, as she looked around at some new customers coming in, "but I must go now."

Bill watched her walk away. He stayed in the cafe for an hour and looked through the window as the people who lived in the Gables made their way to work. There was no sign of Jasmine, but he was not too downhearted. At least he now had confirmation that he was looking in the right place, and if he could find someone who knew her, he might still manage to track her down. When the time came to pay for his breakfast, Bill looked around for Hayley. He wanted to thank her and leave her another tip. He waited several minutes but could not see her anywhere, and he was surprised that he felt so disappointed. He paid at the counter and left.

"Silly old fool," he muttered to himself, at the thought that a nice young woman like that could be interested in a middle-aged man like him.

Bill showed the photo to dozens of people that morning but he had no more success. In the evening Jonathan asked him for help with his homework. When Bill went up to the top room, Jonathan was sitting at his computer. Bill knocked on the door and waited to be invited in.

"Hi, Jon. Your mum tells me you're looking for help."

"Yes, please, Uncle Bill. It's science. Dad used to help me with it and I can't find all the answers."

"I'll do my best, but there's no chance I'll know as much as your dad. Why don't you leave the computer for now and show me what you have to do."

"But it's all on the computer. They give you a worksheet, or you can log on to the school computer and enter the answers direct on the screen."

"You're kidding! Let's have a look. Wow, this is different from my day. We had things called books."

"So do we, but it's more interesting like this."

"I can see that."

"What were you like at school, Uncle Bill?"

"Me? I did alright. I got my O levels and A levels, but I could've done better, I suppose. I could've done more than I did. Take my advice, Jon. Grab all the opportunities you can when you get the chance."

"I've decided I'm going to try really hard from now on. I talked to Mum about it and she said I should get to university if I work hard."

"Good for you, Jon, and I bet you will too."

"See, I've got most of these right. We're doing a project on bacteria. A lot of it's about this French bloke, Louis Pasteur. I found out a lot about him on the internet."

Bill was pleased with how much he was able to help his nephew. Bill had always enjoyed learning. It was sitting behind a desk being taught that he had found difficult. But all his life he had read widely, especially about history and travel, and he had accumulated a wide general knowledge. Soon they had answered most of the questions about the French wine and silk industries, which Pasteur had helped to save. They investigated his work on rabies and pasteurisation and now they had only a handful of questions left. Bill was surprised at how much he had enjoyed himself.

"How about this one, Uncle Bill? 'How can you delay milk turning sour?'"

"Let's see. What have you put? 'Keep it in the cow.'"

Bill looked at Jon, and Jon looked back, and then they both burst out laughing.

"Actually, Jon, that's a bloody good answer. Keep it in and see what your teacher thinks of it."

"Do you want to see something really funny, Uncle Bill? Wait a minute. Come here. Look at this."

On the screen was a photograph of Susie. "Watch this," Jon said, and in a few seconds he had blacked out her front two teeth and extended her nose by three inches. She looked grotesque.

"That's terrible, Jon. How can you do that?"

"It's a photo workshop. It comes with my digital camera. You can change your pictures on it to make them look better."

"I don't think you've done Susie any favours. Hang on a minute. You might be able to help me with something. I'll be right back."

Bill went down to his room and in a minute he was back with the picture of Jasmine.

"Can you make this any clearer for me? It's a bit fuzzy."

Jonathan put the photo of Jasmine on his scanner and brought it up on the screen. Gradually he sharpened the outline of her face and her features and zoomed in closer.

"Can you print that off for me?"

The printer produced two copies and Bill studied them. Jon kept working on the computer and started to laugh.

"Look at this, Uncle Bill. Look at her with no hair."

Even the beautiful Jasmine now looked bizarre.

"Can you do something else, Jon?" Bill said.

"What?"

"Give her brown hair going back from her face."

Bill felt goose bumps go up his arms and up the back of his neck as Jon worked on Jasmine's picture.

"And can you take that lipstick away, and the dark stuff around her eyes?" he asked.

"Oh, my God," said Bill. "Now can you change the colour of her eyes from green to hazel? Light brown, I mean."

Bill slumped down on the bed.

"What a complete idiot I am!" he said. "Jon, you have done your old Uncle Bill a huge favour. You are one clever boy."

The next morning Bill was at the café in the Gables when it opened at 7.30. He sat at the table by the window and the same waitress came over to take his order.

"Good morning again, sir," she said.

"Good morning, Jasmine," Bill replied in a cold, humourless voice.

Hayley showed very little reaction.

"Ah, so you've worked it out at last," she said. "I'm quite flattered that it took you so long."

"Why should you be flattered?"

"Because Jasmine was so effective. It was such a good transformation."

She smiled at Bill as she spoke and opened her eyes wide as if she expected him to share her enthusiasm.

"I suppose you were having a good laugh at me looking out the window for Jasmine, when all the time she was right there serving me my bloody coffee."

"I wasn't laughing at you. I recognised you right away and I was going to say something, but then decided not to. I just thought it was a bit of fun, that's all. I was just waiting for you to work it out."

"Well, it's not fun for me, Hayley, or whatever your real name is."

"Hayley is my real name. And if you're going to get heavy about this, Mr Knight, I'll get someone else to serve you and I'll not bother you any more."

"No, Hayley. Please don't do that. I'm sorry if I'm overreacting. It's just that you, or Jasmine rather, are the only person who can help me just now."

"Well, Jasmine can't help you, I'm afraid, Mr Knight. I'm not resurrecting her for anyone."

190

"My name is Bill. Please call me Bill. And please don't walk away. Do you know what happened after that night? Has Benny told you?"

"I haven't heard a thing from Benny, and I don't expect to."

"Well, you won't hear from him for a while. He's in hospital and he can hardly speak."

"No. Really? What happened to him?"

"He had an accident. Look, will you please meet me just once, so that I can explain everything that's happened? I promise I'll be more pleasant than I was just now. The truth is, I quite liked Jasmine. I felt quite sorry for her that night. I have absolutely no intention of being unpleasant, I assure you, Hayley. It was just the realisation of how ridiculous I must have seemed, that's all."

Hayley folded her arms and looked down at him, her head on one side as if she was considering the risks. At last she smiled.

"Okay, Bill. I'll take a chance with you, that you're not some kind of criminal maniac. Besides, anyone who likes Jasmine can't be all bad, I suppose. Do you see that pub over there, the Gardner's Arms? I'll see you in there at eight o'clock tonight."

Chapter 21

Bill got to the pub early and sat down with a pint of bitter. Hayley arrived at 8.10 and Bill stood up to greet her. Her appearance had changed again, but this time it was only a change and not a disguise. Her light brown hair was no longer swept back and tied on top, but framed her face in a neat cut. She had only light make-up on, hardly noticeable but just enough to emphasise her hazel eyes, high cheekbones and delicate features. She was wearing a suede jacket against the November cold, and a brown skirt with cream-coloured tights and brown ankle boots. She looked gorgeous and Bill nearly told her so, but then thought better of it.

"Thanks for coming," he said. "Can I get you a drink?"

"A dry white wine, please, Bill."

When Bill turned round from the bar, he saw that Hayley had taken off her coat and was sitting back looking at him.

"I think I'm going to call you 'the Chameleon'," he said, as he placed the wine in front of her. "Every time I see you, you've changed your appearance. I still can't believe that Jasmine in the casino was you. How did you do it?"

Hayley laughed and took a sip of wine.

"You men make it easy," she said. "If you put on a blond wig and have it coming down just enough to touch your bare shoulders, they'll hardly notice anything else. Then you add a bit of cleavage and a bit of leg in a small red or black dress and they're not really seeing you. They're just seeing body parts. And that's just the start." She took another sip of wine and smiled. "It can be fun sometimes playing little games like that."

"If that's just the start, what else is there?"

"Accentuate the eyes, change the colour with coloured lenses, and wear bright red lipstick. Very few people will pick out your real facial features, if you do that. And with men you have your hair parted to one side so that it keeps falling over one eye and you're looking up at them all the time. Then keep brushing your hair away from your face as you look at them and they lose all reason."

"You make us men sound really stupid."

"No, don't get me wrong. I love men. It's just the way you're programmed, I guess. You see what we wear, not what we are. It just makes you predictable and easy to manipulate. Most of you, anyway."

"Well, you got me right enough. I believed in Jasmine so much I came to Medford hoping to find her."

"No, Bill. I don't think you fell for Jasmine's tricks at all. When you talked to me in the casino you were treating me as a person, not as a pair of boobs and legs. You seemed to be really concerned for me. I really liked you for that. I thought you were really nice. None of Jasmine's tricks worked on you."

"The problem I've got now, of course, is that I don't know whether you mean that or whether you're just manipulating me again with flattery."

"No. I promise that Hayley is for real, and I don't do what Jasmine does. If I say or do something, it's genuine."

"Where did you learn all these tricks about disguise and things?"

"It's my training. I'm an actress. We did a huge amount of work on make-up. A really top make-up artist can make you look as if you've had plastic surgery. They use eyeliner to change the shape of the eyes. Lip-liner gives fuller lips and it's amazing how much you can alter the shape of someone's face with the right blusher and the right hairstyle."

"I didn't realise make-up could be so interesting. Is that what you want to do?"

"Make-up? No, I didn't study for three years to become a make-up artist. I want to perform. I just love performance. It's so exhilarating. But at my level at the moment you have to be able to do your own make-up as well."

"Where did you study all this then?"

"At the Metro in London. The Metropolitan School of Dramatic Art."

"Sounds impressive. How's it going?"

Hayley leaned forward and put her elbows on the table. She looked at Bill and smiled.

"You may remember that you tracked me down waiting tables in a café."

"Yes, but it's a very posh café," Bill said, smiling back at her. "Besides for all I know you could be researching a role."

"No, Bill, believe me, I *am* waiting tables."

They both laughed and Bill took a drink of his beer.

"But I have got something coming up," continued Hayley. "I'm starting rehearsals for the pantomime at the Theatre Royal next week."

"That's great. What is it?"

"Cinderella."

"And what part are you playing?"

"Guess."

"Well, you're definitely not one of the ugly sisters, that's for sure," said Bill, and then immediately regretted it.

"Bill Knight, are you flirting with me?"

"No, sorry, it's just that you are really...you know."

"No, I don't know. What am I?"

"You're a really beautiful woman. A really beautiful *young* woman and I think I should keep my thoughts to myself in the future. Anyway, with your skill at make-up I suppose you could be an ugly sister."

"No, I'm actually Prince Charming. It's a traditional version with a girl as the leading boy and men playing the evil women's roles. It's going to be great fun."

"I can tell. Who's Cinderella then?"

"Mandy Miller, the soap star. But I'm thrilled with what I've got," said Hayley. "There's plenty of singing and dancing, and in this business it's all about showing what you can do and building up a reputation. I can't wait."

"Is that why you came to Medford? To do the panto?"

"No, this is my home town. I was working in a summer show in Bournemouth and I came up here to earn some money for the winter. Then two weeks ago someone dropped out of the panto and I was in the right place at the right time. I can't believe my luck really. Everything's suddenly started working out really well for me."

"I'm really pleased for you, Hayley. I'll come and see the show over Christmas."

"I won't forgive you if you don't."

Bill stood up. "I'll get some more drinks."

"No, you won't," said Hayley, "it's my turn to buy you one."

"Don't be silly. I'll get the drinks."

Hayley stood up and took his glass. She came close and looked up at him. "Sit down," she said, "and do as you're told. Nowadays women buy the drinks too, you know."

Bill sat down and watched her at the bar, as she shared a joke with the barman. This beautiful woman was young enough to be his daughter, but she was so sure of herself that in some ways she made him feel the more inexperienced one. Before he could explore the thought any further Hayley was back with their drinks.

"So, tell me all about Benny and this accident," she said. "Tell me what happened to him?"

"How much do you know?"

"As I told you this morning, I don't know anything. I haven't spoken to Benny since that crazy night at the casino. Please tell me how he is."

"He had a bad fall in the woods near his house, and he's done a lot of damage to his face."

"Oh, the poor old thing, how bad is he?"

"He fell and hit the right side of his face against a tree. All that side of his face is badly damaged. The eye socket, the cheekbone, his jaw, are all broken. And he's lost some teeth. He'll need a lot of surgery, I'm afraid."

"Oh, poor Benny. When did all this happen?"

"Last Sunday. A week ago yesterday."

"Does anyone know how it happened?"

"Yes, I do. I was there with him."

"Tell me then."

"We were arguing and Benny rushed at me to try and hit me with something, and I tried to get out of his way, but I caught his leg and he fell forward into the tree."

"And you got him to hospital?"

"I called an ambulance, yes. How do you know that?"

"I just thought it's what you would do in the circumstances."

"Goodness. Thankyou, Hayley. You're not going to ask me if I attacked him then and beat him senseless?"

"No, why should I? You just told me what happened."

Bill looked at her and shook his head slowly, as Hayley smiled at him and took a sip of wine.

"How did you meet Benny then?" Bill asked her.

Hayley leaned forward and started to speak with new enthusiasm.

"Well, when I first came back to Medford after the summer season I stayed with my parents. I should've gone to London really, that's where all the real work is, but I just couldn't afford it. The prices there are so ridiculous. I thought I'd try to save some money and move up there in the New Year. So I signed on with a temp agency and they got me some hospitality work."

"What does that mean exactly?"

"It means standing around at conferences and trade fairs looking glamorous, handing out brochures and getting people on mailing lists. Half the time you end up as a glorified waitress serving drinks."

"And that's how you met Benny?"

"Yes, it was one of the first ones I did. It was a really posh do at the Conference Centre selling exclusive houses in Marbella. I mean really exclusive, by invitation only. You know the sort of thing. They told us to really turn on the glamour, so I created Jasmine especially for the occasion. Benny started chatting to me and told me he had some work for me, which would pay extremely well. Then he asked if he could take me to dinner to discuss it. So I did. Nothing ventured, nothing gained, as they say."

"Did you go as Jasmine or as yourself?"

"As Jasmine. Benny definitely wanted to be with Jasmine."

196

"Wasn't that a bit unwise meeting up with a stranger like that?"

"You mean I should be wary of men who chat up waitresses and ask them for a drink because they want something from them?" she said, frowning.

"Sorry, I deserved that."

"You were beginning to sound rather fuddy-duddy, don't you think?"

"Yes, I was and I really apologise. It's just that I know what Benny can be like. I don't know if any young woman's really safe with him."

"I know Benny's loud and crude sometimes, but there is another side to him as well. When he stopped trying to impress me, he had quite an interesting story to tell. He seemed like a very unhappy man."

"What did he tell you?"

"He told me about his father," she said more slowly. "About how he used to beat his mother and make her life hell. His father sounded like an awful man. You can see where Benny gets his attitude to women from."

"It's a funny thing," said Bill. "I knew Arthur Horseman really well and I would never have guessed all that about him. He was a hard man. He kept everyone in the yard in line, that's for sure, but he was always fair with the men. I never knew he treated his family so badly. Benny was always the bully at school, but I suppose that's not such a surprise really, after the way his old man behaved in front of him. I have a lot of sympathy for Benny over all that."

"I'm surprised to hear you say that. To hear him speaking you'd think you hated one another."

"I used to hate him, but recently I've learnt that I was really just using him as a focus for all the anger and frustration I really felt about myself."

"Wow! That's sounds like one major insight. How long did that take you?"

"About 30 years," he said with a smile, hardly able to believe the truth of it himself. "I just wish he would bury the hatchet and let me get on with my life."

"Well, you can hardly blame him, can you?" She leaned forward and spoke in a whisper. "You have been stealing his money for years."

"Is that what he told you?"

"I saw you do it."

"You saw me do it once, but that was the only time. If Benny told you anything different, he was lying."

"Well, you chose the worst possible night to do it then. What made you do it on that particular night?"

"I don't want to go into it all now, Hayley, if you don't mind. I just had dreams, things I wanted to do with my life, and I needed money to do them. Benny knew how I felt and he deliberately put the temptation in my way. And I succumbed. He got lucky, and I got very unlucky. It was my fault. I don't blame him or anyone else any more. Anyway, why did you get involved?"

"Lots of reasons," she said. "The excitement, the buzz, the money. I really needed the money."

"So you took part in all that for money?"

Hayley picked up on the change of tone in his voice, and the smile disappeared from her face.

"Don't you dare judge me, Bill. You're not the only person who's allowed to have dreams, you know. And I need money for my dreams as much as you do for yours."

"I'm sorry, Hayley. I didn't mean to sound judgemental."

"Well, you did. Judgemental and narrow-minded."

"Okay, I apologise, but tell me what Benny wanted you to do."

"You've got to remember what Benny told me about you. He said you were this awful person who smarmed his way in with his father so that you could take over the firm. He told me about how you froze him out of his own firm and started to steal money from behind his back. He said he couldn't catch you at it, so he needed a reason to get rid of you before you did too much damage to the business. And he thought I might be able to help. It all sounded dramatic and exciting, and I make no apology for liking drama and excitement. He did make you sound like a horrible man."

Bill felt his anger towards Benny resurfacing and fought hard to control and conceal it.

"So what was your role going to be?" he said.

"Benny told me he had your office under video surveillance and he might need me purely as a witness. But he also said that if he couldn't catch you in the act of stealing his money he needed to find another reason to fire you."

"What did he want you to do?"

"What did he want Jasmine to do, you mean?"

"Okay. What did he want Jasmine to do?"

"He wanted her to come on to you and get you acting in a way that would give him grounds to dismiss you."

"And how far was Jasmine prepared to go with all this?"

"Is the thought starting to excite you then?"

"I don't know. I'm just curious that's all."

"Well, I'm pretty sure Benny wasn't going to get the full-blown porno movie he was hoping for, but I think Jasmine would have played her part."

"And that would be alright with you, would it?"

"Bill. You're starting to sound judgemental and pompous again."

"But surely you were being just as judgemental towards me. You'd found me guilty just on Benny's say-so. You didn't even know me then."

"I'm not asking for your permission. We all have choices. I had a choice and I chose to go along with it. I'm not asking you to like me for it. Anyway, if Jasmine had gone into your office, you would have had a choice as well. You could always have turned her down. And I expect she would have talked to you and realised you weren't as bad as Benny made out. She would have given you a chance."

"Why do you talk about Jasmine as if she's a different person than you? It's still you doing those things."

Hayley's cheeks reddened and she sat upright in her chair.

"You are judging me," she said, raising her voice. "Damn you. I'm an actress, you fool. Jasmine is a role I was playing. There are plenty of highly respected actresses who do a lot more on the screen than I was prepared to do that night. I'm interested in character and what makes people tick. That's why I find people so fascinating, even the Bennys of this world."

Bill could see how much he had upset her. Hayley turned her

head sharply to the side away from him. She breathed out deeply before turning back to look at him.

"I need to get experience. I need to find out what motivates people," she said. "Everyone has a story. Everyone in this pub has a story. And most of them are fascinating. You're like so many people, Bill Knight. You think yours is the only important story and you don't bother to see where other people are coming from."

She picked up her wine and drank what was left in one go.

"I'm sorry. I didn't mean to offend you, Hayley."

"Well, you have offended me, not because you question my morality, but because you're narrow-minded. Remember that I came here to meet you tonight knowing what you've done, and I still gave you a chance. Remember that. Remember, I sat there and saw you stealing Benny's money. And then you warn me about receiving dinner invitations from people like him. What about people like you?"

"That's the only money I ever took from Benny, Hayley. He was lying about me stealing from him before that. I'm not really a thief."

"No, but you are self-righteous and I'm not sure what's worse."

"But I'm not a thief."

"Okay. You're not a thief and I'm not a tart. I think I'm going home."

She stood up and brushed away Bill's attempt to help her on with her coat. Bill followed her out into the cold November air. He stopped by the entrance but she kept on walking.

"Look, Hayley, I know I made a right mess of things in there. Will you please let me try to make it up to you?"

She kept on walking.

"You'll never meet anyone as screwed up as I am right now. Think of all the good material you'll be missing out on."

Hayley stopped and turned to face him. When he saw her smiling he felt a huge sense of relief.

"Do you know what really annoys me?" she said. "I agreed to meet you tonight even though I saw you steal that money and nearly gamble it away. I watched you do it. But I met you anyway, because I sensed that you were a good person, and because you said you needed my help. And I didn't pigeon-hole you, and I didn't judge you. And you still haven't told me what help you want from me."

"I know, I know. Give me another chance, Hayley. I know I get a lot of things wrong but I'm not a lost cause yet."

She walked back towards him.

"No one can be pigeon-holed like that, Bill. I told you. Everyone's got a story to tell, even the Jasmines and the Bennys of this world. Don't judge them."

"Friends?" he said, and he took off his glove and offered her his hand to shake. Instead she reached up and kissed his cheek.

"It's a good job I like lost causes," she said. "Meet me here at eight o'clock on Friday and you can take me to dinner. You can tell me about your dreams and who you really are."

Chapter 22

Bill knew he ought to tell Natalie Barry about finding 'Jasmine' but he decided against it. After all, he had not even asked Hayley yet if she supported his version of what had happened at the casino, let alone get her agreement to testify in his defence. He was also afraid that once Natalie learned that he had found Jasmine she might insist that he have no more contact with her, since she was now a potential witness. And Bill was looking forward far too much to seeing Hayley again on Friday night to risk that. So he contacted no one in Bramport until Thursday. That afternoon he had at last found himself some work, and in the evening he phoned Angie to tell her about it. She seemed very pleased with the news.

"I must say, Bill, I am really relieved. I was getting really worried about the way our savings have been going down. There's a bill here for your mobile, and a lot of forms from your solicitor about legal aid. What do you want me to do with it all?"

"Send it all to me at Liz's, love, and I'll deal with it. They're going to pay me weekly, by the way, and I'm starting on Monday, so I should be able to pay in at least £100 at the end of next week. And they say there's plenty of overtime, so I should be able to up that to £200 most weeks. That'll cover the mortgage and most of the household bills."

"That's good, Bill. It'll be so nice to have some money coming in at last. I was beginning to really worry."

"Do you want to know what it is I'll be doing, Angie?"

"Yes, of course, love. I meant to ask."

"I'm labouring on a building site."

"Oh, Bill, you can't do that."

"Yes, I can. I'm still in good shape. It'll do me good to be outside and get more exercise. I'm quite looking forward to it."

"Couldn't you get an office job or something?"

"They ask too many questions, Angie, and they all want references, and I don't think a reference from Horseman's is going to do me any favours at the moment, do you?"

"Oh, Bill. But you're right back where you started."

"No, I'm not, Angie, believe me, I'm not. Honestly, I really am looking forward to it. I want to work outside and let off some steam. It'll do me good. Besides, they ask no questions and it's all cash in hand. There's no problem."

"If you say so."

"I do, love. Just don't worry about me. As long as you're alright, I'm alright. I've got to go now, Angie, because I want to phone the boys and I want to speak to Stoner about how Benny is."

"Oh, you can speak to Mark now, Bill. He's right here with me in the lounge."

"Mark?"

"Yes. Mark. I mean Stoner. Anyway, here he is."

"Hello, my old mate."

"Stoner. That was lucky catching you there."

"I just popped in to see how Angie was getting on. How are you?"

"I'm finding my feet, Stoner, and staying out of trouble. Angie will give you all the details. What I really wanted to know was how Benny was doing."

"Not good, Bill, I'm afraid. He's still in hospital and he lost an eye."

"Oh, dear God, no."

"I'm afraid so, Bill. Apparently fragments of bone went into the soft tissue and they couldn't save it. They were worried about infection, so they decided it was safer to take it out."

"That's terrible news. How's he taking it?"

"Not well. I saw him two days ago and he's pretty sedated because of all the painkillers. They reckon he could be out in about ten days."

"Is he still blaming me?"

"I think he blames you for the rain on a summer's day, Bill. There's no change there. But the police have interviewed him again and I'm pretty sure they're not going to pursue it."

"Well, I won't ask you to give him my best wishes, because I know he doesn't want them, but I am genuinely sorry to hear about how bad he is."

"I know you are, mate. I do realise that."

There was a pause and Bill was just about to end the conversation when Stoner spoke again.

"Listen, Bill. I'm coming up to Medford tomorrow. I collect Benny's rents up there on a Friday. Perhaps we could meet for a drink. There are some things I really need to talk over with you."

"That would be good, Stoner, but I'm already booked up tomorrow. Will it wait until next Friday?"

"It'll wait for a week, but no longer. I'll call you on your mobile to arrange it for next Friday."

"Okay, Stoner. I'll see you then. Give my love to Angie."

"I will, my old mate. See you soon."

On Friday evening Bill met Hayley again in the Gardner's Arms. This time when he got up to greet her, she came straight up to him and kissed him on the cheek and declined the offer of a drink. She hoped he did not mind but she had booked a table for them at a French restaurant for 8.15, and she suggested they go straight there. As they walked along the Gables Hayley linked Bill's arm and she chatted animatedly about the week's rehearsals, and how wonderful the show was going to be.

Eventually they turned down a narrow side street and came to a dimly lit restaurant squeezed in between two antique shops. When they entered they heard the opening bars of Charles Trenet's *La Mer*. As a waiter helped Hayley off with her coat Bill looked around to see that all the dozen or so tables were occupied except for one in the far corner. When he turned back Hayley was standing there in a short black cocktail dress. She seemed to have on very little make-up and she was wearing a simple gold necklace with a single diamond pendant. The waiter led them to the small table in the corner. Hayley sat on the inside so that Bill was looking into an alcove with photos of old Montmartre on the walls. The waiter lit the candle on their table and handed them their menus. When he asked them if they wanted aperitifs Hayley ordered two kirs.

"I just love the food here," she said, and added in a whisper, "and it's very reasonable too. They have excellent fixed menus just like in France."

The kirs arrived and they clinked glasses.

"Salut," said Hayley.

"Here's to a wonderful acting career," offered Bill.

"Thanks. And to you fulfilling your dreams, whatever they may be," she said.

When the waiter came back, Hayley ordered for both of them.

"I'll have the *soupe de poisson à la catalane* and the *blanquette d'agneau* and my friend would like *les escargots de Bourgogne et le rôti de veau cevenole*," she said in a perfect accent.

Bill ordered the wine in English. "That's very impressive," he said. "Where did you learn to speak French like that?"

"Oh, my parents have had a house down in Languedoc since Jed and I were little. We spent every summer there and we spoke French with the neighbours' children. I love speaking French. It gives me a chance to show off."

"Jed's your brother?"

"Yes, he's two years younger than me."

"And your parents live here in Medford?"

"Just outside in Burnell Village. Dad's the professor of molecular biology at the university and Mum's a GP."

"And what do they think of you being an actress?"

"Ooh, that's a sore point. They're not keen at all, especially Dad. He doesn't regard it as a 'proper' career. They would like me to have been an academic, or gone into medicine or the law or something."

"Did they put a lot of pressure on you?"

"Yes, terrible pressure. We had dreadful rows but I wouldn't give in. In the end they refused to support me at drama college, or help me financially since I left. That's why I'm saddled with all this debt. I find it completely impossible to live with them."

"Because you argue all the time?"

"Because they're so negative about everything I try to do. I don't need people who try to belittle what's really important to me. I feel they're just waiting for me to fail."

"It must have been really difficult for you to go against their wishes."

"Not really. I had no choice. Ever since I can remember I've known what I wanted to do. I feel that it's a gift if you're given a clear idea of what you want to do with your life. And who has a right to stop you? Who has a right to presume they know better than you what's good for you? I won't let anyone do that to me."

"And you've always been that sure, have you?"

"I've always loved dressing up and performing and creating characters."

"I have a friend who would probably tell you that you do that because you're not happy with the person you are."

"No, that's completely wrong. It's not that at all. It's not about escape. I'm very happy with who I am. I just like exploring feelings and finding out what it's like to walk in other people's shoes, and acting allows you to do that. Plus, it's great fun."

The wine waiter arrived and showed Bill the bottle for his approval. Hayley was so animated by what she was saying that she carried on talking as the wine was served.

"The buzz of being on stage and knowing you've got the audience on your side is just so exhilarating. Your confidence grows and the adrenalin surge is incredible. Performance is like a drug. I just feel incredibly lucky that I find it so fulfilling. I know I'd just be miserable if I'd given in to my parents and become a solicitor or something, working in an office. It would've totally crushed me."

"I think it's admirable that you're so single-minded about pursuing what you want to do," Bill said. "I envy you your courage."

He picked up his wine glass. "Here's wishing you a career that always keeps you so fulfilled and enthusiastic, Hayley," he said, and they leaned towards one another and touched glasses.

"Thanks, Bill. That's such a nice toast," said Hayley. "I'll happily drink to that."

After a short while the waiter arrived with their first course and Bill looked down at the six snails on his plate. Beside the plate lay a small pair of tongs and an instrument that looked as if it was for picking locks. Hayley saw the puzzled look on Bill's face.

"I've personally never been keen on those," she said. "My brother used to call them bogies with crash helmets." And she put a hand over her mouth to stifle her laughter.

"I don't know whether I'm very keen on them either now you've said that," said Bill, joining in with her laughter. "I've never had them before. I just thought it was too good an opportunity to miss."

"Good for you, Bill. I like people with a sense of adventure."

"I don't know, Hayley, the last time I indulged my sense of adventure it didn't work out too well."

"Well, the way I look at it is like this," she said picking up her glass of wine, "if it weren't for your sense of adventure you wouldn't be here with me now. And I'm really pleased you are."

"Thankyou, Hayley, that's a really nice thought. I'll drink to that too." And they clinked glasses again and started to eat.

"You know, Bill, you've asked me all sorts of questions about myself, but I know next to nothing about you."

"What do you want to know?"

"Well, I know you're married, because you're wearing your wedding ring."

"A bit of a give-away, is it?"

"I like the fact that you wear it. Why shouldn't you? I can't stand men who try to pretend they're not married. They dress appallingly, make no effort to stay fit or in shape, and usually have no idea about grooming, but then they think that taking off a wedding ring suddenly makes them exciting and available to all women."

"Well, I'm glad I didn't fall into that trap then."

"No, you're not like that at all. For a start you're in very good shape. I bet you do lots of sport. And you dress nicely, and you smell nice."

"I won't after I've eaten these snails. They're full of garlic. But I am grateful for your compliments, Hayley. After what's happened recently I'll take all the compliments you've got."

"How long have you been married then?"

"Twenty-nine years."

"No! That's not possible. How old were you at your wedding for goodness sake? Ten?"

"No, I've got a son of 28 and another of 24."

"I don't believe it! I thought you were about 39 or 40."

"I wish, Hayley, I wish."

"Well, all I can say is you've looked after yourself really well. What are your sons called?"

"The oldest is Mickey. He's married to Cheryl and they're expecting a baby next summer, so I'm actually going to be a grandfather. He's a wonderful man. He's steady, reliable, honest. You could depend on him for anything. And Dave is two years younger. He's single and a bit of a live wire. He's funny and impetuous, and he shows no signs of settling down yet."

"You're obviously very proud of them."

"They're everything to me. Everyone says they love their kids, but I think the intensity of feeling towards your children is more like being *in* love. It's unshakeable. You have no choice, and it's completely selfless. And it's forever."

"They're very lucky boys to have a father who feels like that about them."

"Like I say, Hayley, I have no choice. I can't feel anything else. They are wonderful, though, I know you would like them."

"I'm sure I would. I'm sure they're everything you say they are. But I have to admit that generally I don't find men of my own age very interesting."

"No? Why's that?"

"Because they haven't experienced enough and yet they think they know everything, and they're often so full of themselves."

"So you actually prefer confused old grandfathers like me then?" Bill said with a smile.

"Yes, I really do. You're courteous and considerate and attentive. Younger men tend to be brash and self-centred, whereas you're just confident in yourself and really interested in me. It's so much nicer."

"So I'm forgiven for being a self-righteous, judgemental prig then, am I?"

"I think so," said Hayley, smiling back at him. "I think everyone should get a second chance. And my instincts tell me you deserve one."

Just then the waiter came to clear their plates. When he had gone Hayley leaned forward holding her glass in both hands.

"Tell me about your wife," she said. "You haven't mentioned her yet."

"My wife? She's called Angie. She's a wonderful mother to the boys. She's a wonderful person really. A bit highly-strung, I guess."

"And what does she think about you being here in Medford?"

"Well, to be honest, I think she's been glad to see the back of me. Things became very difficult after that night at the casino."

"So are you separated then?"

"Not officially, no. We're just having some time apart. I don't think it's more than that. This whole business with the money put us under a lot of pressure. I think she just needs some peace."

"And what do you need?"

"What do I need? Well, I don't think I'm looking for peace. I'm looking for answers to a lot of things, I suppose. And I need help."

"You need help from me?"

"I think I might do, Hayley, yes. Do you know that I was arrested the day after I saw you at the casino?"

"No, but I thought you were going to tell me something like that. You said something to me in the café about you going to prison."

"I was arrested for stealing £20,000 from the safe in my office."

"But you did steal it, Bill," she said in a whisper. "I don't see how you can change that."

"But it's only stealing, you see, Hayley, if you intended to keep the money. In law they call it 'permanently depriving the rightful owner of their property'.

"And didn't you intend to do that?"

"No, I didn't. I've asked myself the question a thousand times, and I know that I have to be honest with myself before I can move on with my life. The honest truth is that I would've returned the money to Benny somehow."

"I believe you, Bill," Hayley said, smiling at him as if they shared a secret. She paused and sipped her wine. "Benny and I watched you playing that night, you know. He could hardly contain himself when you were losing it all."

"He was angry, was he?"

"No, the complete opposite. He was laughing, saying that he'd got you at last, and how the more money you lost the more money he was making. It made no sense."

"Oh, it makes sense alright," said Bill. "Benny had more than one reason for wanting me sacked from Horseman's. The main one is simply because he hates me, but there's a more practical reason too. I was about to be made redundant, you see, and he was going to have to pay me a lot of money for all the years I'd worked there."

"How much?"

"One hundred and fifty thousand as a lump sum, and about £25,000 a year for the rest of my life."

"And he's saved all that because of what you did that night?"

"Yes, he has."

"That explains so much to me."

"It does?"

"It explains why he was getting so agitated when you started winning the money back. I told him to go over and confront you and grab his money, but I see now that's the last thing he wanted."

"No, he wanted me arrested, sacked and imprisoned. He's got the first two already, and he'll probably get the third."

"But it doesn't change the fact that you stole his money in the first place, Bill."

"Took his money, Hayley, not stole it. You asked me if I intended to keep it, and I said I want to be honest about it. Well, I know without question that when I got that money back again at the tables, I had made up my mind to put it all back in the safe."

"So why didn't you?"

"Because Benny barged in and 'borrowed' it off me. Don't you remember?"

"Yes, he took your seat and was playing while we had a drink. Do you know, Bill, he didn't really lose that money. I thought he had, but he still had it when we got back to my flat later."

"I know about that. When I saw him that day in the wood he was bragging about it. But the point is, you see, Hayley, he's lied to the police about it. He's made a statement swearing I didn't pay him back any money in the casino, and I can't prove any different."

"What about the croupier. He must remember."

"No, the casino refuses to get involved in any of it. Bad publicity, I suppose. And we've been through the CCTV, but it proves nothing."

They both sat back from the table as the waiter brought their main dishes. Bill poured some more wine.

"This looks good," he said. "Do you mind if I tell you a bit more about what happened while we eat?"

"No, I don't mind. I want to know what happened."

"That night after I left you I stayed in a hotel, and that proved to be a major mistake. I had the other £10,000 in a money belt, you see, and I intended to get to my office early on Saturday morning and put £9,000 of it back. Then I would tell Benny on Monday that I'd already taken the £11,000 he owed me, and everything would be fine."

"But it wasn't?"

"No, Benny must have realised what I intended to do, so he nipped into the office on Saturday morning before me, 'discovered' the theft and called the police."

"That explains something else," Hayley said, frowning.

"What?"

"The way Benny behaved on that Friday back at my place. He was so full of himself and he threw all this money up in the air, and he was popping champagne. I thought it was because he had his money back and because he'd got the evidence he needed on video to put an end to your stealing." She put her hand to her mouth. "Whoops. Sorry, Bill, but I didn't know then that you hadn't done it before."

"That's alright. Go on."

"Anyway, I knew he was going to make a pass at me and I had my opt-out clause ready when suddenly he just stopped, swore a lot and collected his money and made a dash for it."

"Because he'd just realised he had to get to the office before me. Otherwise I could ruin his plan by putting the money back. What a nasty devil he is."

"I expect that was it. But don't get worked up, Bill. Enjoy your veal. Is it good?"

"Very good, thanks," he said with little enthusiasm. "But you know, Hayley, this business gets worse. On the Saturday morning when I heard the police wanted to interview me, I did something really stupid. I went round to Benny's place just outside Bramport and tried to sort it out with him. At that point I didn't realise that his only real intention was to stitch me up. So I gave him back the other £10,000 from the money belt. And I pleaded with him to call off the police. I really grovelled. But he threw me out. He wouldn't give me a chance."

"So he really does have all his money back then?"

"Yes, he does, but I'm still accused of stealing the lot and keeping the lot, you see. I've already confessed to taking the money, plus he's got the video, of course. He swears that he never received the £10,000 at the casino and never received the other £10,000 the next morning, and somehow I've got to prove that he's lying about it."

"Oh, dear," Hayley said. "I think I can see now where I come in."

"You can?"

"You need me to testify that Benny's lying about getting back the money in the casino, don't you?"

"Yes, I do. You did see me with that £10,000, didn't you?"

"Yes, and I saw him take it off you. I made him promise to pay you back £11,000. Don't you remember?"

"Yes, I do. I could have hugged you for that."

"Let me think about this, Bill. I think I may have lost my appetite now."

She put her knife and fork down on her plate and leaned forward on the table.

"What exactly do you want me to say?"

"Simply that Benny's not telling the truth. Once I can prove that he's lying about one thing, it will destroy the rest of his story, and I can be judged simply on what I really did."

"But if I testify against Benny he'll do anything to get back at me, you know. He'll say I was paid money to try to entrap you. If that came out in court I'd be finished. I might gain some notoriety in the tabloids, but I don't think I'd be taken seriously again. My parents would completely disown me, and my agent probably would as well."

"There's no way I'd want you to pay a heavy price like that, Hayley."

"Bless you for saying that," she said, and she reached out her hand and placed it on his. "I don't want to make you any promises that I may not be able to keep, Bill. Will you let me think about it for a few days? I know how important it is to you, but it's a really big decision for me too."

"I know, Hayley. Whatever you decide, I'll accept it."

"Come on," she said, taking up her knife and fork, "let's not waste this wonderful food."

They left the restaurant just before 11.00 and walked through the Gables to Hayley's flat. Hayley took Bill's arm again as they strolled along, but this time she held on to him with both hands.

"There's something I have to tell you," she said, "something I feel quite bad about."

Bill immediately felt butterflies invading his stomach.

"What is it?"

"That night with Benny. The money he took off you at the casino. He gave me £2500 of that money for helping him that night."

"Was that the deal?"

"No, there was more. He gave me a contract on my flat for 12 months, and it's all rent-free. That's how I was able to move out of my parents' place so quickly."

"And were there any strings attached?"

"He said that I mustn't use my Jasmine character ever again, and in six months I'd receive another £2,500. I knew it was too good to be true. I couldn't understand why he was paying me so much, but it was just too good to turn down."

Bill stopped walking and stood facing her with his hands on her shoulders.

"Is that all?" he said.

"Is that all? Isn't that enough? I've got some of the money you're accused of stealing. It's the money you could go to prison for."

"I don't care, Hayley. I just don't care. If that's all you want to tell me. I'm just glad at least one of us has done alright out of Benny."

"Oh, I'm so relieved," she said, and she wrapped her arms around his waist and put her head on his chest. "You don't hate me then for helping Benny against you?"

"No. I most definitely don't hate you."

"Come on, then," said Hayley taking his hand, "come back to my place and I'll make us both some coffee."

Hayley's flat was above a bridal shop, almost exactly opposite across the green from the café where she worked. She opened the street door with a Yale key and they climbed the stairs to a solid white door, which she opened with a second key. She hung her coat up on a peg in the small hallway and Bill did the same with his. There were three more white doors leading off from the hallway. They were all closed and Hayley opened the one on the right.

"Through here," she said.

Bill followed her into a lounge that was almost filled by a large sofa and two armchairs. They all had beige-coloured throws over them and matching cushions. The throws and cushions looked new. Hayley bent down and lit the gas fire. Then she switched on a stainless steel standard lamp and disappeared through an archway into a small kitchen. The lamp threw light up into a corner of the ceiling.

"How do you like your coffee, Bill?" she called out.

"White with one small sugar, please. Who plays the piano, you?"

"Yes," she answered, popping her head around the corner, "that's my precious baby."

Bill looked at the upright piano next to the standard lamp. It was a Steinway.

"What sort of music do you play?" he asked.

"All sorts. Ragtime, classical, everything."

"Any rock 'n' roll?"

"What were you thinking of? Elvis? Or Bill Hayley perhaps?"

"It seems appropriate. But I was trying hard not to say it."

"I was afraid you might try a line like us 'making sweet music together'."

"I wouldn't say anything like that," Bill objected.

"I know you wouldn't. You're far too nice," she said, smiling at him. "Here's your coffee."

"Thanks."

Hayley sat down on the sofa, but Bill stood with his coffee in his hand looking at the contents of Hayley's bookcase. There were books on mime, ballet, puppetry, plus Shakespeare and Sartre and half a dozen Lonely Planet guides. Around the bookcase were photos of Hayley with her family and friends. There was Hayley skiing, Hayley on the stage, Hayley on a beach with some girlfriends, and Hayley with a tanned young man holding a tennis racket.

"You really are a girl with many talents, aren't you?" Bill said.

"I've got a wide range of interests. I don't know how talented I am at them all. Sometimes it scares me when I think of all there is to learn about in the world and I know so little."

"I know exactly what you mean," said Bill. "I think of all the books I haven't read and the music I haven't heard. I can't even speak another language or play a musical instrument like you can."

"Why don't you learn?"

"You're right. There's nothing to stop me now, is there? Before it's all been about bringing up children and keeping on top of things at work, but I've got no excuse now, have I?"

Bill turned to face her. She was sitting with her legs crossed and one elbow resting on the arm of the sofa. She seemed to be studying him.

"You're very sensible doing so much while you're young, Hayley."

"Don't be silly, Bill. You're still young. Michelangelo was 83 when he designed the cupola of St Peter's, you know. And Picasso, Titian and Verdi were all over 80 when they did some of their greatest work. Compared with them you're hardly out of nappies."

"Well, I suppose if you put it like that…"

"I do. You've got all the time in the world, Bill. Half the battle is knowing what it is you want. If you know what your dreams are, you have to go for them."

"Is it that simple, Hayley?"

"It has to be, otherwise you deny yourself what's really important to you, and I don't see much point in that. But you still haven't told me what your dreams are. Are they to do with learning languages and music?"

"No, not really. I'd like to do those things, but my real ambition has always been to travel. You say it scares you thinking about how much you don't know, and how much there is to learn. Well, it scares me when I think of all the places I've never seen and all the experiences I've never had. All the cultures, the people, the food, the music out there and I've had so little contact with any of it. I'm sorry. I'm not explaining it very well."

Bill went over and sat down in one of the armchairs. He sat forward with his forearms resting on his knees and his coffee mug held in both hands. Hayley kicked off her shoes and drew her legs up onto the sofa. She rested her head on her hand and looked straight at Bill as he spoke.

"I always say it's about travel," he said, "but it's more than just travelling. I know I could make a list of countries and sights and buy a ticket and just tick them off as I go. But it's more than that. It's hard to explain."

"Try. I want to understand."

"I don't want to just visit places, you see. I want to be part of wherever I am. I want to be able to belong anywhere, to be able to react to any situation that comes my way. That way you learn about the sort of person you really are. I suppose it's a very vain thing really, because it's all about me. I'm the raw material and I want the world to be my testing ground."

He put his mug on the coffee table in front of him, and he looked at Hayley. She smiled at him but offered no comment.

"I feel I've squandered so much of my life. Staying in the same place. Repeating the same things day after day after day. Why do we do that when the world's so full of different people and places and cultures? Imagine, Hayley, facing new experiences and new challenges every day, instead of the same ones over and over. I'm not talking about risk and high drama all the time. But I am talking about variety and change, where the only constant is you. It's about treating your life like a work in progress instead of something you just have to get through."

He stopped and looked at Hayley, who still had not moved a muscle as he spoke.

"Does this make any sense to you, at all?" he asked her.

"Of course it does," she said, and she raised herself slightly and pulled her dress down over her knees. "I think you're describing a variation on acting. I look for new characters and try to get into their shoes and inside their heads, but you're not talking about trying to *imagine* what it's like to be someone else. You want to find out what it's like just to be you interacting with as many situations as you can. You'd like the whole world as a backdrop to your life."

"That's it, Hayley, that's it," said Bill and he stood up, walked back to the bookcase and turned to face her again. "The whole world is there to be a backdrop, like a canvas, for your life. Just like your acting provides you with an endless possibility of characters, the world supplies us with endless situations and experiences."

He started pacing between the window and the bookcase and his face became more animated as he spoke.

"You know, I see our lives as a gift, Hayley. We look after our bodies and try to give them the things that are best for them, but we treat our lives so recklessly. Our lives shouldn't be something that just happens. Life should be treated as a separate entity, like a work of art, with care taken over it so that it's full of interest and colour. And at the end of it we should hope we created something beautiful and worthwhile."

"And within the broad canvas you could create a lot of smaller canvases, couldn't you?"

"How do you mean?"

"There's no reason why every day shouldn't hold something new and stimulating for us, is there?"

"Exactly," said Bill. "If you open your life up to all the world offers you, there's no reason why every day shouldn't be rich and full of new experiences."

"So it would be like starting a new canvas every day."

"Why not, Hayley? Why not? Every day like a new canvas. Every day like a new life."

Bill came back to his chair and sat down.

"You know, I've never found anyone before who understood what I meant by all this. I remember when I was younger; I used to think, 'Why live a small life when you can live a big life?' And I was convinced I was going to be different and I'd do and see so much. I was so determined not to be one of those people who spend their whole lives in the same place, in one speck on the map, repeating the same day over and over until their time runs out."

Bill slumped back in his chair and Hayley watched the excitement and exhilaration slowly drain from his face.

"So come on, Bill. Why haven't you lived your life like that then?"

Bill sat forward again and looked down at the coffee table as he spoke.

"It's funny, Hayley. I always thought I would. Even as a little lad I used to dream about it. Other kids wanted to be Buck Rogers or Dan Dare, but I wanted to be crossing the Sahara on a camel with Bedouins, or riding a motorbike around India, or sailing down the Amazon, that sort of thing. I used to read all the books about these places I could get my hands on. I loved the library, but I hated school."

"Why do you think that was?" asked Hayley.

Bill looked up at her.

"I was like a caged animal at school. Sitting in one place all day was torture for me. But I stuck it out. I had this plan to leave home and get out of Bramport as soon as I was 18, even though I knew it would break my parents' hearts. But at 18 I got Angie pregnant, and the rest, as they say, is history."

"You could have gone anyway."

"I don't think so. I couldn't be that selfish."

"Maybe it would've been unselfish. Maybe selfish was doing something that made you unhappy and resentful."

"No, don't get me wrong, Hayley. I wanted to stay with Angie. I loved her to bits. It's just that I thought she shared the same dreams as me."

"But she didn't?"

"No, she didn't. She wanted security and a settled home for herself and the children, and the only way I could provide for it was by working my whole life at Horseman's."

"And do you blame her now for that?"

"Not really. She's done what every mother wants to do. Provide a warm, safe nest for her young. She's done that and I bless her for it."

"You make her sound like a sparrow," said Hayley, smiling at him.

"Sorry, I didn't mean to sound patronising towards her. It's just that I understand what's important to her and I respect her for what she's done. I couldn't just leave her without my support."

"So what's going to happen about your dreams now then?"

"I don't know. That's what the £20,000 from the safe was all about. I was going to leave Bramport and live out the dream for a while, but I needed money so Angie could survive for a year or so. I knew I couldn't just steal it so I had this crazy idea about winning at the casino and funding it that way."

Bill looked down and shook his head.

"It really was a bloody crazy idea," he said. "I don't even have the excuse that I was drunk. I was just desperate, I think. I just couldn't go on any more."

"You poor old thing, Bill. I feel so bad about what I did. I was watching you from Benny's car, and you were pacing up and down and then sitting at your desk, and then pacing up and down again. I wish now I'd gone in and got talking to you."

"I wish you had too," said Bill, looking up at her.

"I'm sure I would've worked out what you're really like instead of believing the things Benny was telling me. I'm so sorry." And she got up and went over to Bill's chair. She sat on the arm and rested her cheek against the top of his head.

"You're a decent man, Bill Knight. You're old-fashioned and naïve, and decent."

"Old-fashioned and naïve. Are those meant to be compliments?"

"Yes, they are, because it means you consider other people all the time and put their needs first. That sort of attitude isn't very fashionable nowadays, but maybe it is a bit naïve. And even a bit dishonest."

"Dishonest? How do you work that out?"

Hayley got up and knelt down on the floor facing him. She held his right hand in both of hers as she spoke.

"It's maybe a bit dishonest because if you don't tell people clearly how you really feel and what your needs are, they're not getting the real you, are they? They're getting a pretend you."

"But if we went around speaking our real minds all the time we'd all be in a constant state of chaos and embarrassment, wouldn't we?"

She pulled his hand in a gesture of mock impatience.

"I'm not talking about sharing every private thought that comes into our heads with everyone around us," she said. "I'm talking about you knowing what you need to make you fulfilled and then not sharing that information with the people you love, and who love you. That's a form of dishonesty, because without that information they're not really dealing with the real you, are they? No one can really know where they are with you. They just have this façade of Bill Knight who spends all his time trying to give people what he thinks they want from him."

Bill said nothing.

"Do you understand what I'm trying to say?" Hayley asked him.

"I think so. An old friend of mine said something similar recently." He looked down at Hayley who was still kneeling at his feet. "Do you think all you're getting from me is a façade?" he asked her.

"No, I don't think that, because I'm sure you're sharing your real feelings with me. But you've got to share those feelings with the really important people in your life."

"Angie, you mean?"

"Absolutely."

"I've tried, but she's never really listened."

"You've got to make her listen, Bill. Look where your silence has got you. You stole, sorry, *took* that money rather than speak to her about the frustrations you were feeling. If it's that important to you, you've got to explain it to her like you did to me just now, and find out where it leads you both."

"She wouldn't be very happy about it, I can tell you. There'd be a right royal drama."

"Well, that's another thing you have to accept then."

"What's that?"

"The consequences. The consequences of telling people how you really feel. You have to accept that people might get angry with you, or even hate you. But at least they'll be dealing with the real you. I know my parents really disapprove of me for what I'm doing, but that's the price I have to pay for being honest with myself and with them."

Bill sat in silence mulling over what Hayley had said. She was still holding his hand and she seemed to be waiting for a response from him, but he could think of nothing to say. As he looked down at her he could only think about how wise she seemed and how beautiful she was. He leaned forward towards her until their faces were only inches apart. Later he realised that this was the moment when everything changed for him.

From the first minute he had seen her he had recognised how attractive she was. He had registered the shape of her breasts and her legs. Earlier when she sat on the arm of his chair he had noticed the outline of her thigh under her black cocktail dress. But up to this point his observations had been matter-of-fact as he fought to look at this beautiful young woman in a purely platonic way. Now as he looked into her face and into her eyes everything about her became sexual and he felt his heart pump faster and his breathing quicken. And he felt ashamed, because she was so young and she trusted him. Bill cupped Hayley's face in his hands, kissed her on the forehead and stood up.

"I don't know where you get all your wisdom from at your

age," he said. "You must be half my age, but you seem to know twice as much about life as me."

"I'm 26," Hayley said. "What are you doing?"

"I'm going home. It's late. People are asleep."

"But I don't want you to go. We were having such a nice time. I was really enjoying talking to you."

"I was too, Hayley, but I just think it's time I went, that's all."

Hayley stood up and smiled at him. "Well, you're a free man, Bill Knight. Free to do as you please. Just as long as I haven't said anything to upset you, that's all."

"Oh, God, no," said Bill, taking a step towards her. "Quite the opposite. What you said made a lot of sense. You haven't upset me. You're a wonderful girl. Intelligent, caring, beautiful. You haven't upset me."

"Will I see you again, Bill?"

"I'm not sure that's a good idea."

"But I have to see you again, don't I?" said Hayley and her eyes lit up. "You need to know if I'm going to help you against Benny."

"God, that's right," Bill replied. He had come all the way to Medford for that very purpose, but now it had slipped his mind. And suddenly Hayley's testimony had a new purpose. It was the excuse he needed to see her again.

"Why don't you meet me outside the Guildhall at nine o'clock on Wednesday," Hayley said. "That's where we're holding rehearsals. I'll have come to a decision by then."

"Okay, I'll see you there at nine o'clock on Wednesday, Hayley."

At the front door Bill kissed her on the cheek and she hugged him. "I don't even know your full name," he said.

"McKenna. My name is Hayley McKenna. I'll see you on Wednesday."

Outside the door Bill stopped at the top of the stairs leading down to the street. "Hayley McKenna," he said to himself.

Chapter 23

Liz's house was about a 15-minute walk from Hayley's flat in the Gables. It was a cold night but Bill was grateful for the chance to walk and clear his head a little. He could not believe his luck in first finding Jasmine, and then discovering that behind the disguise existed another young woman who was intelligent and sensitive and equally beautiful. Hayley was the first person who seemed to understand how he wanted his life to be, and talking to her had had a liberating effect on him.

But now as he walked along Bill's mood changed slowly and he grew angry with himself. He had been determined to treat Hayley in a purely platonic way and to behave with a reserve that he always adopted in his relationships with women. To act any other way was demeaning, potentially very embarrassing and not like him at all. What an old fool he was being! Misreading the situation like that and letting his imagination run away with him right at the end of a wonderful evening. She had been interested in his ideas. She had been friendly and attentive, and that was all. It was pathetic and disrespectful of him to read any more into their evening than that.

Bill paused as he opened the door to his sister's house, and confirmed these final thoughts in his mind before he went in. But somewhere in his head where there is no place for logic, he saw a picture of Hayley kneeling on the floor and looking up at him, and he knew that he could not wait to see her again.

When he opened the front door Bill saw a light on in the lounge. He looked at his watch. It was a 12.45. He pushed the lounge door open gently and Liz peered over the back of the sofa to look

223

at him. She was in her dressing gown.

"Hello, Bill love," she said, "did you have a nice time?"

"You haven't been waiting up for me, Liz, have you?"

"No, of course not. There's no curfew for you here, Bill. I'm not your wife or your mother. You know you can come and go as you please."

Bill felt stupid for asking the question, but he could not escape the feeling that somehow he must be accountable to someone for his evening out.

"Thanks, Liz. What's the film?"

"*Now, Voyager* with Bette Davis. It was always one of Mum's favourites, remember? But you can stay and talk to me if you like. I haven't seen much of you over the past couple of days."

Liz pressed the mute button on the television and Bill sat down in the armchair opposite her. When he looked over at his sister it was obvious that she had been crying. "Fancy a cup of tea?" he asked her.

"Yes, that would be nice. Thanks."

From the kitchen Bill heard the sound come on again and he recognised the last line of the film, 'Jerry, don't let's ask for the moon. We have the stars'.

When Bill came in with the tray, Liz muted the music playing over the closing credits.

"A bit of a weepie, was it, Liz?" he said.

"It's a classic two-hankie weepie this one. But I must admit I don't need much of an excuse for a cry at the moment. It's been a hard week."

"Do you want to talk about it?"

"It's partly work. The kids are so difficult at the moment, especially my Year Nines, and I've got all the GCSE orals to organise. But the big problem is Steve. You know he saw Susie and Jon on Wednesday and promised to take them to Bristol this weekend to stay with his parents? He phoned up tonight to cancel. Susie's been in tears and Jon's hardly speaking to anyone. It's not been a good end to the week."

"I'm sorry I wasn't here for you, Liz."

"No, don't feel like that, Bill. You've got your own life to lead."

"So how do you feel about it all?"

"I'm bloody furious. I've dealt with the hurt I felt back in the summer, and I'm even trying to be understanding about Steve and Charlotte, but the way they're playing with my children's emotional health is making me bloody mad."

Bill could see that his sister was fighting to hold back her tears, but some found their way through and she dabbed her eyes. Bill wondered how Steve could possibly live with the guilt of all the misery he had created. Then he saw Liz's face tighten and her eyes widen as her pain turned to anger.

"I'm sure it's that stuck-up bitch who's stopped him from taking them," she said. "He says he's got too much work on, but I bet it's more to do with her posh bloody friends inviting them out somewhere, or something like that."

Bill thought of his evening with Hayley and then the evening his sister must have gone through, and he could not help feeling bad about it.

"I know what we'll do, Liz," he said. "I'll drive us all to Bristol tomorrow and we'll have some lunch somewhere. Jon and I can go to see Medford play Bristol Rovers in the afternoon while you and Susie do the shops again, and then we'll meet up in the evening to see *Gladiator*. I know Susie and Jon are keen to see it, because I heard them talking about it yesterday."

"That would be wonderful, Bill. Can we really do all that?"

"Yes, why not? The children will love it, and two hours of Russell Crowe's legs will do wonders for your spirits, Liz."

"Oh, that's really cheered me up. Well done, Bill."

"And on Sunday I'll do the dinner so that you can have some time for your schoolwork. How about that?"

Liz got up and came over to Bill and kissed him on his forehead.

"I think you're wonderful," she said. "You've always been my favourite brother. You've really got me looking forward to tomorrow now."

Liz put the teapot and cups on the tray and carried them through to the kitchen. When she came back in she did not sit down.

"I'm really tired, Bill," she said. "I'm going to go to bed. I think I might manage a decent night's sleep at last. Oh, by the way,

Angie phoned tonight. I told her you were out."

"What did she say about that?"

"Nothing. There was no inquisition at all. No questions about where you were, who you were with or anything. She seemed very perky actually. Not like Angie at all."

"It must be doing her good having me out the way."

"I don't believe that, but she did seem different to normal. She was interested in me and how I was, and she even said I could call her if ever I needed to talk things over. She was really quite chatty."

"Really? Perhaps I underestimated how much stress I've been putting her under. I'll call her in the morning."

"Okay, Bill. I'll be off then. Did your evening work out alright?" Liz asked at the door.

"I saw the girl who was with Benny at the casino. She's going to let me know on Wednesday if she'll testify on my behalf."

"How important do you think she'll be to you?" asked Liz.

"I don't know," said Bill. "I really can't say."

On Monday morning Bill walked into the centre of Medford and was picked up outside the town hall at 7.30 by a minibus belonging to Carter Construction Limited. He must have been the last pick-up because the van was already full with 13 others, plus the driver. The guy in the front passenger seat turned round to greet him.

"Grab yourself a seat, mate. My name's Tony. I'm the gaffer. Who are you then?"

"I'm Bill, Tony."

"I'll be havin' a word when we get there, Bill. We'll be about 20 minutes."

"Cheers, Tony."

"We don't call him Tony," offered the young man next to Bill without looking up from his paper. "We call him Piles."

"Why's that then?" asked Bill.

"Because he's a fucking pain in the arse," said someone from behind him.

Bill laughed but said nothing. Early on a Monday morning after a busy weekend no one wanted to say much. Half the men were reading a paper and nearly all of them had cigarettes on the go.

The van was full of fug, and condensation ran down the windows. Bill had never smoked, because of his sport, and he did not find the journey easy. It was turning light when the bus finally pulled into the site.

Nobody at the Jobcentre had bothered to tell him exactly where he would be working, only that it would be local, that he would be employed by Carter Construction Limited, and he should be outside Medford town hall at 7.30 sharp on Monday morning. So when Bill saw the sign at the entrance of the site it came as a complete shock to him.

"Oh shit!" he said. "I don't believe it."

"What's the problem, Bill?" said the young man beside him. "Had enough already?"

Bill studied the sign as they passed it, turning his head to glean every detail.

Against a blue and green background was a picture of a large detached house and a bird swooping in front of it. 'SWALLOW HOMES,' it read. 'Energy Efficient Homes For The New Millennium.' And in smaller letters in the corner he could just make out, 'Contractors: Carter Construction Limited and Horseman's Heating'.

"My God," thought Bill, "so this is the Meads."

The Meads was the new development of 75 houses on the outskirts of Medford, which had provided Horseman's with their biggest contract ever. Bill had negotiated for weeks with Peter Smale, the contracts manager at Swallow Homes, and had only signed the contracts on the 20th October, two days before the visit to the casino. Swallow wanted their new development to boast some of the most energy-efficient houses in the country, and Bill had planned and researched for weeks to make sure Horseman's could give them what they wanted. Besides the usual double-glazed units and wall and loft insulation, the electrical and hot water systems were to be state of the art.

Bill decided that the electricity to run appliances and lighting would be generated by solar photovoltaic tiles and panels. There would be grey solar tiles on the roof to match the normal roof tiles, and the conservatory on every house would be fitted with transparent cells and panels, which provided shading as well as generating electricity.

But the real breakthrough was to be hidden underground. Bill had contracted Horseman's to provide each house with a ground-source heat pump to provide central heating. This involved taking heat out of the ground like a fridge takes heat out of the air, and then using the heat for open-space radiators. Just like a fridge the system needed a heat pump, a compressor and a condenser, and the beauty of the system was that the electricity for these came from the solar tiles. Everything worked in energy-efficient harmony.

Now the man who had worked everything out, and who had secured the contract for Horseman's Heating, stood in the mud waiting for the gaffer to lay down the rules for his day's work.

"Right, lads. Most of you know me, and you know I won't put up with any fucking nonsense on any of my jobs," said Tony. "And those who don't know me will soon fucking learn."

There was a general murmuring but no one said anything. Tony was about 6ft 4, around 18 stone and not much of it was fat.

"This is a hard-hat area at all times," he went on. "Anyone I see without a hard hat on is sacked on the spot, right?"

"Did yous say we 'ad to 'ave a permanent 'ard on all the time we're work'n, Tone?" came a voice from Bill's left.

"Is that you, Scouser? You're fucking sex mad, you are," said Tony.

"Yeah, I've been practis'n all weekend, Tone. A'm gett'n frigg'n' great at it, 'n all," Scouser answered back.

"I know," said Tony, "I've heard all you need now, Scouser, is someone to do it with."

Everyone laughed, including Bill, whilst Scouser eyed the floor. Everyone knew that it was never enough just to be a hard man to stay in charge of a group like this. You had to have a mouth on you and quick wits as well. Everyone understood that Tony was the boss.

"Now, if you'd all like to shut the fuck up, I'll tell you what the score is," he continued. "See those three portacabins over there. The one on the left is for the suits. The one in the middle is for us gaffers and the one on the right is for you lot. Same with the portaloos. There's going to be 75 houses on this site and we're on phase one. That's the first 15 here."

Everyone looked around at acres of mud full of machinery and piles of bricks and breeze blocks. Stuck into the mud as far as the eye could see were plastic yellow poles connected by string, and alongside the poles and string ran lines of concrete.

"Right," said Tony, "you can see for yourselves, the foundations are in but that's about all. You lot are here because we need to speed things up a bit. So there'll be no pissing about, right?"

He eyed everyone and waited for any comment. There was none.

"Now, I've got some good news and some bad news. The bad news is the suits want phase one finished by the 25th of March."

There was a lot of swearing amid expressions of disbelief. "The good news is that there'll be loads of overtime." There was more swearing amid expressions of pleasure.

"The day finishes at half four for those who want it to. For those who want the overtime you can go on 'til half five under the arc lights. Overtime is time and a half weekdays and Saturdays and double time on Sundays. You all know the score."

Bill was pleased at the thought of all the money he would be able to send to Angie with all the overtime on offer. And he also understood more than anyone else standing there in the mud why Carter Construction needed the men to work such long hours.

Peter Smale had made it clear to Bill during his negotiations with Horseman's that Swallow wanted to ride the back of the housing boom, which promised to stretch into the new millennium. Swallow were determined to build through the winter and catch the surge in demand in the spring with their first phase. But this was a double-edged sword for both Carter Construction and Horseman's Heating. Swallow were prepared to pay top money to their contractors, but the penalties for late completion were severe.

All the men chose to work on and take the minibus back into town at 5.30. Bill had enjoyed his day working out in the open. The men had built up some camaraderie during their first day together and the atmosphere in the van was much livelier on the way home. Bill was the first to be dropped off just after six and there was a chorus of comments aimed at him as he left.

"Cheers, lads, see you in the morning," Bill replied to them all.

Tony wound down his window as they drove off.

"Nice one, Bill, I like to see a grafter. Same time tomorrow, okay?"

"Sure. See you, Tony."

Bill walked back to Liz's in the darkness, which had descended quickly in the last half hour. He thought about Tony's last comment to him and took pleasure in it. Bill had surprised himself on the site with how fit he still was, and he had enjoyed the graft. Most of the lads were much younger than him but he reckoned he had kept up with the best of them.

None of the men were offering specialist skills, although it was obvious that some of them knew most things about building work. Their job was basically to do anything Tony or one of the skilled bricklayers, or the operators of the mechanical diggers, told them to do. Bill had spent most of the morning with Scouser and a young lad called Sam clearing some small trees and bushes from a corner of the site. In the afternoon the three of them started digging ditches for the drainage and utility supplies for what was going to be the show house. Bill wondered what all the lads would say if they knew how involved he had been in the planning of these houses. And what would Tony say if he knew just how much specialist knowledge Bill really had?

It did not matter, thought Bill, because he was quite happy with the job he was doing and there was no need for anyone to ever know anything different.

That night Bill slept more soundly than he had for months. When the alarm went off at six o'clock he was in a deep sleep, and as he got out of bed every muscle in his body seemed to object. The walk to the town hall loosened him up a bit, and he was in place when the bus arrived at 7.30 exactly. Unlike the previous day everyone greeted him as he got in.

"Here's Bill, me old gardening mate," said Scouser. "He loves nature, don't ya, Bill? In spite of what it did to ya."

Everyone laughed.

"Yeah sure, Scouser," Bill replied.

"I heard you had that brain transplant, Scouser," Bill said, as he took his seat, "but I see it rejected you." And everyone laughed again, including Scouser.

"Nice one, Bill," said Tony from the front seat. "Listen everyone," he said, "I know Scouser looks like an idiot and talks like an idiot, but don't let that fool you. He is a fucking idiot."

The journey was boisterous and the conversation was mostly loud and foul-mouthed, but by the time they got to the site everyone was in good spirits.

Bill, Scouser and Sam spent most of that morning finishing the ditches for the show house. The brickies worked alongside them to get the show home up as soon as possible. Swallow wanted it finished before Christmas so that they could start selling off-plan. Then they could raise money for phase two on the back of the sales of phase one. The timing and finance was tight, as it usually was in the building trade, and they were taking a big risk with the weather.

On Tuesday afternoon Bill, Scouser and Sam worked with the digger excavating the trenches for plot two, and by Wednesday lunchtime they were starting plot three. By that time Bill was starting to get seriously concerned. All the drainage ditches were getting dug ready for water supply in and waste water out, and there were the usual trenches for the normal utility supplies. That was the problem. Bill knew that the utility supplies to these houses were anything but normal. By mid-afternoon on Wednesday Bill felt that he had to say something to someone. He tested Scouser out first.

"How much do you know about these houses, Scouser?" he said while taking a rest on his shovel. "Aren't they meant to have some fancy energy-saving ideas built in, or something?"

"Fucked if I know, Bill," Scouser replied, standing up to face him. "We're do'n what we always do, aren't we?"

"That's the point, Scouser. We should be doing things a bit different with these houses." He pointed along the length of the ditch they were standing in. "What do you think this one's for?"

"What's this, Bill, frigg'n Mastermind?"

"No, tell me. What's this one for?"

"I dunno," said Scouser. He sounded impatient. "That one over there's the mains in. That's the sewer. This must be the gas."

"There you are, see," said Bill. "These houses don't have gas. They've got PV solar energy and ground-source heat pumps."

Scouser looked at Bill in disbelief and curled his lip. "Bill, me old mucker," he said, "I think yous must've mistak'n me for someone oo gives a fuck."

"Do you think I should say something to Tony?" asked Bill.

"Oh yeah. Good idea, Bill," said Scouser as he returned to his digging. "Go and tell Tone he's a stupid twat oo doesn't know what the frigg'n hell his gang should be do'n. Rather you than me, mate."

Bill decided to keep his thoughts to himself and he went home without a word to anyone. As he walked back to Liz's house he had soon forgotten all about Swallow Homes. All he could think about now was meeting Hayley at nine o'clock.

Bill arrived at the Guildhall early and waited outside on the steps. By ten past nine there was no sign of Hayley and he went into the large entrance hall to get out of the cold. From a room on his left he heard a piano and then two or three male voices singing falsetto, "Sisters, sisters, we are such devoted sisters...." Bill heard the song through and then started to become impatient. It was 9.15 when a stern male voice from within the room boomed out, "I want that one more time before anyone can *think* of going home."

Bill felt increasingly edgy and nervous and it was not all connected with his impatience to see Hayley again. It was also about what she was going to tell him and what the consequences of her decision might be for him. He thought about Medford Prison, which he passed every morning in the minibus on the way to the Meads. The Victorians had built the prison on green fields outside the town so that the townsfolk were not threatened by having the criminals in their midst. It was an irony that in the course of the next 150 years the town had expanded to embrace the prison, and the green fields further to the north were now prime building land. Bill wondered if any part of the Meads would be visible from the highest of the tiny barred windows spaced symmetrically along the neat brick prison walls. And the thought that one day he might have a chance to find out had really started to scare him.

His thoughts were interrupted by the crash of the double doors to his left as a dozen or so people spilled out into the entrance hall. They were talking animatedly and laughing far too loudly. They waited at the main doors, still talking and laughing and looking back to the room they had just come from. After a minute Hayley came through the double doors in conversation with a tall, blond man of about 35.

"Come on, Hayley. Come on, Giles," called several members of the group.

"I'll be along in a minute," Giles called back.

"See you both in the Bull then," someone said.

"No, I'm going out with my friend Bill here," Hayley replied.

Bill smiled and nodded in the general direction of the group by the entrance.

"Lucky Bill," said Giles.

"Lucky Hayley," said a short, chubby man with red cheeks from amongst the departing group, who all immediately started to laugh again.

Hayley approached Bill with her arm linked to Giles. When they reached Bill she let go of Giles and leaned forward to kiss Bill on the cheek.

"Bill, this is Giles. He's the producer and director of the show," Hayley said, stepping back to stand next to Giles again.

"Giles, this is Bill Knight, a dear friend of mine."

The two men shook hands. "A friend of the family, are you, Bill?" Giles asked.

For some reason the question annoyed Bill and he gripped Giles's hand a little too tightly. "No, I'm just a very good friend of Hayley's actually, Giles," he said.

"Okay then," Giles said deliberately, as if he was taking time to think something over. "I'll see you on Saturday then, shall I, Hayley? To iron out the details?"

"Yes, I'll really look forward to it," she replied, and they kissed one another on the cheek, and he walked to the main door. "And thanks, Giles," Hayley called after him. Then she turned back to Bill.

"Do you mind if we go to my place, Bill?" she said. "It's been such a long day. I can't wait to get home."

Hayley took his arm as they walked to her flat and she sensed his irritability.

"Have you had a hard week too, Bill?" she asked him.

"I've enjoyed the work," Bill replied, "but all in all I guess it hasn't been easy."

"I'm cold," Hayley said. "Will you put your arm around me?"

Bill put his arm around her and squeezed her shoulder. She smiled at him and then they walked back to the Gables without another word being spoken.

The flat was cold and Hayley immediately turned on the gas fire. When she took off her coat Bill saw that she was still wearing her waitress uniform, and he understood just how long her day had been. Bill went into the kitchen and made some coffee and sandwiches whilst Hayley had a bath. When she came back she had on a long white towelling robe and fluffy slippers. She sat in front of the fire and ate her sandwiches and drank her coffee. The light of the fire was the only light in the room. Bill sat in an armchair and made her laugh with stories about Tony and Scouser and the rest of the boys.

"I'm glad you're enjoying the work, Bill. It's great when you have a good bunch of people to work with. I'm having such fun with *Cinderella*. They're such a good company."

"You seemed to be very popular with everyone. Especially Giles."

"Actually, I need to talk to you about that. Giles asked me something tonight which I'm afraid might change things a bit between you and me."

234

"Go on."

Hayley fiddled with the end of the belt on her dressing gown, and did not look at him.

"You know what I said the other night about being true to ourselves and living with the consequences, even if it makes people disappointed in us?"

"Yes."

"Well, I'm going to disappoint you, Bill, because I can't do what you want me to do."

"What do you mean exactly?"

"What do I mean? I mean I can't be a witness for you, Bill. I can't stand up in court and be cross-examined by Benny Horseman's lawyers. I've been torturing myself all week about it, and I want to help you so much, but I just can't."

Bill leaned forward and reached out his hand. Hayley took it for a moment and then released it suddenly. She looked up at him.

"Don't be so nice about it, Bill," she said, "you've got a right to be disappointed or angry or something."

"It's alright, Hayley. I understand."

Hayley stood up and went over to sit on the arm of the sofa.

"It's not alright, Bill," she said. "It's alright for me, but it's not alright for you, is it? Tell me how you really feel about it, will you, and don't be so understanding. Just be honest."

Bill looked at her and felt his own impatience rising to the surface.

"I am being honest," he said. "I *am* disappointed. I don't want to go to prison, that's for sure, and you could probably stop it, but I understand your reasons."

"You understand why I need to say no?"

"I think so."

"That's not good enough, Bill. Why should my needs be more important than yours. Why aren't you angry with me? Why accept what *I* need? Why don't you fight for what *you* need?"

"I don't know, Hayley. Because I respect your decision, I suppose."

"I know you do. And I love that you respect my decision, but I still don't know what you really think and feel about it."

"What does it matter what I think or feel. You've made up your mind and that's that, isn't it? I'll just have to get on with it, won't I?"

"By all means just get on with it, Bill, if that's what you want. But just make sure when you bottle up all your feelings instead of expressing them, that you've worked out how they'll eventually come out."

Bill stood up suddenly. "Alright, Hayley, alright! You want to know how I really feel? I'll tell you how I really feel. I feel that in every bloody decision that's made around me I come in a bloody poor second every time. And why the hell is that, eh? I'm always putting everyone else before me. So why just once can't I come first for a change, eh? You tell me that!"

He looked straight at Hayley and stabbed a finger in her direction. "So go on, Hayley, you explain it to me then. Why the bloody hell *won't* you help me, eh? I'd do anything for you, so why won't you help me?"

He glowered at her. "And one more thing. What's that long streak of piss Giles got to do with any of this anyway?"

Bill sank back down in the armchair, scarcely able to believe how he had just spoken to her. Hayley sat down on the sofa.

"Phew. Thank goodness for some honesty at last," she said. "Now at least we can really talk about it."

Hayley came back from the kitchen with two more mugs of coffee. Bill poured them both large cognacs, as she had asked him to.

Bill returned to his armchair whilst Hayley sat back on the sofa. She raised her glass.

"Here's to us always being honest with one another," she said.

Bill held his glass up and took a drink.

"Let me start then," he said. He was calm now and he sounded tired. "I really haven't been uptight this week about what your decision would be, Hayley. Not until tonight anyway, while I was waiting for you."

"I wonder why that was?"

"A couple of reasons, I think. First of all, I don't think I've actually been able to imagine being in prison before, but tonight I saw it really clearly." He paused and breathed out deeply. "We pass Medford Prison every day on the way to work, you see, and one of the guys has done time there and was talking about it. Perhaps all that brought it home to me at last."

"I can see why. And what's the other reason you're uptight tonight?"

"You, Hayley. I've been thinking about you this week, far more than about any decision you might make. You did ask for honesty."

There was a silence, before Hayley spoke.

"I've been thinking about you too, Bill," she said, "and I've been agonising all week about what I should do. But tonight Giles asked me something that confirmed what I think I already knew. I can't risk losing the chance of doing the one thing I've always wanted to do."

"Perform."

"To be a successful performer, yes. Tonight Giles offered me a chance I wouldn't have dreamt of only a few weeks ago."

"Tell me."

"Giles is actually a very talented director, Bill."

"Not just a long streak of piss then?" said Bill, smiling at her.

"No, that was a dreadful thing to say," said Hayley, smiling back at him. "I know he can be terribly opinionated sometimes, but he actually formed the company that are doing *Cinderella*. They… we, are called the Limelight Players. The company has a really wide repertoire; from panto and musicals right through to JB Priestly and Samuel Beckett. He's asked me tonight to become a permanent player, and… I can hardly believe it."

Hayley shook her head and clapped her hands together.

"He wants me to play Sally Bowles in *Cabaret* for two weeks at the end of February at the Congress Theatre in Eastbourne."

"Oh, that's wonderful, Hayley. I'm really pleased for you."

"It'll be my first lead in a fairly big production. They're showing a lot of faith in me. It's actually a really serious company. But if all that business with Benny came out I'd be a laughing stock."

"You don't have to explain, Hayley."

"Yes, I do, Bill. You deserve an explanation, for heaven's sake. We've just been through all that."

"Go on then."

"One day I hope to be a well-known performer, Bill. I've worked so hard at all of it; the acting, the music, the dance, everything. I feel that I'm right on the verge of something. I can almost reach out and touch it. Imagine if I make it and some hack somewhere dredges up an old story about me in court being part of a honey trap. I'd lose everything I want from my life. I'm so sorry, Bill."

"I do understand, Hayley, I honestly do. Honestly, honestly," he said smiling at her.

"But I'm sorry for being part of Benny's plan against you," she said. "You're such a wonderful man. I wish I could change what I did, but I can't."

Bill could see her joy of a few moments earlier turning to distress. He went over and sat next to her and took her hand. She turned to face him.

"I have a choice, you see, Bill. I can help you and risk losing my career at any moment in the future, or I can protect the dreams I have for my life and risk you hating me."

"I'm not going to hate you, Hayley."

"I think I'd rather you hated me for what I am, Bill, than like me for what I'm not."

"I understand that, Hayley," said Bill. They were sitting so close that their knees were touching, but neither of them attempted to move away.

"It's time that you listened to me," he told her. "I've only known you for a few days, but it feels much longer. In that short time I've learned so much from you and from all that business with Benny. I have no regrets about it now, and I'm prepared to pay the price for it."

"Tell me what you think you've learned?"

"What you've been showing me. That we're very lucky if we know what we really want to do with our lives, and that, if we do know, we have a responsibility to ourselves, and to those close to us, to fulfil our lives in that way. Like you're trying to do."

"You used to think that was selfish."

"I know I did, but now I realise that not following our dreams, and then being resentful about it, is the really selfish thing to do."

Bill looked down and laughed quietly to himself.

"What is it?" asked Hayley.

"I'm thinking of the irony of all this," said Bill. "I spent all my life playing it straight, but basically being dishonest about myself. And then I have to break the law to learn what being honest is really about. Sometimes I find it all very confusing."

Bill sighed deeply and looked down. His shoulders slumped forward as if he could no longer bear the weight they were carrying.

"I'm exhausted with it all," he said.

Hayley stood up and kept his hand in hers. She pulled him up gently from the sofa.

"Come on," she said. "I'm having no arguments from you this time. Tonight you're staying here with me."

Hayley kept hold of his hand as she led him through the small hallway and into her bedroom. She turned on the lamp on the bedside table.

"I won't be a minute," she said, "I'm just popping to the bathroom."

Bill stood by the bed unsure of what he should do. He had slept in several different beds over the past five weeks, but he had not shared a bed with another woman in 30 years.

"You can use my toothbrush, if you like," said Hayley as she came back into the room."

Bill stood there and looked at her. She was still wearing her white towelling robe, which reached down almost to her ankles. She smelt of toothpaste. The whole situation seemed more domestic than erotic, and he felt relieved.

"Go on," said Hayley, turning him around and pushing him gently in the direction of the bathroom. "Just stop thinking," she told him.

Bill went into the bathroom and brushed his teeth. He tried hard to follow Hayley's advice and not to think too much, but he found it impossible. He took his mobile phone and called Liz's house. It was 11.30 and they would all be in bed, but the phone would only ring in the lounge so it should not disturb them.

"Hi, it's Bill," he said softly to Liz's answer machine. "Just to say I'm staying over at a friend's house tonight. I didn't want you to worry about me. Bye."

Bill put his hand on the lock of the bathroom door and paused. "God, what do I want from this?" he said to himself. He did not know the answer. There had been other opportunities in his life to sleep with other women, but in the past he had always known he never wanted to. But for some reason this was different. All he knew now was that Hayley was lying in the room next door and he just wanted to be with her.

He went into the bedroom and saw that Hayley was already under the duvet. He could only see the back of her head on the pillow and she did not move as he stripped down to his boxer shorts. He went out to the hallway and turned out the light. The curtains were quite thin and let in enough moonlight for him to make his way around to the other side of the bed. Hayley had still not made a sound and he thought she must have gone to sleep. It did not matter. Just being close to her would be enough. Bill climbed as quietly as he could into bed next to Hayley, trying not to disturb her. But she was not asleep.

"You took your time," she said, as she moved her body next to his. She put her arm around his waist and pulled him close to her. She was naked.

"Let's take these shorts off," said Hayley, as she pulled his boxers down over his buttocks. Bill raised his hips and kicked the shorts to the bottom of the bed.

"Now I'm going to relax you and make you hard for me," she said, and she stroked him gently up and down as they kissed.

Bill had made love to only one woman in his entire life and Hayley's eagerness to take control came as a shock to him. He ran his hands down her back. Her skin was tight and smooth. She stopped kissing him and nuzzled up to his ear. "I can feel you swelling in my hand," she whispered. "Do you like me talking to you like this, Bill?" she asked him.

"Yes, Hayley, I love it," he said. "Tell me some more."

"Now I'm going to take you in my mouth," she whispered, "because I want you really big when you make love to me." And she threw the duvet back and slowly slid down his body. Her breasts brushed against his chest, then his stomach and finally his thighs. Bill's eyes had gradually grown accustomed to the moonlight in the room, and with one hand Hayley moved her hair away from her face so that he could see everything she was about to do to him.

As Bill watched her in the moonlight he concentrated on the pure intimacy of the moment and knew that he would never forget it. Gradually the feelings grew more and more intense for him, and he did not want it all to end too soon. He put his hand gently on her head. "Stop for a moment, darling," he said. "Come here to me." And he took Hayley and lay her gently down on the bed. He took a pillow and placed it under her hips.

"Now it's time for you to relax," he said to her. He slid down the bed and gently coaxed her legs apart. She was soft and wet, and her taste made him feel so much part of her that his tongue slowed and quickened with every sound she made. He heard her breaths become shorter as her pleasure intensified, and he felt the muscles in her back and legs tighten. Then she let out one long gasp of pleasure and thrust her hips forward, holding the same position before lowering herself down onto the bed.

Bill moved up and lay next to her and kissed her. "That was so beautiful, Bill," she said. "Now I just want you to come inside me."

Bill lay between Hayley's legs and they moved onto their sides facing one another. He entered her slowly and not too deeply. They looked into each other's faces as he swelled up again inside her. Gradually his movements became their movements and they quickened and started to kiss passionately. Bill felt the pleasure grow until it was concentrated in one intense part of him. His face tingled as the blood rose in him and his breathing became so short he had to release his mouth from Hayley's. Suddenly he could hold it no longer and he felt the release. For some moments he held Hayley in a tight embrace and did not want to let her go. When he finally released her he lay with his arm around her, and he stroked her hair until they both drifted into sleep.

They were both woken by the alarm going off on the bedside cabinet. Bill did not bother looking at the clock. Instead he lay on his side looking at Hayley.

"Did you sleep well?" she asked him.

"I kept waking up, but then I remembered I was with you, and I felt so relaxed I just went straight back to sleep again."

Hayley nuzzled up to him. "Mmm," she purred, as their bodies touched, "you seem very excited this morning. But we'll have to be quick. I've got to be at work by eight o'clock."

"Hayley, what time does your alarm go off?"

"Seven o'clock."

Bill looked at the alarm clock for the first time. It was 7.06. "Oh hell," he said, "I've got to be outside the town hall by half past."

"We could both throw a sickie," suggested Hayley.

He leant over and kissed her and then climbed out of bed. "I'd love to, darling," he said, "but it's only my fourth day, and I would've needed to phone the gaffer last night to do that."

"I hope you're going to save that for me then," said Hayley, pointing at the clearest sign of his excitement.

"You're so gorgeous," replied Bill, as he bent over to kiss her, "I think I'm going to have this with me all day."

"Will I see you tonight?" she asked.

"Try and stop me. Why don't I come over about seven with a Chinese or something?"

"That would be lovely. And I'll get a bottle of wine," she said.

Bill went into the bathroom and then came back to the bedroom to get dressed as quickly as he could. He kissed Hayley one more time and hurried down the stairs. He ran down the dark street with a big smile on his face and every now and then his smile turned to bursts of laughter. When he arrived at the town hall he was out of breath and there was no bus. He looked at his watch. He was five minutes early.

Chapter 24

The five minutes waiting outside the town hall gave Bill time to realise how much stick he was going to get from the lads when the bus did at last arrive. It was not unusual for someone to turn up for work in the same clothes that they went out in the night before, but the price they paid was merciless mickey-taking.

"Fuck me," said Scouser, as Bill climbed aboard, "oo dressed yous this morning, Stevie fuck'n Wonder?"

"Alright, Bill?" asked Tony, turning round in his seat. "What was it, mate, on the piss or on the pull?"

"Maybe it was both, eh, Bill?" ventured young Sam.

"For fuck's sake, save your breath, Sam," said Scouser, "you'll be needing it to blow air into the only frigg'n girlfriend you're likely to get."

"I've got a proper girlfriend," Sam protested.

"Yeah, and I bet her mother's got a loud bark," offered someone from the back of the bus, and everyone except Sam and Bill laughed.

Bill felt sorry for the young lad, but he was relieved that the attention had moved away from him. He had only been a youngster himself when he started as a coalie at Horseman's yard all those years ago, and he knew how ruthless the mickey-taking could be. The humour and language might be crude, but if you wanted to survive you had to be as well-armed and in control as in any university debating society. Poor Sam still had that lesson to learn.

The banter carried on all the way to the Meads and Bill was pleased to be out of it. The contrast between the atmosphere in the bus and the time he had spent with Hayley could not have been more stark. He could still smell her on him and could almost sense her with him, and he was not ready yet for any intrusions.

When the bus stopped everyone filed past Bill as he stayed in his seat.

"Come on, Bill. Get over to the cabin," Tony shouted to him. "There's plenty of spare wellies there, and you'll find one of my old donkey jackets somewhere. Help yourself."

"Thanks, Tony," Bill called back.

Scouser poked his head inside the bus door. "Better wrap up, mate," he said. "It's colder than a penguin's bollocks out 'ere."

Within ten minutes Bill, Scouser and Sam were starting another day of digging trenches.

Bill found it hard to enjoy the work knowing that they were doing it all wrong. Their digging was making no provision for the systems Horseman's were contracted to install later. He knew that the ground-source heat system he had recommended needed a length of pipe about ten metres long buried in the ground in a horizontal trench. The pipe was a closed circuit filled with water and antifreeze, which would be pumped around the pipe absorbing heat from the ground. The pump, compressor and condenser for each house would be in a small room at the back of the garage, so the length and depth and placement of each trench was crucial.

Bill had signed up for two of the heating technicians at Horseman's to go on a two-week course with the manufacturers to get the latest updates on the technology. Ideally one of the technicians should be on site now supervising the placement, or at the very least Tony should have the trenches marked on his plans. Bill knew the plans must be in the gaffers' portacabin and he would have liked to have gone over and taken a look. But no one on a site like this liked a clever dick greasing up to the gaffer, and anyway, what loyalty did he owe now to Horseman's Heating?

Bill arrived home at 6.15. He had already phoned Liz to tell her he was going out for dinner that night. After he had showered Liz knocked on his bedroom door.

"Sorry to disturb you, Bill," she said, pushing the door open tentatively. "I just wondered if you were staying out again tonight."

"I expect so, Liz. I hope it doesn't put you out too much."

"No, it's just that I prefer to know, that's all, so I can double lock when I go to bed."

"Yes, you do that, Liz." Bill looked away from his sister, knowing that he was going to lie to avoid upsetting her. "I've met some nice people and we stay up talking, and they've got a spare room, so…."

"You don't have to explain to me, Bill. I'm not prying. As long as everything's alright with you."

"Everything's fine, Liz. In fact, it couldn't be better. We'll have a good chat soon and I'll bring you up to date with everything."

"Perhaps tomorrow night then?"

"Yes, why not? No, wait a minute; I'm meeting Stoner tomorrow night. I spoke to him last week. There's something he needs to talk to me about apparently, so I can't put that off."

Bill was annoyed at the thought that meeting Stoner tomorrow would deprive him of an evening with Hayley.

"Why don't we all do something on Saturday then, Bill?" suggested Liz. "The children loved the trip to Bristol last week, and they seem to really enjoy themselves when you're around."

Bill knew that Liz would not deliberately try to make him feel guilty, but that was the effect she was having. Perhaps she had caught it from her mother and was not even aware when she was doing it. Then he remembered Hayley's advice to be honest with people and tell them how you feel; to give them the chance to make informed choices, and to take the risk that they might not like you for it.

"To be honest with you, Liz," Bill said, "I don't think I can make plans for the weekend at the moment…."

"Oh, that's alright, I only wondered if you might like to do something."

"No, let me finish, Liz. I just don't want to make promises I can't keep, that's all. I'll know by tomorrow what time I'll have free and we'll make arrangements when we both get back from work. Is that okay?"

"Yes, Bill, that's okay. I'd like to tell the children tonight and give them something to look forward to, but we'll do it tomorrow instead."

"Liz," said Bill, putting his arms around his sister. "You know that I love Susie and Jon second only to my own two, but I can never take Steve's place, you know. I can't fill that gap for them."

"I know, I know," said Liz. "I'm not expecting you to." She sounded dejected and defeated. She broke away from Bill's embrace and turned her back on him. "Don't worry. I'll sort it all out myself," she said and closed the door behind her.

Bill sat on the bed. His honesty had not given him the sense of freedom he expected. In fact, he felt terrible. "So this is what's meant by accepting the consequences," he thought to himself.

Bill was carrying two bags when he arrived at Hayley's flat at seven o'clock. In one he had the special set menu for two from the Canton House, and in the other he had a change of clothes for work in the morning. He was not going to get caught out again.

As soon as he stepped inside the hallway of Hayley's flat she put both arms around his neck and kissed him passionately.

"I've been waiting to do that all day," she said, "I've been feeling wonderful after last night. I really missed you."

It was exactly what Bill wanted to hear. "I couldn't wait to see you either," he said. And he put down his bags, put his arms around her waist and pressed her close to him as they kissed again.

Bill took off his coat and followed Hayley into the lounge. The table was set, and the only light came from two red candles on the dining table and a third one on a small shelf next to the piano. Hayley went into the kitchen and started to put out the food. A CD of classical music was playing. Bill recognised it as the music from an 80s film. He racked his brain to locate it. "Gabriel Byrne, Greta Scacchi – *Defence of the Realm,*" he said to himself and smiled at his own cleverness.

"What?" Hayley called from the kitchen.

"Nothing. I just wondered what this beautiful music was called. I know it so well but I just can't get it."

"It's Pachelbel's *Canon,*" said Hayley appearing from the kitchen. "Come and open this wine, Bill, will you, please?"

Bill stood in the doorway of the small kitchen and Hayley turned around to hand him a corkscrew and a bottle of Alsace wine. He could not believe how good she looked. Her light brown hair was soft and shiny and seemed to flow when she moved her head, just like a girl on a shampoo advert. Bill guessed she must be wearing make-up, but it was not noticeable except for the general effect of making her lips well-defined, her eyes bright, and her skin smooth and fresh. She was wearing a blue three-quarter sleeve dress, which stopped just on her knees. It was silky and shaped at the waist, which highlighted the shape of her hips. Around her neck she wore the same gold chain and single diamond pendant that she had worn in the French restaurant a week ago. Her legs were bare and her delicate sandals were such a light shade of brown that her feet looked bare too.

After the meal Bill cleared everything away. He was standing at the sink when Hayley started to play the piano. Bill dried his hands and stood in the archway between the lounge and kitchen. Hayley had taken off her sandals and replaced them with black satin slippers. Bill had no idea that she was such an accomplished musician. The movement of her head, hands, fingers and feet seemed to be choreographed, and the music they produced held Bill in a trance. Bill was helpless. However much he had resisted before, there was no resisting this. This beautiful young woman, the thoughts of her intimacy with him, and now this wonderful music gave him no chance. Later he learned that he had been listening to Chopin's Polonaise, and later he also recognised that this was the moment when he knew he was in love for the second time in his life.

When Hayley stopped playing they drank coffee and talked for over an hour. Then they poured cognac and took their glasses to the bedroom, where they made love until the small hours. Afterwards they lay facing one another as Bill stroked the hair away from Hayley's forehead. Her eyes were wide open and she kept them fixed on his as he continued smoothing her hair away from her face.

"Have you ever had a day which was so perfect and so full you wish every day could be like it?" he said.

"Yes, I have."

"That's how I feel about this. Being with you, talking to you and making love with you is all so perfect. So much of life is forgettable, but I'll never forget this."

"I don't want you to ever forget me."

"Oh, my darling Hayley, I could never do that," he said, and he held her closer and kissed her. "I wish I could spend the rest of my life like this."

"Don't say that, Bill," said Hayley, and she broke away gently and lay on her back with her head still turned towards him.

"Why not?"

"Because you're right. This is wonderful and I love being with you as much as you love being with me. You're a wonderful, generous man. You wouldn't believe how many men are not like you."

"So why shouldn't I want my life to be like this?"

Hayley turned back and placed her hand on his cheek and kissed him. "Because I'm not your dream, Bill. Think of the dream you were describing to me here just one week ago. You've had that dream all your life. Since you were a child. It's survived all that time and nothing's been able to change it. It's probably the longest, most constant feeling you've ever had. You can't replace it with me."

"But it would be so easy to love you, Hayley."

"And I feel the same about you, Bill, but don't mistake this for your dream, or you'll never be happy." She kissed him again. "Now sleep, darling," she said.

Chapter 25

Bill had set the alarm on his mobile for 6.30 and he left before Hayley got up. Everything he did and said at work that day was filtered through thoughts of her. At seven o'clock that evening Bill made his way to a pub around the corner from Liz's house to meet Stoner. Bill knew he should not begrudge giving up an evening with Hayley to spend time with his oldest friend, but he could not help feeling impatient about it. He hoped that whatever Stoner wanted to see him about was important enough to justify the sacrifice he felt he was making.

The Horse and Groom was an old coaching inn that now boasted a Harvester restaurant, and several function rooms. Bill looked around the large bar area to see if Stoner had got there before him, and eventually found him sitting in a quiet corner away from the other drinkers. The two men shook hands and greeted one another warmly. To both of them it seemed a lot longer than two weeks since Bill had moved out of Stoner's flat to come to Medford. Stoner went to the bar to get Bill a pint of the local Cathedral Ale.

"There you are, Bill, my old mate," he said, putting the beer on the small circular table between them. "So, tell me how you're getting on in Medford then."

"Thanks, Stoner. Cheers." Bill took a long drink. "I'm doing alright. I've got a job labouring with a good bunch of lads. I expect Angie told you about that."

"Yes, she did say something about it. You can still swing a pick then, can you, Bill? It's not all flab yet then?"

"Solid muscle, Stoner" said Bill, clenching his fists and tightening his arms and shoulders. "I'm really pleased at the shape I'm in, considering all the years I spent behind that desk. How are things at Horseman's anyway?"

"I don't go in there much now, Bill. I think Hugh Turner's struggling a bit though. I bumped into your Mickey a couple of days ago. He said it's a nightmare doing contract work for them now. No one seems to be organised."

Bill was not surprised to hear it, but he decided to keep quiet about his own experiences at the Meads.

"I phoned Mickey and Dave earlier in the week," he said. "Neither of them mentioned Horseman's at all then. All Mickey wanted to talk about was Cheryl's ultrasound on Monday. It seems to me as if Cheryl and Angie have got season tickets to Mothercare."

"Tell me about it, Bill. By the time next June comes around, mate, your house will have more toys in it than an Early Learning Centre."

The two friends both laughed and each took a mouthful of beer.

"Are you missing things back in Bramport then, Bill?"

"I miss Angie and the boys, Stoner, but I'm in touch with them a lot by phone. I can't say I miss anything else. Frankly things are a lot better for me here."

"How do you work that out then?"

"Well, all that crazy business with Benny. It got to the point where I couldn't relax walking down the street in Bramport. I'm anonymous here. I have to report to the police station twice a week as part of my bail conditions, but apart from that I feel I've got a new start."

"I've got to say, Bill, my old mate, you do seem a lot more relaxed than I've seen you for a long time."

"I am, Stoner, I am. I'm really enjoying it with Liz and Susie and Jonathan."

"I haven't seen Liz's children for years."

"They're really good kids. We have a great time together. You know their dad left home last summer, do you?"

"I probably did, but I forget the details."

"He went off with a younger woman," said Bill, and suddenly he became aware of how hypocritical he was about to be. "That's his business, I suppose, but the way he's treated those two kids has been bloody terrible."

"Yeah?"

"He makes no attempt to see them or explain things to them. And they're both so vulnerable at their age. He's left them as insecure as hell."

"And what part are you playing in all this then?" asked Stoner.

"Part? I'm not playing any part. I know Liz appreciates having someone to talk to and having some support."

"You're not doing the old 'Bill Knight riding to the rescue bit' then?" said Stoner with a smile.

"I like to think I've helped them, especially Jon. He was really screwed up, holding everything in, and he manages to let things go a bit with me."

Stoner shook his head, still smiling at Bill.

"Okay, Stoner, okay. What is it?"

"Nothing, Bill. I just hope you're not making the same mistake here as you did in Bramport, that's all. Making everyone more and more dependent on you."

"It is my family, Stoner. We're not talking about complete strangers here."

"Alright, Bill, but just allow me a little test. You can tell me to mind my own business, if you like."

"No, go on."

"You've been in Medford for two weeks, haven't you?"

"About that."

"I just wonder if there's anyone you can think of, outside your family, who has become in any way dependent on you."

"I don't see…"

"No, let me finish. And you've been working for five days since Monday, right? I wonder if you haven't already found something at your work that you feel is wrong or needs improving, and you think it might be your responsibility to fix it."

Bill was shaken by what Stoner had said, and the fact that his friend had such insights about him annoyed him too.

"Bloody hell, Stoner, have you got bloody spies on me or something?"

"So I'm right then?" said Stoner, slapping the table and laughing.

"Well, no, you're not actually. I've learnt a lot in the short time I've been here in Medford, and I've already said to Liz that they mustn't all become too dependent on me. And it was bloody difficult saying it, I can tell you. I hate disappointing people."

"You hate risking being unpopular, you mean."

"I hate letting people down, Stoner, but I'm learning."

"Being honest and disappointing someone isn't the same as letting them down, Bill."

"I'm slowly getting to realise that, Stoner. And you're only partly right about work too. I have noticed some things that aren't quite right there, but I realise it's not my job to fix it so I'm keeping my nose out of it."

"Good for you, Bill."

"No, Stoner, it may be good *for* me but I'm not so sure it's good *of* me. But I'm starting to realise the less you get involved the simpler life is. Maybe it's just selfish, I don't know. But I do understand at last that you can't be everything to everyone. Now, do you want another drink?"

Bill brought the pints back to the table. The two of them had decided to make a night of it and Stoner had gone off to book a table for dinner and a room for himself for the night.

"Right, that's done," he said when he came back from reception. "I've booked dinner for nine o'clock."

"My treat, Stoner," said Bill, "to thank you for letting me stay with you that time, and because you're such a bloody clever dick."

"I don't mean to wind you up, Bill, but I don't think it's a good idea for you to make too much of a life for yourself up here in Medford."

"Why not?"

"Because at some point you've got to come back to Bramport."

"For the Benny thing, you mean?"

"No, Bill. For Angie."

"I assumed it was Benny you wanted to talk to me about tonight."

"No. Benny came out of hospital on Wednesday. He's already back to his old ways driving Sandra and everyone at Horseman's round the bend. I don't want to talk about him. I came here to talk to you about Angie."

"She's alright, isn't she? I only spoke to her yesterday. She sounded really happy."

"That's the point, Bill. Angie *is* a lot happier. But do you really want her to be happier without you?"

"I think it's doing us both good to have some time apart, Stoner," said Bill. "All this business with the money took a lot out of Angie, you know. She doesn't find upsets like that very easy to handle."

"I do know," said Stoner. "I also know that Angie has to be a hundred times stronger than most people to deal with these things."

"What do you mean by that?"

"Because of her illness. The extra strength she needs because of her illness."

Bill was starting to become agitated by his friend's assumption that he knew more about Angie than Bill did. He liked seeking Stoner's opinion, but he was not sure he welcomed it offered so freely.

"What illness, Stoner? Do you mean her panic attacks?"

"Yeah, of course I do."

Bill took his pint and sat back, relieved that Stoner had nothing more in mind.

"God, I know all about Angie's attacks, Stoner. She's been to the doctor's hundreds of times over the years. They've treated every symptom she's ever had. The nausea, the chest pains, the high blood pressure. Angie's had more tests than Len Hutton. That's just the way she is. She's very highly-strung, the same as her mother."

"Well frankly, Bill, the doctors are talking out of their Hippocratic arses, the same as you are right now. All any of you can see is the symptoms and not the cause."

Bill was taken back by the vehemence in Stoner's voice.

"Well, by all means be frank, Stoner. It's only my wife we're talking about."

"I'm sorry, Bill, I'm sticking my nose in too far. Let's change the subject."

"No, Stoner, no. It's me that should be sorry. You're my friend. I trust what you say and your motives for saying it. If you've got something to tell me about Angie, let me hear it."

Stoner put his drink down and leaned forward.

"The thing is, Bill," he said, "Angie is the bravest person I've ever met."

Stoner was looking Bill straight in the eyes as if to check that his words had landed with the impact he intended. They had. Bill opened his mouth to speak but nothing came out.

"Do you remember when Angie had her first panic attack?" Stoner asked him.

"Yes, it was on our honeymoon in '68… we'd been having a great time… but then she got incredibly homesick… and felt really insecure. I tried to make her feel safe with me, but I couldn't."

"And how many more has she had since then?"

"Dozens."

"How often?"

"It varies. Every month or so. Sometimes she can go three months or more without one. The Valium helps."

"Yes, well, the less said about that chemical rubbish the better," said Stoner. "Did you ever notice a pattern with her attacks?"

"Sometimes they come right out of the blue when we're having quite a nice time. But you can almost guarantee one if we go away anywhere. In fact, we can't really go away any more. But you know all about that already, Stoner. I've bored you enough with it over the years. Why do you need to know all this?"

"And what would you say is the worst one you've ever seen?" asked Stoner, ignoring his friend's question.

"Probably the one in New York about five years ago. We had to call the paramedics. I thought she was dying, having a heart attack or something. The hotel called 911 and got her to hospital. She had tests but she was okay physically. They gave her loads of sedatives and we got an early flight back."

"But she isn't always that bad?"

"No, she usually takes herself off to bed when she gets an

254

attack and stays there until she's over it."

"Poor old Angie," said Stoner shaking his head.

"Hold on, Stoner. I know it's rotten for her, but why are you giving it so much emphasis. I always think it's best to play it down, for her sake. Not to make too much fuss about it."

"Bill, Bill, Bill," said Stoner. "When I said Angie is the bravest person I know, I damn well meant it. Do you know the main feeling a person has when they have a panic attack? I mean a real panic attack, not just a feeling of anxiety or being stressed out."

"No, but I want to know."

"Terror, mate. Sheer bloody terror. Overwhelming, uncontrollable dread, as if you're about to die or lose your mind. And dear old Angie has hidden that terror from you on all those occasions for all those years."

"Are you sure about this?" said Bill.

"Yes, my old mate, I'm sure."

"But why? Why would she hide all that from me?"

"That, Bill, is one of your dumbest questions ever. She hides it because she feels guilty towards you. And because she hasn't wanted to upset you and your boys."

Bill sat forward and put his glass on the table. For a few moments he sat staring at his hands clasped tightly together on his lap. Then he looked up at Stoner.

"So do you really think that Angie has felt that terror every time she's had an attack?" he asked him.

"I'm afraid so, Bill."

"Oh, bloody hell," muttered Bill, and he studied his hands again for some time thinking of all the pain Angie had endured without his understanding.

"And how have you found out all this then, Stoner?" he said.

"Well, you asked me to look out for Angie while you were away, and one evening I called in on her and we just got talking about alternative medicine and she told me all about her attacks. I recognised the symptoms she was describing. I haven't wanted to push her too far about it yet, so I thought I'd better see what you could tell me."

"And have you been able to help her?"

"I think we've made a start. A crucial first step is to help people understand why these things happen in the first place and what triggers the attacks. Getting Angie to understand what's causing her attacks is the first step to helping her get rid of her fear of them."

"Well, I've always thought her problems started with the insecurity she got from her father's comings and goings."

"And I think you're right," said Stoner. "Most people's attacks can be traced back to chronic insecurity in childhood, and poor old Angie had that in bucket loads."

Stoner leaned forward and held up his left hand. He counted off his fingers as he spoke.

"Think about it, Bill," he said. "She was an only child, continually being uprooted, never in one place long enough to nurture friendships, and never knowing what was happening with her parents."

"And I suppose the poor girl didn't just lose her father once, like my nephew Jon," added Bill. "She kept losing him over and over again."

"Exactly."

"I know she's always been terribly insecure. She's always been afraid of me rejecting her, you know, Stoner."

"I know she has. It's just a classic pattern for attacks to start and recur."

Stoner started to count again.

"Childhood insecurity, fear of abandonment, low self-esteem, intense feelings of helplessness. After a while something has to give and people usually have their first attack in their late teens or early twenties."

"So when we were in Greece on honeymoon Angie suddenly got hit by…what exactly?"

"Loss of security, I expect, and a realisation of the huge responsibility she was about to take on."

Bill sat forward and cupped his hands over his face.

"This is terrible, Stoner," he said. "Do you know at the time I just thought she was fed up with me? I was actually quite hurt by it. And then for ages afterwards I was on to her about going back to Greece with Mickey to carry on travelling. It must've been a bloody nightmare for her to hear me saying that."

"That's why she's been so brave, Bill. For years she's knowingly put herself back into positions where an attack might happen, just so she didn't disappoint you. Like your holidays in France and the trip to New York. Most sufferers would do anything to avoid a situation like that."

"Such as what?"

"Some simply refuse to go out. They just refuse to put themselves in any situation where an attack might happen."

"Become agoraphobic, you mean?"

"It can lead to that. Agoraphobia isn't really a fear of open spaces, like most people think. It's actually a fear of putting yourself in a position where an attack could happen. It's the attack itself which people fear."

"But Angie isn't that bad," said Bill. "She still goes out into Bramport. And to Mickey's and Dave's. And her mother's."

"No, she's not that bad, thank goodness, but she's probably developed a hell of a lot of avoidance strategies over the years. You'd know more about that than me."

Bill thought of all the times Angie had found excuses not to go anywhere and not to get involved with other people. In the beginning, when her father finally left for good, she would use any excuse to spend time with her mother and miss out on parties and weekends away. Then she would use the boys as her reason for staying as close to home as she could. Later no excuses became necessary as Bill understood that it was best not to mention holidays, or even social events which might mean meeting even a few new people.

Now Angie openly admitted that she had no ambition to go anywhere outside Bramport. She was not interested in a job, and she had no life plans outside the boys and her mother and Bill. Bill knew that she still loved him, but she seemed to live in constant fear that one day he would leave her for someone else.

The strange thing was that it had never occurred to Bill to leave Angie for another woman. In spite of all the disappointments he felt about their life together, he always loved Angie. He always believed that the only thing that could ever take him away from her would be his dream of travelling, never another woman. At least that was the way it had been until last night.

"What can we do to make things better for her?" he asked Stoner.

"Well, there are lots of different therapies, and the good news is that a lot of them work."

"And you think Angie should come off the Valium?"

"I do, but very slowly and only when she's a lot better. Coming off something like Valium too quickly could make Angie ten times worse. I think you should both discuss all that later with her doctor."

"Yes, I will, Stoner."

"In the meantime I'll carry on helping Angie to understand what triggers her attacks. Once someone understands how to separate the attack from the trigger, the trigger loses its power."

"I don't quite get that, Stoner."

"Well, take someone's fear of flying, for example. Most people who suffer from that understand logically that the plane won't crash. What they're afraid of is that their irrational fear will trigger a panic attack, which they know will be truly terrifying. They're not afraid of flying in itself, but only because it's their trigger for an attack. They're actually afraid of fear itself."

"And Angie's trigger is a feeling of insecurity?"

"Yes, I think so. And of being left alone and abandoned, especially in a strange place. We'll have to see what more comes out over the next few weeks."

"God, I can't tell you how grateful I am to you, Stoner, for taking all this trouble over Angie."

"You don't have to thank me, Bill. You and Angie are my oldest, closest friends. When I think of all the times I turned up on your doorstep over the years, and not once did you ever turn me away. Can you imagine how that made me feel, knowing that wherever I was in the world, I always had two people in Bramport who would welcome me into their family? Money can't buy that, Bill."

"No, I guess not, Stoner."

"That's why I think you should come back to Bramport and be with Angie, Bill. The two of you are meant to be together. You belong together."

"Married life isn't always that simple, Stoner. I really think Angie and I both need time apart at the moment. We cause one another a lot of stress, you know. I've been a lot happier here, and you said yourself that Angie's a lot happier in Bramport without me."

"Yes, she is better, but I never said it's because you're not there. I think she's better because she's getting rid of a lot of the baggage she's been carrying around all these years. You could help her, Bill, with some of the relaxation techniques. You could do aromatherapy with her. And meditation and breathing exercises and that sort of thing."

"Stoner, believe me, you are a thousand times better than me at all that. Do you mind doing it for her?"

"As if I would, Bill. Like I said, Angie and you are my dearest friends. I'll help you in any way I can."

"I think it's best if I stay here for now, Stoner. I know Angie's in good hands and my being there could unsettle her. I'll be down to visit in a week or two."

Stoner got up and picked up the two pint glasses, which had stood empty on the table for the last ten minutes. He looked at Bill.

"I believe what you're saying about you and Angie, Bill, and you could be right about unsettling her," he said. "But I also know it's not the only reason you've got for staying in Medford. I'll get us another drink, my old mate, and when I come back you can tell me what else is keeping you here."

Bill waited until Stoner was out of sight. Then he cupped his hands over his face. "Shit, oh shit," he said, and he rubbed his eyes and breathed out deeply. How could Stoner possibly have guessed the secret that Bill had already decided not to share with another living soul? God knows how grateful he was to Stoner for the help he was giving Angie, and God knows how much he admired his old friend, but hell, he could be such a pain in the ....

"Here you are, Bill, my old mate. Get that down you. Cheers."

"Cheers, Stoner. You've got to tell me, Stoner, what makes you think I've got other motives for staying in Medford?"

"Because there's no way you could ever stay away from Angie for ten seconds if you thought you could help her. Not after what

I just told you. So what other reason is there, Bill?"

"We both need space?"

"Not enough of a reason, my old mate."

"I'm earning good money and it gives Angie security?"

"Not enough."

"Liz needs me?"

"No. Won't do."

"I've fallen in love with someone else?"

"Yes, that'll do," said Stoner, and he sighed deeply. For a few moments neither of them spoke. Eventually it was Stoner who broke the silence.

"Bill, Bill, Bill. What's to be done with you? I knew you wanted to turn your life upside down to get a fresh start. I even admired you for it. But I always thought you and Angie were sacrosanct. I just can't believe it. How could you let that happen? You've only been away from Bramport for a couple of weeks."

"I know, Stoner, It's a shock for me too. And believe me, I tried hard to stop it happening, but in the end it was out of my hands."

Stoner said nothing. He just looked at Bill with a disbelieving smile on his face and shook his head.

"I know this sounds corny, Stoner, but it doesn't really mean I love Angie any the less."

"I'm sorry, Bill, but I don't see how that one works. But, listen, I'm not here to judge you and I'm sure as hell not going to lay any guilt onto you. I'm pretty damned sure you'll take good care of that for yourself. I'm glad you told me though, because I need to know what to say to Angie."

"You're not going to tell her, are you?"

"I'll pretend you didn't ask me that question, Bill. Of course I won't damn well tell her! I'll go back to Bramport and give Angie all the help I can, but I won't be encouraging her to get you back to Bramport any more, will I?"

"No, I guess not. But I don't understand why you're not angry with me, Stoner."

"It's not my place, Bill, is it? Besides, you'll sort your life out somehow. But I am interested in knowing what's so special about this new lady."

"Stoner. Where do I start?"

Bill sat forward as he spoke. His elbows rested on the wooden arms of his chair, his hands were clasped in front of him and his chin almost rested on his chest. He spoke slowly and softly, almost as if he was talking to himself.

"I can talk to her about anything, you see. With her I can express myself as freely as I like. In fact, the only thing she insists on from me is honesty. I'm totally open with her, and she's the same with me. And she's so beautiful."

"So is Angie."

Bill looked up.

"I know that, Stoner, but with Angie the last thing she wants from me is honesty. I've had to spend my whole life being dishonest with myself and with her, because all Angie's ever insisted on is that there should never be any change in our lives."

"Well, at least we understand now *why* she could never cope with too much change, don't we? Give it time, my old mate. It strikes me both you and Angie are trying hard to understand yourselves. I expect one day you'll be able to talk honestly with one another."

"I hope you're right, Stoner, but it's something I just can't imagine for now."

"Like I say, Bill, give it time."

Stoner took a long drink and brought his glass down heavily on the table.

"Anyway, let's try and lighten things up a bit," he said. "So what's your lady's name then?"

"Hayley."

Stoner laughed. "Bloody hell, mate. Bill and Hayley, rocking round the clock. Now all you need are the bloody Comets!"

"Well, I'm glad you're taking it so well, Stoner," said Bill, trying unsuccessfully to laugh with his friend. If anything, Stoner's reaction to his news about Hayley was unnerving him.

"To be honest, Stoner, I thought you'd be really annoyed with me if ever I told you about all this."

"No. Bill. Like I said, it's not my place or my style to judge or condemn. I suppose in the end no one can choose who they fall in love with, can they? Love makes fools of us all sooner or later. Come on, my old mate, let's get some food. I could eat the hump off a camel's back."

Chapter 26

Bill could not see Hayley until Sunday evening. Stoner's news about Angie had unsettled him so much that he hardly slept on Friday night. On Saturday he worked a full shift at the Meads to earn some valuable overtime. Angie had sent three letters up with Stoner and they were all bills.

On Saturday night Susie went to a birthday party at the house of one of her friends. Bill and Liz stayed in with Jonathan and watched *The Truman Show* on video. Bill enjoyed the story of a man who thought he was free, whereas in reality his whole life was programmed, and he was really only free within the limits other people had set for him. In order to keep the hero trapped in his artificial life the creators of his world afflicted him with two emotions guaranteed to stop him breaking away – fear and guilt. Truman Burbank's biggest problem was his fear.

Bill Knight could tackle fear, but he still had little defence against guilt. It was a prison that he kept his thoughts in. Everyone was advising him to be honest about what he wanted for himself and to live with the consequences of the choices he made, and the advice seemed so rational and mature when spoken by Stoner or Hayley or Liz. Bill wondered if they ever felt any guilt, and knew immediately that they did not. At least not the same sort of guilt that he felt. The sort that weighed him down with feelings of obligation and responsibility for other people's happiness. The sort that took away his freedom to be himself, and sabotaged the pleasure of any moment that was too self-indulgent or not earned by hard work or sacrifice. At least he could understand his renewed guilt towards Angie, and to a lesser extent towards Liz after he upset her on Thursday. But for the life of him he could not understand where his feelings of guilt towards Hayley were coming from.

Ten minutes before midnight Bill drove to pick Susie up from her party. Liz had had an argument with her daughter earlier in the evening about the length of Susie's skirt and the logo on her tee-shirt, 'Rehab Is For Wimps'. Liz had been edgy and withdrawn all evening and Bill was pleased for an excuse to get out on his own.

On Sunday Hayley had a full day of rehearsal and was not free until seven o'clock. So in the afternoon Bill took Jon and Susie bowling. Liz was still quiet and self-contained and told Bill that she needed time to herself whilst he took the children out. Bill really enjoyed being with Susie and Jon, and it was obvious that they felt the same about him. He could relax with them and had great fun playing the joker. On these occasions he was the person he wished he could be all the time. As much as Bill loved his niece and nephew he did not feel directly responsible for them, and that helped a lot. It was much easier playing the role of uncle than most of the other roles he had in his life.

When they got home at about five o'clock Liz was in the kitchen. She shouted out to Bill as he put his coat and scarf in the cupboard under the stairs.

"Bill, can you spare me a minute?"

When he went into the kitchen, Liz was standing at the hob preparing a stir-fry. When she turned to face him, Bill was relieved to see that she had a smile on her face.

"Sit down and pour yourself some wine," she said. "I just wanted to thank you for what you said to me the other night."

"Thank me? I was afraid I'd upset you."

"Well, maybe it did for a while, but you made me think, and it did me a lot of good. I know you don't find things like that very easy, Bill, so I just needed to tell you I appreciated it."

"Thanks, Liz. I've been feeling really bad about it. You've seemed so miserable over the weekend."

"No, I haven't been miserable, Bill. You know me. I'm not a sulker. I've been a bit quiet because I've been thinking things over, that's all." She picked up her wine from the worktop and turned to face Bill.

"I realise you were absolutely right about what you said, Bill. I've been doing everything to plug the gaps left by Steve, including expecting you to be a stand-in father to Susie and Jonathan, and it's got to stop. I was on the phone to Steve while you were all out and told him straight."

"Good for you, Liz."

"I told him I don't care if he doesn't want to see me, but he has to bring some stability back into the children's lives. They've only got one father and he'd better start acting like one before he does lasting damage to them."

"You're dead right."

"I said, 'You can trade me in, if you want to. I don't care any more. But you can't get rid of your responsibility to the children. It's there for life.' I really went for him, Bill. And do you know what he said?"

An even bigger smile came over her face. "He said, 'I don't want to trade any of you in, Liz. I miss you all.'"

"Bloody hell, Liz. That's a result."

"Isn't it just? I think it's because I was really worried about the children after what you said, and I really didn't care any more if he didn't want me. I think when I said that it must have really shocked him."

She came over to Bill and put her arms around his neck and kissed him on the cheek.

"Oh, thanks, Bill," she said, like an excited teenager. "We're meeting on Wednesday night. He wants to discuss everything over dinner. Do you think you could stay in with the children that night?"

He looked at the glow on Liz's face, caused partly by her excitement and partly by the wine.

"Of course I will, Liz," he said. "You know I'd do anything for you."

"I'll tell you one thing, Bill."

"What, Liz?"

"I'm going to make sure the rotten sod takes me somewhere bloody expensive," she said, and she started to laugh.

And suddenly Bill felt a whole lot better about everything.

At seven o'clock that evening Bill was at the Guildhall again to meet Hayley from her rehearsal. He had been waiting for 20 minutes by the time the double doors of the rehearsal room opened and a dozen or so people came out and stood around chatting in the entrance hall. He recognised Giles in deep conversation with an attractive young woman, who Bill was sure he recognised from somewhere. Giles either did not recognise Bill or chose to ignore him as he walked past.

Hayley was the last to appear. She was laughing with the short, chubby man with the ruddy cheeks who Bill had noticed the week before. They both came up to Bill and Hayley put her arms around him and kissed him. Her display of affection in front of all her friends made him feel good.

"Bill, I'd like you to meet Roly. Roly is Baron Henry Hardup in the production.

"Roly, this is Bill Knight, my dearest friend."

Bill held out his hand and Roly placed both his hands lightly around it and held on as he spoke.

"I am so pleased to meet you, Bill. Hayley's told me all your wicked secrets. She's such a lucky girl."

"Really?" said Bill turning to Hayley.

"No, not really, Bill," she said. "Roly, you are such a terrible tease."

Roly let go of Bill's hand and laughed. "It's jealousy, Hayley dear. I admit it. I just wish I had some wicked secrets with someone like your lovely Bill here."

Bill decided to change the subject as quickly as he could.

"Who's that over there with Giles?" he asked. "I'm sure I know her from somewhere."

"That, my dear boy, is the star of our show, Mandy Miller. You doubtless recognise her from Colby Street. She's wonderfully typecast as the bitchy barmaid in the King's Head."

"Now, now, Roly," said Hayley, "retract those claws. You know what Giles would say. She's the one who's going to put bums on seats."

266

"True, true, Hayley dear. But it annoys me when I compare the likes of her with real talent like yours.

"Do you realise how talented this wonderful girl is, Bill? If our Hayley isn't a major star one day, there's absolutely no justice left in this wicked world."

"Yes, I think I do understand how wonderful she is, Roly."

"Well, there you are then. Now who's coming to the Bull to buy old Roly a G and T?"

Hayley took Bill's arm. "Do you mind if we join everyone for a drink, Bill?" she said. "I think Giles is expecting everyone to be there."

"That's fine, Hayley. I'm happy to do whatever you want."

"Oh, isn't he a darling," said Roly. He stood between them and linked their arms, and they were still linking arms when they arrived at the Bull a few minutes later.

Some of the group were already in the lounge bar putting chairs around in a circle with two tables in the middle. As Bill was buying drinks for Hayley and Roly, Giles arrived, without Mandy Miller, and sat in the biggest chair in the circle. It was the only one with arms. A young man at the bar who Bill did not recognise asked Giles if he wanted a drink.

"Make it a double, Tom, would you? I'm absolutely whacked," Giles called back.

"I see he's arrived sans our marvellous Miss Miller," observed Roly. "The great Lothario must be losing his touch."

"Oh, Roly, do behave yourself," Hayley whispered to him.

"Here's your gin and tonic, Roly," said Bill. "And your dry white wine, Hayley."

"Thankyou, Bill dear," said Roly. "Here's to actors the world over. The less ability they have, the more conceited they are. Which is why, of course, dear Hayley is so modest."

"Thankyou, Roly," said Hayley, and the three of them clinked glasses. "Now you will promise me, won't you, Roly, that you won't have too many gin and its and disgrace yourself again?" She gave Bill a knowing look.

"I shall be the soul of moderation and discretion, Hayley dear. You may depend on it."

"And you won't let your tongue run away with you?"

"Hayley, my love, I shall follow the advice of the greatest of all actors. 'Talk low, talk slow, and don't talk too much'."

"Who said that, Roly?" asked Bill. "Laurence Olivier?"

"No, dear boy. John Wayne."

They all laughed and Roly ordered another round. "Make mine a special this time, will you, Joyce?" he said to the barmaid.

"A special?" Bill whispered to Hayley.

"A triple," Hayley replied, shaking her head.

By now all the seats in the circle had been taken and when Giles rapped his knuckles on the table to get everyone's attention, Hayley, Bill and Roly sat on stools at the bar.

"I just wanted to thank everyone for their hard work today. I feel it came together much better than last week.

"As you know, we start rehearsals at the theatre on Wednesday between five and seven. There will be full orchestra rehearsals all day next Sunday, the 5th, and the following Sunday, the 12th. That will give some of you a chance to polish up your vocals. There will be full-day rehearsals during the week starting Monday, the 13th, and as you all know we open on Thursday, the 16th of December for just over four weeks."

There was a restrained cheer and tapping of the tables in approval.

"And the end-of-show party is upstairs here after our last performance on Saturday, the 15th of Jan."

The cheers became louder.

"Are there any questions?" asked Giles.

"Yes," said Roly," how many rehearsals will Miss Miller be required to attend?"

Bill could hear Hayley sigh, and he noticed that Roly had already started another 'special'.

"Oh please don't get on your high horse about that again, Roland," said Giles. "It's such a bore."

"I just wondered, that's all," said Roland. "An innocent enquiry, I assure you, dear chap."

"As you know, Roland, I shall be travelling to London several times over the next fortnight to go through the part with Mandy. She's been given Sunday, the 12th, off from her filming schedule to do a full orchestra rehearsal, and Wednesday, the 15th, for a full dress and orchestra rehearsal with the rest of us here. Is that alright with you?"

"Absolutely, dear chap. I just wondered if you would be reminding Miss Miller whilst you were in London that acting is about being able to express emotion, not just being emotional."

There was some muted laughter. Giles just shook his head.

"I've told you before, Roland, we're very lucky to get Mandy to join us on this. She's a big draw right now. Bums on seats, Roland. Bums on seats. No Mandy, no money. Remember?"

"I do, Giles, I do. I realise, alas, that the altar of the theatre is no longer the stage, but the box office."

"It always has been, Roly," said Giles. "You know that from your own efforts at producing and directing. You know damn well that without subsidies or patronage the Limelight Players have to pay their own way. So we have to give people what they want."

Roly held his empty glass up to the barmaid without bothering to look at her and she prepared him another drink. "Here we go," she said under her breath.

"Surely the primary function of the theatre is not to please itself or the audience," expanded Roly Upperton, "it is to serve talent."

Several of the company started to groan. Giles tried to remain patient.

"First we make money from the panto and from *Cabaret*," he said, "and then we'll be able to afford to do something innovative, Roly. I've just been looking at something from a new young writer. It's very promising, but it'll probably lose money first time out. It's the money that Mandy Miller brings in that pays for innovation, Roly. That's the way it works."

"No production of mine ever depended on a strumpet from a soap operetta," sniffed Roly.

"But all your productions failed!" said Giles.

Roly tried to stand up, but toppled forward. Bill caught him and helped him back onto his stool.

"Failed?" said Roly. "No play of mine ever failed. As dear Oscar once observed, 'The play was a success. The audience was a failure'."

Some people laughed, others groaned. Giles had lost his patience.

"Oh, for goodness sake someone get the drunken old fool away from me," he said.

Roly made another attempt to stand up, but his legs went again and Bill had to hold him up.

"Alas, the dove of inspiration has flown away from the theatre and on its roof now, the commonplace crow caws candidly," boomed Roly.

"Sean O' Casey," he said, turning his smiling face to within inches of Bill's.

"Yes, I thought it must be," replied Bill, and he put Roly back on his stool.

"You're very naughty, Roly," said Hayley. "You promised to behave yourself. You're very unfair to Giles."

"Don't be annoyed with poor old Roly, my dear Hayley, my sweet Beatrice. Why do you stay with these people? What purpose has a sundial in the shade?"

"I like these people, Roly, and if you had any sense you'd realise we're all lucky to be in this company. Giles is really ambitious and he's got some marvellous ideas. He's worked so hard building this company up from nothing."

"I know, I know, Hayley dear. It's just Roly having some fun. Another special over here, Joyce, if you please."

"And it doesn't matter who gets the credit," said Hayley. "It can be Mandy Miller or Mickey Mouse, as far as I'm concerned, as long as we work together and achieve what we want to. Don't you think so, Bill?"

"Yeah, I suppose I do. But we all need praise and reward. And I agree with Roly. It's best if our success is in some proportion to the effort we put in."

"There speaks a man of wisdom," said Roly. "Praise given and not merited represents devaluation of a precious currency. Hayley is the true star of our show, as we all know too well. But alas, all actors have an infinite capacity for acclaim, whatever their accomplishments, and all feel they have a right to it."

Roly leaned back to empty his glass of another special and kept leaning, trying to tease the slice of lemon out of the bottom. He had forgotten that he was sitting on a bar stool and that the only thing that would eventually halt his backward movement was the tiled floor. Bill suddenly glimpsed Roly arching further backwards, the glass still to his lips and a look of confusion in his eyes, as he wondered where he was headed.

Bill made a last-minute lunge to catch him. He just managed to get his hands under Roly's head and neck before they made contact with the ground. Roly lay there with his eyes now staring in bewilderment and disbelief. He was shocked and bruised, but nothing worse, and he was slowly coaxed to his feet.

He was clearly so drunk that he could not stand unaided. He sat in a chair muttering to himself. Hayley called a taxi from her mobile and Bill bent down to check that Roly was alright.

"Well, that shut you up alright then, Roly," he said in his ear.

"My dear boy, even I know when it is best to say nothing," whispered Roly. "First lesson my old friend Johnny Gielgud taught me, 'be profound, be funny, or be quiet'. Since the first two are currently clearly beyond me, I think I shall seek refuge in the third."

"Bloody good decision in the circumstances, Roly," said Bill. "There's a taxi coming. I'll take you home in a minute."

"Do you mind if I stay here a while, Bill?" said Hayley from behind Roly's chair. "I think Giles still has some more things he needs to tell us. Here are my keys. Let yourself in and wait for me." She bent down and kissed him on the cheek, and then kissed Roly too.

Giles came over and placed his hand on Bill's shoulder. Bill stood up to face him and Giles led him over to the bar.

"I just wanted to thank you, Bill," he said. "That could have been really nasty if you hadn't managed to react so quickly."

"That's alright, Giles. I shouldn't have just stood there and watched him drink so much all night."

"You'd have a damned hard job keeping Roly Upperton away from his gin, Bill. It's a shame really. He's a damn fine actor when he's sober."

"He certainly likes the sound of his own voice."

"He can be a pain, old Roly, but we all love him in spite of it. He's played with the greats, you know. Olivier, Gielgud, Richardson. His Falstaff for the RSC back in the 70s is considered by some to be the best ever."

"So what happened to him?"

"He missed out on a few parts he felt should've been his and he allowed himself to become bitter about it. He hit the bottle, and what you see now is the result. I'm afraid Roly's just terribly frustrated and unfulfilled. It's a shocking waste.

"Anyway, thanks again for helping him. Are you going to see the show?"

"I hope so."

"You should. It's actually very good, and your Hayley is sensational."

"The taxi's here," someone shouted.

"Thanks again, Bill," said Giles, and he held out his hand.

"I'm pleased I could help, Giles. It's been nice talking to you."

In the taxi on the way back to his digs Roly was a changed man. The euphoria induced by the alcohol and by performing in front of his fellow players had been replaced by melancholy. He was slumped in the corner with his head down, and only occasionally did he look up and open his eyes to remind himself where he was and who he was with. Eventually, with his eyes still closed and his head hanging forward, he spoke.

"So you're the wonderful man," he mumbled.

"What was that Roly?" asked Bill.

"You're Hayley's wonderful man."

"Am I?"

"Well, she's always going on about you. 'Roly, I've met the most wonderful man.'"

"That's nice to hear, Roly. Thanks. I still can't quite understand why she thinks that, but I'm not complaining."

Roly opened his eyes and lifted his head slowly. He struggled to get Bill into focus.

"Character, dear boy. Hayley likes men with character, like you and Giles. She also likes *characters* like me, bless her. Hayley is a first-class student of the human condition, as all good actors should be."

"You make me sound like a research project, Roly."

"Nothing so shallow, dear Bill. Hayley will like you for what you've been, what you are, and most importantly what you're capable of being. She understands, you see, that all the arts we practice are apprenticeships. The real art is life itself."

"All the world's a stage, and each man must play his part, eh, Roly?" ventured Bill.

"Ah, the Bard. *As You Like It.*"

"Well, no actually. I was thinking of Elvis. *Are You Lonesome Tonight?*"

They both laughed and Roly patted Bill's knee.

"Ah, touché, dear boy, touché. But the King was right. We each play our part, but some of us, I fear, go through life not liking our part and not believing in the play. And take it from me, my dear Bill, that is a fate best avoided."

"This is it, gents. Ten Rose Gardens," came a voice from the front of the cab.

"Ah, the sweet abode of Mrs Doreen Harris, landlady to the stars," said Roly. He leaned over to Bill and whispered.

"I suppose you wouldn't care to come in for a nightcap and tuck dear old Roly up in bed, would you?"

"Sorry, Roly, not my style at all, I'm afraid."

"Ah, just my luck to be taken home by a straight man," said Roly. "My dear, I can't even *think* straight."

Roly rummaged in his pockets.

"I'm terribly sorry, Bill, but I appear to be out of funds."

"Don't worry, Roly, I'll get this."

Roly opened the door and stepped out onto the pavement. As soon as the fresh air hit him he started to perform again.

"That money talks, I'll not deny," he announced to the residents of Rose Gardens. "I heard it once, it said 'Goodbye'." And he promptly stumbled into the garden gate.

Bill got out of the taxi and helped Roly to his front door, and then up the stairs to a dimly lit room on the first floor. Roly slumped into the only armchair in the room and was asleep almost immediately. Bill covered him with a quilt from the single bed by the wall behind the door. As he was about to turn out the light and leave, he looked around Roly's room. There were no personal mementos anywhere to be seen. No photographs, no letters, no papers. The only items that seemed at all personal to Roly were on an old fridge in the corner by the window. They were a bottle of Tesco's own brand gin and a large plastic bottle of tonic.

Bill closed the door quietly, went back out to the taxi and on to the Gables to wait for Hayley.

Chapter 27

Hayley asked Bill to keep the door keys she gave him the night they all went to the Bull. Over the next week Bill saw her almost every day. And every day Bill went to work at the Meads, where things were going from bad to worse.

Tony kept Bill, Scouser and young Sam together as a team working on the show house, which was supposed to be completed by Christmas. Tony made it clear that whatever the skilled men – the brickies, chippies, sparks, plumbers or plasterers – told them to do, they had to do it.

The three of them worked well together. For a while it seemed that Scouser's relentless 'wit' aimed at young Sam would be too much for the lad, but once Bill let it be known that he had seen Sam out in Medford with his girlfriend, and that she was a 'real stunner', Scouser's mickey-taking tailed off.

It was just as well that the three men were a good team, because the problems at the site were mounting. The weather was being kind to the contractors. It was dry most days and quite mild, so the brickies were able to work flat out and the carpenters were able to start on the roof. That is when Bill knew for sure that Horseman's were not keeping a close enough eye on the job.

No one at the site seemed to even understand the principle behind getting electricity from solar energy, although it was simple enough. The latest solar cells did not even need sunlight. Daylight on its own was enough. And the panels that Bill had ordered for the Meads came disguised as grey tiles to match the rest of the roof. There was no problem in any of this, except that the solar tiles were heavy and the whole roof needed special strengthening.

Bill looked at the chippies at work and saw clearly that this extra strengthening was not being done. He cursed Hugh Turner and Benny for being so slack and allowing things to get so out of hand. Where the hell were the people from Horseman's who should be sorting all this out? Bill was quite happy to have a quiet word with the Horseman people when they arrived. He would almost certainly know them anyway. But he was sure as hell not going to make any of this mess his own responsibility.

Most days Bill got back from the Meads just after six. He took it in turns with Liz to prepare the evening meal, and Jonathan usually came down to lend a hand and to talk when his uncle was in the kitchen.

Liz did not seem to mind Bill going out most evenings just after eight and coming home either well after midnight or not at all. She was pleased just to have her brother there and to see him enjoying himself in Medford, given all the problems he had arrived with only three weeks previously. Liz was a lot happier herself after her dinner date with Steve. Bill had stayed in with the children on that Wednesday night, and when Liz came home she was triumphant, and could not wait to tell Bill everything that had been said between her and Steve.

Steve's new partner, Charlotte, had waved him off thinking he was going to ask his wife for a divorce. Charlotte had decided that her apartment was too small for the two of them, especially if one day they were to start a family. To buy a bigger place they would need Steve's share of the equity in the house he had bought with Liz. But Liz realised that Charlotte had miscalculated. She was moving too fast for Steve and he was not ready for such big and irreversible changes in his life. Instead of asking for a divorce he spent most of the evening trying to persuade Liz to take him back.

"And are you going to?" Bill asked his sister.

"I haven't said yes yet, but I probably will. For the kids' sake, if nothing else."

"Is that enough of a reason, Liz?"

"Yes, it's the best reason, Bill. Besides, I still fancy him, you know, and deep down somewhere I expect I still love him."

Liz looked at Bill with a wicked smile he had not seen since she'd put Tabasco sauce in her mother's favourite ketchup after one of their many rows.

"Do you know what I'm going to do, Bill?" she said.

Bill laughed. "No, tell me."

"I'm going to have an affair with the bugger first. He can start lying to his precious Charlotte for a change, and I'll have some of the excitement. I'm meeting him again on Friday. We're having dinner at the George. I'm going to book a room in advance, get all dolled up and seduce him."

"He won't know what's hit him."

"No, he won't. I've held back too much in my life. He's going to see another side of me. That snooty bitch Charlotte won't stand a chance."

There was fire in Liz's face.

"Are you going to tell Susie and Jonathan?" asked Bill.

"What? That I'm going to seduce their father in a hotel room with every deviant move I can think of?"

"Nooo. Are you going to tell them that their dad's coming home?"

"Not yet. I'm not taking anything for granted, not even the way *I* feel about it all. We'll see how it goes. It's funny, isn't it, Bill. You can never predict what's going to happen, can you?"

"As far as I can make out, Liz, that's the only real certainty we have in life."

"So Steve does feel guilt, after all," mused Bill, as he sipped another whisky alone in his room once Liz had gone to bed. Or perhaps it was not guilt at all that he felt. Perhaps he was just shitting himself with fear of the unknown. Maybe he did what he did for the same reason Bill went to the casino that night. Maybe Steve just wanted something to change in his life.

"Who knows, and what right have any of us got to judge?" Bill said to his whisky glass.

The only thing Bill could be sure of for now was the love he felt for Hayley and the guilt he felt towards Angie.

Poor Angie, going through all that alone for all those years. And Bill remembered the resentment he had felt towards her when they had not been able to join in socially with other people. The countless excuses they had made to Harry and Alison Woodford for not accepting their invitations to go down to their villa in the South of France. The time only last year when Mickey and Cheryl had asked Bill if he could persuade Mum to go to Mauritius with them, and Bill had not even wasted his time mentioning it to Angie, because he could not be bothered listening to her excuses. And if he was honest, he had to admit that at times over the last year or two his feelings towards Angie had gone beyond frustration and resentment. He had started to feel contempt.

Now, as he sat in his room in Liz's house in Medford, he was paying for those feelings in guilt. He replayed Stoner's words, 'terror, mate, sheer bloody terror. Overwhelming, uncontrollable dread as if you're about to die or lose your mind.' And he felt so much remorse and regret and responsibility that he just wanted to tell Angie how sorry he was, and find out if he could do anything to make it up to her. Perhaps Stoner was right. Perhaps his proper place was back in Bramport with Angie.

But what about Hayley? Could he ever bring himself to leave her? He knew that he was not going through the same emotions as Steve clearly was. Steve seemed to be guilt-free, but he feared where a future with Charlotte would lead. Bill was not afraid of a future with Hayley. Quite the opposite. He would embrace a future with Hayley. Any future. He did not even feel guilty for loving her. His feelings towards her were genuine and honest, and anyway he had no choice but to love her. At least on that level he felt he belonged more with Hayley right now than he did with Angie. He had more affinity with Hayley after three weeks than he had managed to retain with Angie after 30 years.

He poured himself another single malt and slumped back down on the bed. He heaved a deep sigh. He knew he was kidding himself.

However much he wanted to stay with Hayley, deep down Bill knew well enough where his proper place was. If she needed him, his place was with his wife back in Bramport. And he knew that sooner or later he would have to speak to her to find out how she felt about him coming back.

For several more days Bill could not bring himself to make the call, knowing that it would signal the end of the time he would spend with Hayley. And his time with her that week was the best time of all.

Hayley was rehearsing every evening now until nine o'clock. And apart from Wednesday night when he stayed in with Susie and Jonathan, Bill went to her flat in the Gables to have a meal ready for her when she finally got home from the Guildhall. Her work in the café followed by nearly three hours of rehearsals was exhausting her, but she did not show it. All she showed to Bill was her pleasure in finding him there every day, and her excitement over the work she was doing with the Limelight Players.

Hayley loved to talk about the theatre and the exhilaration she felt in everyone's commitment and performance. And as Hayley talked, Bill questioned her in an attempt to understand how anyone could pursue their dream as single-mindedly as she did. And Hayley and Bill were perfect listeners, because although neither of them mentioned it, each of them sensed their time together was running out, and they both wanted to learn as much as they could about one another whilst they still had the chance.

On Saturday they both took a day off and they stayed in bed for hours sharing a bottle of wine, making love, and watching old movies that Bill had chosen from the video store across the Green. Bill had Peg to thank for his love of classic films, but he doubted that she would be very pleased to know how she had contributed to such a perfect day.

Hayley had been teasing Bill all day about a 'treat' she had for him in the evening, and no questioning could get her to give anything away. So at 7.30 Bill was surprised to find himself standing in the foyer of the Theatre Royal in Medford while Hayley went over to the box office.

"Here you are. The mystery's over," she said, and she handed Bill a ticket. It read, 'Puccini's *Madam Butterfly*'.

"You told me you'd never been to the opera," said Hayley, "so I thought I'd treat you. I know you're going to love this."

"I don't know what to say, Hayley. It's a wonderful idea. Thankyou, darling," said Bill, and he took a step forward and hugged her, not caring where they were or who was watching.

"It's my favourite Puccini and I wanted us to see it together," she said softly, as their cheeks touched and they held one another.

From the first note Bill was captivated. He could count on the fingers of one hand the number of times he had been to the theatre in his life, and he had never thought of going to the opera. Very soon he understood what he had been missing. Even before the curtain went up the orchestra had begun to create the atmosphere of Japan, and the first scene transported the audience to a Japanese home with terrace and garden. In the background lay the harbour of the town of Nagasaki.

Bill always thought opera might be rather dull, but how wrong he had been. The story of love and betrayal was carried along by the music and Bill understood how recurring musical themes were illustrating the different characters and the varying moods. Before he knew it the first act was drawing to an end with the love duet between Captain Pinkerton and Madam Butterfly. As Pinkerton tried to calm the fears of the much younger Butterfly the beauty of the melody increased until the lovers were singing with passionate abandonment, before their voices became tender and soft and the curtain fell. Bill thought he could never hear music more powerful than this, but he was wrong.

When the deserted Butterfly gave up her child at the end of the opera and then took her own life the dramatic power of the scene was strong enough on its own. But then it was combined with music so beautiful and a melody so haunting, that when the last strident chord was played and the curtain fell, Bill sat motionless whilst everyone around him was applauding rapturously. After a full minute he turned to Hayley who was smiling broadly whilst still clapping with enthusiasm. When she looked into his face she stopped clapping and grasped his arm.

"Bill. Darling. Are you alright?" she said.

For a moment Bill could not understand what the question meant, but then he realised that tears were streaming down his cheeks. Hayley flung her arms around him and kissed his face.

"I won't ask you what you thought of it then," she said. "Come on, let's go home."

The rain that had been falling when they arrived at the theatre had now stopped and it was quite a mild night for early December. Bill and Hayley decided that they would walk back to the flat. Bill moved to the outside of the pavement as he always did and put his arm around Hayley's shoulder. He pulled her close and she put her arm around his waist.

"Blimey, I'm sorry about that," he said. "They ought to put a government health warning on those tickets. 'This opera can seriously upset your emotional equilibrium'."

"Don't apologise, Bill. I'm thrilled that it meant so much to you."

"The strange thing is I was completely in their world. I didn't even know I had tears in my eyes."

"And on your cheeks, and your chin, and your jacket."

"Did I make a real fool of myself?"

Hayley stopped and turned to face him.

"My dear, lovely Bill," she said. "It's the exact opposite. The way you reacted shows how alive you are. It means you're not just existing. You're not just walking around breathing in and out like most people do."

"Aren't I?"

"No. Your receptors are full on, and you're always ready to open yourself up to experience new things. I think it's wonderful that you're like that."

Hayley kissed him and they walked on past the town hall.

"The thing is, Hayley, I just can't believe how powerful all that was. I don't know how to describe it. It wasn't just emotional. It was almost like a spiritual experience."

"I think it is a spiritual experience. Beethoven called music 'the mediator between the spiritual and sensual life'."

"Well, there you are then. Even Beethoven agrees with me."

"I can promise you, Bill. You and Beethoven aren't the only ones who feel like that."

"Do you know, Hayley, if I could write one song from that opera, or one book, or even one beautiful poem I would die a happy man. Can you imagine creating something that beautiful?"

"But that's why I love performing in the theatre so much.

Interpreting something in your own way through your performance is a way of creating something unique to yourself.

"And isn't that what you said about your travelling too, Bill? That you'd treat each day like a performance with a new setting and new characters and new interpretations? That sounds pretty creative to me."

"That's exactly how I see it, Hayley. You've got such a wonderful way of putting these things into words. You seem to understand it better than I do myself."

Bill stopped, put his hands on Hayley's shoulders and looked into her face.

"You're so wonderful," he said. "I do love you so much."

"I know you do, Bill," said Hayley and she put her hands around his waist and her head on his chest. "We have to talk about all this, you know," she said. "We have to decide what we're going to do."

"I know that, darling. I've just been trying to avoid facing up to it, that's all."

Hayley broke away from him and then took his arm and led him towards the Gables.

"We don't have to avoid anything, Bill," she said, as she quickened their pace.

"Remember, as long as we can always be honest with ourselves about what we really want, we can both get to wherever we want to go."

Chapter 28

It was 10.30 by the time they reached the flat in the Gables after their night out at the opera and Hayley was tired out. She had a full-day rehearsal starting at nine o'clock in the morning and it was clear that any conversation about their future would have to wait for now.

Bill walked with Hayley to the Guildhall the next morning and as they kissed goodbye they arranged to meet at the flat again that evening. Bill was already dreading it. It seemed a strange feeling for once not to be looking forward to seeing Hayley. The streets were deserted on a Sunday morning and the steady drizzle did nothing to lighten Bill's mood as he walked back to Liz's house.

Liz could see immediately that things were not right with her brother. She offered to make him a drink and invited him into the kitchen for a chat, but Bill declined both. Instead he went upstairs to his room. When he reappeared he was wearing thick clothing and hiking boots and carrying his windjammer.

"I thought I'd have a day out on the moors, Liz," he said to his sister without allowing her to catch his eye. "I'll get the bus to Maybridge and walk from there."

"You haven't chosen a very good day for it, Bill. Will you be back for lunch? Steve's invited himself over."

"No, Liz, I'll look after myself today, if that's alright. I fancy a bit of time to myself."

"Okay, love. Look after yourself then. Bye."

Bill was opening the front door when Liz appeared in the hallway.

"Wait," she said, and she came up and kissed him. "I haven't wanted to pry, Bill, but I want you to remember something. Whatever it is that's troubling you, you're my big brother and I know nothing can ever beat you."

"Thanks, Liz. Don't worry. I'll be alright."

It took 40 minutes for the bus to reach Maybridge and Bill was the only passenger on it for the entire 20-mile journey. Maybridge was no more than a village, but in the summer months it was so popular with tourists that it often became crammed with cars and visitors. Now all the tea rooms and B&B's were closed for the off-season and the main village street was deserted. Bill looked at his watch. It was 11.50 and even the pubs in the village were not yet open. Not that Bill wanted a drink. He did not want any company. He wanted to walk and get as far away from other people as he could.

Bill left the village on the path that led along a fast-flowing stream up to Braytor, a hill 800ft high and known locally as 'Mount' Braytor. Usually Braytor could be seen clearly from Maybridge, lying about two miles to the north of the village, but today it was totally obscured by the light drizzle that had been falling since the previous evening. Bill was pleased with the conditions. It would mean that he was unlikely to encounter anyone else on his walk, and it would also make his climb up the steep path to the top of Braytor more of a challenge.

Bill had attempted the climb once before, when he was about ten. It had been a hot summer's day then when his dad's brother, Uncle Les, brought them all out from Bramport in his Morris Oxford. Bill remembered his uncle staying with them on two or three occasions in the summer when Bill was a boy. Uncle Les was as unlike Wilf and Peg as it was possible to be. He had never married and he left Bramport as soon as his employers, the Great Western Railway, offered him a job at Paddington Station. Peg often referred to Les as a 'dandy' and clearly disapproved of him. Bill remembered Les making the walk to Braytor in a white linen suit, a panama hat and suede shoes. He had even carried a silver-topped cane.

Bill smiled at the memory. Uncle Les was great fun, and very generous towards Bill and Liz. At least he tried to be. He loved laughing and joking with them, and he liked to give them treats as much as he could, but more often than not Peg would put a stop to it. Maybe Uncle Les did overdo it a bit, but Peg was always a little too anxious to make sure her children were not spoilt. She always seemed to want to curtail their pleasures rather than encourage any enjoyment of life. Bill felt that he and Liz were never left in peace by their mother. She clearly worried about their welfare but why did she always have to show it through carping attention and disapproval of whatever they wanted to do? She could never just let them be. And she was far worse with Bill than she was with Liz, because it was always Bill who seemed to be the more excitable and adventurous one.

Bill had never forgotten the argument he'd had with his mother when they reached the foot of Braytor. He was desperate to make it to the top, and would happily have gone on his own, but she would not hear of it. She had no intention of taking any risk herself and certainly her children were not going to take any, although in truth Braytor was not really dangerous to climb. It was just damned hard work. Liz wanted to go with her big brother but she was only eight at the time and easily dissuaded. Uncle Les was not really the type for strenuous outdoor activity and was very apologetic for 'not being able to help out on this one'. But Bill recalled clearly that on this occasion he had the bit between his teeth and would not let go.

No one even considered that Wilf would volunteer to go up with the lad, since he had already done well enough walking along the uneven path beside the stream to get where they were. But Wilf could see that Bill was determined to go, and he wanted to keep an eye on the boy and stop the damned arguing, which he hated. In fact Wilf's decision only made Peg worse. She now went on to Bill about how selfish he was for making his father take such a risk with his leg, and how he would be to blame if anything bad happened to him. Bill stood there angry and frustrated and resentful. After all, all he wanted to do was walk up a bloody hill on a nice summer's day and see the view from the top.

As Bill started his second attempt to climb Braytor he winced and shook his head at the recollection of that day in 1961. And as he remembered the feelings he'd had then as a young boy he was surprised to find he was experiencing the same emotions again nearly 40 years later. He stopped and breathed out deeply to try to regain his equilibrium. He looked over to the spot by the stream where he and his father had left the others sitting whilst they'd set off up the hill.

Bill had started with all the energy of a fit and strong young boy, while Wilf followed on with the help of Les' cane, his efforts hopelessly compromised by the clumsy wooden prosthesis strapped to his left leg. It was tough going, and they got halfway up the hill to a stone viewing table, before Wilf said that he was sorry but he could go no further. At the time Bill had been disappointed with his father for stopping. He wanted his father to be strong and to lead him, and not the other way round. And maybe he had even felt a bit annoyed with his dad. He could not be sure any more.

But he did remember that the climb back down took the two of them even longer than the climb up. It was a terrible struggle for Wilf to get down, but he did not complain or say anything much at all really. And for his part Bill could not recall sympathising very much with his father or trying to help him in any way.

"What a selfish little brat I must have been," he muttered to himself.

The words were similar to the ones Peg had used on him when he and Wilf eventually rejoined the others at the foot of Braytor. Wilf was all in by then, and he sat for about half an hour bathing his stump in the cool water of the stream, before he could once again put any pressure on it.

Bill remembered his mother coming over to him and being furious with him. She'd told him over and over how irresponsible he was for insisting on doing the climb, and putting himself and his father in such danger. As they walked back to the village Bill had been as miserable and defeated as it was possible to be. His embarrassment in front of his Uncle Les was particularly painful. Uncle Les had always treated Bill as an equal and talked to him like an adult, so being belittled by Peg in front of him meant a loss of status for a ten-year-old that could never be recovered. Bill walked behind everyone as they made their way back in silence to Maybridge, and he could see his father limping badly in front of him. Given different treatment the young boy might have managed to appreciate what his father had tried to do for him that afternoon, but instead each limp made Bill feel more resentful and angry and confused. The guilt came later.

Bill looked up at Braytor through the drizzle and realised that all desire to climb it today had left him. He turned his back on the hill and walked down the same path that he had followed nearly 40 years before. He had come here to get some peace, but he had not found any. Instead his head was filled with accusations.

Why had he failed to understand the seriousness of Angie's illness just as he had failed to appreciate the extent of his father's disability? Was there some basic feeling missing in him? Was it possible that he was the selfish person his mother always said he was? But how could he be selfish when he constantly felt responsible for other people's well-being, and when he spent so much of his life trying to do what was right? Try as he might, he had no answers to his questions.

Except one. There was one thing he was now certain about. He could not desert Angie. If she wanted him to go back to her, he would.

He had listened to Stoner and Hayley's advice about looking within himself to find what he needed to live a fulfilled life. About making informed choices based on what he wanted to be and what he wanted to do. But with some decisions there was no choice. Some decisions made themselves. He would go back to Angie because it was just simply the right thing to do.

She was his wife and the mother of his children and she needed him. And she was a wonderful mother who had nurtured and encouraged her boys, so that they had grown into happy, well-rounded young men. And he owed it to her to make up for the negative feelings he had harboured towards her at times over the years, when he had been ignorant of the torment she was going through.

Besides, how could he stay with Hayley and attempt to build a future with her based on Angie's unhappiness? It was a recipe for disaster. He could never live with himself. He had to go back.

It all made sense, but Bill knew that all these reasons were still not enough. He stopped on the path and bent down to pick up a handful of stones. One by one he threw them into the fast-flowing water with all the force he could muster. Then he picked up a large rock, which lay to his right, and with a great effort he held it with two hands above his head. With a loud roar he hurled it into the water, and then he checked all around him before he let out another huge roar that came from the pit of his stomach and lasted until he had no more breath in him. Twice more he picked up huge rocks and hurled them into the water until he started to feel so light-headed he was forced to sit down on a boulder. He was exhausted, but he felt a damn-sight better and at last his head started to clear.

"There's only one good reason for going back to Angie, you bloody fool," he said out loud to himself, "and that's if you still love her."

And he did still love her. It might not be a love as fresh and as easy as his love for Hayley, but it was a love that was fighting to survive the most traumatic period of their marriage, and he could not give up on it now. Bill's decision was made. He loved Angie and he would go back to her. It was what he wanted. Now it was time to tell Hayley.

Chapter 29

Bill had arranged to meet Hayley at her flat at eight o'clock that Sunday evening. He stood at the door and waited for a minute before ringing the bell, and when there was no answer he let himself in. He was about to put the keys back in his jacket pocket when he decided to leave them on the bookshelf instead. He saw the brandy bottle and poured himself a large measure. Just then he heard another key in the front door and Hayley appeared.

She looked tired but her face lit up when she saw Bill and she came straight over to kiss him. Her hair was tied back, but loose strands fell over her forehead and there were few traces of the make-up she had put on at the start of her long day. Bill put his arms around her and held her close to him. He breathed in her familiar smell and it reassured him. They stayed there by the bookcase, holding one another but not speaking. Eventually Hayley leaned back a little so that she could look into Bill's face.

"You're a sight for sore eyes," she said.

"And so are you, Hayley. You look beautiful."

He stroked the loose strands of hair away from her face.

"It's so good to see you," he said. "It felt like a long day without you."

"What did you do today?"

"I went out onto the moors at Maybridge."

"In this weather?"

"I wanted to climb Braytor."

"In the middle of winter? I think you're slightly eccentric, Bill Knight."

"I wanted to be on my own for a while. I had a lot of thinking to do. Hayley, I…"

"Don't let's talk about that just yet, Bill."

She kissed him again and broke away to go through to the kitchen. She had found new energy from somewhere.

"Let's have a hot drink first," she said. "Coffee?"

"Yes, that would be lovely. Did you have a good day?"

"Yes, it was great fun. I was working on one or two of my numbers. We've got a few new songs, but we've taken most of them from the shows. I was doing *Memory* from *Cats* today. I sing it after the ball when I think I've lost Cinderella forever. Roly calls it 'mammaries' because Mandy Miller's breasts are just about falling out of her costume most of the time. Giles said it'll keep the dads happy, so of course that set Roly off again. 'But where's the artistic integrity, dear boy?'"

Hayley came back with the drinks. She was smiling.

"I've never heard you sing," said Bill.

"Tickets available at all prices from the box office, sir," replied Hayley, as she put the mugs down on the coffee table in front of him. She turned on the gas fire and sat on the rug in front of it, as she always did when she first got home. Bill looked down at her from the armchair.

"I have to talk to you about what I need to do, Hayley," he said.

"I know," she said, staring at the fire. "Let me have a sip of your brandy and then you can tell me anything you want to."

Bill held out his glass and she took it.

"Aah, that's better," she said. "Okay. Let's hear it straight."

"The thing is, Hayley, I've decided to go back to Bramport to be with Angie."

Bill waited for Hayley's reaction. There was none.

"I don't know whether you remember me telling you about a good friend coming to see me about a week ago. He told me a few things I didn't know before. He explained to me just how ill Angie's been over the years, and how much she's still suffering from it. He thinks I can help her."

Bill paused again, expecting Hayley to speak, but still she said nothing. Instead she turned her head and looked up at him and smiled.

"I find it very unnerving when you don't say anything, Hayley. I don't know what you're thinking."

"You just talk to me, Bill. I'll let you know what I think when I've heard everything you have to say."

"OK then, if that's what you want. Just before I came to Medford Angie and I had been through a really bad time. I think we'd become just about the worse thing for one another in a way. We both needed a break, that's for sure. I wasn't offering her much apart from a load of anxiety and I think she was relieved just to see me go in the end. I came here to find Jasmine and earn some money, and to get some damned peace, quite frankly. Finding you, and falling in love with you, wasn't part of the plan at all."

Hayley was still looking into the fire and showed no signs of saying anything.

"The thing is, now I've learnt how bad Angie is and how much she needs my help, I just can't turn my back on her. We still love one another in our own way, I suppose, Angie and me. God knows, I'm so bloody confused. I could stay here with you, Hayley, but I don't think I should. But at the same time I feel bad suddenly leaving you like this."

Hayley got up and Bill watched her go over to the sofa and sit down with her legs tucked beneath her. The way she always sat.

"Right," she said, "let's deal with the last bit first. For a start you have no reason to feel bad towards me, Bill. I always knew your situation and I accepted it. You and I became involved because we liked one another and fancied one another. Neither of us made any silly promises. All I ever asked of you was to be honest with me and to treat me with respect. And you've done much more than that."

"I hope I have."

"Of course you have. You've been so loving and supportive towards me. I've loved being with you, Bill. The past three weeks have been the happiest weeks of my life, and I'm going to miss you like mad, but you haven't done me any damage. You've made me feel wonderful."

Bill was sitting forward with his head bowed.

"Listen to me, Bill, will you?" He lifted his head to look at her. "You are not responsible for my happiness. Do you understand that?"

"I do understand that, Hayley. I understand that you made a free choice to get involved with me and you accept the consequences, and all that stuff. But it doesn't change the fact that I'm hurting you, and I don't want to do that. I love you."

"But that's the point. You're not hurting me, Bill. You've never lied to me or deceived me or broken any promises. You've got a tough decision to make and you're making it. I respect that."

"God, you're always so positive about everything, and so generous about people, Hayley. I think it's what I like most about you, but I don't know how you do it all the time."

"Probably because I take responsibility for my own life and my own happiness, and I'm not looking for other people to blame for anything."

"But I'm the one bringing everything to an end, just when things are so good between us. And my timing's terrible with all you're involved in at the moment."

"Bill, Bill, what am I going to do with you? There's no reason why you need to feel so guilty about any of this. For a start, I'd much rather deal with this now than wait until I'm in the middle of the run. Of course I'd like things to carry on between us, but remember I'm leaving Medford too in a few weeks. And nothing's going to stop me doing that."

"I could've come with you."

"You could. And maybe I would've wanted you to, but sooner or later I would want you to leave me. I'd be disappointed with you if you didn't."

"Why the hell do you say that?"

"I've already told you why. Because I'm not your dream, Bill. You can only achieve your dream on your own, by doing it for yourself. If you stayed with me you'd remain unfulfilled, and eventually you'd become frustrated again and start to resent me. I'm not signing up for that nonsense. You get out there, Bill Knight, and do whatever you have to."

"And you really think I'm allowed to do that, do you?"

"You have to be. But you'll wait forever if you hang around waiting for permission from everyone in your life."

"I wish I could be as single-minded as you are."

"You have to preserve the things that are vital to your happiness, Bill. In the long run it's a lot kinder to everyone around you, even if it makes you appear selfish. We could stay together here in Medford. I could testify for you against Benny. But it would be the end of everything I've ever wanted, Bill, and without that I'd stop being the person you love. We'd be together but it would be a disaster for us both."

"So you're saying it's a good thing for us to part?"

"Yes, I am. If we stay together neither of us can do what we need to do. Of course, it's sad, but we should be excited about it too. You can be excited for me, because I'm moving forward with my dream, and I want to be excited about your future too."

"And aren't you?"

"I could be if I thought you could go back and help Angie but not compromise what you have to do for your own happiness. Do you think you can do that?"

"I'm sure as hell going to try."

"Wouldn't it be wonderful, Bill, if you and Angie could help one another through all your problems and then support one another to live the life each of you want."

"It would be a bloody miracle, Hayley. But I'm going to give it a go."

"And one day you'll send me a postcard from a far-off place telling me all about your new life. The life you always imagined for yourself."

"I'm going to really try, Hayley."

"No, Bill. I want you to do more than try. When you leave here tonight I want us both to be looking forward to a really exciting future. Otherwise I'll feel we got nowhere together. I want us to be optimistic and excited. And happy for one another."

Bill got up and sat down on the sofa next to Hayley. He took her hand in both of his and they turned and faced one another, as they leaned back against the cushions.

"Whatever I do for the rest of my life, Hayley, I'll never forget all the wonderful things about you, and what you've shown me."

"But you have to promise me, Bill, that you won't let go of your dream. Promise me."

"I promise you that I'll never let go of my dream, Hayley."

"Good," she said, and she put her arms around his neck. Bill could feel her warm breath on his cheek as she spoke.

"Now I can let you go," she said. "And we can leave one another feeling stronger, because we've helped one another get closer to what we want to be."

She got up and pulled Bill to his feet. She led him to the front door.

"I'm not going to allow us to be miserable," she said. "We'll say goodbye and we'll both be okay."

Bill put his arms around her and they held on to one another, knowing it was for the last time.

"I've got one more thing I want to say to you, Bill. You've been wonderful to me. You're the most loving and thoughtful man I've ever met. I want you to remember that you leave here free of any obligation or guilt towards me. That's my gift to you."

Bill tried to speak, but Hayley placed her fingertips on his mouth and kissed him on the cheek.

"Now go," she said, "and don't forget to send me that postcard."

Bill went down the stairs towards the street. He heard the door close behind him. He stopped at the foot of the stairs and looked back up. He felt elated and wretched in the same moment. He stared at her door and imagined her standing behind it.

"Hayley McKenna," he said to himself. And then he walked out into the Gables and back to Liz's house.

Chapter 30

Bill waited all day on Monday before he made the phone call to Angie to tell her that he was coming back to Bramport. He had taken Hayley's advice to heart and he drew strength from her optimism and from her faith in him. He pushed himself hard during the eight-hour shift at the Meads, as if the physical effort could reinforce his conviction about the decision he had made. The digging and the lifting and the thinking set up a rhythm together, and by the end of the shift he was sure he had worked out a positive vision of his future with Angie.

The first priority was to help her with her attacks so the two of them could live a more normal life together. Maybe with Stoner's help it might even be possible to stop the attacks completely. They could bring honesty back into their marriage and learn from each other what they each needed to be happy and fulfilled, and then help one another to achieve it.

He and Angie had faced tough times before in their lives together and they had always got through them. And they would get through this. Bill would get the court case behind him and deal with whatever the consequences were, and then they would get on with their lives again. And they would be good lives. Bill was determined about that.

Tony dropped Bill off outside the town hall as usual at about ten to six. Bill raised his hand to acknowledge all the lads as the van drove off, and they treated him to a wide variety of signs and catcalls. Bill winked at Sam and smiled at him. Bill had decided to say nothing yet to Tony or anyone else about his plans to leave

Medford. He had not even discussed it with Liz. He thought it better to speak to Angie first.

As he walked past the town hall he searched in his phone book for the single word 'Home'. He pressed to connect and within a few seconds a tentative voice answered, 'Hello?'

"Hello, Angie, it's me, love."

"Hello, Bill. This is nice."

"Yes, I'm sorry I haven't been in touch for so long, love, but I've been pretty busy up here."

"Yes, it's been well over a week. I was starting to worry about you."

"You can always leave a message on my mobile, Angie. Or phone me at Liz's."

"You know I don't like doing that, Bill. You know I never feel very comfortable with Liz."

"Never mind that, love. How are you all? How are the boys?"

"They're fine, but I think they miss you not being in Bramport."

"I spoke to them both at the weekend. They seemed okay about it then."

"I expect they don't want to upset you."

"What do you mean, Angie? I don't understand that."

"I don't mean anything, Bill. I just think they prefer it when you're more available for them, that's all."

"That's what I wanted to talk to you about, Angie. I'm thinking of coming back to Bramport."

"Oh, right. What's brought that on all of a sudden then?"

"Well, you know I met Stoner up here about ten days ago?"

"Yes."

"He told me all about how you've been feeling and how much he's been able to help you."

"Oh, right. What did Mark say exactly?"

"I can't get used to you calling him Mark, love. I'll have to say 'Stoner'."

"So what did Mark tell you, Bill?"

"He told me about how bad you've been and how I didn't understand just what you've been going through all this time."

"You've got to realise, Bill, that it's been very lonely for me here."

"I know, Angie. Don't upset yourself. And I'm so sorry I haven't understood that, and haven't helped you as I should've done."

"That's alright, Bill."

"No, it's not alright, Angie. I should've been there for you more, instead of being so bloody self-obsessed all the time. I want to come back and put it all right."

"Oh, right. But you must understand, Bill, I don't want any more upset. Things are so lovely and calm here at the moment, and I'm so much happier in myself."

"I won't do anything to upset you, Angie. I promise. I just want to help. I want us to help one another."

"Well, why don't you just come back for a visit then, Bill? And we'll talk about everything and see what's best for everyone."

"Okay, Angie. I was thinking of coming back this weekend. I thought I'd get the train down on Saturday morning. Is that okay with you?"

"Next Saturday, the 11th, you mean?"

"I think it's the 11th. I'm really looking forward to seeing you, Angie. I want you to realise that I understand now, and I just want to help you get through everything, and we'll go from there."

"It's lovely to hear you say that, Bill. It's such a relief to me. I'll see you on Saturday then, shall I?"

"About twelve o'clock love. Give my love to the boys for me. Bye, Angie."

"Okay, Bill. Bye. See you on Saturday."

When he got back to Liz's house that evening Bill found a letter from Natalie Barry of Robinson and Reed Solicitors waiting for him. She asked him to contact her at his earliest convenience. Bill phoned Natalie on Tuesday and Wednesday during his lunch breaks but she was out of the office. Her secretary insisted that Ms Barry needed to see him, so he brought his trip to Bramport forward a day and made an appointment for two o'clock on Friday.

Tony, the gaffer at the Meads, was not best pleased when Bill told him he needed Friday off, and that he would be unavailable for overtime at the weekend. The weather had turned and they were falling behind schedule, and Bill was one of his best men. Tony was obviously a worried man, and Bill's original disappointment at only going home for a weekend visit was eased a little by not having to quit for good and add to Tony's problems.

Bill caught the 12.05 train from Medford Station, arriving at Bramport Junction just after one o'clock. Horseman's had allowed him to keep his leased Ford Mondeo until the beginning of December, but Bill had returned it before he left Bramport, and ever since he had relied on public transport. He did not mind. Not having a car had slowed his life down, and if anything he felt freer without it.

He had a pint and a sandwich at the Railway Hotel when he arrived in Bramport and was at Natalie Barry's office ten minutes early. When she returned from lunch and saw him waiting she greeted him with genuine warmth.

"Bill, how lovely it is to see you. My, you look ten years younger."

Bill shook her outstretched hand.

"Hello, Natalie, it's good to see you too."

"Come on through. You can leave your bag there with Linda."

Natalie opened the door of her office and Bill waited for her to go in first.

"So what's it like being back in Bramport then, Bill? Seen any familiar faces? Please sit down."

"Thanks, Natalie. No, I haven't seen anyone yet. I'm quite relieved about that really."

"I wouldn't worry too much about other people's opinions of you, Bill. In my experience most people have very short memories and their main pre-occupation is themselves. So what are your plans whilst you're here?"

"I'm staying until Sunday. I'll be spending my time with my wife, and I expect I'll see my sons and my parents at some point."

"And how are things at home, if I may ask?"

"Good, Natalie. I'm very positive about everything. I'm actually more relaxed now than I've been for years. I want to put everything right with my wife, Angie. And then I want to get through this court business and start afresh. I'm actually managing to see all this as a chance to make things better for myself. And for the people that matter to me."

"Well, Bill, I can't tell you how delighted I am to hear you talking like that. Getting away to Medford's obviously done you a power of good."

"It has, Natalie."

"Good, good. Now, obviously I've asked you here today to bring you up to date with everything."

Natalie took a buff-coloured folder from the corner of her desk. She opened it and started reading. During the short silence Bill felt butterflies invade his stomach.

"We have a court date now, Bill," she said, without looking up. "Yes, here it is. Monday, the 28th of March at Medford Crown Court. It'll be a jury trial, of course, because of your 'not guilty' plea. And it'll be in front of a circuit judge. We don't know who yet. There's only one indictment. 'Theft contrary to section one, paragraph one, of the Theft Act 1968.' That's about it."

The butterflies were now going crazy.

"God, this makes me very nervous, Natalie."

She looked up at him.

"That's understandable, Bill, but there's very little here that we didn't know before."

"No. I realise that, Natalie."

"Our biggest problem is our lack of any witness to contradict Mr Horseman's account of what transpired at the casino on October 22nd. Our people have had no luck at all in tracing this Jasmine character. How about you, Bill? Any luck in Medford?"

"No, none. At one point I thought I'd found her, but it turned out to be someone completely different. I don't see the point of searching any more really. Even if we did find her we couldn't make her testify, could we?"

"Oh yes we could. We can issue a Witness Summons on her under section two of the Criminal Procedure Act. If she fails to comply she's in contempt of court, and if she lies she's committing perjury."

"So you're going to keep looking for her?"

"Absolutely. Finding Jasmine would make things very straightforward for us."

"What do you think our chances are without her?"

"They've not changed. It could all come down to who makes the better witness, you or Mr Horseman. The prosecution can obviously show that you took the money. It will be incumbent upon us to explain your motives for doing so. Then we have to convince the jury that you always intended to return it, and that you actually did return it. Then technically no theft has occurred and there's no case to answer. A lot will come down to their faith in your good character. And there I have some good news for you."

"I like the sound of that."

"We have a very good list of people willing to act as character witnesses for you, Bill. Yes, here it is. Harold Woodford, Mr Horseman's accountant. That's a coup for us. I expect the prosecution would like to have him."

"I'll be damned. Good old Harry," said Bill. He knew it would mean Harry and Alison would lose the Horseman account, but they were going to speak up for him in spite of that.

"Mr Woodford approached us initially and he suggested other names who have since stated their willingness to appear on your behalf. There's Lionel Summers, chairman of the Bramport Chamber of Commerce, and two borough councillors, Gareth Williams and Jenny Perryman.

"God, I'm really touched by that, Natalie. That's so good of them. Gareth's father was one of my teachers at the old grammar school, you know. Goodness, that has restored my faith in human nature."

"Yes, well, you've obviously made some good friends here over the years, Bill. The only person we can't use unfortunately is your doctor, because he appears to be a stranger to you, in spite of all the stress you've been under. I'm going to have to ask you to describe to the jury yourself the stress that occasioned your actions. But don't worry. I'll have you well prepared."

"So how optimistic are you about it all, Natalie?"

"If I can undermine Mr Horseman's statement to the police in front of the jury, I'm very confident. Otherwise it's hard to say. I don't like making predictions."

"The bottom line for me is, Natalie, whether I'm going to prison."

"I realise that, Bill. I can't promise you anything, but I'll do all I can to make sure it doesn't come to that."

"I know you will, Natalie. Whatever happens, I'm determined to remain positive."

"I'm pleased to hear that Bill, because I'm afraid one more cloud has appeared on the horizon."

"That sounds ominous."

"Yes, it's extremely vexing. I received a letter from Tom Wiltshire at Wiltshire, Stanford and Cross last week. That's really why I had to speak to you in person today. Tom is Mr Horseman's solicitor, as you know. Apparently Mr Horseman is determined not to let this terrible incident of Sunday, 7th November rest. You know he lost an eye as a result of that incident, do you?"

"Yes, I heard all about that."

"Well, the CPS has made it clear that it has no case against you, but Mr Horseman intends to sue you, I'm afraid."

"Oh God, no. Why the hell can't Benny just move on from all this?"

"Well, he hasn't had time to come to terms with his injuries yet, I suppose. Maybe he'll have a change of heart once the immediacy of it all has passed."

"So what does it all mean exactly, Natalie?"

"Tom Wiltshire says that Mr Horseman is instructing a barrister and that we'll be hearing from him or her in due course. Tom's doing me a favour really in giving me prior warning of all this. Mr Horseman is suing you for trespass on his land, and for his injuries resulting from an assault."

"But there was no assault."

"Exactly, and hopefully Mr Horseman will receive advice from his silk not to proceed. But Tom tells me off the record that his client is pretty set on going ahead in the face of any advice to the contrary."

"Yes. That sounds like Benny alright. What does all this mean in practical terms, Natalie?"

"It means that we have little or no defence against the claim for trespass. But on its own that's a minor matter that might occasion a token award of damages. The injuries claim is potentially more serious. Tom Wiltshire thinks Mr Horseman wants to sue for a sum above £50,000, which would mean a hearing in a high court."

"Oh my God, Natalie. That sounds really serious."

"Steady on, Bill. Mr Horseman may be scoring an own goal here. We could turn this around to our own advantage."

"How?"

"Well, *we* know there was no assault, and the police and CPS accept that there's no evidence of an assault. Indeed, it was you who called the police and kept Mr Horseman alive until the ambulance arrived. We'll find the people who can verify that. We might even put in a counter claim for the trauma caused to you by Mr Horseman's threats with a loaded shotgun. I shall seek a second opinion on that matter. But whatever happens I think we can use this civil action to help in the criminal case against you."

"In what way, Natalie?"

"Well, let's assume that the civil case comes up before the criminal case at the end of March, and that we win it, as I expect us to. We can use that at your criminal trial to show that Mr Horseman has given false evidence in the past, and that he has ulterior motives for doing so."

"But what if he wins the civil case?"

"I don't think he can, and therein lies his own goal. But I must say that I think it's unlikely the civil case will precede the criminal trial. But that still gives me the chance to cross-examine Mr Horseman about it in March. I think we can show him to be a liar, and that he has a history of giving false statements to the police. It could help you no end, Bill. I hope to see you acquitted in April and then in a good position to counter-sue in the civil case, if we think it advisable."

"Or I could be in Medford prison in March waiting for Benny to sue me for £50,000."

"I do urge you to try to remain positive about all this, Bill."

"Oh, I am, Natalie. I promise you I'm trying. I'm really trying."

Chapter 31

Bill meant what he said in Natalie Barry's office. He was determined to remain positive in spite of the news he had received. He knew it would be unfair to Angie to go back unless he was ready to help her with her problems. And that meant he must come to terms with his situation and do nothing to add to her anxiety.

As he walked through the centre of Bramport towards the bus station, Bill felt sure he could remain positive and optimistic. He knew he was ready to overcome any obstacle to make the future right for him and Angie. He kept rehearsing in his mind his plan to make her strong so that they could be honest and open with one another. So that they could move on and shape a future together which suited them both. The court cases and even prison, if it came to it, were just things they would get through together. He would not let anything beat them.

Bill grew more determined as he walked, and then the sun came out briefly and lifted his mood even further. He even found he was enjoying being back in his home town. He felt better about the place somehow. The last time he was here it had seemed as if every pair of eyes was watching him and judging him, but now the town felt friendly and reassuringly familiar. Perhaps Natalie's news that so many people were willing to stand up for him in court made him realise that he was among friends here after all.

Bill would have welcomed bumping into a familiar face on the way to the bus station, and even stopping for a chat, but he met no one he knew that well. As he waited for a bus to take him to his home in Westgate, Bill thought about phoning Angie to tell her that he was in town a day early, but just then the bus pulled up and he decided against it. He would give her a nice surprise, and if she was not at home he had his own door key anyway.

Bill had not been on a bus in Bramport since he was 19, and only a few short weeks ago he would have been too impatient to have considered it. He would have got a taxi or phoned for a lift. But even in this small way he had changed. He was more flexible and relaxed about such things, and he was more tolerant of himself and other people. As he got nearer to his stop Bill felt excited about the thought of seeing Angie again. It was four weeks since he'd left Bramport to go to Medford, and so much had happened in that time. It was the longest time that he and Angie had ever spent apart, and as he stepped off the bus at the end of his road Bill felt as if he was returning from a long and eventful journey.

He walked past the mock-Georgian houses of Beauchamp Crescent until he came to number 17. It was just starting to get dark. Bill put his holdall on the front door step and rang the bell. For some reason it felt like the right thing to do, rather than barging in unannounced. As he waited he felt unexpectedly nervous.

A light went on in the hallway. The door opened and there was Angie. Her hair was cut in a younger style and she had on more make-up than usual. She had lost some weight and was wearing loose white trousers and a white top, which showed off her figure. Instead of the flat shoes she normally wore indoors she was wearing sandals with a heel. She looked good.

"Bill," she said, "what are you doing here?"

Bill stepped inside and put his arms around her.

"Hello, love, I thought I'd surprise you."

"Well, you've certainly done that," said Angie looking flustered. "You'd better get your bag and come in."

Bill stepped outside again, picked up his bag and followed Angie through to the lounge. All the furniture was arranged differently, and there was a very strong but pleasant smell, which Bill did not recognise.

"I hope it's alright me coming a day early, love," he said.

"Well, it's a bit of a surprise. But don't worry. It'll be okay."

Bill stood in his own front room with his coat on feeling very awkward. Angie also seemed ill at ease, saying nothing, but rubbing her hands together as if to keep warm.

"It's just that I had to see my solicitor unexpectedly this afternoon, and I thought I'd come straight round rather than phone. I'm sorry, Angie. It was obviously a mistake. I should've warned you."

He moved towards her and held her arms gently.

"We don't have to feel awkward with one another, do we?" he said, and he pulled her towards him. "It is lovely to see you, and I must say you look fantastic."

Angie perked up on receiving the compliment.

"I love the new hairstyle, and is this a new outfit?" asked Bill.

"Yes. Are you sure you like it? I thought it was time I had a bit of a makeover. It's all part of self-awareness and a positive self-image. I'll tell you all about it later."

"And you've changed the room around. I like it. And that's new, isn't it?"

"Yes, it's a futon for my shiatsu."

"For your what?"

"Shiatsu. It's a type of Japanese massage to help with anxiety. I'll explain it all later. Can I get you a drink, Bill?"

"A cup of tea would be nice."

"Come through to the kitchen then, and we can carry on talking. Would you like some herbal tea, or just the ordinary?"

"What's the herbal tea?"

"Camomile, mint, or jasmine."

"Since when have you been drinking that stuff, Angie? Don't tell me. Since Stoner's been working his magic."

"Mark recommended it, yes. But I really enjoy it. It's very good for relaxation."

Bill laughed. "No, thanks," he said, "I've been treated to Stoner's tea before. It's taken me this long to get over the last cup."

"It's not that bad," said Angie, and as she spoke she turned and smiled at Bill in a way that seemed almost flirtatious.

"I can't get over how fabulous you look, Angie. I'm so pleased to see you so relaxed."

"I am so much better, Bill, and I really want to stay that way.

You must promise me you won't do anything to upset things this weekend."

"No, of course not, Angie. The exact opposite. I've learnt a lot while I've been away. All I want to do is help us both to be relaxed and happy. I promise you the last thing I want to do is upset you. Or myself, for that matter."

Angie went into the lounge carrying two cups of tea. Bill followed. He stood beside her as she put the drinks on the coffee table. When she stood up he put his arms out and Angie at last responded by stepping towards him and putting her arms around him.

"I'm sorry I've made such a mess of everything," he said. "I just want to make it all up to you, if I can. I'm so pleased to find you so well and so happy."

Angie moved away and sat down in an armchair. Bill sat in the other armchair facing her across the coffee table.

"You look a lot better too, Bill. You seem to have got broader across the shoulders, and you look about ten years younger."

"Thanks, Angie. You're the second beautiful woman to say that to me today."

"Who's the other one?"

"Natalie Barry, my solicitor. Sorry, Angie. I know you don't like me saying things like that. Natalie's alright though."

"No, it's okay, Bill. Comments like that don't upset me like they used to. I'm a bit more relaxed about silly things like that nowadays."

"Is it Stoner that's helped you with all this?"

"Oh, Mark's been marvellous, Bill. I wish I'd listened to him a lot more in the past. He knows so much about everything, and he seems to understand exactly how I feel. I've never felt anyone realised what I was going through before. Not even Doctor Corrigan. Mark seems to be able to share everything with me."

"I know, Angie. He's been like that with me. Sometimes I think he knows more about me than I do myself."

"I don't know what I'd do without him."

"Has he stopped your attacks?"

"I had one just after you left, but I haven't had another all the time you've been away. I'm almost at the stage now where I feel

I could go on without ever having another one. I'm sorry, Bill. But it's the truth."

"No, that's alright, Angie. I'm delighted you can say that. I realise I haven't done much to help you in the past. I want to try and change all that."

"Mark's helped me to understand about my triggers, you see. He's explained it all to me. He says once you understand what causes attacks you can start to control them. He says my main trigger's been my insecurity."

"And how do you control it?"

"It's hard to explain. Mark can do it better than me. Now, let me get this right. It's all about staying in the present moment. I used to be afraid about having attacks in the future… because I remembered how bad they were in the past… even though nothing was happening in the present moment. So really it was my thoughts that were the problem. Thoughts of the past and the future. Does this make sense?"

"Yes, love. It makes perfect sense to me."

"So if I can stand back a bit, I can become aware of my thoughts almost like someone looking in from the outside. I can see that nothing bad is actually happening to me right now. So I just have to stay in the present moment. I mustn't relive past attacks or be afraid of ones that might not even happen in the future."

"It's so wonderful to hear you talking like this, Angie. I understand completely what you're saying. I feel the same in a way. My problem is that I'm always guilty about the past, about something I've said or done. And I've been negative about the future because I didn't like what I saw there. Now I realise that I do have control over my life. I have control over what I do right now in the present. It's the same as you said. We shouldn't live forever controlled by the past or frightened by the future."

"And did Mark teach you that?"

"Not really. I've been doing a lot of thinking while I've been away in Medford. I've had a lot of help from different people, and I think I've helped myself too. I'm so thrilled that we can have a conversation like this, Angie. More than anything I want us to be open and honest with one another. And I want us to be able to help one another."

"I want us to be honest as well, Bill, but I don't want any upset. You must understand that."

"I do, Angie. I promise I won't upset you. Tell me more about how Stoner's helped you."

"Oh, I don't know, Bill. He's helped me so much. He's helped me feel better about myself. About how I see myself. And he's helped me to create a living space where I feel good. And he's helped me to learn how to relax in my own space."

"So that's why you've changed the furniture round?"

"It's about creating space that you've made for yourself."

"And what's that lovely smell? Is that part of it all?"

"Yes, that's my oil burner. It's lavender, sandalwood and nutmeg. It soothes stress."

"I must say, Angie, it is nice. Better than when I used to bring home my smelly old stuff from the coal lorries, eh?"

Angie smiled at him and shook her head.

"Oh, don't remind me of all that, Bill."

"You'd have one basket full of Mickey's nappies and another one full of my stuff caked with coal dust."

"I don't know how I coped with just an old twin tub."

"I can remember you wringing it all out in the bath in the evenings, love. Your hands used to be red-raw."

"And then I'd hang it out to dry in the stairwell."

"And old Mrs Hargreaves came out one night and accused us of running a laundry business in a rented property. Do you remember?"

"Yes, I do. She said she'd report us to the landlord, and so we made up a sign, 'Knight's Dry Cleaning and Laundry Services' or something, and we put it on the main door of the block just to annoy the old bag."

"That's right, Angie. We did. And someone left a bagful of filthy old stuff with a note saying they'd pick it up at six o'clock after work!"

"And I was so embarrassed I washed and ironed it, and you charged them seven and six for it!"

"We must have been mad, Angie. But they were good days, weren't they, love?"

"They were good days, Bill. We had some fun, didn't we?"

They were both laughing and Bill got up and went over to Angie and kissed her on the forehead.

"We did have fun, didn't we, Angie?"

"Of course we did, Bill."

"And I'm bloody determined we're going to have a lot more fun in the future too, Angie. I tell you what; I'm going to pour myself a whisky. Can I get you something, love?"

"Why not, Bill? I'll have a port and lemon, please."

"One port and lemon coming up."

Just then they both heard someone put a key in the lock of their front door. Angie jumped out of her chair and ran into the hall.

"It's alright. Wait. I'm coming," she shouted.

"Hi. Alright, darling?" someone asked her.

"Hello, Mark," Angie said. "Bill's here. He decided to come a day early."

Bill got up and waited for his friend to come into the lounge.

"Hello, Bill. We weren't expecting you 'til tomorrow."

"Hello, Stoner," said Bill, holding out his hand. "Good to see you. Where's Angie gone?"

"I'm here," said a voice from the hallway.

Angie came in and stood just behind Stoner. Bill noticed her rubbing her forehead and looking very red in the face.

"Would you, uh, like a drink, Stoner?" Bill managed to ask. "I was just having a whisky."

"Thanks, my old mate. I'll join you in one. So what brings you down here a day early then, Bill?"

"Had to see my solicitor. Problem with Benny. Won't talk about it just now, if you don't mind. Here's your drink, Stoner. Excuse me a minute both of you. Must pay a visit."

Bill left the room quickly and went upstairs to the bathroom rather than go to the cloakroom in the hall. He locked the door behind him and stood there for a minute catching his breath. He looked around the room. Two toothbrushes. He opened the cabinet above the sink. Shaving stuff. Not his. Roger et Gallet aftershave. Not his either.

Bill walked slowly down the stairs. He was in a daze and could not focus on one particular thought. When he went into the lounge Stoner was sitting on the sofa and Angie was back in her armchair. Stoner was talking to her about nothing in particular, but Angie looked anxious and was not joining in with his attempt to make conversation. Bill picked up his whisky and stood in front of the mantelpiece and the coal-effect gas fire. There were too many thoughts going in and out of his head for him to say anything.

"So have you left Medford for good then, Bill?" asked Stoner.

"Surely Angie's told you, hasn't she, that I'm just back for the weekend?"

"Yeah, that's right. Of course she did. So how are things in Medford with everyone then?"

"I don't know, Stoner. Pretty shitty, I suppose. Just hang on a minute. Let me get this straight. Are you living here now or something?"

"No, of course not, Bill. I've got my own flat. You know that."

"I know you've got a bloody flat, Stoner. That wasn't my bloody question. Are you living here with Angie? You've got a front door key and all your stuff's in my bathroom."

Angie leaned back and put the palm of her right hand against her forehead. "Oh no," she moaned. "I don't want all this."

Stoner leaned towards her as if he wanted to help her. But he was sitting a good eight feet away and could not reach her. He remained leaning towards her as if he was aching to get up but was restrained in his seat.

"It's alright, Angie. Stay calm," he said.

"You haven't answered my question, Stoner. Are you living here in this house with my wife? I'd like a straight answer."

"Okay, Bill. I stay here from time to time." He kept looking over to Angie as if his conversation with Bill was a mere distraction. He looked worried. "If we've been talking or doing some shiatsu or meditation, then sometimes I stay over. Yes."

"And what room do you stay in?"

"I don't know, Bill. What do you want to know exactly?" Stoner could see the clamminess in Angie's face, and that she was starting to take short, shallow breaths.

"I want to know, Stoner, *my old mate*, if you're having an affair with my wife."

"Stop this!" Angie shouted. "I don't want this. Stop it, both of you!" She clasped her chest and fought for breath.

Bill and Stoner both went over to her. Stoner shot forward as if he had been waiting for a starting gun and got there first. Bill stood back feeling useless.

Stoner had his arm around Angie and was coaxing her to her feet.

"Easy, Angie. Easy. We're just going to flow through this together. Remember what I taught you. Breathe in through your nose and push out through your mouth. Let me hear it."

"I can't, Mark." Angie fought to breathe as she spoke. Her face was no longer flushed red. It was deathly white. "I can't.... I can't feel... my hands... my feet... I think... I'm going... crazy."

"No, you're not, Angie. You're absolutely alright. Do everything I say. Feet apart. I've got you. Breathe through your nose, and out through your mouth. Force it out. That's right. Plenty of noise when you force each breath out. That's good. Well done."

Each time Angie breathed in Stoner raised her arms slowly above her head. Angie clasped her fingers and stood there with her hands above her head, palms up and her head tilted back.

"Well done, Angie. One more breath in and then drop your hands to your side and push that air out. Let me hear it."

Angie exhaled with a noise, which pushed out the anxiety and panic from deep within her.

"That's it," said Stoner as he walked Angie up and down. It had taken him only a few minutes to get Angie's breathing back to normal and the colour back into her face.

"Where's your special handkerchief, darling?" he asked her. "I want you to breathe in the lavender."

"In my pocket."

Stoner reached into the right-hand pocket of Angie's trousers and took out her handkerchief. The gesture was natural and intimate, and Bill, who had been looking on with begrudging admiration up to now, saw red.

"I think you can take your hands off my wife now, Stoner. I think I can look after her myself from now on."

"No, Bill. Just be patient, mate. Let's just make sure Angie's alright first. That's the main thing."

"Do you think I don't know that? I'll look after my own wife now, thankyou, Stoner. And if you call her 'darling' again in front of me, I might just smack you in your smug face."

"Stop it, Bill!" said Angie. "Just stop it, will you?"

"I'm sorry, Angie. I just want to look after you myself."

"Well, it's a bit late for that, don't you think?" she said.

And she turned to Stoner, who still had his arm around her, and rested her forehead against his shoulder. "Just make him go away, Mark. Please."

"Him? Is that what I am here now – 'him'? Bloody hell. I can't believe what's going on here. You've got some explaining to do, Stoner."

"I will explain, Bill. I promise. But for Angie's sake, not here, not now, eh? Just leave it for now, and I'll see you at my flat in two hours. I promise, Bill. Two hours. Please. Neither of us wants Angie to have another attack, do we?"

Bill looked at Angie hoping that she would say something to encourage him, but she did not even raise her head from Stoner's shoulder. He looked again at Stoner.

"I'll see you in two hours," Bill said, "and you'd better be there." Then he went into the hall, picked up his holdall and left the two of them together.

Chapter 32

When he reached the end of his road Bill phoned for a taxi, which took him to a pub in a village ten miles out of Bramport. Luckily the lounge bar was deserted, as he was hoping it would be. He ordered a double brandy. He had not managed to drink any of the whisky he had poured himself back at the house, and the thought of his drink sitting on the sideboard in the same room as Angie and Stoner made him spitting mad. Everything had changed so quickly that he was in a state of shock. He realised he had to control his anger before he met Stoner, and he had to stay sober. God knows what he might do if he did not stay calm.

Bill had just one more drink before the same taxi came back as arranged and took him into the centre of Bramport. He checked his watch when he arrived at Stoner's flat in Castle Square. It was 7.20. Nearly two and a quarter hours since he had left them together back in Westgate. He climbed the steps of the Victorian house and pushed the first of three silver buttons.

"Come up," said a voice through the intercom, followed by the sound of the buzzer unlocking the front door.

The stairs up to the second floor were covered with a dirty red carpet. Bill climbed them slowly so that he would not be out of breath when he reached the top. The front door of Stoner's flat had been left wide open. Bill went in, threw his holdall down on the floor of the hallway and pushed the door to. It slammed with more force than he intended, but he did not care.

Stoner was sitting at an old oak table, rolling a cigarette. Bill kept his coat on and stood in the middle of the room.

"I thought you gave those up years ago."

"I did, but I thought it was a good time to take it up again. Do you want one?"

"Nothing in this world would make me touch one of those bloody things."

"You're a funny one, Bill. You're always so keen on being physically fit, but you… No, it doesn't matter."

"Go on. But what?"

"I was going to say, but you're prepared to take so many risks with your mental and emotional health."

"I'd better warn you, Stoner. This isn't a good time for any of your clever bloody insights. I think we'd better have a good look at your bloody character for a change, don't you? What the hell do you think you're playing at?"

"Don't you want to know how Angie is first?"

"Of course I do."

Stoner looked up at him at last.

"I dropped her off at her mother's. Her breathing's better but she's had to take a Valium, which is a real backward step. I should be there really to help her through it."

"You've made yourself that bloody indispensable, have you? My God, Stoner, you're a real snake in the grass. I can't believe you'd betray our friendship like this after all these years."

"It's not about you and me though, Bill, is it? It's about Angie. She's not far off being seriously ill, you know."

"So having sex with her is your miracle cure then, is it, Stoner?"

"It's not like that, Bill."

"Oh, no, I'm sure with you it's all got to have some higher purpose, because you've gained some clever bloody insight the rest of us struggle to understand."

Bill started to pace up and down the room.

"Calm down, Bill."

"No, I won't bloody well calm down. Don't worry. I'm not going to beat the crap out of you, like you think I did with Benny Horseman. I may not have your fine philosophy on life, Stoner, but I'm not a thug."

"I know that."

"For God's sake, Stoner, explain to me why you've done this to me, when you've been my closest friend for all these years."

"It isn't about doing anything to you, Bill. It's about helping Angie."

"But you're the one who's always telling me not to make people dependent on me, and then you do exactly the same thing with Angie."

"Angie won't be dependent on me for long, Bill. Once she's been through the therapy and she has her relaxation techniques all worked out, she won't need anyone but herself. She'll be able to cope on her own."

"But that's what I wanted to do for her. That's why I've come back, for Christ's sake!"

"But I didn't know you were coming back, did I? You made me think you were going to stay in Medford with Hayley. You'd hardly been in touch with anyone here for weeks."

"Don't you try and make me feel guilty about this, Stoner. Don't you use Hayley as an excuse for what you've done. You made me tell you about Hayley when I didn't intend to. What's happening here is not my fault. Not this time."

"But it's no one's fault, Bill. It's just life."

"Don't give me crap like that. Of course this is someone's fault, Stoner. It's your bloody fault, you hypocrite. You've had sex with your best friend's wife!"

"It wasn't meant to be like this, Bill. I went round your place today to pick up my things. I persuaded Angie that she had to give you a chance to put things right. I was going to stay completely out of your way. None of us knew you were coming back today, and Angie wasn't expecting me over until later tonight."

"So screwing my wife was alright as long as I didn't find out, was it? Is that what you're trying to say?"

"Don't keep using expressions like that, Bill. That's not what it's all about."

"Oh, come on, Stoner. Come and join me in the real world, where you have to feel shitty about yourself sometimes. Because you know deep down you've acted like a real bastard.

"You can wrap this up any way you like with your clever philosophy, Stoner, but it comes down to what you know is right and wrong. And you know what you've done is wrong."

"Wrong for you, you mean, Bill?"

"No, you clever bastard, wrong full-stop. All this bollocks about freedom to choose as long as you take the bloody consequences. As far as I can see that's just an excuse to do what the hell you like and not have a conscience about it. We're not free to choose all the time, Stoner, because some things are just not bloody right. Like betraying my trust and our friendship."

"You may not like it, Bill, but I did have a choice about that, and I am prepared to live with the consequences of it. And I know one of those consequences may be the end of our friendship."

"You can be bloody sure that's one of the consequences, Stoner. Nothing you can say to me can excuse what you've done."

"Are you not even going to give me a chance to explain?"

"You can try, but I don't hold out much hope for you."

"I'd like to try anyway, Bill."

Stoner lit his cigarette and took a long draw on it before he spoke.

"Look, it was pretty obvious to me after you went to Medford that Angie's anxiety was bordering on a phobia. And at first I was able to help her just by listening. Once she got to understand why she's felt so anxious for most of her life, the change in her was incredible. You could see that for yourself today. Then it was a case of building on her new confidence and teaching her how to control her anxiety. But at that point I realised that all this was bringing us very close together. Too close really. That's when I phoned you in Medford and told you I needed to see you."

"When you asked me to come back, you mean?"

"That was a week later. You couldn't meet me 'til a week later, remember?"

"Of course I remember. That's when you got me to tell you about Hayley. After that I had no choice but to come back to Bramport."

"But I didn't know you'd decided that. I thought you were staying there with her. You were telling me how much in love with her you were, and how much better your life was there."

"Well, that sure as hell turned out to be true, didn't it?"

316

"I was just really worried for Angie, Bill. I could see how hurt she was going to be when you left her. So I decided it was better in a way if I stopped holding back."

"So you thought I'd given you the excuse you needed to come back here and start having sex with your patient."

"You've got a nasty streak in you, Bill. Do you know that?"

"Funny thing, Stoner, but sometimes people do things that bring the nastiness out in me."

"But why do you have to keep bringing it all down to sex all the time? My relationship with Angie isn't about that."

"What the hell is it about then?"

"For me it's about helping her with her illness. That's all I care about. It's about Angie learning to understand herself and accepting herself. I know Angie doesn't love me, but she needs me at the moment. When she doesn't need me any more I'll be gone."

"Do you love her?"

"Of course I love her. I've always loved her."

"What, all these years?"

"Yes, but I would never have done anything about it, or said anything."

"Bloody hell, Stoner. You've been a right cuckoo in the nest, haven't you? You were the best man at our bloody wedding!"

"You've never had anything to worry about, Bill. Angie's always loved you. Everyone could see that. She still loves you now, but she's always been so insecure about you. You said yourself she's always been afraid you'd leave her."

"But I never would. I've come back now, haven't I? She must know I'd never really leave her."

"But you've always treated her like a child, Bill. Like a troublesome child. You've always made her feel like a liability getting in your way."

"She told you that, did she?"

"She had to admit it to herself, Bill, so she can understand her feelings and move on."

"And you treat her differently, I suppose, do you?"

"I do, yes. I treat her like an independent adult who's ill and who needs help."

"You know, you're doing it again, Stoner, you clever bastard. You're starting to make all this into my fault."

"Stop trying to see everything in terms of blame, Bill. None of us will ever get anywhere like that."

"But there is blame, you devious sod. You're to blame for what you've done. You're just trying to stand right and wrong on its head, by proving there's some great life-affirming principle involved here. But there isn't. In the end it's just a simple case of a sad bastard cadging sex off a vulnerable woman."

Stoner pushed his chair back as if he was about to stand up, but then he thought better of it. The fingertips of his left hand tapped furiously on the table as he spoke.

"Now hold on, Bill, you're going too far now. You know I'm not capable of something like that."

"I don't know what you're capable of any more."

"Well, let me ask you a question for a change, Bill. Why exactly did you decide to come back to Bramport?"

"You know bloody well why. I wanted to help Angie."

"But why did you want to help her?"

"Because I love her, of course, and because I felt bad towards her after what you told me."

"But you loved Hayley and you didn't stay with her."

"I felt bad about leaving her too, but not half as bad as I did towards Angie."

"So your decision was based on feeling guilty towards Angie?"

"I suppose so. But there's nothing wrong with feeling some guilt, Stoner. I wish you'd damn well feel some now."

"So you came back because you love Angie. You also love Hayley but you feel more guilty towards Angie so that has the bigger pull on you. Besides it's your duty as a husband to be with her, I suppose. "

"You can throw that in if you like. There's nothing wrong with acting in a decent way, Stoner."

"There is in my book if it's just driven by guilt and feeling bad towards people. You sound like a damned robot that's programmed to act with no real feeling. Where's your feeling, man? Where's your compassion? Where are *you* in all this? People don't get the

318

real you, do they, Bill? They get this husk that acts out of guilt and duty. It's mean and it's condescending, and as far as I'm concerned Angie deserves a whole lot more than you're offering her."

Bill stood in the centre of the room, his hands deep in his coat pockets, hunched over and red in the face, but saying nothing.

"Do you remember when you were staying here in my flat a few weeks ago, Bill? I asked you a question about Benny. Do you remember?"

"Vaguely."

"It was when you found out that Benny had lived a miserable life because of the way his father treated him. Benny hadn't been able to enjoy a penny of the money he'd made out of Horseman's."

"I remember well enough. You asked me if I felt better knowing Benny was an even bigger loser than me?"

"I think I used the word 'victim'. Did you feel better knowing Benny was a bigger victim in all that business than you? That was the question. Did you ever work out an answer?"

"Yes, I did. Knowing Benny had a crap life helped me feel better about the crap I was in. But that's just human nature, Stoner. I don't see that makes me any different from most other people, and I don't see what the hell it's got to do with what's going on here now."

"I think it's got lots to do with it, Bill. Just tell me one more thing, will you? Did you feel anything else about Benny after you found out in that wood what a damaged person he was?"

"I don't know. I suppose I did. I suppose I felt bad about always hating him so much, when he'd been so bloody miserable all his life."

"So you even felt guilty towards Benny Horseman in the end then?"

"I suppose so. But I think I might get over that easily enough now."

"But don't you see all of these feelings are doing you no good, Bill. You can't base all your decisions and actions on the level of guilt you feel towards people. It's not fair on you and it's not fair on them. Not Benny, not Angie, not Hayley, not anyone. People need your compassion not your guilt. They don't want you to feel bad about them. They want you to feel good about them."

Bill stood up straight, took his hands out of his pockets and started to do up the buttons of his outdoor coat.

"You know, you really piss me off, Stoner," he said. "I've had enough of your bloody lectures and your bloody wisdom. I came back here to Bramport feeling good about everyone and everything. I just wanted to make things work out, that's all. I know my feelings about all of this are right, whatever you might say. But I've had enough of it all. Tell Angie I'm really sorry to leave her again, but I'm going back to Medford. I'm sure you'll be happy enough to look after her, won't you, Stoner… my old mate?"

Bill went out into the hall and picked up his bag. Stoner followed him and Bill was sure that his friend was about to say something, but all he heard was the door closing behind him. Bill went straight to the train station and caught the 21.17 back to Medford.

Chapter 33

Bill could not go to Liz's when he got back to Medford. She was not expecting him until Sunday evening and he could not face the explanations he would have to give if he walked in now. He also knew that he could not go back to Hayley. They had parted with such optimism and she had shown such faith in him. This would be her last day of working at the café before she started full-time rehearsals for the pantomime next week. If ever he saw her again it would not be just to use her for shelter and to comfort his wounded pride.

From the station Bill walked in to the city centre and booked into the Ibis Hotel for two nights. He decided he would say nothing at all to Liz, but just turn up as usual on Sunday evening as if he had spent the weekend he had originally planned. And he would not worry about the expense of the hotel either, since he would not be sending Angie back any more money from now on. If Stoner had taken his place in their house he could take care of the damned bills as well.

Bill bought a half bottle of Teacher's when he got off the train, and he drank most of it in his room before he went to bed. But he still spent a restless night. He could not get the image of Angie's intimacy with Stoner out of his head, and again and again he turned over and sat up in bed trying to come to terms with it. He knew he was being a hypocrite after his own relationship with Hayley, but this was not about Angie and someone he did not know. It was with Stoner, their closest friend, and it was not about coming to terms with just the last two weeks. It felt like a betrayal that tainted more than 30 years of his life.

As he sat on the bed looking out over Medford at three in the morning Bill felt more insecure than he had ever done in his life. Whatever problems and frustrations they might have had together, he had always had Angie. Now at this very moment she was with someone else, and it undermined the bedrock of his life. His boys felt further away from him, and his home had just vanished. Where did he belong now? Where was home? Everything in his life would have to be redefined.

Bill was relieved when the morning came, and the daylight brought some respite from the insecurity. He knew he could not spend the whole day alone with his thoughts, so at ten to eight he made the short walk to the town hall to meet the minibus to the Meads. The Meads seemed the best place to keep out of everyone's way, and there was always plenty of banter to stop you from brooding. All of the lads on the site must have had their own private problems and worries at some time, but there was no place for such things once they all got together. The banter came in thick and fast, and in many ways it was a good therapy if you could handle it.

As soon as they saw Bill waiting outside the town hall in his weekend clothes again, it started.

"Aye, aye, Bill. Been out all night on the razzle again then, have we?" shouted someone from the back of the van.

"I don't know what look you were going for this morning, Bill, but I think you missed it, mate."

"Morning, lads," Bill said as he climbed aboard.

"Oo wuz the lucky girl, Bill?" asked Scouser. "'Cos you know, lads, the last judy I saw wi' Bill got kicked out the zoo 'cos she scared the frigg'n animals."

Bill searched for a quick answer but none came. It was not a good idea to enter a verbal battle with Scouser unarmed, and he was relieved when Tony entered the fray for him.

"I met a girl last night who says she knows you, Scouser," Tony said. "Says she's always seeing you at the place she works."

"Oh, yeah. What does she do then, Tone?" asked Scouser, his curiosity raised.

"She's a receptionist down the clap clinic," said Tony, and the laughter of everyone in the bus at last made Bill smile.

The day at the Meads was as good as any day was going to be in the circumstances. Bill would have worked there for nothing just to keep himself occupied, but in fact he was earning time and a half, and tomorrow he would be on double time. In his whole life this was the first day's work that Bill had ever done just to earn money for himself and no one else, and it was a strange feeling.

Just after six he entered the lobby of the hotel and went into the bar for a beer before going up to his room. As he looked around in the bar he realised he was anonymous, and that no one in his life knew where he was, and no one would be looking for him. What was it that made a person independent, he wondered? Was it when no one was dependent on you, or was it when you were not dependent on anyone else?

Bill took his drink and sat at a corner table studying his glass. Only one week ago tonight he had been at the opera with Hayley and he had felt wanted by her. But he always understood that she never needed him. It was her decision not to need anyone for now. But he really felt that Angie needed him and depended on him, and although it weighed heavily on him sometimes, it had always been a central fact of his life. Now not having one single person dependent on him felt just as bad as having too many.

And he blamed Stoner for the situation this time and not himself. Maybe he should have gone home sooner, but how could he possibly have guessed that Stoner would betray him like that? Stoner had robbed him and Angie of the chance of reaching a new phase in their lives, where they could have needed one another without being too dependent on one another. Bill would never forgive him for that.

Bill took his mobile from his pocket and switched it on. He had to call Dave and Mickey and his parents to let them know he would not be seeing them that weekend. When he entered his pin a text message appeared. It was from Stoner.

"Angie much better. But very worried about u. R u ok?"

Bill stood up, downed his pint and stabbed out a reply. It read, "What the hell do you think?"

Back in his room Bill sat on the bed and phoned Dave. When his son answered Bill could hear cheering in the background.

"Hello, Dave's Fish and Chips."

"I'll have a large cod with mushy peas, please."

"Nice one, Dad. Speak up, will you? I'm in the pub watching the rugby. Hold on a minute, I'll go outside... That's better. I'm out in the car park. What'ya doing then? I just phoned you at home to see if you wanted to come down here for a pint. Mum says you're back in Medford. Everything's alright, is it?"

"Yeah, everything's alright, Davie. I'm sorry to disappoint you, son, but I had to come back. Mum doesn't find it very easy with me around at the moment with the court case and everything."

"You can spare me the details, Dad. We all know what Mum can be like."

"It's not her fault, Dave. She's working hard to get better and I don't want to do anything to upset her."

"I hope it's got nothing to do with that Mark fella who's always sniffing around. He's a bit of a creep, if you ask me."

"No, he's helping your mum out a lot, Dave. I think it's best to let Mum sort herself out. As long as she gets better. That's the only important thing."

"Okay, Dad. Whatever you say's fine by me. Listen, would you like me to come up and see you in Medford. I don't like the thought of you being up there on your own."

"I'm fine, Dave. I've got Auntie Liz and Jon and Susie. But I'd love to see you if you can."

"Okay, Dad. I'll give you a bell about it next week. I can pick your brains about the new business. It's going really well."

"That's great, son. I'll look forward to hearing all about it."

"By the way, Dad. Before you go. How do you spell 'cod'?"

"C-o-d."

"You forgot the 'f'."

"There's no 'f' in 'cod'."

"Yeah, I'm sorry about that. Bye, Dad."

"Bye, son," said Bill, with a big smile on his face.

Dave had set up on his own after he left Horseman's. He was selling security systems for homes and businesses and he drove around in a van with the slogan, 'I'll alarm you but my prices won't' on the side. Dave was a natural salesman and Bill was very proud of him. He was proud of both his sons who were now each running their own business. Bill liked to think that maybe their sense of adventure and enterprise was something he had passed on. But who could tell? At least both his sons had the sense to keep the money from their own hard work and not give it all to someone else.

Mickey was not in when Bill phoned him.

"He's out on a rewiring job," explained Cheryl.

"What, at this time on a Saturday night?" Bill asked her.

"You know what Mick's like. He works all hours. He's been out all day."

"He always was a hard-working boy, Cheryl. How are you both?"

"I'm fine, Bill. I'm 15 weeks now. I'll be into maternity clothes soon."

"And you're feeling good, are you? Not working too hard at that nursery?"

"No, I'm really fit and healthy. Dear old Mick is so excited. I think that's why he's working so hard now. He wants to be able to have some time later with the baby."

"He's a sensible man. I wish I'd spent more time with my boys when they were younger."

"Well, whatever you and Angie did must've been right, Bill. There's no better man than my Mick. And I've got a feeling Dave's going to make a pretty good uncle too. He's a bit off the wall maybe, but I'm sure the baby will get down to his level. I've got a feeling Dave's going to be marvellous with children."

"Thanks, Cheryl. It's nice to hear you say all that."

"Mick's going to be really disappointed to have missed you, Bill. But you're coming round tomorrow, aren't you?"

"I'm sorry, Cheryl, but I'm afraid I won't be able to make it. That's why I'm phoning. I'm not in Bramport. I've had to come back to Medford."

"Oh, no. Mick will be disappointed. He was only saying the

other day how much he missed seeing you. Do you want to leave him a message, or anything?"

"You could tell him how wonderful I think he is, and how proud of him I am. And of you, Cheryl."

"Okay, Bill. I will. Are you alright? You sound a bit upset or something."

"I'm a bit tired, Cheryl, that's all. I'll call again soon, alright?"

"Okay, Bill. Take care."

Bill struggled to finish the call. He was ashamed of himself for ever thinking that there was no one now who really needed him. His boys would always need him and he would always need them. It did not matter what happened with Angie or with Stoner. This was something that no one could ever break. And when Mickey's baby was born there would be a new bond with his grandchild that no one would be able to break either.

Bill felt that he had some peace at last. He lay on the bed with the mobile in his hand and he closed his eyes. He had to phone Peg and Wilf, but he would leave it a few minutes first to regain his composure. When he opened his eyes again there was no noise in the hotel or outside in the street, and it took him several moments to work out where he was, and what he was doing there. He looked at his watch. It was 5.30. He had been asleep for over ten hours.

Bill was not able to phone his parents until his lunch break at the Meads at 12.30. He knew his mother would be busy preparing Sunday lunch and that she hated being interrupted, but he took the chance that his dad might answer. When he heard Peg's voice Bill's heart sank, knowing there was no chance she would make things easy for him.

"It makes no difference to me, William, but your father's going to be very disappointed."

"But you're not, eh, Mum?"

"I've learnt not to let things disappoint me, William. Or to expect too much of people."

"I'm really sorry, Mum. Like I said, Angie and I are going through a bad time at the moment. I just couldn't stay there."

"That shouldn't mean you can't come over and see your father and me. None of you seem to make any effort with us any more. It's all self, self, self."

"I know, Mum, it is bad of me. I'm sorry. Please trust me though. I had no choice."

"None of you do when it comes to thinking of us. That's your trouble. And I've got the Christmas presents for Liz and her two here. I wanted you to take them back to Medford with you."

"Oh hell, I really am sorry, Mum. I'll send you the postage. Will that help?"

"Don't bother. I'll work it out somehow. I can't stay here talking, Bill. I've got the carrots to do."

"Can I speak to Dad? It'd be nice to have a chat with him. I'd like to explain to him what's happened."

"He's not here."

"Where is he?"

Bill could hear his mother tutting.

"He's where he always is. In his shed. He's been in there for well gone an hour. He won't be out before one. And he thinks you're going to be here then."

"Oh, damn. I feel terrible, Mum. Can you get him for me?"

"No, I can't, William. I've got the dinner to see to. You're just like your father. You want waiting on hand and foot."

"Okay, Mum. Tell him I called, will you? And that I'm sorry to disappoint him. I'll call again in a few days."

"I'll tell him, but he's going to be very upset. I don't know why, but this has always been your problem, William."

"What has?"

"You never think of other people."

Bill walked into Liz's house that evening as if everything was normal, but as soon as his sister started to ask questions about his weekend he knew he had to tell her about the rift with Angie, although for now he decided to say nothing about her involvement with Stoner. Liz was shocked, and she was anxious to sympathise with Bill, but that was exactly what he was hoping to avoid. Sometimes the only need he had was to remain private, and at those times he could not stand people fussing over him. Later as he sat in his room he worried that he might have been too dismissive towards his sister.

The routine of work carried on as normal that week. There was no chance they could possibly finish the show house by the Christmas break, and the strain on Tony was making him short-tempered with everyone. Bill felt for him. He had spent enough sleepless nights over the years worrying about deadlines to know what Tony was going through. If Tony only knew how far the show house differed from the original Horseman plans, Bill doubted whether the poor man would ever get any sleep again. Bill still lived with the dilemma of whether to tell Tony about the discrepancies, but it would mean explaining his whole background with Horseman's to everyone and that was exactly what he was trying to get away from.

Every time they broke for tea or for lunch Bill checked his phone to see if there was any message from Angie, or maybe even from Hayley. But there was nothing. Everyone was getting on with their lives without him, and Bill felt that his own life was standing still again. All he could do now was wait for his court cases before he could make any plans for the future. It was as if the world was going on around him, but that he was not part of it.

All the talk was of Christmas and the millennium celebrations at New Year. Swallow originally planned to shut the site down from Christmas Eve until Monday January 10th, but they were so far behind that it was decided to open again on the third of January and offer everyone double time for that week. Everyone jumped at the chance and spirits were pretty high on the day it was announced. Bill was pleased enough about the money, but the real relief for him came at having one week less with time on his hands to spend brooding about Angie and Stoner and Medford Prison.

Chapter 34

Bill did not hear one word from Angie and it seemed unlikely now that he would be going back to Bramport for Christmas. Dave was going skiing with a group of his friends, Mick and Cheryl were going to her parents, and it did not occur to Wilf or Peg that Bill might want to go there. They had their routine and had chosen to spend every Christmas on their own for nearly 30 years. Then Liz announced that Steve was coming home at Christmas and that she was expecting it to be a permanent move, and Bill realised that things were not looking too festive for him in Medford either.

Liz, Mickey and Dave all offered to include Bill in their Christmas plans somehow, but he reassured all of them that he was fine and that he had a lot of things going on with friends from work. He also persuaded Liz that he had been intending for some time to find a place of his own in Medford, and the following weekend he started looking. Bill had hoped to find a flat somewhere, but with two months' rent in advance, a month as a deposit and an agency fee, the cost alone meant it was out of the question.

Eventually Bill did find some accommodation he could move into right away, and on the Saturday night he took home a bottle of wine to Liz to 'celebrate'. He told her how lucky he was to have found such a nice place so quickly and how excited he was by the challenge of making it into a nice home for himself. Liz was relieved that he was so positive and that he had found something so good at such short notice. She even got out a double duvet cover for the bed and a throw for the sofa that Bill described with such enthusiasm.

He had a real job persuading her not to get out saucepans, utensils and a baking tray for his kitchen, but eventually amidst a lot of laughter she relented. It was just as well too, because Bill's new place did not have a kitchen. It did not have a sofa either, come to that. Or a double bed.

The only accommodation Bill had been able to find five days before Christmas at a price he could afford was a bedsit around the corner from Roly Upperton's place. It was in an old Edwardian terrace that had seen much better days. The room itself was dark and cramped and had only a single bed, two old armchairs and a coffee table. There was a single aluminium sink on a kitchen unit against one wall and next to it on an old fridge stood a plug-in hob with two electric rings. The only heating was provided by an electric fire that swallowed pound coins faster than a fruit machine.

On the next landing was a bathroom which Bill shared with the tenants of the other seven bedsits. It was far from ideal, but the landlord only wanted one week in advance plus one week as a deposit and it was available right away. Bill had no intention of staying there longer than a few weeks, but for now it gave him some independence, and if he exaggerated the amenities of the place just a little it stopped people worrying about him.

Bill moved out of Liz's house on the Monday before Christmas. Liz was keen on having a look at Bill's new home, but he asked her to wait until after the New Year to give him a chance to 'smarten it up a little bit'. One thing Liz did insist on was taking Bill out for a Christmas treat. She explained that he would be doing the whole family a favour if he accepted, because the children thought they were too old now for this family tradition, but they would certainly come along if Uncle Bill was going too. Liz also insisted on keeping it a secret, but she asked Bill to be at her house by 6.45 on Wednesday evening. When he arrived Liz was in the hallway with her coat on ready to face the December cold.

"So, what is it, Liz? A visit to Santa's grotto?"

"I'm only telling you once you promise not to back out."

"Okay. I give in. I promise. Where are you taking us?"

"The panto, Bill. *Cinderella* at the Theatre Royal."

Bill looked shocked and mumbled something incoherent.

"It's not that bad, Bill, for goodness sake! Some friends at work went on Saturday and said it was really good. Mandy Miller's in it."

"No... uh... no, Liz, it's a... it's a nice idea."

"I don't know what's wrong with all of you. Honestly, you're a right bunch of killjoys. I've got the tickets now. We've got to go."

"No, Liz. I'm sorry. It's a great idea. Come on. Get the kids. It'll be wonderful."

By the time they got to the theatre it had sunk in with Bill that he was going to see Hayley again, and he was behaving like a child whose nervousness made him overexcited. He was certainly confusing Liz.

"I don't know, Bill. One minute you act as if I'd invited you to a funeral, and the next minute anyone would think going to the panto was one of your life's ambitions."

"Perhaps it is, Liz. I love the theatre."

"Do you?" asked Liz, puzzled by a side of her brother she had not known about before.

"Could I have a programme, please, Uncle Bill?" asked Susie.

"And some sweets," chimed in Jonathan.

Bill put an arm around each of them and ushered them towards the kiosk in the foyer.

"I'll tell you what. We'll have a programme each as a souvenir," he said, "and it's my treat for whatever sweets anyone wants."

Bill looked back over his shoulder at Liz, as if seeking her consent. At first she shook her head at her brother in mock annoyance, but then she gave him a broad smile that signalled her approval and her relief.

They took their seats in the third row of the upper circle and Bill looked through the programme to find details of the cast. And there on page five was a black and white photo of Hayley McKenna staring back at him.

'Hayley McKenna – Prince Rupert (Principal Boy). Hayley is a graduate of the Metropolitan School of Dramatic Art. In 1993 she won the prestigious Grosvenor Prize for Music (Classical Guitar) and in 1994 she won a bursary to study at the Actors' Workshop in New York. Hayley has appeared in musicals and repertory theatre in Bristol, Leeds, Doncaster and Brighton. Her TV credits include appearances in Grange Hill, Byker Grove, the Bill and Colby Street. This is Hayley's first production with the Limelight Players.'

As the theatre filled and the time approached curtain-up Bill felt very nervous for her. He imagined Roly backstage being obnoxious to Mandy Miller and Giles after having had one too many of his specials, and he could see Hayley trying frantically to calm everyone down. Bill felt a nudge from Liz who pointed to his hands and gave him another quizzical look. Bill realised that he had his fingers crossed.

"It's an old theatrical tradition," he said without conviction, and Liz's confusion over her brother's behaviour grew.

Bill need not have worried. From the moment the orchestra started to play and the curtain rose the fun started and did not stop. And there was Hayley in the very first scene with her father, King Cuthbert the Convivial, discussing the need for the prince to find a bride. Within minutes Hayley was singing 'I need a bit of Erica in my life…' from *Mambo Number 5* and the stage was soon full of courtiers dancing the mambo with a brass section behind them. The audience was clapping along and one or two revellers in the front of the stalls were already on their feet dancing to the Latin beat. It was a risk by Giles to attack the audience so early on, but the gamble worked. Hayley, dressed in traditional tights and short tunic, drove the number along, working the audience and the stage as she went, and at the end of it the whole auditorium applauded wildly.

The mood was set. The production kept strictly to the traditional *Cinderella* story, but Giles played to his strengths and brought in as many musical numbers as he could. Mandy Miller managed to be sweet and innocent but voluptuous at the same time, and Giles chose songs for her that came with a lot of backing support, so none of the momentum was ever lost. The stage management was slick and dynamic, and the transformation scene where pumpkin, mice and rags turned to a carriage with horses and a beautiful ball gown left the audience gasping. There was a collective 'Aah' as four Shetland ponies and a gold carriage appeared in seconds from behind a cloud of smoke, with Cinderella standing beside it dressed immaculately with an extravagant coiffure. Bill never did work out how it was done.

Roly Upperton was a revelation. He doubled as the dame and Cinderella's wicked stepmother and this gave him the most difficult job of all, because he had to maintain a fine balance between comedy and villainy. He had to bully the unfortunate Cinderella, which he seemed to enjoy, but to achieve the comedy he had to keep the warmth and sympathy of the audience. And Roly played the audience like the old pro he was. He insulted them, took them into his confidence, made them laugh, and made them love him one minute and hate him the next. He brought children from the audience onto the stage and had everyone singing along to *Always Look on the Bright Side of Life* with the words changed to make fun of the fears everyone had about the millennium bug. As Bill watched Roly in total control of nearly 1,000 people of all ages he finally understood what Hayley meant by the addictive power of performance.

The first act ended with the ball at the prince's castle, and the music and dancing on stage had everyone in the audience singing, swaying and clapping along. Then the clock struck midnight, and after several more millennium jokes Cinderella disappeared into the night, leaving the prince in the middle of the stage. Slowly the other members of the cast slipped away, the lights went down, the audience went silent, and alone under a single spotlight Hayley started to sing.

'Midnight, not a sound on the pavement...' she started. Bill knew he was going to struggle with this. 'Memory. All alone in the moonlight. I can smile at the old days...' Her voice was clear and pure but it had a strength that gave her total control. 'Daylight. I must wait for the sunrise. I must think of a new life and I mustn't give in...' Bill felt his own control slipping away as he thought of Angie and Hayley and all that he had lost. The song reached a crescendo and Hayley hit the note perfectly. 'Touch me, it's so easy to leave me, all alone with the memory of my days in the sun..." Bill gritted his teeth so hard that his jaw ached and his neck nearly went into spasm. Then it was over. The spotlight went out, the curtains went across and Hayley was gone. The audience started to applaud and showed no signs of wanting to stop until the lights in the theatre went up and a gentle murmuring and shuffling took over.

Bill wiped his eyes as if in reaction to the light. "Who fancies a drink?" he asked as he looked down pretending to search for something on the floor.

"I fancy an ice cream," said Jon.

"Please," Liz corrected him.

"Ice creams all round then," Bill said.

"Yes, please. Raspberry ripple tubs, please, Uncle Bill."

"I'll get them," offered Susie, "if I can have the money. I want to walk about a bit."

Bill stood up with Liz to let Susie past. He wiped his eyes again and shook his head as if he could shake away some of his emotions.

"Are you alright, Bill?" Liz asked him. "You are enjoying it, are you?"

"Absolutely, Liz," he answered, and for the most part it was the truth. But it was hard to enjoy completely something that threatened at any time to expose his rawest emotions.

"I actually think it's fantastic," he added.

"So do I," said Jonathan. "I like the fat man in drag best."

"He's called the dame, Jon," said Bill.

"I think the girl playing the prince is wonderful," said Liz. "She's got a fabulous singing voice, and she's a great dancer."

"She's a great musician too," said Bill a little too enthusiastically.

"I don't remember her playing any instruments."

"No, but I'm sure I read it somewhere in the programme."

Susie returned with the ice creams just before the curtain rose again.

If anything the second half was even more of a spectacle than the first. You had to hand it to Giles. He knew how to target an audience and keep everyone happy.

There were acrobats performing at the castle for the crestfallen prince, and a suicidal knife-juggling act by Buttons to amuse Cinderella. Bill noticed that Mandy Miller stood well to one side for this scene and he did not blame her. There were lots of 'oohs' and 'aahs' from the audience, and a lot of people turned away as blood poured from Buttons' hands. It ended with each knife soaring into the air and landing point first into the stage floor in quick succession like the rat-tat-tat-tat of a machine gun. Then a towel was thrown onto the stage and Buttons wiped his hands to show that he had no real injuries at all, and the audience applauded loudly with admiration and relief.

But for real showmanship no one could upstage Roly Upperton. He invited people up from the audience, and they must have been stooges because Roly subjected them to one of the messiest and funniest slapstick routines that Bill had ever seen. At this point he looked over at Susie, Jon and Liz and saw all three rocking back and forth with laughter as a well-dressed lady of middle age received yet another custard pie full in the face.

Roly was a hard act to follow but Hayley managed it. Giles planned the music so well that it gave the show pace and continuity all evening, and it was so well performed that the mood in the theatre could be changed in an instant by it. And the musical star of the show was undoubtedly Hayley McKenna. She played the harpsichord, serenaded Cinderella on the guitar, and sang and danced for all she was worth. When she performed a duet of *Love Changes Everything* with Cinderella's father, Baron Hardup, the harmony of their strong soprano and tenor voices brought the longest and loudest applause of the night so far.

Then came the finale. As the prince placed the slipper on Cinderella's foot the scenery that was the drab kitchen in Hardup Hall transformed itself before the audience's eyes into the sumptuous luxury of the ballroom at King Cuthbert's castle. It was unusual for an audience to applaud a scene change, but this transformation deserved it. A fireplace became a grand staircase, a large old dresser rose and became a balcony and huge chandeliers appeared from nowhere. Then the prince appeared with Cinderella in glittering clothes, and they walked slowly down the staircase for the wedding scene to even more applause from the audience.

The wedding celebrations brought more singing and dancing from the main players until gradually the whole cast was involved, and the music became faster and louder. Eventually the audience at the front were on their feet as Hayley led everyone from sing-along to rock and roll. The energy was contagious and those in the audience who could not get up and dance were clapping and singing in their seats. As the last bars of the final number were played the whole cast came forward and took a bow and the whole of the audience stood and applauded. Bill held his hands in the air and clapped as hard as he could.

"Well done, Hayley! he shouted. "Well done."

Then the cast stepped back and the principals came forward one by one, until finally the prince and Cinderella took their bow together. Bill nearly called out again but thought better of it. Hayley looked around the theatre to acknowledge the applause, and then she looked up. For a moment Bill imagined she was looking at him, and at that moment Hayley waved. Bill was about to wave back, but then he realised she could not possibly have singled out any one face in the darkened auditorium. His euphoria slowly faded as the curtain fell and the applause died. As the lights killed the illusion it felt as if he had lost Hayley all over again.

After Susie and Jon had gone to bed Bill and Liz stayed up for a nightcap, and Bill decided it was the right time to tell Liz the whole story about Hayley and Angie. Liz listened and for once she was speechless.

"You must say something, Liz, even if it's to tell me what a bloody fool I've been."

"I'm still trying to catch my breath. I don't know what's shocked me most. You and that beautiful young girl tonight, or Angie and Mark Stone."

"To be fair on Angie, Liz, her affair with Stoner started after me and Hayley."

"I thought you said she doesn't know about Hayley."

"She doesn't unless Stoner's told her. But I don't think he will."

"Well, then she can't use what you did as an excuse for her affair, can she? Stop taking all the blame, Bill. You're always letting Angie off the hook like that."

"But it was my feelings for Hayley that stopped me going back to Bramport when I should've done, Liz. Angie and Stoner would never have happened if I'd gone back right away."

"It's no good, Bill. You're always taking responsibility off Angie and putting it all on yourself. You've got to stop doing it."

"So you don't condemn me for Hayley then, Liz? I thought you would."

"No, silly, I don't condemn you. A few months ago I might've done. Six months ago I would've taken all adulterers out and shot the damn lot. But I know now if I'm going to take Steve back this week I've got to try to understand it all a bit more."

"Don't ask me to explain any of it to you, Liz. I'm totally bloody confused by what makes people do what they do. Including me."

"It doesn't take a lot of working out why a man would be attracted to that girl in the show tonight."

"Believe it or not, Liz, I resisted her at first. I've never been unfaithful to Angie, nor wanted to. But it wasn't just about Hayley being beautiful."

"What was it then?"

"Oh, I don't know. I suppose she saw things in me that I hoped were there but couldn't ever be sure were worth anything. Hayley persuaded me that all my dreams and ideas about life weren't just a waste of bloody time. When someone believes in you that much, it's pretty powerful stuff. Especially at my stage of life."

"We're not old."

"No, I know we're not, Liz, but it's pretty damned amazing that a girl like that saw so much in me."

Liz laughed.

"Dear Bill, you don't understand women very much, do you?"

"Don't I?"

"No. I'll tell you what Hayley saw in you. First of all, you're a very good-looking man, but leave that aside. Women like men who make them feel good about themselves. Men who are interested in them. I'm sure Hayley gets certain types ogling her all the time and wanting to impress her. And then along comes Bill Knight. Unassuming but confident, always vulnerable but at the same time always strong and dependable. And very appreciative of her, not only because of how she looks, but because of who she is. She'd love you for it. Especially if you never pressured her, which of course, my lovely brother, you never would."

Bill looked at Liz and smiled. "You couldn't write all that down for me, could you, Liz?" he said, and they both laughed.

"So there's definitely no future for you together then, Bill?"

"With Hayley? No, at least not any future I can see at this moment. You saw her tonight, Liz. Hayley's really going places and I've got this Benny Horseman business to get over first."

"And what about you and Angie?"

"I think I'm where you were with Steve a few months ago. I'm too bloody angry at the moment to think too clearly about it. But I'm more angry with Stoner than I am with Angie. Angie and I both put our trust in him, and he used that trust to come between us. I'm as shocked about all that as you are."

"He was always turning up on your doorstep whenever he came back to Bramport, wasn't he? You don't think he and Angie…?"

"No, I don't, Liz. I just think Angie's become more and more vulnerable because of the business with the money and everything, and that gave Stoner his chance."

"What a rotten sod he's been to you."

"Yeah, he has. But I've also got to admit he's making Angie a lot better."

"Maybe you're better off leaving them to it, Bill."

"I don't think I've got much choice at the moment. But you know, Liz, as strong as my feelings are for Hayley and as much as I know I'm going to miss her, I still feel that Angie and I belong together. Hayley and I left one another because we both needed to, so there's sadness there but there's no pain. This thing with Angie and Stoner feels like my insides have been ripped out."

"I think I know all about that, Bill."

"I know, Liz, I'm sorry."

"No, don't apologise. In many ways all this is helping me. If I can understand what you did and not condemn you, there's a good chance I'll understand what Steve did one day."

"I hope so."

"And what you say about belonging together is true too. Steve belongs here with me and the children. But it's a bit different with your two being grown up, I suppose."

"I'm not so sure about that, Liz. I think Mickey and Dave would still be hurt if Angie and I got divorced. Even at their age."

"It won't all come to that, Bill. But whatever happens you mustn't put all the blame onto yourself. I know you too well."

Liz got up and went over to Bill and kissed his head.

"Come on, Bill. We'll never get to work in the morning. You can stop over if you like."

"No, Liz, I'll get back. I quite like my new place," he lied.

"Now, Bill, are you absolutely sure you won't come and spend Christmas with us? I can't stand the thought of you being on your own."

"No, Liz. Don't worry. I've been invited out by some people from work," he lied again. "Besides, it's really important that Steve has you and the children all to himself. Uncles don't make fair competition."

"If you're sure?"

"I am. Thanks for a wonderful evening, Liz. I don't think I'll ever forget it."

"Happy Christmas, Bill. Call me soon."

"I will, Liz. Have a wonderful Christmas together."

Chapter 35

Christmas for Bill was a lot harder than he thought it would be. Work finished early at the Meads on Christmas Eve and in the van on the way back into town the only topic of conversation was how and where everyone was going to spend the long Christmas and New Year break. Scouser had given up on his latest girlfriend because 'Moses 'imself couldn't part 'er knees', and he was off back to Liverpool. Tony was flying to Tenerife with his family that afternoon and young Sam could not stop talking about being invited by his new fiancée's parents to spend the holiday at their home. Bill offered no information about his Christmas plans and he was pleased when no one asked.

A few of the younger lads were staying in town and were off right away to spend the rest of the day 'pubbing and pulling'. They invited Bill along but he turned their offer down, and instead he spent a couple of hours in a packed supermarket buying a portable TV and the ingredients for a Christmas dinner that could be cooked on two electric rings. On the way home in the taxi he looked out at the streets and shops teeming with people making their last minute preparations for the long millennium holiday. They had an urgency about them and a sense of purpose which he envied.

Later when he sat in his bedsit drinking his second can of beer Bill regretted turning down the chance to go out with the young lads from work. He had been determined to make something positive out of this time on his own, but it was an uphill struggle from the start. Once it began to get dark outside, the single bulb hanging from the ceiling struggled to light the room and the bedsit became a gloomy, depressing place.

Any peace of mind Bill thought he might achieve here on his own was undermined by thoughts and feelings that kept turning up uninvited. And however hard he tried he could not keep them out. He stood at the window and looked out at Runnymede Terrace. Most of the houses up and down the street were showing some kind of Christmas decoration. Perhaps that was what this place needed? Perhaps some Christmas decorations would have made it feel more like home? He smiled at the craziness of the idea. Santa Claus, Rudolph and all their little helpers together would struggle to make Flat 6 at 12 Runnymede Terrace feel festive.

Bill set up his new TV and kept it on as a permanent distraction, but he could not concentrate on anything for long. His thoughts kept returning to what a normal Christmas Eve would be like at home in Bramport. He would be in the kitchen now drinking sherry with Angie. It was a bit of a tradition on Christmas Eve. She would make the brandy butter and he would prepare the stuffing and cranberry sauce ready for Dave, Mickey and Cheryl's visit the next day.

He started pacing the floor of his small room, six small steps to the window and then six more back to the door. He fought to clear his head of all thoughts that stirred up his emotions, but it was a losing battle. The grief about Angie, the anger with Stoner, the sadness over Hayley, and the anxiety about the court cases. It was all too much. He sat down on the edge of the bed with his head in his hands, and he felt the tears trying to break through his defences.

"I'm not having that, you bloody fool!" he shouted, jumping up and immediately turning his sadness and anxiety into anger against himself.

"It's a bit bloody late to start feeling sorry for yourself now, you prat."

Bill knew there was no place for self-pity in any of this. His actions alone had been the start of the mess he was in now, and he had to live with it. It could all have been avoided and he knew it. Angie and Stoner. Being on his own in this stinking rat-hole of a place. Facing the new millennium with a prison sentence hanging over him. It all led back to one thing. His decision to take Benny Horseman's money out of the safe just nine weeks ago tonight.

On Christmas morning Bill woke up with a headache. He had drunk far too many cans the night before and the headache was not the worst price he had to pay for it. Far worse was having to go out into the freezing hallway, which stank of cat's pee, and up to the next landing every time he wanted to go to the toilet. After each visit it actually felt good getting back to the privacy and relative warmth of his own room.

Bill boiled some water in a pan to make some coffee and switched on the television. He searched for a channel with a live transmission to give him more of a feeling of contact with the outside world, and then he opened his Christmas presents. Liz had got him a bottle of Glenmorangie single malt whisky and a video of *The Magnificent Seven*. From Jon there was a chef's apron and hat, and from Susie a selection of liqueur chocolates. Mickey and Cheryl had given him a copy of Halliwell's *Film Guide* and a boxed set of six Alfred Hitchcock films. And from Dave he got a map of the world, a pair of binoculars, a compass and a metal file. Bill put on his chef's apron and hat, poured himself a glass of whisky and stood at the window testing his binoculars. It was drizzling outside and he could not see very far. He bit into a liqueur chocolate, took a generous mouthful of whisky and wished himself a Happy Christmas

At 10.30 Bill changed channels for a film, which had always been a favourite in the Knight household. Peg loved James Stewart, and every Christmas she had insisted that everything stopped whilst they all watched *It's A Wonderful Life*, the story of George Bailey, a decent man whose life falls apart when he faces financial ruin. Bill came to love the film too but this Christmas, alone in his room, he found it hard to watch as George Bailey once again wished that he had never been born and then found his wish granted by his guardian angel, Clarence.

"Get me back!" George Bailey cried out in desperation, as he realised that not only were the bad things in his life erased, but so too were his relationships with his wife and family and friends, together with all the good deeds he had done in his life.

The film always made Bill choke up, even though he knew every scene and every speech off by heart, but this Christmas the full force of the film's emotional power smashed into him, as George Bailey realised that he would gladly face all the bad things in his life again if only his position in his family could be restored.

'Get me back. I don't care what happens to me! Get me back to my wife and kids!' George Bailey pleaded. "Help me, Clarence. Please. Help me. I wanna live again.'

Bill clenched his fists, he clenched his teeth and screwed his eyes shut, but it was no good. At last his defences were breached and he sat on the edge of his bed and sobbed. For several minutes Bill could do nothing to stop the flow of tears as the film played to its end and George Bailey's family life was restored to him by his guardian angel, and his lesson was learnt for another year. 'Appreciate what you have now, before you lose it.'

Bill got up, switched off the TV and went to the window. He realised he still had his chef's hat on, and he took it off and wiped his face with it. "For God's sake, man, pull yourself together," he snapped. He leaned on the window sill and looked out at the grey sky and drizzle that hung over Medford.

"Not much chance of a guardian angel out there for you, Bill, old son," he said out loud.

By the time Bill had cooked his turkey steak, mashed potato and peas and drunk a bottle of South African chardonnay it was getting dark outside. His phone had not rung all day, but he knew that everyone would be taken up with their own arrangements. He regretted telling everyone that he was busy celebrating Christmas with friends, but still he decided against making any calls himself. They would have to wait until he had a bit more self-control and he could guarantee not to make a damn fool of himself.

By the early evening Bill could have sworn his room was getting smaller. He turned the sound down on the television. It was not a comfort any more. It was getting on his nerves. Then he turned it off completely, but then there were no distractions in the room at all and after ten minutes it went back on again. Bill realised he should have provided himself with some books. He read Halliwell's *Film Guide* for 20 minutes, but could not concentrate.

"A fine traveller you'd make," he said to himself. "One day left to your own devices and you're climbing up the bloody wall."

Bill stood at his door and listened for any sound on the other side. Then he became aware of what he was doing and felt annoyed at his pathetic behaviour. He knew people were out there in the other bedsits and the sensible thing to do was just to go out and knock on someone's door. But the longer he thought about it the more difficult it became.

It was strange. He had never had a problem before talking to new people of any age or background. It was something he was good at. Something he enjoyed. But in the past he had never felt this desperate for company. There had always been plenty of people in his life to provide all the social contact he needed, and if anything he would often crave a bit of time on his own. But this was different. Being in this room for hours on end was not independence or a chance to have some time to yourself for a while. This was being alone when you did not want to be, and feeling wretched about it. He would never choose this. This was just loneliness, plain and simple.

And it was not helped by thinking of what other people might be doing now, especially Angie and Stoner. The thought of the two of them together in his house – and in his bed – made his feelings of isolation and helplessness much, much worse. He was trapped in this bloody room, and he was trapped by time that passed so damned slowly. Bill looked at his watch. Five thirty. He had not even reached the evening yet. How was he going to get through all those hours until the morning? But then Boxing Day would be another day exactly like this with no one expecting him, or waiting for him, or needing him to be with them.

"I'm not damn well hanging around here putting up with this," he growled, as he put on his coat and stuffed his keys and phone into the pocket.

Outside it was a miserable evening of damp and drizzle and deserted streets, and walking around with nowhere to go did nothing to lift Bill's spirits. There was not one other person to be seen and not one shop or garage or pub was left open. It was as if all the life had been sucked out of Medford and was concentrated now in small groups of people gathered behind closed doors. The usual life of the town had simply disappeared.

Bill walked in a large circle, and after 30 minutes he found himself back again only a few hundred yards from Runnymede Terrace. As he came nearer he thought of his small room and the hours left of the day he would have to spend shut away there. "My God," he thought, "this must be what prison'll be like. Shut away day after day. No chance of your life ever expanding or changing." It was exactly the opposite of everything he had always wanted for himself and the full meaning of what he might face in the New Year hit him harder than ever. Bill turned into Runnymede Terrace and pictured the confines of his tiny room.

"Why do they call a prison sentence 'doing time'?" he wondered. "It should be 'doing time and space'."

Back in his room Bill thought he could go mad. Time had now slowed to a crawl and the need to talk and to interact with someone had become oppressive. Even more oppressive than the four walls that marked the boundaries of his pacing up and down. He went to the window again and looked out hoping to see a sign of some activity. Nothing. No one. Not one single person out there to give the place some life.

Bill picked up his mobile and scrolled down the names in his phone book. Who could he call? Who was there to help him out of this deep pit he was sinking into? *Angie.* No chance. *Benny.* Even less. *Dave.* Why not Dave? He was in Austria skiing, but he could still take a call, and it would be lovely to speak to him.

Bill felt excited and relieved as he pressed to connect. *'Kein Anschluss unter dieser Nummer. Kein Anschluss…'* Bill tried again with the same result. He struggled to shake off his dejection and disappointment but kept scrolling. *Harry.* Out of the question. *Hayley.* My God, how he would love to call Hayley and to see her. But it would be so unfair to her. *Liz.* She needed some peace. *Mickey.* He could try Mickey. But Mickey's phone was switched off. *Mum and Dad.* The last thing he needed was criticism. *Stoner.* Bastard. *Tony.* The mood had gone. The moment had passed. There was no one he could turn to. He was completely alone.

Bill opened the door to get some air. There was not a sound coming from anywhere in the house. Maybe he was the only tenant there and all the other rooms were empty. He went back in and closed the door. He was feeling desperate now. He could not face any more hours alone being tortured by his thoughts. He went to the sink and splashed cold water on his face in an attempt to shock himself back to some normality.

"What am I going to do?" he whispered. "What am I going to do?"

Slowly Bill raised his head and saw someone looking back at him. He studied the face for a long time. The face was so familiar and friendly that he smiled at it and was instantly reassured.

"My God. I'm not alone at all, am I?" he said. "You're with me, aren't you? You're always with me."

And at that moment Bill knew that he would be alright. He had company after all. He liked the person he saw in the mirror and he was never going to let him go again. Bill knew that with him he could get through anything.

The next day at twelve o'clock Bill made his way round to a pub he had passed on his walk the previous evening. He was not desperate for company now as he had been then. Now he just wanted to socialise a little, and he appreciated the world of difference that existed between the two. As Bill stood at the bar ordering a beer he heard a familiar voice.

"Bill, old chap, whatever lures a respectable man like you to the iniquities of the Runnymede Arms?"

Bill looked up and saw Roly Upperton sitting at the end of the bar holding his glass up in salute. Bill went over and shook his hand.

"Hello, Roly. It's very good to see you. Can I get you anything?"

"Thank you, dear chap. One of my specials would be most acceptable."

Bill ordered a triple gin and tonic.

346

"Cheers, Roly. A very Happy Christmas to you."

"And likewise to you, Bill. Let our toast be 'alcohol'. Proof positive that God loves us and wants us to be happy."

Bill took a mouthful of beer whilst Roly emptied most of his glass.

"So don't you have a performance today then, Roly?"

"Matinee at two, evening curtain at 7.30. When we shall once again seek to revive the spirit of Grimaldi and the Commedia dell'Arte. Or dish up more mayhem for the Medford masses. Whichever way you may care to look at it."

"I saw the show on Wednesday, Roly. I thought it was really good. Great pace, great variety. I thought it was a fantastic spectacle."

"You honestly enjoyed it?"

"I really did, and so did everyone else there. I wasn't really expecting to, if I'm honest, but you and Hayley were just superb."

"Steady, Bill, old chap, or you'll choke on your own hyperbole."

"No, like it or not, Roly, I really thought the way you and Hayley played the audience was sensational. You were both a class apart. And that's as much as you're getting, my friend."

"Bill, you are clearly a man of some discernment. It will be my pleasure to purchase for you a beverage of your choosing."

"Thanks, Roly. A pint of Thoday's would be nice."

"And a special, landlord, if you please."

"So, Bill, what brings you to the Runnymede on the Feast of Saint Stephen? Hayley told me you'd moved on to other climes."

"Yes, that was the original plan, Roly. But it didn't quite work out. How is Hayley, by the way?"

"The same as ever, dear boy. Keeping the peace. Healing wounds. Giving her all to everything she does. She's even done the impossible. Stolen the heart of an old misogynist like me."

"She's a fantastic girl."

"So why, dear heart, did you ever leave her?"

"That's a question I'm asking myself right now. Look, Roly, I don't mean to involve you in any deceit or anything, but I'd really appreciate it if you didn't tell Hayley you'd seen me here today."

"Don't worry, dear boy, I've learnt many times in my life, alas, the need for discretion above all other considerations."

"Don't get me wrong, Roly. I'm not cheating on Hayley or anything. It's just that we've said our goodbyes and wished for the best for one another, and I don't want her to find out what a bloody mess I've made of it already."

"Your presence here already forms no part of my recollection of the day's events. What have you done?"

"It's what other people have done. It's not easy to talk about."

Bill waited for Roly to change the subject but it was clear he was not going to.

"Anything you say to old Roly will be locked securely away forever, my dear Bill."

"Well, okay. I left Hayley to go back to my wife in Bramport, to try and start again, but when I got there I found she was having an affair with our oldest friend."

Roly leaned back and his eyes bulged in surprise.

"Your problems don't come in easy-fit sizes, do they, dear boy?"

"If only you knew, Roly, that's only the half of it. But you can see that it's not something I'd want to share with the world."

"Quite, dear chap. Quite. So what are you doing now?"

"I've come back to Medford because my work's here and my sister's here."

"And she's providing you with sanctuary and solace, I assume?"

"She was, but I've just moved out on my own to a place round the corner in Runnymede Terrace."

"Oh dear. The nether reaches of bedsit land."

"It's all I could get."

"And will you rest there over the festive period?"

"I'm living there, Roly."

"Oh dear. I do feel for you, Bill. It's not easy cooped up in one of those rooms, is it?"

"It was difficult at first, but I'll be alright now."

"Good man. There's nothing worse than the day a fellow discovers that he bores himself."

"I haven't found that yet, Roly."

"And let's hope you never do, Bill dear. Let's hope you never do. It is a wise man who finds comfort in his own company."

"I know, Roly. I've learnt the truth of that just recently."

"They say that wisdom comes with age, dear Bill, but alas, for some of us age comes alone."

Roly looked down into his drink and frowned before quickly downing the entire contents and rattling the glass on the counter.

"Come on, come on! Let's get in the festive spirit. We are forced to grow old, but nothing says we have to grow up. More drinks here, please, landlord. I've got to be off soon."

"My round, Roly."

"Bless you, Bill. Cheers. You know, Bill, I know it's an old cliché but time is a great healer, you know. A bloody awful beautician, but a great healer."

They both laughed and Roly emptied most of his glass.

"Are you going to be alright this afternoon, Roly? It's none of my business, but how the hell do you perform like that on top of all those specials?"

"My dear Bill. Imagine, if you will, standing in the wings of a theatre waiting for five, ten or 15 minutes for your cue to step out in front of hundreds of people. Knowing everything you are about to say and do will be scrutinised, dissected and discussed. Believe me, my dear fellow, there exists no greater sobering experience."

"So it's not about Dutch courage or anything?"

"Bill. I shall share something with you. I drink not to make myself more interesting. I drink to make other people more interesting. Although in your case, dear chap, that is of course never a necessity."

"Thanks, Roly. I think."

"And I shall be delighted to share your company again. Shall we meet here on the eve of the new millennium? You will be staying up to see the New Year in, I suppose?"

"No. I'm not staying up to see the New Year in, Roly. I'm staying up to make sure the old bugger leaves."

"Good fellow. Good fellow. We shall meet on Millennium Eve and make our resolutions together. Farewell, my dear Bill."

"Bye, Roly. Give Hayley a kiss for me, but don't tell her where it came from."

"I shall be your Hermes and your Eros," boomed Roly as he

walked out through the bar, waving his hand in grand gestures above his head. As dozens of pairs of eyes sought out Bill, he turned and stared into his beer.

It was now so noisy in the bar that it took Bill a while to work out that the mobile phone he heard ringing was his own. By the time he answered it the call had gone onto his voice mail. Bill dialled 121, put his right index finger to his ear and struggled to decipher the message. He caught the words, 'Mick'… 'urgent'… 'as soon as possible' and immediately hurried out into the relative quiet of the car park. Thoughts raced through his head and none of them were comforting. He was sure it was Mickey's voice he had heard, and he sounded very upset.

"Oh God," thought Bill. "Not the baby. Please God, not the baby."

Then he thought of Dave skiing in Austria and his heart pounded in his chest and blood rushed to his head as he prayed out loud.

Somehow with both his hands shaking Bill managed to retrieve the message, and this time Mickey's strained voice came over more clearly.

"Hello, Dad, it's Mick. I'm sorry to phone you with such an urgent message, but you must call me back as soon as possible."

Bill fought to control his reactions as he pressed to return the call. Mickey answered immediately.

"Mickey, I just got your message. What is it, son?"

"Oh, there you are, Dad. Listen. I'm afraid I've got some bad news."

Bill looked to the heavens, breathed in hard and closed his eyes.

"I'm afraid it's Grandad. He's had a heart attack."

Bill could hear Mickey's voice cracking, but in the car park of the Runnymede his own tension subsided and he said a silent prayer of thanks. He was sure his father would understand.

"How is he, Mickey?" he asked in a steadier tone.

"I'm so sorry, Dad," his son said through his tears. "Grandpa died an hour ago."

Bill walked the three miles to Liz's house. No taxi was available for at least half an hour, and anyway he needed the time to clear his head and work out how he was going to break the news to his sister. Liz had always been much closer than Bill to their father, and he knew how hard this was going to be for her to take.

The news had not really hit Bill yet and he wondered when or even if it was going to affect him more deeply. He remembered the last time he had seen his father nearly two months ago, when they had probably got on better than at any time in their lives. Wilf had listened whilst Bill explained the trouble he was in at Horseman's, and for once he had tried to understand Bill and be supportive instead of judging him. Bill regretted not seeing his father on his last visit to Bramport. For whatever reason he had allowed Wilf to become an increasingly peripheral figure in his life over the years and now it was too late to ever do anything about it.

After 40 minutes Bill arrived at the end of Liz's road. He stopped on the corner to try yet again to work out how he was going to break the news, but in the end he knew there could be no script or rehearsal. He went to the door and rang the bell.

Susie answered.

"Uncle Bill's here," she shouted back into the house and then kissed him on the cheek.

Liz came out of the kitchen with a chef's apron on, smiling broadly. As he stepped into the hallway she put her arms around him.

"Bill, what a wonderful surprise!" she said. "Come in. You're just in time for lunch."

Jonathan and Steve appeared from out of the lounge.

"Hello, Bill," said Steve, holding out his hand. "Long time no see."

"Hi, Uncle Bill," said Jonathan excitedly. "You've just got to see the Playstation Mum and Dad got me for Christmas."

"I will later, Jon. I just need a word with your mum and dad for a few minutes, okay?"

Liz was the first to sense that something was wrong.

"Are you alright, Bill? You're looking terribly serious."

"Can the three of us go into the kitchen for a minute?" he said.

He ushered Liz and Steve into the kitchen, and just before he closed the door he whispered to Susie, "Go and look after your brother in the lounge. I need some time with your mum and dad. I'll explain later."

Bill took a kitchen chair and asked Liz to sit down. He sat facing her and held her hand. She was smiling nervously.

"Liz, my darling," he said. "We've all got to be really strong today. I'm afraid it's Dad."

"What's happened?"

"He had a heart attack this morning. I'm afraid he's gone."

"Gone? What do you mean 'gone'?"

"My darling," Bill said, as he put his arms around Liz and held her. "Dad died this morning."

They held on to one another for a long time while both of them wept. Liz cried for her father and Bill cried for her.

Chapter 36

Two hours later Bill was on his way to Bramport in Liz's car. There had been a long debate about whether Liz should go with him, and in the end it was decided to try to keep Christmas as normal as possible for the children. The fact that Peg and Liz might be a volatile mix at such an emotional time was left unsaid. Bill would look after his mother and make all the necessary arrangements, and Liz and her family would follow on later in the week.

Mickey had assured Bill that he and Cheryl would stay with Peg until Bill got there, so when he arrived at Shangri-La he was surprised to find his mother on her own.

"Oh, it's you now, is it?" she said when she saw him on the doorstep. She walked away as Bill stepped inside. "It's funny how everyone turns up when it's too late."

Bill followed her into the front room.

"Don't be like that, Mum," he said. "I got here as soon as I could. Where are Mick and Cheryl?"

"I told them to go. There's no point in them hanging around here upsetting themselves. Especially with her with the baby and everything."

"I expect they just wanted to be with you, Mum. We all care about you, you know."

"Do you? So where's your sister then?"

"Liz wanted to come, but we all persuaded her to keep things normal for the children's sake. I don't think it would've been good for her anyway. It's all hit her really hard. But she'll be down later."

"She hasn't called."

"I think she's too upset, Mum. You know how she's always doted on Dad. She'll be in touch with you later, for sure."

Peg sat down in her usual spot at the dining table and stared out at the garden as she always did.

"Can I get you anything, Mum? A cup of tea? I'd like to make myself one."

"I'll have one if you're making one anyway."

When Bill brought the tea in, his mother was still looking out of the window. When Bill put the cup and saucer in front of her she said nothing.

"Do you feel up to telling me what happened with Dad?"

"He was out there," she said, without turning to face him. "Where he always is. In his precious shed. I went to call him in for morning coffee and found him lying on the path. I knew right away what it was."

"You didn't think he'd fallen or anything?"

"No. I knew it was his heart."

"But he's never been ill in his life. Apart from his leg giving him trouble."

"His stump, you mean?"

"Yes, I suppose I do."

"You never could stand anyone using that word, could you, William? His infected stump is what you mean."

"Yes, alright, Mum. That is what I mean. Apart from that I've never known him to be ill."

"You'll never understand, will you, William? All the stress your father's been under."

"Stress about what?"

At last she turned to face him.

"About you, of course. What do you think? He's been worried sick about you and all that business with Horseman's."

"Are you sure, Mum?"

"Of course I'm sure. He's never stopped going on about it for the past couple of months. About how you might be going to prison. It was torture for him. I told him, 'It's not our problem,' but he never listened to a word I said."

"Oh, hell," said Bill. He put his head in his hands. He felt exhausted at the mere thought of the hours he was bound to spend dealing with what his mother had just told him. But he could not even consider thinking about it now.

"So was he able to speak or anything?" he asked.

"He was trying to speak, so I came in and called an ambulance. They were here in a few minutes, and they took him to the General."

"I'm sorry, Mum. It must've been awful for you."

"You just get on with it, don't you? I went in the ambulance with him, but I could tell he'd gone."

"How could you?"

"They weren't doing much for him after a while. And when we got to the General they weren't rushing. You know."

"Yes. I understand what you're saying."

Bill wanted to go over to his mother and comfort her, but he knew it would make them both feel too awkward. He decided instead to keep practical.

"So when did they tell you he'd gone?"

"About half past twelve. They asked me if I wanted to contact anyone so I called Elsie next door. She'd come out when the ambulance arrived. She tried to call you at your place, but I'd forgotten you weren't there. I think she called Michael then."

"Yes, I think she must have, because he called me about one o'clock."

"Well, that's it then. Your father's still at the hospital. They said family can go and see him, if you want."

"Maybe I will, Mum. I'll have to think about that."

Peg got up and leaned on the table, gazing once more out of the window onto the garden.

"I'm going for a lie-down," she said. "You can put your things in your old room if you're planning to stay."

"I was planning to, Mum. I can help out with all the arrangements."

"Please yourself, if you want to. It's up to you."

Peg paused at the door and took something out of her pocket.

"There is one thing you can do for me, William. Your father

was holding this key to his shed when he died. Perhaps you could sort out whatever's in there. I don't want to do it."

"Of course I will, Mum. You go and have a good rest."

Peg stayed in her room for the rest of the day. Bill went to check on her at about eight o'clock.

"I just want to be left in peace," she called out to him through the bedroom door. "There are eggs in the fridge if you're hungry. I'll see you in the morning, William."

Bill was happy to leave his mother to herself. He was tired, and talking to her was always hard work. Bill decided he would leave sorting through his father's things until the morning, and he turned in early too.

It was the first time Bill had slept in his old room in his parents' house for nearly 30 years. The room had not changed much. The wallpaper was different, of course, and the old Formica desktop which had been built into the alcove for him to do his homework on had been replaced by a chest of drawers. But the built-in wardrobe was the same and so too were Bill's feelings as he lay in bed trying unsuccessfully to go to sleep. It was still an unhappy house. He wondered if there was any truth in what his mother had said about him causing his father so much stress. Was she really saying that he was responsible for his father's heart attack?

Bill lay on his back thinking of the child who had stared for hours at the same ceiling. The little boy always felt that his parents were unhappy, and that they were unhappy with him too, and he always thought that he was responsible for both.

After breakfast Bill went into the garden to sort out Wilf's shed. The shed had been there as long as Bill could remember. It was not very big. Probably about 5ft wide by about 9ft long. It had concrete supports under each corner, which raised it about 6 inches off the ground. Bill remembered how as a boy he was always having to retrieve balls from underneath it whenever he and Liz played in the garden.

Originally all the garden tools were kept in there, but a year or two after Bill and Liz left home the tools were moved to the garage and Wilf had claimed the shed as his 'den'. He'd covered the window with brown paper on the inside and put a heavy padlock on the door. And every summer Wilf gave his den a fresh coat of wood preserve, and every third summer it received a new felt roof.

'Your father's out in his precious shed' became Peg's stock saying whenever Bill phoned or called round, and it brought amusement to everyone in the family apart from to Peg herself. She seemed to be the only one who could not work out why Wilf spent so long out there.

Bill undid the padlock and opened the door. As he stepped inside he was first of all surprised by the warm air that hit him, and then he was even more surprised by what he saw. A light switch hung from the roof and he pulled it to get a better look. There was a fan heater standing in the middle of the lino-covered floor and next to it an easy chair. Wilf must have left the heater on when he was called back into the house for his morning coffee. Bill switched it off. There was a desk-top built along the far wall and on the desk top were paper and a pile of envelopes, some large books, and what looked like a large tin cash box. The walls of the shed were lined with what appeared to be plasterboard, but Bill could not really be sure because every available inch of it was covered with photographs. Hundreds and hundreds of photographs.

Bill turned to the wall to his right to take a closer look. All the photos on that side were of Liz, starting with her as a baby and working through her school years to her graduation and wedding photos. As Bill followed the photos back along the wall towards the door they turned into pictures of Mickey and Dave and Susie and Jonathan. Going the other way there was a large section full of photos of Bill from his birth through his rugby-playing days right up to the picture of him and Angie in New York, which he used to keep on his desk at Horseman's.

On the far wall above the desk all the photos were of Wilf and Peg. And right in the centre was a large black and white portrait of a very pretty girl. It was almost certainly a studio portrait because the background was smoky grey and the girl was in a pose, turning slightly and looking up with the hint of a smile. You could only see her head and neck and the top of her shoulders, which were uncovered. She looked like a film star. Her auburn hair appeared thick and soft and moved away from her face and forehead in waves. Her skin was absolutely smooth and her eyes looked into the distance, bright and full of life. Bill could hardly believe that this was a picture of his mother, but it was. It was Peggy Thornton, aged 17.

Wilf was there too. He was there as a baby with Gran and Grandpa Knight, and he was there in his school uniform looking very serious and determined. Bill had never known that these pictures of his parents even existed. He wanted to take some of them off the wall to get a closer look but Wilf had attached each one with a small pin tack in each corner and Bill did not want to disturb what his father had done. He looked at pictures of his father, fit and strong, wearing the same rugby kit for Bramport Chiefs that Bill had worn. And then he saw the portrait that Wilf Knight had sat for in 1943 in the uniform of the 1st Airborne Division. He still looked very serious and determined, but handsome too, and ridiculously young to be going off to war.

Bill looked down at the papers on his father's desk. They were letters. And each letter had the same address in the top right-hand corner – 26 Wilmhurst Road, Bramport – the address of Grandad Thornton where Peg lived with her widower father before she married Wilf. Bill picked up one of the letters. 'My Own Darling Wilf', it began. Bill was shocked at the thought of invading his parents' privacy. He quickly folded the letter and put it in one of the empty envelopes on the desk.

There must have been 100 envelopes with letters already in them and another half dozen open on the desk. He put them all away and placed them in three neat piles in the corner. He cautiously opened one of the large books. It was a scrapbook and inside were all Liz and Bill's school reports and certificates. In another were newspaper cuttings from the Bramport Herald covering just about every rugby match Bill had ever played in.

Bill went over to the easy chair to sit down and try to make sense of all that he had seen. On Wilf's chair was another letter lying open. Bill picked it up, sat down and glimpsed the first line. Once he had started reading his mother's words to his father all those years ago he could not put the letter down.

26 Wilmhurst Road
Bramport
10-9-44

My Dearest Darling Wilf,
I hope this letter finds you as well, my darling as it leaves me. It seems such a long time since I have seen your dear face.
Today I have read your letters over and over again each time as if for the first time. I want you to try to write to me as often as you can my darling because I miss you and worry about you so.
I know how selfish I am darling, to be so happy that you are out of danger so far but all I want my dear is to have you safe here with me. With you beside me forever I know we can face all the future has to give.
Darling Wilf I do not want you to worry about me. I have your ring my darling and I shall never take it off. I know rings are nothing really darling but it is what they stand for and mean that really counts. It means that I belong to the best man in the world, one that I love very much and one I shall be proud to give my whole life to.
I know that I mustn't harp on my darling but I pray every day that God will keep you safe for me. I think about your last leave and wish that I could have you close to me again. I know how difficult it is for you darling to be always on your best behaviour and sometimes I am amazed how we have managed to be as good as we have. Soon we shall be together forever my darling and I shall be the girl you want me to be and I promise our life together will be the best.
I think I must close now my darling. I shall keep my chin up for you my dearest Wilf and I shall kiss your photo as I do every night. My father says I must not grizzle so much but I find it so hard when I miss and love you so dearly. Your mother has been so kind to me. I call her Mum Knight and love her as if she were my own mother.

God bless you again my darling and keep you safe. Each day is one less towards you coming home to me.
  Your everloving sweetheart and wife to be
  Peg
  x x x x x x x x x x x x x x x x x x x x x x x x x x x x xx x x x x x x x x x x x x x x x

Bill put the letter in his pocket, locked his father's den and went back to the house to try to explain to his mother what he had found.

When Bill came in the back door Peg was at the kitchen sink washing some clothes.

"They're Dad's things, aren't they?" he said.

"They're his dirty things. There's no point in wasting them. Once they're done I'm giving them all to the charity shop."

"You don't want to do that now, Mum. Give yourself a bit of a break. Let me take you out for a drive or something."

"I haven't got time for all that, William. There's no point in moping about feeling sorry for yourself. It's best just to get on with things and make the most of it."

She kept her hands in the sink and turned her head to look at him.

"That's what you should've done at Horseman's. Accepted what you had and got on with it. Then maybe none of all this would've happened."

Bill was ready to raise a hundred objections but thought better of it and decided to change the subject.

"Don't you want to know what I found in the shed, Mum?"

"Not really. Unless you need to tell me."

"I don't need to tell you, but I think it might be nice for you to know."

Peg said nothing but looked out of the kitchen window onto the garden as she kept pounding Wilf's clothes. Bill sat down at the kitchen table.

"Dad seems to have built a family archive out there or something. He had a chair and a heater and hundreds of photographs of us all on the walls. He must've sat there surrounded by us. There's you, and me, and Liz and all the children. And there are loads I've never seen of you when you..."

"I'm not really interested in all this, William."

"Really?"

"All this dredging over the past. Your father was always far too soft about everything. I used to tell him, 'Just get on with things the way they are', but he never wanted to listen to me."

"He was just proud of us all, Mum. Proud of his family. That's all."

"He was always worrying about his family, you mean, and fussing around me about it all. He drove me mad with it."

"Did he worry about us that much?"

"Of course he did. 'What will Lizzie do now?' 'What'll happen to Bill if... this or that or whatever?' He never stopped."

"Poor old Dad."

"Oh, yes, 'poor old Dad'. I never hear 'poor old Mum'."

Bill took the letter from his pocket. He checked that Peg still had her back to him at the sink. He unfolded the letter, glanced at the first line and quickly refolded it. He shook his head, looked to the ceiling and took a deep breath.

"Mum, there were some other things in Dad's shed, including this letter."

Peg turned her head to look. When she saw the letter she first looked surprised and then turned right round and kept her eyes fixed on it as she dried her hands on a tea towel. Bill got up and handed the folded paper to her. Peg stood with the letter in her left hand, and as she read it she placed her right hand over her mouth. When she had finished she gently folded the letter and looked away to one side. For a second he saw the girl in the photo with the bright eyes. She looked confused and vulnerable. And then in an instant the girl was gone and Peg thrust the letter back at him.

"I can't waste my time on things like that now," she said, returning to her washing. "Your father had no right keeping things like that. All that was years ago."

"I think he kept every letter you ever sent him, Mum. There must be over 100 of them out there."

"Well, he had no right keeping any of them. If I'd known all he was doing out there was moping over the past…"

"Obviously it was really important to him."

"That may be, but it's no good dwelling on things. Like I said, he was too soft, your father. That was his trouble. Too soft at his work and far too soft with you. He let you do whatever you wanted and look where it's got you."

"Steady on, Mum. Dad wasn't too soft with me. He was always ordering me around when I was a lad. Telling me what I ought to be doing."

"But you didn't listen to him though, did you? Your father had his heart set on you going to university. And it broke his heart too when you started on those coal lorries. All we sacrificed for you and you end up delivering coal."

"Well, I think I did a bit better than that, Mum."

"Oh, yes. You've done really well, haven't you? Bringing all this disgrace on us. Causing us all this worry. Well, it's killed your father."

"That's a terrible thing for you to say to me, Mum. You nearly said as much yesterday and I let it go, but you mustn't say it again."

Peg turned round and wiped her hands furiously on her apron.

"Oh, I mustn't? If you knew what your father and I gave up to help you, William. If we'd had just half the chances you've had in your life…"

"Hold on, Mum. I appreciate all you and Dad have done for me, but you can't make me responsible for what you missed out on. I'm responsible for my life, not yours."

"Oh, don't you worry. I know none of you care about me any more."

"I didn't mean that, Mum. I care about you very much, but I hate seeing you so bitter and disappointed."

"Well, I am disappointed with you, and I don't see why I should have to hide it."

"No, Mum. You're disappointed with your life and you're trying to make it all my fault. But it's not my fault if you and Dad weren't happy."

Bill knew he had gone too far. Peg made a movement towards him and he hunched his shoulders as he always did as a child when he knew a slap around the back of the head from his mother was imminent. But Peg stopped just short and stood over him wagging her finger.

"How dare you speak to me like that, William! I don't know who the dickens you think you are, but things between me and your father have nothing at all to do with you."

She slammed the door and went out into the front room. Bill sat for several minutes in the kitchen before he decided he had to go in to her. She had taken up her usual position at the dining table. She was holding a handkerchief and looking out into the garden.

"I'm sorry, Mum. I don't mean to upset you, but I can't let you go on saying such terrible things to me. Not any more."

"Your trouble is, William, you just don't like to hear the truth."

"But you're trying to make everything my fault, Mum. Even Dad's death. That's a terrible thing to do."

"Well, it was your fault! Stealing money. Leaving your family. Your father never got over it. I don't know why you did it to him."

"But I didn't do it to him, or to you, Mum. I was just trying to live my life, that's all. I made a mistake. We're all allowed to make mistakes, aren't we?"

"It's not the way we brought you up, William. It's not what your father and I taught you."

"No, Mum. You taught me to feel bad about myself. That I don't deserve to be happy. And you taught me that it's my fault too if you're not happy."

"Don't be so ridiculous."

"But you did, Mum. And you're still trying to do it. But you can't make your child responsible for your happiness."

"But we can expect you to behave decently and show us some consideration."

"I do consider you, Mum. Far too much for my own good sometimes. God knows I love you and Dad and I'm sorry he's gone. And I'm sorry that you're so unhappy, but you can't make it all my fault."

"I've never heard such nonsense, William. I don't know why you're trying to upset me."

"Please believe me, Mum. I'm not. I know it can't have been

easy for you. I would love you and me to try to help one another to feel better about everything. Can't we do that?"

"You don't understand, William, what it's been like for your father and me going into town over the past few weeks. We've known people were looking at us and talking about you and the money you stole. Especially when that Horseman boy was lying in hospital. And we've been so ashamed…"

As his mother talked Bill knew there was no hope. He wanted to go to her and comfort her, but she had made her defences stronger and stronger over the years, and Bill knew that no word or action from him would ever get through to her now.

That afternoon Bill went back into his father's den. He sat in Wilf's chair and looked around trying to see things as he would have done. But try as he might Bill could not understand his father. Why had he settled for so little in his life? And how had he put up with Peg for all those years? The constant nagging and the belittling comments. How often as a boy had Bill heard his mother undermine Wilf with some remark or other about the lack of money he was earning, or his inability to carry out some task around the house? Maybe that was why Bill never felt the respect for his father that he would like to have done. If only Wilf had asserted himself a bit more over Peg, and a little less over Bill, maybe all their lives would have worked out better.

But one thing was for sure. Wilf had cared about his family. Liz was certainly right about that. He may have been weak in dealing with Peg, but no one could doubt how strongly he'd felt about his family. Whenever he entered his den Wilf had surrounded himself with the people who mattered most to him. Bill got up to take another look at the photos. Then he moved to the desk and studied the scrapbook his father had made of all his children's achievements.

Bill knew the shed would have to be cleared of everything at some point, but he decided to leave it until after the funeral. Or at least until Liz had had a chance to see it all. Then Bill noticed the metal cash box in the left-hand corner of the desk. He picked it up. It was not heavy but there appeared to be something inside it. The box was locked. Bill searched on the desk for a key, but there was none there. He looked on the floor and on the chair, but there was no sign of one anywhere.

Peg had gone to her room before lunchtime, and she was still there when Bill went back into the house. He thought it best not to disturb her just to ask about the key. It was possible that Wilf had it on him when he collapsed, and Bill decided it was the excuse he needed to go to the hospital to collect his father's things.

At Bramport General Bill was taken to a small room and asked if he wanted to see his father, but he could not face it. Eventually he was given a plastic bag containing Wilf's clothes and a plastic box containing his personal possessions. Bill had to check that everything corresponded to the list made out when Wilf was admitted, and then he had to sign for it all. A Timex watch, a pair of reading glasses, £1.25 in change, and a small key.

Chapter 37

When Bill got back from the hospital Peg had still not emerged from her room. Bill went out to his father's den with his clothes and the few personal items. He took the clothes out of the bag and placed them neatly in the middle of the desk. Then he put the watch on top of them and the small change by the side. He took the key and sat down in the chair with his father's box.

"I hope it's alright with you if I open this, Dad," he said.

Inside the box was a maroon beret with a metal badge. Beneath it were more photos and some papers. Bill took out the beret and the papers and saw that underneath them lay five medals. Bill put the beret on his lap, placed the papers and photos on the floor next to him and examined the medals one by one.

They all had ribbons on them and three of them were star-shaped. Bill read the inscriptions. 1939-45 STAR. AFRICAN STAR. FRANCE AND GERMANY STAR. The remaining two were round and the size of an old half-crown. One had a picture of George VI on one side and a lion standing over an eagle on the other with the simple inscription 1939-1945. The final medal had the dullest ribbon. A vertical dark blue stripe in the middle with rust coloured stripes on either side. On one face of the medal was another engraving of George VI and on the other was an inscription.

FOR DISTINGUISHED CONDUCT IN THE FIELD

Bill examined the medal more closely. There was more engraving around the rim. He held it up to the light and read 3189201 CPL W H KNIGHT.

Bill knew nothing about medals, but he guessed that if one had a personal inscription on it, it must have been awarded for something important. He put the box on the floor and picked up the papers. One was like a very thin magazine, almost like a pamphlet.

FIFTH SUPPLEMENT to THE LONDON GAZETTE
of FRIDAY, the 25th MAY 1945

There were only six pages in the *Gazette* and Bill found what he was looking for on page two:

DISTINGUISHED CONDUCT MEDAL

The KING has been graciously pleased to approve the
following awards in recognition of gallant and distinguished
services in North West Europe:

No 3189201 Corporal Wilfred Henry KNIGHT
2nd Parachute Battalion
(The Parachute Regiment) (Bramport)

Bill had heard of the DCM, but he did not know how it ranked in importance. But it must be quite important. It was on page two and the only thing before it was a citation for a Victoria Cross. He looked again at the papers and photos. There were three photos, all of young men in uniform and all wearing the same beret and badge as Wilf had kept in the box. The badge showed a parachute with eagle wings topped with a crown and a lion. One of the photos was a formal group of about 50 men, all seated. Bill looked to see if he could recognise his father in it, but it was impossible without a magnifying glass. The other two photos were informal. One was of three young lads in their berets, all laughing and clearly in high spirits. Bill recognised the boy on the left as the young Wilf Knight. In the final photo a group, six men in full kit were walking as if in a queue or a line and not looking at the camera at all. It was just possible to make out the tail of an aeroplane in the background.

Under the photos was a piece of folded paper that was so thick it was almost like parchment. It was buff-coloured but around the edge and where it was folded it had become brown with age. Bill started to read it.

REGIMENTAL REPORT
In support of the award of the
DISTINGUISHED CONDUCT MEDAL
to
No 3189201 Corporal Wilfred Henry KNIGHT
The Parachute Regiment

Corporal Knight was part of a machine-gun section of the 2nd Battalion, The Parachute Regiment, which was dropped on the 17th September 1944 with the task of seizing and holding the bridge over the Rhine at Arnhem.

The north end of the bridge was captured and late that evening Corporal Knight was a member of a platoon ordered to assault and capture the southern end of the bridge. The attack was pressed with the utmost determination but the platoon was met by a hail of fire from two 20mm quick firing guns and from machine guns of an armoured car. Almost at once Corporal Knight was shot through the shoulder. Although there was no cover on the bridge, and in spite of his wounds, Corporal Knight continued to press forward with his platoon commander until casualties became so heavy that they were ordered to withdraw.

Later that day Corporal Knight was placed in charge of five men with three Bren machine guns and ordered to occupy the top floor of a house which was vital to the defence of the bridge.

Throughout the next day and night the enemy made ceaseless attacks on the house, using not only infantry with mortars and machine guns but also tanks and self-propelled guns. The house was very exposed and difficult to defend and the fact that it did not fall to the enemy must be attributed in large part to the courage of Corporal Knight and his section.

On 19th September the enemy renewed his attacks, which increased in intensity and Corporal Knight's section, although constantly exposed to enemy fire, held out until the house was set alight and had to be evacuated.

During that night and the next day Corporal Knight constantly sought out new defensive positions to cover approaches to the bridge. On countless occasions he took part in a series of fighting patrols which prevented the enemy from gaining access to houses in the vicinity, the occupation of which would have prejudiced the defence of the bridge.

On the morning of Thursday 21st September Corporal Knight occupied a slit trench in the final defensive perimeter with the two surviving members of his machine gun section. During an enemy assault a stick grenade was thrown into the trench, and Corporal Knight, without regard to his own safety, first shouted a warning to his men and then placed himself between them and the grenade, subsequently taking the full force of the explosion and sustaining serious injuries, for which he is still hospitalised.

From the evening of 17th September until the morning of 21st September Corporal Knight showed courage and devotion to duty, which are beyond praise. Although in pain and weakened by earlier wounds, short of food and without sleep, his resolve never flagged.

Finally Corporal Knight directly hazarded his own life in what proved to be a successful attempt to save the lives of his comrades. Young in years and experience, his actions throughout were those of a veteran, and followed in the proud tradition of His Majesty's Armed Forces and of the Parachute Regiment.

Brigadier G W Lathbury   Major-General R E Urquhart
(Commander 1st Parachute Brigade)   (1st Airborne Division)
Twenty-second day of May, 1945

* * *

Wilf's funeral was set for two o'clock on Wednesday, the 5th January at the Fernvale Crematorium. Liz and Steve and the children did not come down until the day of the funeral and were planning to return to Medford that same evening. Liz did not want to spend any more time with her mother than was necessary. She could still not forgive Peg for being so judgemental towards her, and for becoming increasingly cold and cruel to Wilf in his final years.

For her part Peg saw Liz's attitude as further proof that her family was forever letting her down. Peg shunned all warmth. She shunned Bill's attempts to tell her about Wilf's bravery, and she shunned Wilf's brother, Les, when he arrived from London the day before the funeral. The irony was that the same drama acted out on the cinema screen would have moved Peg, but played out in her own life everything left her cold.

Two days before the funeral Angie phoned. She wanted to be there, and she asked if Mark Stone could attend if he sat at the back away from the family. If Bill had any objections it felt like the wrong time to express them, and on the day Stoner sat in a corner on his own, whilst Angie sat at the front with Bill, Mickey, Cheryl and Dave on one side of Peg, and Liz and her family on the other side with Uncle Les.

The local vicar of St Paul's Church conducted the service. Wilf had not been a churchgoer and the vicar did not know him personally, but Wilf and Peg had been married in St Paul's 53 years previously and in his address the Reverend Smith soon referred to it.

"...to celebrate the life of Wilfred Henry Knight, who was a true son of Bramport. Wilfred was born in the town in 1924 and was married to Margaret in the parish church of St Paul's in 1946.

"We read in the gospel of St John that, 'Our love must not be a thing of words and fine talk. It must be a thing of action and sincerity', and such was Wilfred's life-long love for his town, and for his loyal wife through 53 years of marriage, and for all his family and friends who are gathered here today to remember him. The way he lived his life was a testament to his love for those around him.

"The Bible tells us, 'God opposes the proud, but gives grace to the humble', and whilst talking over the past few days to people who knew Wilfred there is no doubt that Wilfred was a man who lived his life with humility. He worked hard, cared for his family and friends and fully merits now the grace of our Lord.

"He was a man who not only loved his family but also served his community. Our Lord reminds us that 'it is more blessed to give than to receive' and in his service to his country during the second war Wilfred gave so much, bearing with great fortitude his own painful legacy of that dreadful conflict.

"So as we come together today to say goodbye to our brother, Wilfred, let us rejoice in the words of our Lord Jesus who said, 'I am the bread of life: he that cometh to me shall never hunger, and he that believeth in me shall never thirst'.

"Please stand and say with me Our Lord's Prayer. Our Father…"

Bill mumbled his way through the prayer and then through a hymn that was drowned out by the organist. He looked around as much as he felt he could in order to see how many people had gathered in the chapel built to accommodate about 200 mourners. Including the family Bill reckoned there could be no more than 25 people in total. He looked at his father's coffin lying on the catafalque. Good old Wilf being sent off with all these half-hearted mutterings. He probably would appreciate the fact that no one was making a fuss; except Liz, of course, who had been sobbing gently right from the start.

Very quickly the vicar arrived at the committal prayers. Bill looked again at his father's coffin with one small wreath on it and suddenly he felt anger rising up inside him. Then to his great surprise he heard a voice cutting through the solemnity of the vicar's prayers.

"Stop! Please," the voice said. "I'm sorry, but I can't let him go like this. I have to say something."

"By all means," said the vicar. "You're the son, aren't you? Would you like to come up here to speak?"

Bill made his way to his father's coffin and stood beside it.

"No, Reverend. I'd like to say something from here if that's alright."

The vicar remained behind the lectern. "Go ahead, please. Go ahead. There's plenty of time."

"Thank you. I'm really sorry to interrupt everything, but there's something I had to tell you all about my father."

Bill put his hand on Wilf's coffin and then looked out into the chapel. Everyone was sitting up straighter now and their eyes were fixed on him.

"My sister, Liz, told me recently that she thought our dad was a hero. I didn't know what she meant really, if I'm honest. To me Dad was just a quiet, unassuming man who just got on with his life. He always had ambitions for me and Liz, but he never seemed to have any for himself. He was just a man who worked hard to keep his family. Forty-three years in the same shop. Day after day. It's unbelievable really. But that's what made him a hero to his daughter. Not to me, I'm afraid, but at least to Liz. Because he was so steady, so reliable. Liz knew that her father would always love her and never ever let her down.

"Maybe boys demand more of their fathers. I don't know really. I suppose boys think their dad's a superman and then never forgive him when they find out he's not. I don't know. I'm afraid I was a bit harsh on my dad sometimes. I wanted him to be more, if I'm honest. More adventurous maybe. I don't know. But I understand what Liz meant now. Dad was good enough just the way he was. I had no right to expect more from him… No right.

"But there was more anyway, you see. And I only found out this week. I found this."

Bill held up his father's medal in his left hand. His right hand remained on the coffin.

"My dad had five medals, but this one's a bit special apparently. It's a DCM. It says on it, 'For distinguished conduct in the field'. My dad won it at Arnhem when he was 21 years old. We always wondered how he got his injuries, didn't we? And we all knew he would never tell any of us."

There was some gentle laughter as people remembered the lengths Wilf would go to in order to avoid all questions about his role in the war.

"Well, I can tell you now how it all happened. Dad parachuted into Arnhem with the 1st Airborne Division on the 17th September 1944. They had to capture the bridge. It was a Sunday. That same day he was shot in the shoulder, but it didn't stop him fighting. He fought on for four more days. He was under fire all the time. On the Thursday they were about to be overrun. A German grenade was thrown into a trench where Dad was firing from with two other guys. He was the only one who saw it. But instead of getting out and saving himself he did the opposite. He put himself between his mates and the grenade and took all the force of the explosion instead of them. All down his left side."

There was a complete hush throughout the chapel. Bill saw Liz staring with her mouth wide open gripping Steve's hand. Peg was sitting with her head bowed. No one was moving a muscle.

"Apparently the medal wasn't awarded until the soldiers who were with Dad at the bridge were released from prison camps in the spring of 1945. By then Dad was in hospital in Bristol recovering. No one in Bramport ever knew a thing about it. Typically, Wilf just didn't want any fuss.

"The only person who knew anything was Uncle Les, and Wilf swore him to secrecy. I was talking to Uncle Les last night and he told me they wanted to give Dad the Victoria Cross. Everyone thought he deserved it, but there was no officer to back up what happened in that trench. The only officer who saw what Dad did was killed later that day. But this medal is second only to the Victoria Cross, and I think it should rest on Dad's coffin and go with him.

"So, you see, Wilf Knight was a real hero after all. As a man and as a father. He lost so much when he was so young, but he knew no bitterness, my dad. He never complained. He just got on with things. And I want to say one more thing. He wasn't the only one to lose out in that war. My mum lost a lot too. Wilf and Peg both sacrificed a lot and I just want to say 'thankyou' to my mum and my dad for what they went through for my sister and me."

For a few moments there was complete silence in the chapel as Bill made his way back to his seat. Then people started to applaud gently and Wilf's brother came over to Bill and shook his hand. The vicar seemed to be encouraged by this unscheduled turn of events and asked a little too enthusiastically, "I wonder if anyone else would like to come forward and share with us similar reflections on the life of our dear, departed brother in Christ, Wilfred?"

The chapel went silent again as people looked around, smiled nervously and then tried hard not to catch anyone else's eye. No one moved except Peg. She stood up and walked over to Wilf's coffin, ignoring the vicar's nod of approval as she passed him. She paused at the coffin for a moment and then picked up the medal that Bill had laid there. And then in front of everyone she clipped open her handbag and placed the medal inside. Then she turned to face the mourners and with her head held high strode back to her seat, all the time looking up towards the far wall of the chapel.

Bill left Bramport the next morning. The wake had been a quiet affair. Peg's neighbour, Elsie, had laid on a few sandwiches and nibbles to go with the drink Bill had bought in. Peg did not stay downstairs for very long. She sat in her chair at the dining table for about half an hour acknowledging people as they approached her, but she was clearly not in any mood for conversation. She left quietly and went up to her room, unobserved by everyone except Bill and Liz, and she stayed there for the rest of the day.

Bill was relieved that Angie and Stoner chose not to come back to Shangri-La, and he spent most of his time chatting to Mick, Dave and Les, and to Wilf's friends from the bowling club. Everyone wanted to talk about Wilf's bravery and the shock they felt at having known so little about the hero who had lived so modestly in their midst for all those years. And Bill decided to tell no one about the other things he had found in Wilf's shed. Except Liz, of course.

By six o'clock everyone outside of the family had taken their leave and Bill and Liz went out to the shed together. Liz stood open-mouthed when she saw what their father had created there.

"The dear man," she said, as she ran her fingers across the photographs. "The dear man. I had no idea half of these pictures existed. And look at this, Bill. He's got all our old school reports here."

"I know, Liz. I've seen it all. It's incredible to think of all the hours he must've spent putting it all together. Mum asked me to clear it out last week, but she told me this afternoon she'd changed her mind. She wants to sort through it herself now."

"She's not going to throw it all away, is she? You never know with her."

"I don't know, Liz. But we're just going to have to leave her to it. I don't think we can interfere."

"But I want to save Dad's things. I don't want her destroying it all. I want him looked after."

"Actually, Liz, there's something I need to ask you. A bit of a favour, I suppose."

"What?"

"Dad's ashes. I've asked Mum and she doesn't mind."

"What?"

"If I choose where to scatter them. And if I take care of it. On my own."

"Is this something that's really important to you?"

"Yes, Liz. It's very important to me."

"Then you don't need my answer, Bill. You know it already."

Bill collected Wilf's ashes on the way back to Medford. The funeral director presented him with a wide choice of urns and Bill opted for the best. And there it rested on the front passenger's seat next to him. A classic chest-styled box handcrafted out of a single piece of cherry wood so that the grain was continuous all the way around. Simple in style but the best they had.

Bill took the box with him into his room at Runnymede Terrace while he got changed, and then he carried it back out again to the car and placed it on the front seat for the drive out to Maybridge and the moors.

It was nearly midday when Bill started the two-mile walk out of the village along the stream to the foot of Braytor. It was a beautiful day. There was a blue sky, the air was crisp and Bill could feel the sun on his back. Braytor was covered in weak winter light and Bill held the box in both hands close to his chest as he strode out towards the mountain.

He did not pause until he reached the viewing platform halfway up. It was the point where Wilf had been forced to turn round on their previous attempt to climb Braytor together. Bill was breathless when he stopped at the stone seat and the small of his back ached from having to bend forward into the mountain to maintain a grip on the steep path. He appreciated how strong and determined his father must have been to get even this far up nearly 40 years ago.

"We're going all the way to the top this time, Dad," said Bill as he started climbing again. "We'll help each other this time."

It was another 40 minutes before Bill took his last step onto the highest point of Braytor. He turned to the south to look out over the moors towards Medford. He was sure he could make out the outline of the cathedral 20 miles away. Bill turned through 360°. This was the right spot. There was no higher point in any direction.

"We made it, Dad," he said at the top of his voice. "And we got here together!"

He took the box and clasped it tightly to his chest. "I'm going to leave you here, Dad. I think you'll be alright here. I want you to know that I've listened to you. I won't let bitterness eat away at me any more. Not like it's been doing with Mum. You said Mum and I were the same. But I'm free of bitterness now, Dad. Just like you've always been."

Bill opened the lid of the box and took a handful of the light grey ash which lay inside. He was surprised how fine it was. Finer than the finest sand. Almost like dust. He held the box at arm's length and spun around to create the effect of the wind on a windless day. It was like playing one last game with his father and he felt no sadness as he repeated the game several more times.

"Goodbye, Dad," he said. "Thanks. Goodbye."

Bill shook the box and put the lid back on. He looked out from Braytor until all signs of the dust had disappeared. He collected some stones and used them to cover the box so it would not be disturbed. Then he started down the mountain.

Usually, descending was harder than climbing, but this time Bill felt strong and sure-footed. When he got to the bottom he felt exhilarated to be alone in this beautiful place. He looked back up to the top of Braytor where he thought he had left his father. But Bill had not left his father there. He knew that Wilf would always be with him, and that the only thing he was leaving at Braytor was the child that had crawled inside him years ago. A guilty child who was always afraid that he could never be good enough.

Chapter 38

The next day Bill went back to work. When the bus arrived at the usual place it was half empty.

"Mornin', Bill," said Tony, as Bill took a seat behind him. "Am I glad to see you here, mate. Half the lads are still on this bullshit Millennium holiday."

"Hi, Tony. Hi, Sam," Bill replied, and he turned and waved a general greeting to the five other men sitting at the back of the bus. "We're not due back 'til next week though, are we, Tony?"

"Not strictly, but I was hoping there'd be more lads than this taking up the overtime this week. This Millennium crap's put us right behind. The bloody show house isn't even ready yet."

Tony punched the back of the seat in front of him. His Christmas break in Tenerife seemed to have done little to lessen the strain he had been under.

"I've been thinking about that, Tone," Bill said. "I need to have a word with you when we get to the site. I'll come over to your cabin, alright? I'm just going to have a quick word with young Sam."

"Don't waste your time, Bill. The boy's lovesick. Face as long as a horse."

Bill went to the back of the bus and sat next to his young workmate.

"So how did you get on with your girlfriend's family then, Sam?"

"It was a bloody disaster, Bill. A right cock-up."

"How come?"

"They're too posh for me, Bill. They've got this big house and everything. Everything was laid out for dinner every night. And then they played games and things. They played this charades thing. I reckon I made a right pillock of meself."

"How do you work that out?"

"All that pulling yer ear and touching yer nose stuff. How many words it's got. And how many sybles."

"Syllables, Sam."

"Whatever. I made a right prat of meself."

"I'm sure it wasn't that bad, was it?"

"It was all making me nervous waiting me turn, Bill, so I had a bit too much wine. Then I got a bit too carried away, I reckon. With me actions and everything."

"What did you have to act out?"

"Moby Dick. But I don't wanna talk about it."

"No. I think I get the picture, Sam. But listen. You get on alright with this girl, don't you?"

"Yeah. Sophie and me have a great time on our own. But they were all laughing at me."

"But that's the whole idea with charades, Sam. It's just meant to be a bit of fun. Listen, Sam. A word of advice. People can't make you feel bad about yourself without you agreeing to it, you know. And they probably didn't intend to upset you anyway. Do you know what I'd do?"

"What's that, Bill?"

"I'd send a nice card and a bunch of flowers to Sophie's mother thanking her for a wonderful Christmas. And I'd do the same for Sophie. And they'll both think you're the bee's knees."

"You reckon?"

"I'm sure of it. I'll help you with the wording, if you like."

"Thanks, Bill. That's a cracking idea."

"And one more bit of advice, Sam. Don't tell any of the lads about this. Especially Scouser."

When they arrived at the Meads Bill followed Tony into his office in one of the portacabins.

"Have a seat, Bill. Tell me what's on your mind."

"Can I ask you, Tony, how much contact you've had with

Horseman's Heating in Bramport over the show house and phase one?"

"Hardly any. They've been bloody useless, that lot. And whoever contracted them needs bloody shooting."

"I can tell you who contracted them. Peter Smale at Swallow Homes."

"How the hell do you know that?"

"Because I did all the negotiations with Peter to get the contract for Horseman's. I used to be the general manager there."

"You what? Are you taking the piss, Bill? 'Cos I can tell you, I'm not in the fucking mood."

"No, really, Tony. I was the general manager at Horseman's for nearly 30 years."

"You? General manager? You are taking the piss."

"No, I'm not."

"What the hell are you doing here in one of my gangs then?"

"Trying to keep my head down."

"Are you being serious?"

"I am, Tony."

"So why haven't you said anything about this before then?"

"Because I came here to get away from Bramport and Horseman's and the last thing I wanted was to get drawn back into it all again."

Tony got up and went to the window. He arched his back and sighed deeply.

"This is fucking priceless," he said, as he returned to his chair and stared at Bill. "So you're telling me that for weeks I've been trying to get some fucking sense out of Horseman's and all the time I've had their fucking supremo expert shovelling shit in one of my gangs?"

"'Fraid so."

"So why are you choosing to tell me all this now then? Why not just carry on keeping your head down. I'd never have known."

"I've been worried about it for a while, Tony, but I just kept hoping Horseman's would start doing their job."

"So what's changed suddenly?"

"I got a reminder over Christmas about doing what's right. And I know it's right to help you with this."

"I wish you'd worked that out before."

"So do I, Tony. But I left Horseman's under a bit of a cloud, and I didn't feel much like helping them get out of this mess. But I can see now I was wrong. I should've been helping you."

"I think you might've left it a bit bloody late, Bill."

"No. It's not too late, Tony. I know exactly what has to be done. We can start with the show house."

"What's wrong with it?"

"Well. The plan is to market these houses as the last word in energy-efficient homes. I know that Peter Smale wants to try for the Millennium Prize from the Energy Savings Trust at the Master Builder of the Year Awards."

"You must be fucking joking!"

"No, Tony. If everything was done right these houses would be the first major building development with state-of-the-art energy systems. It's been done with one-off houses but never with a big development like this."

"So what do we have to do on the show house?"

"Take a deep breath, Tony. Off the top of my head… you need triple glazing, not the standard double glazing Horseman's have sent you. The roof needs strengthening to take the solar tiles. And some of them are facing the wrong damn way. We haven't even dug trenches for the ground source heating and you need bigger water tanks with thermostatic mixing valves to prevent…"

"Whoa! Stop. For fuck's sake, Bill, you've made your point. Look. I'm way out of my depth here. We need one of the big boys down to sort all this out. I'm going to give Mr Smale a call. Is that alright with you?"

"It's fine with me, Tony. I'll help in any way I can."

Peter Smale came down from Swallow's head office in Birmingham on Monday morning. Everyone was back from the long holiday now and Bill was digging trenches with Sam and Scouser when he was called into Tony's office.

"Hello, Bill," said Peter Smale as he stood up and held out his hand. "It's good to see you again."

"Hello, Peter. I'm afraid my hands are a bit dirty."

"Don't worry about that. I'm just pleased to see you here. Take a seat. Tony's been telling me about all the problems with phase one."

"It's nothing that can't be fixed, Peter."

"Good. But I must say, Bill, we're all a little disappointed you didn't say anything earlier."

"I don't work for Horseman's any more, Peter."

"I know that, but you must see that these delays could be disastrous for everyone."

"Peter, I took a job seven weeks ago as a labourer for Carter Construction. I had no idea I was coming to this site until the morning I arrived. And I chose not to say anything because the last thing I needed then and now is to get involved again with Benny Horseman. You must know what went on there?"

"I only found out on Friday when I got in touch with Horseman's about all this."

"So you know Benny sacked me for theft and that there's a criminal prosecution pending?"

"Yes. I got the details on Friday."

"And do you know Benny is suing me in the civil court for assault?"

"Yes. I heard that too."

Bill caught the look of astonishment on Tony's face.

"So you must understand, Peter, that my first priority hasn't been to help out Benny Horseman. I could've just kept quiet and let you and Carter's sue the arse off him for his incompetence and then watched while the takeover by SCP fell flat on its face."

"So why didn't you?"

"Because it's not the way I choose to be. And Tony here doesn't deserve all the things that have been going wrong here."

"I just wish we'd been alerted earlier that's all," said Peter Smale.

"But that's not my fault and it's not Tony's fault either. He's had no help from Horseman's. He's just had to work with what they sent him. And I've got to say he's performed miracles making things work the way he has."

"Thanks, Bill," said Tony, rubbing his eyes.

"I honestly think Horseman's forgot all about the special plans for this site, Peter," Bill continued, "and they've just been sending out the standard fittings. And Tony here has been getting them fitted as best he could. They even sent combi boilers, for God's sake, and you can't have that with ground source heating."

"Oh, don't tell me any more," moaned Tony.

"It's alright, Tony. We can fix all that."

"You're really sure you can fix it, are you, Bill?" asked Peter Smale.

"Yes, I am, Peter. I know the specs for the plumbing inside out. I'd arranged for two fellas from Horseman's to go on a special course so you'd have one man on site permanently. But it doesn't look as if it's been done. But if I'm here, it'll be just as good."

"Probably better," said Tony.

"And can you have the first phase ready by the target date, Friday, the 25th March?"

"We'll have a bloody good go, won't we, Tone?"

Tony smiled and nodded. Little did he or Peter Smale know that three days after that date Bill would be in court and likely to be unavailable again for another two or three years.

"Well," said Peter, "I've asked Benny Horseman to put you back on his payroll but he's having none of it. I told him the trouble we're in here and the penalty clauses that kick in if he fails to deliver. But I honestly think he'd prefer to be sued and lose millions from a failed takeover than take you back, Bill. I think the guy must have a screw loose."

"The poor man's certainly got problems, Peter. But I don't need to be working for Horseman's to do what's needed here."

"But you'll need new terms of employment."

"If you say so. I'd help anyway."

"No. We need to formalise this. I suggest we change your role to that of a consultant, Bill. Swallow will give you a contract starting today until the end of March. Can I discuss the details in front of Tony?"

"I've got work to do," said Tony. "I'll leave you both to it. Goodbye, Mr Smale. See you later, Bill."

Peter Smale waited until Tony had closed the door.

"Now, Bill. Swallow will pay you as a consultant until the end of March at a salary rate equivalent to £120,000 per annum. In addition we will pay you a bonus of £50,000 if you deliver phase one on schedule by the 25th March. What do you say?"

"I say that's very generous, Peter."

"Not really, Bill. We'll be suing Horseman's for everything we have to pay you. And remember we expect you to be on call morning, noon and night as part of the contract."

"I understand that, Peter. By the way I think I can sweeten the pill a bit for you over what you're having to pay me."

"How's that?"

"Did you know you can get a renewable energy grant of £500 for every house you construct with solar panels? And £1500 for every house with a ground source heat pump?"

"No, I didn't!"

"That's £2,000 for each of your 75 units. One hundred and fifty thousand pounds. I'll get the applications in, shall I?"

"I'd appreciate that, Bill. I think we've got a deal."

Bill gave himself six days to fix all the problems with the energy systems in the show house. It had to be ready before the rest of the first phase could be properly marketed. And whilst he supervised the show house he made sure the other 15 units were prepared properly for the right energy systems to be installed.

Bill was earning his money the hard way from before seven in the morning until after seven at night. To begin with it was not easy for the craftsmen to take orders from Bill, when only a few days before they had been telling him what to do. But Bill understood what so many bosses and managers do not understand. That if you want a job done efficiently and well the most precious resource you have is the goodwill of the people you are relying on to do it. And so everyone was treated with an even hand, and if a job proved particularly difficult Bill would roll up his sleeves and get stuck in with the rest of them.

He bypassed Horseman's completely and went straight to the manufacturers to get the right parts, on one occasion even sending Scouser and Sam on a 200-mile round trip to get a special tank needed for the extra hot water storage.

The show house was open on time, but by the following weekend Bill was exhausted. With his new income he had allowed himself the luxury of moving back into the hotel and hiring a car to get to work, but in over two weeks he had spent only one evening away from work or from thinking about work. It was the evening he went back to the Runnymede Arms in the hope of seeing Roly Upperton.

Bill felt he owed Roly an apology for not turning up on New Year's Eve as they had arranged. But Roly did not come to his local that night. Then it dawned on Bill that the Players were already in rehearsals for *Cabaret* and that afterwards they always went to their usual pub by the Guildhall. He wondered how Hayley would be shaping up in her starring role, but he already knew the answer to that. How he would love to walk into the Bull and talk to her, or even drive past and just catch a glimpse of her. But it would be a mistake. They had both made their choices and if there was ever going to be a time for them to be together, it was not now. Bill left a note for Roly behind the bar explaining what had detained him on the eve of the new millennium and then went back to his hotel for an early night.

Chapter 39

By the end of January teams of brickies were at work on all 15 houses. Modifications had been made to incorporate all Bill's original plans and all the delivery dates for the necessary installations had been agreed. Bill had been working 14-hour days, seven days a week, for nearly three weeks now and he decided it was time at last to take a Sunday off. So he called Angie and Peg, Mickey and Dave and arranged to drive down to Bramport to see them all.

At first Angie was reluctant to see Bill at all without Mark Stone there, but Bill was insistent that he wanted to see her alone. It was only when he assured Angie that he only needed an hour of her time, and that he had only good news for her, that she finally relented. It was agreed he would arrive at eleven o'clock, in time for morning coffee.

Angie asked Bill to wait in the lounge while she made their drinks. Bill sat in a familiar armchair and looked around him. Not a lot had been changed in the room since his last visit at the beginning of December. One of Stoner's Tibetan prayer wheels stood on the sideboard, which might suggest that he had moved in permanently, but Bill decided not to mention it. The house still smelled strongly of lavender or sandalwood or something that Bill could not identify. He picked up the book lying on the coffee table. *Feng Shui And The Theory of Yin and Yang.*

Angie brought the drinks in. Coffee for Bill and herbal tea for herself. She had had her hair cut shorter since the funeral and Bill thought how much it suited her. And she had lost even more weight, which he was not sure suited her at all. Neither of them spoke whilst she poured Bill's coffee.

"Thanks, Angie. Did Mickey and Dave tell you I'm taking them out for lunch today?"

"I think Dave might've mentioned it."

"Yes. I thought I'd take them to Leonardo's. Something special since I don't see them too often."

"You know how expensive it is, do you?"

"Yes, so I've heard. But I've had a bit of promotion at work so I reckon it's a pretty good way of spending my money."

"Promotion? I thought you were labouring?"

"I was. But they need my help with the pipes and pumps, so I've been made a consultant. That's what I really wanted to talk to you about."

"Why? Does it affect me?"

"Well yes, it does, because it means I can give you a bit more money for a few weeks."

"That's alright. Mark's been helping out, so I think I can manage."

"Oh, I see."

"I hope you're not going to get funny about it. It was terrible the last time you were here."

"No, Angie. Relax, love. I'm not going to get funny about anything. What you and Stoner... sorry, I mean Mark... decide is fine by me. But I'd like you to let me give you what I can. Let's face it, Angie, I'm not going to need it where I'm likely to be going. I've got a cheque here. I want you to have it."

He reached into his jacket pocket.

"I don't know, Bill. I can't work you out."

Angie took the cheque and read the amount.

"Four thousand pounds! I don't understand it. Four thousand pounds? How can you afford this? How much are they paying you?"

"Enough for me to give you this and pay my own way in Medford."

Angie took a handkerchief from the sleeve of her white blouse and held it to her nose. She breathed in the aroma.

"I don't know, Bill. I never know what's going on with you.

You do such unexpected things nowadays. I get so nervous around you."

"It's alright, love. You can relax with me now. I just want to help you if I can. That's all."

"Can I really relax with you, Bill? What about Mark?"

"That's alright too, Angie. I don't pretend it's what I wanted, but you've had to make a difficult decision and I accept it. I wouldn't be here otherwise."

"But no one would even speak to us at the funeral. That's why we didn't come back afterwards. I didn't want any funniness towards Mark."

"Well, you wouldn't have got any from me. Mind you, I can't speak for Mum and Liz. They're pretty formidable on their day, I suppose. On second thoughts you probably did the right thing."

Bill tried to laugh and Angie half smiled at him.

"We both thought what you said about your dad at the funeral was really lovely, Bill. I always liked Wilf."

"I know you did, Angie. And he loved you too."

"And are you getting over it now?"

"It's not a question of getting over it, Angie. I learned so many wonderful things about my dad during that week after Christmas. I feel so close to him now. It's changed a lot of things for me."

"What sort of things?"

"The last time I saw Dad was just after I took the money. He could see how upset I was. You know, angry and frustrated about everything."

"Yes. I think I know all about that, Bill."

"Of course you do. But my dad gave me some simple advice. He said, 'Don't let bitterness eat away at you, Son'. And when I found out how much he sacrificed and suffered and how little he complained, it all meant something to me. I understood what being free really is."

"So what is it then?"

"Being free isn't about not having any responsibilities, like I thought it was. It's not about having no work or no ties. It's a state of mind. It's about being free from whatever plagues you inside. And having compassion for people. Including yourself."

"So what's happened to all the frustration you used to go on about?"

"It's gone, Angie."

"And all the anger about the job and the way Benny Horseman treated you?"

"That's gone too. I had no right to blame anyone else for what was going on inside me. But I did. I blamed Benny, and my dad, and I blamed you sometimes too, Angie."

"I know you did. I always felt it."

"I know, darling. I'm sorry."

"You were always so restless. There was always something you had to get out of your system. It was the worst possible thing for me."

"Because it made you so insecure?"

"Because I always knew it would make you leave me."

"I'm sorry, Angie. I thought I was being so heroic ploughing on through all my frustration. But I was just being bloody stupid. My mother's been the same and look what it's done to her."

"It's not been just your fault, Bill. I know I haven't been easy to live with sometimes."

"But you've been ill, love. You've done so well dealing with it. And without much help from me."

"But I haven't been fair to you either, Bill. When I think of you…"

Angie held the handkerchief to her eyes.

"Don't upset yourself, love. There's no need," Bill said.

"No. I have to say it. When I think of you when you were young. When we first met. You were so full of hope. You were so positive and full of adventure. And I watched…"

Angie started to cry. Bill leaned forward but held back from going over to her.

"And I watched you get more and more disappointed with your life over the years. But I couldn't stop it."

"It wasn't your fault, Angie. It wasn't anyone's fault."

"But I could've encouraged you. But I…"

"But you had your own stuff to deal with. I know that, Angie."

"But now I'm feeling better I can see it more clearly. I feel so guilty about it all sometimes."

Bill got up and sat down next to Angie on the sofa. He held her gently by the shoulders and turned her towards him. She stared down at the handkerchief in her hands.

"Now listen to me, Angie. I won't have you wasting time feeling guilty about me or anything else. You and I are both finished with guilt forever."

"How do we manage that?"

"By forgiving ourselves. We're allowed to make mistakes, you and me, Angie."

"So don't you feel guilty about anything any more, Bill?"

"I don't, Angie. Because I understand that my mistakes in the past have come through not being honest about myself. About how I felt."

Angie looked up at him.

"So what's changed in you now then?" she asked.

"I accept myself and I can be honest now about what matters to me. And I intend to be honest with the people around me too. So they can accept me for what I am. Or choose to have nothing to do with me, of course."

"I don't think that'll happen."

"But the point is, Angie, I don't need to blame you or Benny or my dad any more. I'm completely responsible for my own life. And you're not responsible for me or anyone else, Angie."

"What about Mark?"

"He'd be the first person to tell you the same."

"But I do feel guilty towards him, Bill."

"Why should you?"

"Because I don't love him like he loves me. But I need him. He's changed my life with all his ideas and his advice. And he's so patient with me."

As they spoke Bill's hands had gradually slipped down from Angie's shoulders until he was holding her elbows. He finally let go.

"Do you mind me talking like this?" she asked him.

"It's not easy, but I understand. It's alright. Go on."

"I need Mark to stay here with me, Bill. I don't want to ever go back to the way I was."

"I really do understand, Angie. Don't worry. It really is alright. I'll just go back and sit in the armchair so we can talk more easily facing one another."

"I have upset you."

"No, really, Angie. I can't pretend I like what Stoner did, but I can see how much he's helped you. Nothing's more important than you being well."

"You know, Bill. I feel I've got my life back. It's like being reborn really. I'm not taking Valium any more. I haven't had an attack since early December. I belong to a fantastic support group and I'm really into meditation."

"That's great, Angie."

"And there's one more thing, but you might not be too happy about it."

"Go on."

"Mark wants me to try some behaviour therapy. It's all about learning to cope with your fears. By confronting them. Controlled exposure, Mark calls it."

"Why would I object to that?"

"Because he wants to take me on a trip away from where all my security is."

"Where to?"

"Thailand. To a Buddhist retreat."

"God. That's where I've always wanted to go!"

"I know. I'm sorry, Bill. I've been dreading telling you."

"When are you going?"

"The flight's on the 28th of March."

"You're joking!" said Bill and he started to laugh. It started slowly and then grew until it had gripped him and he could not stop. Angie looked at him and smiled with a bemused look on her face.

"What?" she asked. "What's so funny? I don't understand. Stop, Bill. What is it?"

Bill eventually regained control and wiped tears from his eyes.

"That's so wonderful," he eventually managed to say. "That's just bloody priceless."

"What is? Please explain to me."

"Angie, my darling, that's the day I go on trial for stealing Benny's money. There's me always wanting to travel the world and I'm locked up in a cell. And there's you never wanting to go anywhere flying off to bloody Thailand."

Bill started laughing again as loud as before, and after a few moments of thinking about it, Angie joined in too.

Bill offered to make fresh drinks and he brought them into the lounge on a tray. He sat down in his armchair holding his mug of coffee and a biscuit and Angie leaned forward from the sofa to pick up her cup of peppermint tea.

"Lovely. Thanks, Bill. I must say, I'm really relieved we can talk all about these things without getting upset. I can't believe how bad it was the last time you were here."

"I know. I was worried about you after I left. But I knew Mark would take care of you. It was just a bit of a shock when he turned up and let himself in like that."

"I thought you would've already guessed something."

"No. I honestly hadn't. I suppose I thought the whole world was working to my timetable. I could just come back here when I was ready and be welcomed with open arms. Pretty naïve of me really."

Angie kicked off her shoes and drew her legs up onto the sofa. She rested her elbow on the arm and tilted her head slightly as she spoke to Bill.

"Did you really come back that day so we could start all over again?" she asked.

"Yeah," Bill chuckled. "When Mark told me how bad you were, I just wanted to come home and take care of you. But it's probably best left the way it is."

"Just for now, eh, Bill?"

"Yes, Angie. Just for now. We've both got a lot to sort out, haven't we? Like I said, that's partly why I've come down to see you today." Bill put his mug down on the coffee table. "I need to go through a few practicalities with you."

"What sort of practicalities?"

"Well, this consultancy contract I've got. It's very generous pay, but it's going to mean I'm working flat out almost 'til the day of my trial. If I get convicted I may not have a chance of seeing you for a while, Angie. So there are a few arrangements we need to make."

"Like what?"

"Well. We need to transfer the house into your name. I hope you don't mind, but I've already got my solicitor working on it. You'll be hearing from her soon. But it means the mortgage has to be just in your name too. But don't worry about that because I'm going to pay it off."

"How on earth are you going to do that?"

"I get £50,000 if I fulfil my contract on time. By the 25th of March, that'll be. It's going to be a push but I'm determined to do it. And when I do I'm going to arrange for the money to be paid direct to you, Angie."

"To me?"

"Yes. I want you to have it, Angie. It'll make you secure and it'll stop Benny Horseman getting his hands on it."

"I don't understand. How could Benny get it?"

Bill sighed.

"I've got to tell you this, Angie, but don't worry about it. Benny's taking out a private prosecution against me for damages, because of the injuries he received back in November. He says I attacked him. But he's lying. I didn't. And my solicitor thinks he's got next to no chance of winning. But just in case I want you to have the money."

"Look after it, you mean? If all goes well I can give it back to you?"

"No, Angie. I want you to have it anyway. Pay off the mortgage and keep what's left. Treat yourself with it. Go on lots of trips."

"I can't do that, Bill. It's far too generous."

"No, it's not. I could never give you enough, Angie. Not after what you've been through for me and the boys. When I think of how wonderfully you brought them up with everything you were going through…"

"I did have some help from you, Bill."

"That may be, but I want you to have it anyway. This is one thing I won't have any argument over."

Angie put down her cup on a side table and put her head in her hand.

"What's the matter, darling?" said Bill as he went over to her. Angie turned towards him and laid her head on his chest as he put his arms around her.

"You're being so kind to me, Bill. So understanding about everything. I think this is harder to take than when you're being angry and bad-tempered."

"Well, I think I prefer being like this if it's alright with you."

"Yes, of course, love, but I'm going to feel so bad towards you. You're on your own and I've got Mark. And I've got so much to look forward to now and you've got…you know."

"The slammer!"

"Don't joke, Bill. I know what you said about not feeling guilty, but I can't help it. Especially for what I've done with Mark."

Bill let go of Angie and eased her away from him. He stood up and went back to his chair.

"There's something else I need to tell you, Angie. It might make you feel a bit differently about all this."

He looked over at Angie. Her face showed no emotion.

"I thought a long time about saying this and I'm only doing it because I hope it might help you not feel quite so bad.

"When I was in Medford before Christmas I met someone who helped me. Just like Mark's helping you. She was patient with me and she got me to understand a lot of things about myself. Just like you and Mark."

Bill's mouth had become bone-dry and he had to drain his mug of lukewarm coffee before he could speak again. He cleared his throat but his voice still wavered.

"For her it was all about…knowing yourself…and being true to yourself. And being honest with other people about yourself."

He looked at Angie and fought to make his voice stronger.

"She made me understand that if something's really important to you, you have to give it priority in your life or you'll never have any peace."

"And she's your priority now, is she?"

"No, she's not. You are, and the boys are. I just want you to be well and happy."

"Well, that's alright then, because we are all well and happy. So now you can be with her."

"No, Angie, you've got it all wrong. I haven't seen her for nearly two months. We were only together for three or four weeks. I doubt whether we'll ever meet again."

"I don't understand what you're telling me then."

"I'm telling you not to feel bad about needing Mark, because I understand how sometimes we need help to work our way through something. And we don't always know where that help's going to come from. I'm saying that I'm okay about you and Mark."

"So why don't you stay with her?"

"Because we both have things which are more important to us."

"What's she called?"

"Hayley."

"And what's so important to your Hayley then?"

"She wants to succeed in her work."

"I don't see why that should exclude you."

"It's like I said, Angie. I've got my own priorities. I want to put you first, and then I've got my own ambitions to think about."

"Travelling."

"Well, yes, I do want to travel a lot, of course, but it's a bit more than that."

"Pit your wits against the world. That's what you always used to say."

"Did I?"

"Yes, you did. Often."

"Well, I do want to pit my wits against the world. I want my life to have some dynamic about it. So it grows, develops, changes. You must recognise that need in your own life now, Angie."

"Yes, I do. But I want to take small steps with my changes,

Bill. That's what Mark says. Small steps. You always used to talk about such big changes all the time. It used to scare me."

"I never meant to scare you, Angie. I'm sorry I've brought all this trouble down on you."

"No. You can stop apologising for that now, Bill. When you first took the money and everything happened so fast I was so angry with you for changing our lives so much. But now I'm actually grateful for it. It's led to me getting better."

"And you don't mind me telling you about Hayley?"

"Three months ago it would probably have made me have a nervous breakdown, but I'm so much more in control now."

"I can't tell you what a relief that is, Angie. I wanted to be honest with you but I was dreading you getting really upset."

Angie shook her head.

"No, I can deal with it, Bill. Was it really serious between the two of you then?"

"Whatever it was, Angie, it was genuine."

"Mark would say this is all yin and yang, you know."

"Would he indeed? Why?"

"Because the Chinese believe things evolve and eventually find a balance, and that's probably what we've just done here."

"I don't know much about Mark's philosophies."

"Yin and yang. Everything in life contains the seed of its opposite. So confusion and turmoil evolve into peace and serenity. Out of all this mess you and I have managed to become happier."

"But not together, eh, Angie?"

"You can't have everything, Bill."

Over lunch with Mickey and Dave it soon became clear they were not at all happy with the place Mark Stone now occupied in their mother's life. 'A weasel' and 'a snake in the grass' were two of the kinder ways they chose to describe him. It took some time for Bill to convince them that Stoner was helping Angie in a way that years of medical treatment had failed to do. And it took even longer for him to persuade them that he was happy to accept the situation if it meant Angie could be free of all the fears that had blighted her life. Even at their age Bill could see how much reassurance his children needed that their parents still loved one another, and that there might be a chance, some time in the future, when everything in their family would return to normal.

Bill was always proud of his boys. Mickey was a bit of a worrier maybe, and Dave was forever making a joke of everything, but somehow each of them had managed to become people who, to Bill's mind, were better than the best bits of him and Angie combined. He sat back and listened to them talking about the businesses they had both set up. Mickey was now employing another electrician full-time and still had more work than he could handle. Dave's security firm was expanding so fast that he had started providing night-time security patrols for other local businesses. The only work they both refused to do was anything involving Horseman's Heating.

"I hope that's got nothing to do with me," Bill protested.

"No, I'll take Horseman's money any time," said Mickey, "but it's always so bloody disorganised now when you do anything for them. Half the time they're not ready for you or they're just plain not there."

"It's since Benny took over before Christmas," added Dave. "He's about as much use as an ashtray on a motorbike."

"No, it was bad before that," said Mickey, "but it's just plain impossible now."

"I didn't know Benny was running things there now," said Bill.

"Yeah, he gave Hugh Turner the push. Just before Christmas, wasn't it, Dave?"

"Yeah. Three days before the holiday. I reckon he was trying to get out of paying Hugo's Christmas bonus. Tighter than a photo-finish, that Benny."

"Honestly, Dad," said Mickey. "I think you're best out of it from what I hear. It's a real sinking ship. I've even heard that takeover deal's a bit iffy now. Benny Horseman could lose millions if that falls through."

"Well, I'm bloody glad," said Dave. "Benny Horseman's the sort of bloke who cheats filling out opinion polls. After the way he treated Dad, he deserves all he gets."

"No, hold on, boys. I don't want you to feel like that about him.

Believe it or not, Benny Horseman's had a hard time of it."

"Yeah, right," laughed Mickey.

"Yeah. I guess it must be hard for him living his life with his head stuck up his arse," added Dave.

"No, really, boys. I'm not joking. I really have changed my mind about Benny. I really do feel sorry for him."

Mickey and Dave looked at one another but said nothing.

"One thing I've learnt through all this madness over the past few months is that there's more to everyone than we think, and we shouldn't judge anyone too quickly."

"Hell. You haven't got religion, have you, Dad?" said Dave. "'Cos we never said grace before we ate, you know."

"No. I haven't got religion, Son. But I am serious about not being angry towards Benny any more. I wish he could succeed at Horseman's. He really needs to for his own self-respect. It's going to be really painful for him if he fails at it."

"Bloody painful, I should think," said Mickey, "if he loses all those millions."

"Believe it or not, Mickey, I don't think Benny will be giving a damn about the money. The only thing he wants is to prove his father wrong for never having any faith in him."

"But he's making such a cock-up of it."

"I know. And I can imagine how much he must be suffering for it. Much more than any of us have ever wished on him."

"But I don't understand what you're saying, Dad," said Mickey. "Benny Horseman's father died years ago."

"Twenty-three years ago this April."

"Well, what's the point of Benny trying to prove anything to him now then?"

"Because of what his father left him."

"He left him a good business."

"I know. But he also left him feeling stupid and inadequate and full of bitterness, and he needs to get rid of all that somehow. I tell you, boys, I look at Benny and I see how lucky I am with what your grandad left me."

"A set of crown-green bowls and his medals, wasn't it, Dad?" said Dave with a smile.

"Give it a rest, Dave," said his brother. "What did he leave you, Dad?"

"Peace of mind, Mickey. Grandad left me with peace of mind."

The three of them sat in silence for a moment, but Dave could not tolerate silences for long.

"So what was all that business with the medal at the funeral?" he said. "Grandma going up to the coffin and taking it like that? I thought she was going up there to tell the poor old bugger off at first. For not being up and about doing something."

"Cut it out, Dave," protested Mickey, trying to suppress a smile. "Show some respect."

"No, it's alright, Mickey," said Bill. "Your grandad was a big enough man to take a joke. But it was strange what Grandma did. If I get a chance this afternoon I'll ask her what it was all about."

Bill was not looking forward to hearing more bitterness from his mother, although he still lived in hope that she might one day take a different view of the world and of the people in it. It was just possible that Wilf's death had brought about some change for the better in her. But when he arrived at Shangri-La he soon found out it was not to be.

"So I'm last on your list again, am I?" she said to him as he walked from the car to the front door in the rain. "You've already seen everyone who really matters, have you?"

"Hello, Mum," said Bill with exaggerated cheerfulness, and he kissed her on the cheek in spite of her efforts to avoid it. "I've seen Angie this morning and I've just had a lovely lunch with the boys. They all send their love."

"I'll believe that when I hear it."

"Oh, come on, Mum. Don't be like that. I'll make us a nice cup of tea."

"It's alright. I'll do it. You'd better come through."

Bill hung up his coat and followed her into the kitchen. He sat down at the table.

"So how have you been since the funeral, Mum? It's been over three weeks now."

"What do you expect, William? That I'm out dancing and

carrying on every night. Or I've moved a new man in already, like your Angie?"

"Whoa, Mum. Steady on. Where's all that come from so suddenly?"

"Do you think no one knows? She had a cheek bringing him to your father's funeral. And he's meant to be such a good friend of yours. Some friend that is. It beats me why you put up with it."

"Well, this is a nice greeting, Mum. Let me take a deep breath. I can try to explain it, if you really want me to."

"Oh, I know everything can be explained away nowadays. I wouldn't bother looking for explanations, if I were you. I'd just get over there now and throw the blighter out. It's your wife and your house he's taken from under your nose."

"Life's not always that simple, Mum."

"Life's very simple, William. You're married and you should be with your wife where you belong. I know you've always been useless at standing up to women, but I thought you would at least stand up to another man."

"That's just not fair, Mum. There are issues here you don't understand."

"Issues? What issues are there when you're allowing another man into your wife's bed? It's disgusting."

"But you don't understand, Mum. Angie and I have both been unhappy for a very long time. Sometimes you have to accept drastic changes to work out what really makes you happy."

"And you're telling me you're happy now. Is that it?"

"I am, Mum. I'm happier now than I have been for years."

Peg shook her head and brought the kettle down hard on the kitchen sink.

"Well, I think the world's gone completely mad. Your wife's doing I don't know what with another man. You're on your way to prison. And you sit there and tell me how happy you are! I give up on the lot of you."

"So, are you happy then, Mum?"

"It's not all about being happy, William. It's about being decent. Standing by your family and getting on with things."

"So, you're *not* happy then?"

"I'm happy that I've always done the right thing by you and your sister and your father."

"But that doesn't mean you've necessarily done the right thing for yourself, does it Mum?"

"Don't you get clever with me, William. You twist words to make them suit anything you want. We all know what's right and wrong, and what you're letting go on in your house is wrong. What must those boys think of their mother and father carrying on like this?"

"They leave it to us to sort out. They know we both love them and they just want us to be happy."

"So they say. I bet they don't tell you what they really feel."

"And you do, do you, Mum? You're really honest about how you feel, are you? You're honest about all the things you feel you missed out on, and you're honest about all the resentment you felt towards me and Liz and Dad, are you? Don't you talk to me about honesty, Mum."

"Don't you be so impertinent, William. And don't you talk about me and your father like that. All we ever wanted was for you and Liz to get on in life. It's a good job he's not here to see the mess you've made of it all. He's in the best place if you ask me."

"And you can stop trying to make me feel bad towards Dad, because I'm telling you it won't work any more. Dad and I are fine together now and always will be. I wish I could work things out with you half as well."

"You can work things out with me well enough by going back to your wife, William, and leading a decent life."

"Act out of duty like you, eh, Mum? Become bitter and lose all compassion because I can't be honest about who I am. Why don't you go out into Dad's den some time and remind yourself who you really are. All his stuff's still out there, is it?"

"I've had enough of this. I think you'd better go, William."

"I think I better had, Mum."

Bill went into the hallway and got his coat. Peg did not follow him. When he came back into the kitchen she was standing at the window looking out onto the garden and dabbing her eyes with a handkerchief. Bill went to her and put his arm around her. She shrugged him away.

"Just leave me alone."

"Mum, I didn't mean…"

"Just go away and leave me be."

Peg turned her head, but not far enough to look at him.

"I don't want you to come here any more, William. Not until I say so, anyway. You just upset me too much."

"I'm sorry you feel like that, Mum. I just want to help you to see…"

"I don't want any more of your fancy words. Just go!"

Bill went into the hallway and opened the front door. He held it open and shouted back, "I love you, Mum." He waited a few moments but there was no reply.

Chapter 40

As Bill drove away from Bramport on his way back to Medford the pleasure he had felt at seeing Angie and the boys had turned into sadness over his mother. He knew he was not responsible for Peg's unhappiness, but it did not stop him worrying about her. She seemed worse, if anything, without Wilf there. Perhaps he acted as a safety valve for her, soaking up all the frustration and anger she felt about her life, and without him everything festered inside her. Or maybe she really missed him and was desperately sad. Who could ever know? She was certainly never going to allow Bill to help her explore her true feelings. And the worst thought was the possibility that Peg might go through the rest of her life without ever being honest with herself about how she really felt.

Ten miles out of Bramport Bill drove past the gates of Aldrington Hall. "And there's another poor devil," he thought, "blaming everyone else for what's wrong in his life." Bill's heart sank as he imagined Benny Horseman brooding in his study, allowing his anger and hate to eat away at him and ruin his life, in the same way that Bill had almost allowed his own life to be ruined.

Only two weeks later Bill received some startling news about Benny. It was Tuesday, the 15th February. Bill had arrived at the Meads as usual just before 7.30, and a couple of hours later he received a call on his mobile from Natalie Barry. She apologised for calling him at work and suggested he found somewhere quiet on his own to sit down. Bill went to his car and sat in the driver's seat.

"Right, this is private enough, Natalie. I can talk now. What's going on?"

"I'm not sure, Bill, but I had to let you know right away. I've just arrived at my office and my secretary has brought me two letters. I've got them both in front of me now. One is from the Crown Prosecution Service and the other is from Tom Wiltshire, Mr Horseman's solicitor. They both say the same thing."

"I'm listening, Natalie."

Bill steeled himself against more bad news.

"Following a new statement from Mr Horseman given to Bramport police on Wednesday, 9th February, all criminal charges against you have been dropped.

"Bill? Bill? Are you still there?"

"Yes, Natalie. I'm still here. I just can't believe what you just said."

"I said, 'all criminal charges against you have been dropped'."

"Yes, I heard. But I just can't believe it. I don't understand."

"Hold on, Bill. It gets better. The letter from Tom Wiltshire goes on to say that Mr Horseman will no longer be pursuing his claim against you for damages in the civil courts. They've dropped everything, Bill."

"But why? I don't understand why."

"You don't sound very pleased."

"I'm delighted. Thrilled. I just can't believe it. Why?"

"Well, listen. Have you got time?"

"I've got plenty of time for this, Natalie."

"Well, I'll read you some of Tom Wiltshire's letter then. It says, '…during recent redecorating work undertaken at my client's residence a money-belt containing £10,000 in cash was discovered under a bookcase in my client's study. My client accepts that this is likely to be the same money-belt that Mr Knight claimed to have returned to my client on the morning of Saturday, 23rd October."

"What a load…!"

"Wait, Bill. There's more. 'This discovery has further led my client to review the events of the evening of Friday, 22nd October and he now recognises that his earlier recollection of that evening may have been impaired by the effects of a small amount of alcohol consumed after taking medicine prescribed by his doctor.'"

"It's nonsense!"

"Does it matter, Bill? Listen to this bit. 'Consequently and in the light of these new facts my client made a new statement to the police on Wednesday, 9th February 2000, accepting that Mr Knight has not permanently deprived, and never intended to permanently deprive, my client of any monies belonging to him.' And finally, Bill. Bill, are you still there?"

"Yes, I'm still here."

"I'll just read the last sentence. 'As a gesture of goodwill to Mr Knight my client is further minded to withdraw his claim for damages pending in the civil court, and offers to cover in full all legal costs incurred by Mr Knight in connection with both the criminal and civil cases involving my client.'

"It's over, Bill. That's as close as they're ever going to come to admitting it was all a pack of lies in the first place. I'd love to know what made Mr Horseman change his mind."

"Perhaps it wasn't a change of mind, Natalie. Perhaps it was a change of heart."

"I don't see what difference it makes, Bill. Either way, you won!"

Angie and the boys were thrilled when Bill gave them the news later that day. Peg seemed relieved too that he had somehow 'managed to get away with it'. And Bill wondered if maybe she was right. He knew he only intended to borrow Benny's money that night in October, but God knows how he would have repaid it if he had lost the lot in the casino. Would borrowing then have become theft? There was still no way Bill could work out the rights and wrongs of it all.

He went to the hotel bar and ordered another single malt. It was his fourth. This was turning into a strange celebration. There was no question about the enormous sense of relief he had been experiencing all day since Natalie's phone call, but the last thing this felt like now was a victory over Benny Horseman.

Bill realised that taking Benny's money was not the worst thing he had done to him over the years. Much worse had been his willingness to withhold his friendship from Benny, and his readiness to replace it with resentment and arrogance. Benny might have become more involved in the business if Bill had not treated him just like his father had done. Like an uncouth, unintelligent bore. They might even have become friends. But neither of them had been able to get beyond their jealousy and envy for what the other had, and which they thought by rights should have been theirs.

Bill downed his drink and went to get another. He decided it would be his last for the night before he turned in. He stood at the bar to drink it, and as he did he made a decision.

It was true that Benny had not exactly played fair with him over the money, especially lying to the police like that. And maybe Bill did deserve some punishment for what he did, but nothing like Benny had had in mind for him. But now for some reason Benny had decided to put things right between them, and the least Bill could do in return was to show he harboured no ill feeling. And maybe, if possible, even extend the hand of friendship.

Two days later Bill received further proof of Benny's new attitude towards him. Out of the blue Harry Woodford called and asked Bill to come and see him either in his office in Medford or at his home. Bill chose to go round to Harry's house in Cathedral Close that same evening.

Harry welcomed his old friend with an enthusiastic handshake and ushered him into the lounge where a log fire burned in the 16th century stone fireplace. Alison Woodford was standing in the middle of the room as if to receive their visitor. She pecked Bill on both cheeks and asked after Angie before leaving the two men to themselves. Harry did not try to hide his disappointment when he learned that Bill had been in Medford for the past three months but had not called in to see him.

"You could have stayed here with us," said Harry, confirming to Bill why he had preferred to keep his presence in Medford to himself in the first place.

"I thought Stoner might have kept you up to date with everything, Harry."

"Not a word, Bill. But you know Stoner. He's not one for gossip.

He's always worked on the principle that if you want someone to know something you'll tell them yourself."

Bill was relieved that Harry seemed to know nothing about Angie and Stoner, and he was pleased when Harry did not probe. The two friends drank a whisky together and laughed as they reminisced about old times.

"I hope you can forgive me for not keeping in touch, Harry, but it's been a difficult few months for me. There was a lot I needed to work through on my own."

"I think I understand, Bill. I must say, you're looking and sounding so much better than the last time you were here. Alison and I are so pleased things are working out for you."

"Thanks, Harry. It's been a strange time. It's as if I've been peeling away layers of...I don't know...layers of useless packaging...that have built up around me over the years. Holding me in and holding me back at the same time, you know? I think it's been the same for Angie. I know it all sounds very 'new-age hippy', but I think both of us have emerged as much happier people."

"That's wonderful, Bill. I'm really pleased."

Harry and Alison seemed to live such ordered lives that Bill knew he would struggle to explain all the changes that had taken place between him and Angie. He was relieved when Harry moved on.

"So, have you been working while you've been in Medford, Bill?"

"Yes, I have, Harry, and you'll laugh when I tell you what I've been doing. When I first arrived here I went right back to my roots. I started again with a shovel. Labouring out at the Meads."

Instead of being amused, Harry seemed shocked.

"At the Meads? Who for? Not Swallow's?"

"Well, Carter Construction, but they're contracted to Swallow."

"You know Horseman's have the heating contract there?"

"I should do, Harry. I negotiated it for them."

"Of course you did! I'd forgotten that. Oh crikey, Bill. If you knew the trouble Horseman's are in over that."

"I've got an inkling, Harry. Swallow's are paying me a consultancy fee for sorting it all out."

"Oh, there's a beautiful irony to this, Bill," said Harry, getting to his feet.

"I didn't set it up like this on purpose, Harry."

"No, I realise that. But you know there's a rumour that Swallow's will be suing Horseman's for damages over the way they're failing to fulfil that contract."

"I'm afraid it's more than a rumour, Harry. I know for sure they intend to sue."

"Well, that's bad, Bill. Very bad. I fear it could spell the end for Horseman's."

"It can't be as serious as that, Harry."

"It is. Benny has antagonised so many people over the past few weeks. He's losing key staff and key customers. I think if Swallow's sue now it'll be the last straw for SCP. I'm pretty sure they'll call off the takeover."

"But I don't understand this, Harry. It's almost as if Benny's destroying his business on purpose."

"No, it's not on purpose, Bill. The problem with Benny is his bull-at-a-gate management style. He gets an idea fixed in his head and he can't leave it. It doesn't matter if it's important or trivial, he'll be fixated with it, ignoring everything else. And he just charges at it. He's got no overview and, as you know well enough, in business that's fatal. The problems at the Meads probably aren't even registering on his radar."

"Poor old Benny. He's his own worst enemy."

"I never thought I'd see the day when you felt sorry for him, Bill."

"Neither did I, Harry, but I mean it nonetheless."

"I know you do. I can tell. And strangely enough Benny seems to have changed his attitude towards you too. That's why I particularly wanted to see you this week."

"What's he done now?"

"The decent thing, at last. I got a letter from Tom Wiltshire earlier this week advising me that all legal actions against you have been withdrawn. I know your solicitor has passed this news on to you. Well done on that, by the way."

"Thanks, Harry."

"But I received further instructions from Benny through Tom Wiltshire in that letter. Namely to reinstate your full redundancy package from Horseman's Heating. The offer is £150,000 lump sum and a pension of half your best salary over the past three years, backdated to October 22nd last year and index-linked. What do you say to that?"

"Bloody hell, Harry. I don't know what to say. It's fantastic news. I just can't believe how good Benny's being to me all of a sudden."

"But wait a minute, Bill. As Benny's accountant I probably shouldn't say this to you, but I think our friendship takes precedence. I think you should take legal advice about a claim for unfair dismissal, or even wrongful dismissal. They're two different things, but a solicitor specialising in employment law could probably get you a lot more than is being offered here."

"No, Harry. I'm not interested in more. All I want is what's due to me for all the years I did. Benny's going out of his way to treat me fairly now and I want to do the same thing back."

"It's your choice, Bill."

"Do you know, Harry, if Benny and I can patch things up it could be one of the best things to come out of all this."

As he drove home that night Bill made the decision to contact Benny to arrange a meeting so that their old enmity could at last be laid to rest. Benny had offered two olive branches to Bill now and the least Bill could do was thank him. And he decided that he was going to apologise to Benny too, for the way he had been towards him over the years.

The next evening Bill made the phone call to Aldrington Hall. It was Sandra Horseman, not Benny, who answered.

"Hello, Sandra, it's Bill Knight. I hope I'm not disturbing you. I was wondering if I could speak to Benny."

"Bill. What do you want?" Sandra replied in a whisper.

"I'd like to speak to Benny, Sandra. I want to thank him for what he's been doing for me."

"Is this a wind-up, Bill? Because I don't think it's very funny, if it is."

"I'm sorry, Sandra. I think we've got our wires crossed. I just wanted to tell Benny I appreciate the things he's done recently. Is he there?

"Yes. He's here, but you're the last person he'll want to speak to. After what you did last week."

"What I did? I don't understand."

"Don't play…"

Just then Bill could hear a voice booming in the background.

"Who is it, San?" it called out.

"It's just Paula, Benny. I won't be a minute.

"Listen, Bill. I've got to go."

"No, wait, Sandra. I'm not leaving it like this. I'm going to come over in the morning to see Benny and straighten this out."

"Don't you dare do any such thing. Listen. Wait 'til Monday when Benny's at work. Where are you nowadays?"

"Medford."

"I'll meet you half way. Monday morning. Eleven o'clock. The Royal Oak Hotel in Westacott Village."

And she put the phone down.

Chapter 41

It was not easy for Bill to take time off on Monday morning, but he took two hours anyway and was in the bar of the Royal Oak when Sandra Horseman arrived. The hotel had a large garden at the back, which ran down to the River Yale, and as soon as Sandra walked in she went straight past Bill's table and through the door to the outside.

"We'll talk out here," she said, ignoring his attempts at a greeting.

Bill followed her into the garden and had no chance to speak before Sandra launched into him.

"You've got a damn cheek calling our home after all you've done. I've come here to say one thing to you, Bill Knight. *Leave my Benny alone!*"

"Hold on, Sandra. I promise you I've got no wish to hurt Benny or you in any way."

"Oh, yeah, I can believe that. You steal his money, put him in hospital, and then send Stoner and that tart round to blackmail your way out of it. Everyone thinks you're so wonderful, Bill Knight, but you're a complete bastard."

"Whoa! Back up a minute, Sandra. I sent Stoner? To blackmail Benny? I'm not sure I know what the hell you're talking about."

"Oh, don't try and play the innocent with me!"

"Sandra, I know nothing about Stoner coming to see Benny. Look, let's walk down by the river and discuss this calmly."

Sandra made no sign she wanted to move from her spot.

"Don't you lie to me, you sod. You sent him with that tart."

"I didn't send Stoner or any tart, Sandra. I haven't spoken to

Stoner for over two months. Not even at my dad's funeral. Come on. Let's get away from the pub and we can talk about it."

"I don't want to go anywhere with you. Who are you saying that woman was then?"

"I don't know, Sandra. Can you describe her?"

"Made up to the nines. Glamorous. Long blond hair. Lots of cleavage. And the bitch had the cheek to come to my home."

"She wasn't wearing a red dress, was she?"

"Yeah, she was. So you did send her?"

"No, I didn't. Did she give a name?"

"Jasmine something or other."

Bill smiled and shook his head. He turned away from Sandra and walked down slowly to the river on his own.

"So you do know her then?"

"Yes, I know her," said Bill without stopping or turning round. "If you want to come with me I can probably explain it to you, Sandra. But you can please yourself."

Even in her high heels Sandra quickly caught up with him.

"Who is she then? I need to know."

"She's a friend of mine. She was at the casino that night in October when I met Benny."

"So she's definitely a friend of yours then? Not Benny's?"

"What are you afraid of, Sandra? That Benny and this girl are involved in some way? And you think I've persuaded her to get me off the hook or I'll tell you all about it. Is that it? You think I'm pulling all those strings?"

"Something like that."

Bill stopped and looked into Sandra's face. She looked more anxious now than angry.

"Well, I can put your mind at rest over one thing, Sandra. There's nothing between your Benny and Jasmine, and there never has been."

"Are you sure?"

"I can guarantee it."

Bill saw the relief come over her face and they started to walk on more slowly.

"So what was she doing at my place with Stoner then?"

"I said I can put your mind at rest over Jasmine, Sandra, but the rest you'll have to ask Benny about."

"No. I'm asking you. I need to know. Why did they come to my house?"

"To try to keep me out of prison, I expect."

"That's what I thought. To put my Benny under even more pressure."

"No, Sandra. To make him tell the truth."

"But he has told the damn truth. You stole his money. And he lost an eye because of you."

"My God, Sandra. What's the truth, eh? Yes, I took his money, but I gave it back. So, did I steal it or borrow it? Damned if I know the truth."

"So you're still going to stick to your story about giving it back, are you?"

"That bit is true, Sandra. Jasmine was there. She saw me give half of it back in the casino. And the rest I gave back the next morning when I came round to your place. Don't you see? Jasmine could prove Benny was lying. Once she came forward he had to change his story. That's why he dropped the charges. And once he did that he had to pay me my redundancy money too."

"But he still lost his eye because of you."

"In a way, I suppose. If I hadn't gone to the woods that day it wouldn't have happened. But I didn't attack him. Benny knows that. It was him who tried to attack me, but he fell and hit his face against a tree."

Sandra stopped and looked up to the sky. "Oh Benji, Benji," she sighed. "What have you done?"

They had come to a bench at the side of the path and by some unspoken agreement they both sat down. A man walked past with a dog and wished them good morning. Bill smiled and nodded in recognition.

"It's not been a very good morning for either of us, has it, Sandra?"

"Well, you're alright. You've had your friends to bale you out. I don't know where this leaves me and Benny though, if what you say is true. If he's been lying to me about all this."

412

"You can choose to believe me or not, Sandra. But I can tell you I didn't ask Stoner or Jasmine to go to see Benny. I haven't spoken a word to either of them for over two months. Hell, I didn't even know they knew one another!"

"That doesn't make sense."

"I know, but it's true. And I'll tell you another thing you can choose to believe or not. I'm gutted that Benny only changed his story because he was made to. I thought maybe he'd managed to find some peace about all this at last, and changed his attitude towards me."

"Huh. There's fat chance of that ever happening."

"So he still hates me then?"

"Do you blame him? When's the last time you showed him any respect?"

"You're right, Sandra. It's true. I haven't been fair to Benny. The only thing I can say in my defence is that I worked hard for him and made lots of money for him."

"He doesn't give a toss about the money. The more you got for him, the more he thought you were rubbing his nose in it."

"Well, I refuse to feel bad about accepting the general manager's job, Sandra. It was over 20 years ago, for God's sake. And it was Benny who offered it to me!"

"Only because he had to because of his father's will. You'll never persuade Benny you didn't have something to do with that will."

"Well, I didn't. And I refuse to apologise for any of it any more."

Bill stood up and looked into the river. The water was running high. It must have been raining over the moors. He turned towards Sandra and saw that she had stood up too. They started to walk back to the pub.

"Maybe if I spoke to Benny I could still convince him I had no influence on his father's decision."

Sandra stopped and grabbed his arm.

"No! Whatever you do, Bill, don't go anywhere near Benny. I swear he'd kill you. Why do you think I came here today? He's got a shotgun, you know. He's talked about topping you."

"What's the matter with him? That's bloody crazy."

"That's the point. I think he has gone a bit crazy. Sometimes he talks about you and his father as if you're one and the same person. But I suppose in a way I can understand that."

"Can you? I'm damned if I can."

"Oh come on, Bill. Don't play the innocent with me. Benny's mother left him when he was seven. His father treated him like a buffoon. Humiliated him. Showed him no warmth or respect. The only thing he gave him was money. Ring any bells?"

"Are you saying he really sees me as another Arthur?"

"Well, you have been, haven't you? Arthur dies. Benny has a chance to prove himself at last, but all he gets is more of the same crap from you."

"And that's what he feels, is it?"

"Yes, of course it is!"

"Hell, Sandra. Just as I thought things were working themselves out around me, you pile this on me again. When I heard Benny had dropped the court cases I really thought he'd stopped feeling so angry."

"I wish he was still angry. I can live with him angry. But he's changed recently. I'm really worried about him."

"What do you mean? How's he changed?"

"He's more depressed than anything else. I've never seen him depressed before. You can't tell me anything about my Benny. I know he's loud and mouthy. I know people find him hard to take. But he can be a real softie too sometimes. And he's never been the depressive sort. It's all this takeover business. He's built it all up in his mind."

"It's that important to him, is it?"

"I'll say! He sees it as his way of proving himself. Getting some self-respect. It was his own idea, you see. I've always wanted to live in Spain. And Benny said he was closing a deal that meant we could move there for good. 'Leave snotty Bramport behind,' he said. But it all seems to be going wrong. I tell you, Bill, if this fails, I'm really worried about him. I think his mind could go."

"I'm really sorry to hear things are that bad, Sandra."

"And so you should be. It's all this business with you that's changed everything. It was all going wonderful 'til you stole that money."

414

"I don't think it's me that's made the takeover go wrong."

"Well, it sure as hell looks like it from where I'm standing."

"I don't think you've got the full picture though, Sandra."

They had arrived back at the same spot in the garden of the Royal Oak and it was as if Sandra had left her anger there before and had just found it again.

"You just think you can sweet-talk your way out of everything, don't you, Bill Knight? All last summer things were going fine for us. Benny was arranging the takeover. We'd never been happier. And then you decide to steal the firm's money so you can take your bit-on-the-side to the casino. And everything's been messed up ever since."

"That's not the way…"

"Oh, why don't you just shut up for once! My Benny might be a bit loud and crude but he's twice the man you are. To think I came here worrying about Benny taking that Jasmine tart to the casino, but it was you all the time. It's always you. No wonder your wife's gone off with someone else if that's the way you treat her. Mind you, why she chose that weirdo Stoner's a mystery to me. And to everyone else round Bramport."

"That's enough, Sandra! Leave Angie out of it."

"Why should I? She's as stuck-up as you are. Always turning down my invites. Never wanting to bother with anyone. Thinking she's too good for us all."

"You know, Sandra. I made a big mistake with Benny. I judged him and made up my mind about him and never gave him a chance. And I was wrong. Because you shouldn't judge people unless you know the truth about them. And you can never know the whole truth about anyone."

"What the hell are you talking about now?"

"Everyone has their own story, Sandra."

"So what?"

"Nothing really. But I won't apologise for who I am. If you and Benny want to have your prejudices against me and Angie, that's fine. That's your choice. But I refuse to waste any more of my life joining in with it. I'm moving on. I've got better things to do."

Chapter 42

As soon as Bill arrived back at the Meads he got on the phone to Peter Smale, the contracts' manager at Swallow Homes.

"Hello, Bill. No problems, I hope?"

"No, Peter, everything's coming along on schedule now. No, I've phoned you about another matter. But I'd really like to discuss it face-to-face. I wondered when you were next down here."

"Tomorrow, as it happens, Bill. I've got a meeting with the landscape people at ten."

"Can I see you after that?"

"Before, if you like. How about nine o'clock?"

"That's great, Peter. Thanks. See you tomorrow."

The next morning Bill showed Peter Smale into the office he now shared with Tony.

"I've got a favour to ask you, Peter."

"Fire away."

"Can you tell me if you're still intending to sue Horseman's for breach of contract?"

"You bet we are. We've got our legal department preparing it now. Should be ready by early next week."

"You know Horseman's are in the middle of takeover talks, do you?"

"Yes, I know all about that."

"The problem is, Peter, if you sue now I think it'll scupper the takeover and Horseman's could be in big trouble."

"So why should that worry you, Bill? I thought you were in

dispute with them too. I would've thought you'd be delighted to see them in the mire."

"It's not like that, Peter. I've settled my differences with Horseman's. The thing is I put in a lot of years building that firm up and I've still got a lot of friends there. I don't want to see them go under and people lose their jobs."

"So what are you asking?"

"I'm saying that if I work with Horseman's and train up their people on site here, so they can get phases two and three right, will you drop your plans to sue?"

"But we don't gain anything with that, Bill. That's only what they're contracted to do anyway. We've still lost out on the mess they made of phase one."

"How about as a favour to me then, Peter? I've already covered your losses by getting you those grants."

"Sorry, Bill. Business is business."

"Tell me, Peter. Were you thinking of keeping me on to see you through phase two?"

"If you deliver phase one on time, yes."

"I will. It'll be ready by the 25th March."

"Well, yes then."

"On what terms?"

"The same. A salary equivalent to £120,000 a year and a terminal bonus for completion by the 30th June."

"The same bonus?"

"Yes, £50,000."

"I was hoping for more. There are ten more units in phase two. I was hoping for £75,000."

"You're asking for a lot all of a sudden, Bill."

"Business is business, Peter. And you know I'll deliver your houses on time. It's got to be worth it to you."

"OK, I can work with that. Can we shake hands on a deal now?"

"We can, Peter, but I have one more alternative proposal."

"Fire away."

"I see phase two through by the 30th June and you pay me no salary and no terminal bonus."

"You are kidding?"

"No, I'm not."

"What's the catch then?"

"You don't sue Horseman's."

"You're prepared to do that much to help Horseman's? What's going on here?"

"I've told you. I've got friends there. With the takeover they've got a future. Without it they haven't."

"I'm not sure I can do it, Bill."

"Come on, Peter. I've got someone at Horseman's I can work with. I'll get things back to normal. We'll use them as our suppliers again and I'll make sure their people know exactly what to do here. Everything's back as it should be."

"I don't know, Bill. We weren't suing Horseman's just for what we were paying you. We were going for punitive damages too."

"Well, I can't offer to pay all of it, Peter, for God's sake. I'm already offering to work for nothing."

Peter Smale stood up to leave.

"I'm sorry, Bill. I can shake hands on your first proposal but not on your second. I've got a responsibility to our shareholders."

"Well, I think you're making a bad decision, Peter. Drop your actions against Horseman's and you get me for nothing. I can almost guarantee you'll be able to market these houses with a Master Builder of the Year Award from the Energy Savings Trust. And anything that says 'energy-saving' and 'environmentally friendly' is going to be very marketable in the new millennium."

"Sorry, Bill."

"Have you considered the alternative?"

"What?"

"You replace me and pay for someone else who you take a chance on. And the Meads becomes known for incompetent contractors, maybe even bankrupt contractors, and possible late completion. Not a good marketing strategy to keep your shareholders happy."

Peter Smale sat down again.

"I suppose you don't think we could keep these problems low-key then, Bill?"

"You know how it is, Peter. These things have a way of leaking out."

"I've never known you play rough before, Bill."

"Business is business, Peter. Do we have a deal? No legal action against Horseman's?"

"I think we do in the circumstances, Bill."

"And we'll keep this arrangement between ourselves, Peter. Agreed?"

"Agreed."

And the two men shook hands.

Later that day Bill contacted Stoner. Stoner seemed apprehensive about the call at first and only agreed to meet Bill when he insisted he needed Stoner's help with an urgent matter. They met in the bar of Bill's hotel on the following Friday evening when Stoner had finished collecting Benny Horseman's Medford rents.

Bill stood up when Stoner walked towards his table and held out his hand in greeting. Stoner looked surprised by the gesture at first and then he looked pleased. He shook Bill's hand more firmly than normal.

"Pint of Thoday's, Stoner? They do quite a good one here."

"Thanks, Bill. That would be great."

A few minutes later Bill put two pints down on the table.

"Cheers, Stoner."

"All the best, Bill," Stoner replied, still sounding slightly unsure of the situation.

They both took long drinks, each hoping the other would stop first and start a conversation. It was Bill who broke the ice.

"Look, Stoner, I think it's best if we clear the air a bit first, don't you? So we're not tiptoeing around one another all evening."

"Sounds good to me."

"I'm not going to be a hypocrite and pretend things haven't changed between you and me. Because they have. At least for me they have. But I accept now that you did what you did to help Angie, and in the end that's all that matters. All I want is for Angie to be okay."

"She is okay, Bill."

"I know. I could tell that when I saw her a couple of weeks ago. To be honest I was bloody amazed at the difference in her. How is she now?"

"She's good. She sends you her love."

"Right. Send mine back, will you?"

"Of course."

They both reached for the refuge of their drinks.

"She told me what you did for her, Bill. With the money, I mean. It was very generous of you. It took away a lot of worry for her."

"She's my wife, Stoner. I can still look after my own wife."

"Yeah, sure. I realise that."

Bill picked up his pint glass but quickly put it down again without taking a drink.

"Anyway, Stoner, the reason I needed to see you is Horseman's. I saw Sandra last week and she told me just how close Benny is to the edge. She thinks if this takeover doesn't happen, it could tip him over. Do you know what I'm talking about?"

"Yes, I know all about the takeover. But I've heard the French are thinking of calling it off."

"If Horseman's don't sharpen up their act, I'm sure they will. And that's what you've got to help me with, Stoner."

"Me? What can I do about any of it?"

"Do you remember me telling you I went back to labouring?"

"Yes."

"Well, it's at a site where Horseman's have a big heating contract. The biggest ever. I signed it just before I left in October. But Horseman's have made a right bloody mess of that contract and that's what really threatens the takeover."

"I still can't see what I can do."

"You can help me put it right. It's a long story but I'm now in charge of the contract for the other side, Swallow Homes, and I need someone in Bramport who can make sure Horseman's deliver – literally."

"And you want that someone to be me?"

"Yes, I do. I need you to make sure I get the men and supplies from Horseman's when I say I need them. Because if there are any more cock-ups Horseman's will get sued and the French will disappear back over the Channel. And God knows what will happen to Benny then."

"I don't know, Bill. I'm not sure I should get involved. I'm not sure I'm up to it."

"You're already involved, Stoner. You can't always sit on the sidelines… Don't worry. I know what we need to do inside out. Just do *what* I ask *when* I ask and everything will be okay."

Stoner looked at Bill and shook his head.

"You're still the knight in shining armour, aren't you, Bill? Coming to the rescue at full gallop."

"Maybe. But if I am, it's because I choose to. Not for any other reason."

"Okay, Bill. For you and Benny, I'll do what I can."

"Good. I'll get us another pint then."

"No, Bill. It's my round. Stay where you are."

Bill was determined to try to be more relaxed towards Stoner when he came back with the drinks.

"Thanks, Stoner. That's good of you."

"You're welcome."

"Sandra was telling me you went to see Benny at the Hall with some mystery lady, Stoner."

"There's no mystery. It's the girl who was with Benny at the casino. The night you were there. Jasmine she's called. You must remember her."

"Oh, yes, I remember Jasmine alright. I just can't work out how you know her."

"Simple enough. She was one of Benny's tenants in the Gables in Medford. I showed her round and gave her the keys when she moved in."

"But of course! You would've done, wouldn't you? So you've known her all this time then?"

"I wouldn't say I know her exactly. I've only met her twice. When she first moved in, and again when she moved out about two weeks ago."

"So why did she go to Aldrington Hall?"

"I'm sure Sandra must've told you."

"No. Sandra thought she was Benny's bit on the side. She was very upset about it."

"It's funny that. Everything points to Jasmine being Benny's bit on the side, as you choose to put it. She lived in that flat rent-free, for a start. But the way she challenged Benny and stood up to him, I don't think she was somehow."

"Challenged him? What about?"

"You! When I went to inspect the flat she knew about my Horseman's connection and she asked me if I knew Bill Knight, the guy she'd met at the casino back in October. She seemed worried about you. Somehow or other she'd heard about you and Angie. And about your dad."

"Roly, you blabbermouth," Bill thought to himself.

"But she didn't get it from me, Bill. You know me better than that. But she said her conscience had been troubling her, because she was the only person who could back up your story. She said she wanted to help you. And could I tell her how she could see Benny?"

"And you told her where he lived?"

"I told her it was a risky business. I've seen what Benny's been like recently. But I could see she was determined to go, so I thought it would be safer if I went with her."

"Thanks, Stoner."

"What for?"

"For getting involved. And for making sure she was alright."

"No need for you to thank me, Bill. Besides, it wasn't Jasmine who needed looking after. It was Benny."

"How do you mean?"

"I tell you. That girl was fantastic. Benny reacted as you'd expect him to. Threats and insults. You know the type of thing."

"What did he say? I'd like to know."

"Oh, he called her a few choice words. 'Effing whore, effing bitch.' You know the sort of thing. He was going to ruin her, crush her, make her life a misery. You know."

"Poor girl."

"Oh no. Don't say that. That 'poor girl' shouted Benny down better than anyone I've ever seen. She was quite quiet in the car on the way over, and she's a lovely-looking girl. But in Benny's study she just turned into something else. She had the foulest mouth on her I've ever heard."

"Really?"

"Every time Benny tried to intimidate her she just came straight back at him. 'Do you know, Benny, you're living proof that shit can grow legs and walk.' She told him if he lied in court, he'd get seven years for perjury and when Benny just laughed, she stood up and shouted at him. 'What colour's the effing sky in your world, Benny?'"

"Brave girl."

"I don't know, Bill. I got the impression she was quite enjoying it. 'I promise you, Benny,' she said. She was standing up, shouting at him. 'If you don't play fair with Bill Knight I'll make sure the whole world finds out what a mean, lying bastard you really are.' In the end I felt quite sorry for him."

"I think I do too."

"She gave him 48 hours to change his statement to the police, or she said she'd go to them herself, and then she'd let his wife know what sort of man he really was."

"And that did the trick, did it?"

"It seemed to. Benny was just speechless in the end. Just slumped in his chair. But then she told him he had to give you compensation for all the trouble he'd caused you. She gave him 48 hours for that too. And she arranged to phone me to check it was all done."

"God. I can't believe it, Stoner. What a wonderful girl she is."

"I tell you, Bill, she must be your guardian angel. You must've made one hell of an impression on her at the casino to make her do all that for you."

"Are you really telling me, Stoner, that you've got no idea who Jasmine is?"

"Jasmine Jameson."

"No. Who she really is?"

"I don't know what you're talking about, Bill."

"Stoner. Jasmine doesn't exist. That was Hayley McKenna."

Stoner laughed nervously and looked suspiciously at Bill.

"What sort of game are you playing now, Bill? I don't understand."

"The young woman who went with you to see Benny was Hayley McKenna."

"You mean, your Hayley?"

"Yes. My Hayley."

"But she's nothing like I imagined you... She was so…so…sassy and in your face."

"Hayley's an actress, Stoner. A bloody good one. If she walked in here now as herself you wouldn't recognise her. Apart from being beautiful she's nothing like Jasmine."

"I can't believe it. I feel I've been tricked."

"You haven't been tricked, Stoner. Benny wanted someone like Jasmine and that's what he got. She couldn't change her role in front of you. But promise me you'll never let Benny know who she really is."

"You know me better than that, Bill."

"You look as if you need a drink, Stoner. I'll get us another."

"Not for me, Bill. I've got to drive back."

"Book a room. Make a night of it."

"It's a nice idea, Bill. But I'd better get back. Angie will be expecting me."

Bill crossed the room to get another drink. As he stood at the bar he looked over at Stoner and saw him checking his watch. He came back with a pint of Thoday's and an orange and soda.

"I got you that anyway, Stoner, but I understand if you need to get going."

"Thanks, Bill. I'm alright for a while. Besides I wanted to ask you something. Why did you go to see Sandra Horseman?"

"It wasn't Sandra I wanted to see. It was Benny I wanted to talk to really. But I'd misread everything and she put me right about it."

"About what?"

"I thought Benny was holding out olive branches to me. I thought he'd got rid of his bitterness towards me. I even had the crazy idea at one point that he was destroying his father's business on purpose. Trying to rid himself once and for all of Arthur's influence. But I was wrong on all counts, of course. Benny hasn't changed."

"So why are you helping him?"

"Because I have changed. I'm finished with thinking badly of other people and then feeling bad about myself. I want to be free of it all."

"You've come a long way."

"I can't believe how I didn't see it all before, Stoner. I always thought I was quite an intelligent person, but I just couldn't think it all through."

"It's not just about thinking though, is it, Bill? You can be told what's good for you any amount of times but it means nothing until you feel it for yourself. But it can be painful finding out about yourself. That's why a lot of people choose not to do it."

"I know you helped me, Stoner, and I'm sorry things have had to change between us."

"Maybe things will change back again, Bill. Who knows what's in the future. What will you do now? Will you see Hayley again?"

"We haven't planned to. I'm working at the Meads until the end of June. Mickey and Cheryl's baby should be here by then. And after that there's a whole world out there that needs exploring."

"You heard I'm taking Angie to Thailand?"

"Yes, she told me. It's unbelievable you've made that possible for her. I do try really hard to feel good about it, Stoner. Deep down somewhere I'm very grateful to you."

"I'm only the physician, Bill. As I said before, when Angie's better she won't need me anymore."

"And as you also said, Stoner, no one knows what the future holds. Just keep taking care of her."

"I will. Look, Bill. I'd better go."

"Okay, Stoner."

The two men stood up and shook hands.

"I'll be in touch about what's needed at Horseman's, Stoner."

"Okay, Bill. Bye then."

Bill watched Stoner walk through the bar and into the reception. His hair was still unruly and in spite of Angie's best efforts his clothes still did not seem to fit right. Bill could still see the unkempt boy in Dai Williams' class at Bramport Grammar. Bill smiled to himself as Stoner went out through the front door. He waited a moment and then he jumped up and hurried after him.

"Stoner!" he shouted across the car park. Stoner stopped and Bill walked towards him.

"Stoner," Bill said, as he put his arms around him. "I just wanted to say thankyou."

"That's alright, Bill, my old mate," said his friend. "That's alright."

Chapter 43

The first phase of houses at the Meads was finished by the March 25th deadline and Bill's bonus from Swallow Homes was paid directly to Angie. Benny's depression got worse and he stopped going to his office at Horseman's, but in a way that proved an advantage, because it allowed Stoner the access he needed to work with Bill on making sure Horseman's fulfilled their contract at the Meads. And with the threat of being sued by Swallow Homes removed, the takeover of Horseman's by SCP at last went ahead in early May.

In the property boom that spring Aldrington Hall was quickly snapped up for several million pounds by a mobile phone magnate and Benny and Sandra disappeared to a large villa in the Sierra de Tolox behind Marbella on the Costa del Sol. Bill received his redundancy money backdated to the 22nd October and from his lump sum he gave Mickey and Dave £25,000 each to help with the expansion of their businesses.

On 26th June Bill and Angie had their first grandchild. A beautiful, healthy girl named Kelly Margaret Knight. At the christening it was hard to decide who looked the most pleased. The proud parents, the equally proud grandparents, or the great-grandmother, after whom Kelly Margaret had received her second name.

Kelly's birth coincided with Bill delivering the second phase of houses at the Meads four days ahead of schedule. Peter Smale promptly offered Bill the opportunity to oversee the completion of the third and final phase, but Bill turned it down. Then, out of the blue in mid-July came another offer. This time from SCP. They had heard of Bill's work at the Meads and they wanted him to take over as the managing director of their new business, which used to be Horseman's Heating, but which was now known as Bramport Energy Systems, SCP Limited. And all salary and benefits were to be payable on top of the pension he already received from them on behalf of the now defunct Horseman's.

Angie tried hard to persuade him to accept the offer. It would allow him the perfect opportunity to give valuable support to the two boys and their ventures, and also to be in Bramport near their first grandchild.

Bill sipped his coffee. The table where he was sitting was right next to the railway line and there was no platform. The train would come straight down the narrow main street within four feet of the shops, cafes and restaurants that lined one side. The street-sellers were already out with their hats, snacks and bottles of mineral water to sell to the passengers as they disembarked.

The first sign that the train was approaching were the vibrations Bill could feel from the railway line in front of him. Then came the sound of the horn of the diesel locomotive in the distance, followed by the rumble of the train itself. It came slowly into view and Bill sat back and enjoyed the spectacle as people waited for the most important event of the day. The vendors, the people hoping to sell accommodation and the porters from the few upmarket hotels all jostled for position. A feeling of complete satisfaction lay over him as he sipped his coffee and watched. There he was in Aguas Calientes in the foothills of the Andes in Peru, watching the backpacker train arrive from Cuzco, and he felt totally at ease and at home. He would never regret turning down the offer to manage Bramport Energy Systems.

Bill had left England in early September and had decided to travel west rather than east. It was only 12 days since he'd arrived in Lima and only six since he too had taken the backpacker from Cuzco, the ancient Inca capital. He spent three hours on the train and chatted happily to an Austrian couple from Linz. The train had climbed slowly out of Cuzco past adobe houses, until it descended into the Sacred Valley with its lush, green fields and colourful villages. Then the great plain narrowed into a deep gorge carved out by the Urubamba River. Bill looked out to see a raging torrent directly below him and above him agricultural terraces with Inca fortresses dotted amongst them.

Bill had not taken the train all the way to Aguas Calientes. He chose to get off at Kilometre 88 and walk the last 50km to Macchu Picchu along the old Inca Trail. It was a four-day hike. Exhausting, precarious at times, and very cold at 13,000ft through Dead Woman's Pass. But Bill loved every minute of it. He loved the challenge, the camaraderie and the new experiences that each day brought. On the fourth morning, as the sun rose, the group of eight, which had formed on the trek, came through another high pass. They reached the point known as the Sun Gate and as Bill passed through it he got his first glimpse of the fabled Inca city. No one spoke. Bill sat on a rock and watched in awe as the sun rose above Macchu Picchu. He was living his dream.

The café where Bill was sitting filled up with new arrivals. Bill acknowledged people as they filled the half-dozen tables around him and he chatted to a French girl who asked his advice about accommodation. People seemed to find it easy to talk to him. Maybe it was because he felt so much at ease anywhere in any company. Two young men sat down at the table next to Bill's. They were from England on a gap year and had arrived in South America only two days before. Bill turned to them.

"Do you mind if I take a look at your newspaper?" he asked.

"Sure thing, mate, but it's Thursday's. Got it at Heathrow."

"I just want to check the sport. I'm not really interested in the news."

"Don't blame you, mate. Go for it."

Bill started reading the paper from the sports pages at the back. Eight pages in a headline in the entertainment section caught his eye.

'A STAR IS BORN': It is not often that one is lucky enough to witness the creation of a new star. Yet last night at Drury Lane's Theatre Royal one more was added to the galaxy of stars who have shone there over the years. If you hurry you might still get tickets to see her before the secret is out and the price of entry becomes a king's ransom.

The show is the new musical *The Streets of London,* written and directed by Giles Coupland, and the star that glitters so brightly from start to finish is Hayley McKenna.

Coupland has created a masterpiece of co-ordination, integrating wonderful new music and writing with startling choreography and skilful direction. As we chronicle the history of ordinary Londoners from the Merry Monarch to the not so merry Millennium we get a feast of catchy music, stunning dancing and barrels of fun. This reminds us why they make musicals in the first place.

Luckily Coupland avoids creating a succession of unrelated tableaux by weaving the story of Becky Smith (McKenna), or rather a line of Becky Smiths, as we chart the development of a vibrant metropolis. McKenna heads a cast bubbling over with charisma and still manages to steal the show. We have a great new talent here, but whisper it gently, and put this one down for an Olivier.

Bill could hardly contain the smile that spread across his face. He looked around to share the news with the people at the other tables, but they were all involved in their own conversations, and he realised that he wanted to share this moment with only one other person. He went inside to the bar where it was quiet and cool and ordered a beer. Bill found a seat in a corner on his own and raised his glass. "Hayley McKenna," he said, and he took a long drink. Then Bill took a postcard and a pen from his rucksack and started to write.

Martin Gillard grew up in Barnstaple, North Devon. He now lives in Brighton and is married with two sons. He spent the major part of his working life as a teacher. This is his first novel.